Moses and Akhenaten:
A Child's Tale

SHARON JANET HAGUE

In memory of
Ursula Murphy

CONTENTS

GLOSSARY

Akhet – season of Nile's inundation, or flooding, (September to January).

Amon – god of the air, chief national god of Egypt during the New Kingdom. (Variations: "Amun", "Amen".)

Aten – aspect of Ra, the sun god.

Children of the Kap – military organisation within the palace, set up to educate the sons of Princes of Nubia and other countries of the New Kingdom of Egypt.

Eighteenth Dynasty – 1550-1292 BC.

Hapi – Nile god of inundation.

Heb-sed festival – celebrated by the king after thirty years of rule, and repeated every three years afterwards.

Imhotep – (2667-2600 BC) Architect of King Djoser, he designed the Step Pyramid, the world's oldest stone building.

Kemet – the black land, another name for Egypt.

Nemes – striped headcloth worn by the kings of ancient Egypt.

Opet Festival – connected with the king, it was a fertility festival of the god Amon and his wife Mut.

Ostraca – pottery pieces, used for sketching (plural).

Peret – season of planting, (January to May).

Pharaoh – king of ancient Egypt.

Ra – god of the sun.

Shemu – season of harvest, (May to September).

Waset – Luxor, capital of southern Egypt during the New Kingdom.

MAIN CHARACTERS

Royal Family

Amenhotep III, Nebmaatre (coronation name) – King of Egypt

Queen Tiye – his wife

Dhutmose – their son

Amenhotep Junior (Akhy) – their son

Maya – their adopted son

Akhenaten, Neferkheprure (coronation name); Amenhotep Junior/Akhy in childhood – King of Egypt

Nefertiti – his wife

Meritaten – their eldest daughter

Ankhsenpaaten – their daughter

Setepenre – their daughter

Kia – Akhenaten's second wife

Smenkhare – their son

Tutankhaten (Tutankhamen) – their son

Royal Relatives

Yuya – Ay and Tiye's father

Thuya – Ay and Tiye's mother

Ay – Tiye's brother, Nefertiti's father

Tee – Ay's wife

King's Men

Ity – High Priest of Karnak

Minthu – tutor at Karnak

Arathamon – Chief of Security

Men – Court Artist

Children's Friends

Abner – Chief Adviser

Horemheb – General

Bak – Court Artist (son of Men)

Scientists

Walter Zars – head of research

Tom Wahlberg – senior researcher

Ernest Jones – Cambridge academic

Karen Smith – researcher from the University of Manchester

Karl Dacek – Austrian geologist

Melissa Simpson – senior researcher

Abel Curry – New Zealand explorer

George Miller – American professor

Divinity

Jesus – man at the well

How various is the world you have overruled,
each thing mysterious, sacred to light,
O sole God
beside whom is no other!

(Hymn to the Aten, by Pharaoh Akhenaten, circa 1353 BC)

THIS IS A TRUE STORY

In 1353 BC Pharaoh refused
to bow to the idols of Egypt.
Instead, he toppled them,
and introduced his country to the worship of one god.

The original composer of Psalm 104,
he radically changed his country's art,
language, and religion.

Finally, together with his Jewish Chief Minister,
he led an exodus of believers into the desert.

His name was King Akhenaten.
The world knows him as Moses.

INTRODUCTION
In the Beginning: Amenhotep-the-Magnificent and Queen Tiye

1.

AMENHOTEP III

I was Egypt's favourite son. Whether Amon loved me or not, I have no idea, but Ma protected me. No child ever won Egypt's throne and kept it, except Pepi-the-Great, who inherited the Double Crown at the tender age of six ... and me.

I suspect Peps kept the throne into his nineties because no one else wanted the job. In his time the country was in ruins. In mine, Egypt was at her zenith. My father and two brothers died in the year of my coronation. Being twelve was both miserable and incredible. I was literally dragged from the harem, where I lived, and transformed into a god-man overnight.

Ma ruled for the first few years, while I was a figurehead. She was an excellent mentor. I was a monarch who had few problems ... until my son came along, but that's another story.

***

"Blast!" cursed the king, removing several small talons from his left forearm.

"Your Majesty might be wise to consider a glove," the court artist, Men, advised.

"Imhotep is female. She isn't supposed to scratch."

"How on earth do you expect a falcon to hold on by anything other than its two-inch talons?"

"One-inch! She's only a baby, aren't you my sweet?"

Amenhotep tickled the brown-and-white chick under her chin. She screeched, spread her feathers, and hooded her eyes to stare malevolently at his companion.

"Your bird is a killer with a bad temper. Only yesterday Arath's horse lost an eye."

"You exaggerate. Our horses are in perfect condition."

Cautiously, the king placed one hand over the tiny falcon, and moved her onto a perch next to a dead mouse. His bird's eyes rounded. In seconds she was tearing at the entrails of the small mammal. Men shuddered, moving away from the ravenous bird.

"Why, by Amon's beard, do you insist on calling her Imhotep?"

"He was our greatest architect and I aspire to his lofty achievements."

"Precisely – *he*. It's bad luck to give a female a man's name. Look at her – she's a menace!"

"My girl's just eating."

"Why not simply call her Sekhmet and be done with it?" said Men, referring to the goddess who had nearly cannibalised all mankind.

"Don't listen to him," Amenhotep soothed, picking up the bird and placing her tenderly in a large wooden cage. "Nap time, sweetie. Sekhmet indeed!" He brushed his hands against his leather corselet. "Now, let's check the blueprints for my latest monument."

***

In her private apartments the dowager queen, Mutemwia received her first visitor of the afternoon, Lord Yuya. Having originally descended from Canaan, the middle-aged man with his hooked nose, and commanding presence, was known as Joseph by his own people. Gifted in prophecy and the interpretation of dreams, there was no one more powerful in the empire, apart from its ruler. One of Yuya's roles was to make reports. This afternoon the heir was the subject of their discussion.

"Your son is extending the temple at Luxor, Your Majesty."

"How old is he now?"

"Fifteen."

"So ... almost a man," Mutemwia reflected. "Do you think it's time I loosened the reins?"

"He has advanced considerably in his royal duties."

The Lord Chancellor's eyes travelled over Mutemwia's left shoulder, as a stocky youth made his appearance. Bowing to the future king,

Yuya departed for his office. Amenhotep planted a giant kiss on his mother's cheek. Crushing her in a bear embrace, his sparkling brown eyes swept the neat, airy audience room where Mutemwia conducted her business. Noticing a fruit bowl, the boy rapidly demolished most of its contents.

"Has Lord Yuya been spying on me again?"

"Reporting. There's a difference. As Egypt's co-regent, it is important for me to keep abreast of your developments."

"The only breasts I'm interested in are Tiye's."

"Amenhotep! Lord Yuya's daughter should be spoken of with respect."

"Yes, Ma," replied Amenhotep in his most annoying tone.

He pushed away an enormous blue bolster from a gaudy couch to lounge among the cushions. Even at fifteen his superb body, unlike his father's lean frame, displayed the muscles of a highly trained athlete.

"Although I hold her family in the highest esteem, Tiye is a commoner."

"I know," Amenhotep sighed wearily.

"Then stop having this conversation with me! As a matter of fact, I was just thinking it was high time we dissolved the co-regency."

The boy winced, remembering the rumour of how the priests of Amon had poisoned his father, Tuthmosis because he dared to change his alliance to the sun god, Ra. It was the reason Mutemwia was constantly encouraging her son to rebuild the god's temple at Luxor.

"Dad was killed by the priests."

"Don't speak of your father's death like that again," Mutemwia said practically. "The walls have ears."

"It doesn't change the fact Dad was assassinated."

"On second thoughts, this co-regency will continue until I see you behaving like an adult!"

Jumping up gleefully Amenhotep seized his mother by the shoulders and bruised both her cheeks with swift, hard kisses.

"Oh, thank you, Ma!" he exclaimed joyfully.

Leaving her apartment with several oranges tucked into his kilt, Amenhotep strode happily down the corridors of Malkata, pleased his ruse had worked.

***

TIYE

We met on a Nile excursion. My parents were there. Amenhotep was Egypt's handsome new king. His honed body resembled a block of sandstone. Tanned and muscle-bound, he was unlike the nobles of the court, who spend all day indoors.

***

AMENHOTEP III

Tiye was tiny. My heart thumped so loudly I thought everyone could hear. Standing ramrod straight, I hoped she would notice my new linen vest. It clung to my torso emphasizing my shapely chest. I was on tenterhooks all morning.

The lovely maiden did not look at me. Not once. In the morning I paid a visit to her father's house.

***

A servant dropped her water pot and ran into the living room where Yuya and his wife, Lady Thuya, were sipping their morning grape juice.

"My lord," she gasped, throwing herself on the floor. "He's outside our gate!"

"Compose yourself, Tani. Now who is it? Take a deep breath before you say anything."

The woman clasped her hands. For a few moments nothing could be heard except her irregular breathing as she attempted to control her excitement.

"It is the Pharaoh of Egypt in person, sire."

Pandemonium reigned as servants sprang into action. Thuya gave panic-stricken orders. A calf was slaughtered, ducks hurled into pots, and vegetables diced. Floors were swept and re-swept. Swiftly appraising the scene, Yuya ordered refreshments in the garden. Tani bowed and vanished into the kitchen. Outside, Amenhotep waited with his bodyguards, who looked fiercely about for hidden assassins.

"Maybe we should go," Men suggested.

"Relax," Amenhotep soothed. "It's early morning. The master is probably still asleep."

"In that case it might not be tactful to pay his daughter a visit."

The youth's stomach knotted.

"It'll be fine," he replied, feeling more uncertain every minute.

Presently a tall, angular man appeared. Smiling graciously, Lord Yuya welcomed his royal guest by rubbing noses with him. To Amenhotep's chagrin, a butler relieved him of Tiye's gift before he could protest. Soon, he found himself in a quiet, tree-filled courtyard. A house cat leapt onto his lap as he took a wicker seat. Curling herself into a contented ball, the striped, grey-and-gold creature promptly fell asleep.

"Maau approves of you." Yuya settled into an ornate wooden chair decorated with papyrus and water lilies. "Speaking of felines, have you been lion-hunting recently?"

"At every opportunity."

"One wonders how His Majesty finds time to attend to the affairs of state."

"I know how to administer my empire's affairs."

Unfazed by the direct reply, Yuya delicately broke a grape off its stalk. Holding it between thumb and forefinger, he bit into it.

"As you should." Gazing into space, his patrician's nose wrinkled slightly.

"I am here to see Lady Tiye with a courtship gift." Amenhotep glanced helplessly towards the house into which his necklace had vanished.

"It is unusual for a member of the royal house to pay court to a subject, however exalted," Yuya remarked, his grey eyes gleaming like Nubian diamonds in the desert sun.

A collective intake of breath escaped from the royal bodyguards as the men adjusted their shields and pretended not to eavesdrop.

"I–I merely wanted to see her," the young monarch stammered.

A rustling broke out behind them, and Tiye appeared. Immediately, Amenhotep's face lit up and, forgetting the cat, he leapt to his feet. Expressing her indignation at being disturbed, Maau vanished into the surrounding palm trees.

"You may have a few moments alone with my daughter," her father said, vacating his chair. "No more." He glanced sternly at his visitor. "Later, I will take this up with Your Majesty's mother."

"You look stunning," Amenhotep blurted when his reluctant host had departed.

Ogling Tiye's curves, accentuated by a simple, clinging white shift, he swallowed convulsively. Tossing her damp, auburn locks which had just been washed, the girl's casual demeanour contrasted starkly to her disciplined and immaculately groomed father. As she took Yuya's seat, however, Amenhotep noticed she fixed him with the same haughty gaze as her sire.

"You shouldn't pay house calls. It's improper."

"I brought a present," her chastened suitor mumbled, finding his tongue. "But they took it away."

"You're Pharaoh," she laughed scornfully. "Tell them to give it back!"

"That would be impolite. But I did so want to drape the collarette around your neck."

"Precisely what great kings give deserving servants! I hope you're a hundred miles from here when Father unwraps it."

"Why do you mock? Don't you like me?"

Taken aback by his frankness, the girl suddenly broke into a sweet smile.

"I spent all day with you on the Nile."

"You didn't even notice me!"

"You never *spoke*, Your Majesty," she pointed out. "Even an aristocrat cannot address Pharaoh, without having first been approached. You knew that, and yet you simply stood there, like a block of stone – looking very handsome – I might add."

Blushing, Amenhotep raked his hands through his thick, dark locks.

"I never know what to say to girls," he confessed. The apprehensive suitor struggled to articulate the words which would not come. Finally, realising they had limited time, Amenhotep threw caution to the winds and pressed his suit. "I once had a waking dream. Do you ever have those, Tiye?"

"No, but priests and kings do."

"It was after my father died. One day, just before the coronation, I fled to my room in tears at the thought of becoming king, when a noise alerted me – and then I saw you."

"But that's impossible!" Tiye laughed incredulously. "I wasn't even born when you were crowned co-regent!"

"I spotted a maiden who looked exactly as you do today, clad in a white shift with long auburn hair."

"She might have been a princess from the harem."

Amenhotep shook his head vigorously.

"It was you. Her hair had just been washed – like yours is now. I recall every detail of her beautiful face before she vanished."

Secretly flattered, Tiye wrinkled her nose in a manner reminiscent of her father.

"Did this apparition say anything to you?"

"Not a word." The king wiped his brow as if he had completed a particularly strenuous lion hunt. "However, I knew she was my future wife."

"In that case you had better ask Father for my hand. Here he comes now."

With Tiye's words ringing in his ears and his heart ready to burst with joy, Amenhotep stood to attention before the intimidating figure of the man he now knew would be his father-in-law.

***

In the firelight of the Great Hall over a hundred priests took their places at the tables assigned to them in order of rank. Temple girls served Mycenaean wine and wild oryx steaks. Animated discussions of the day took place between bright young acolytes and seasoned priests. Rarely were such meetings called. Most of the clergy led their own lives and, while a board of carefully selected individuals met on a weekly basis, it was unusual for the entire temple staff to assemble at the same time. Conflicting schedules, and the elitism of priestly cliques, ensured most kept to themselves.

Late in the evening a young cleric rose from his jewel-encrusted armchair. He clapped his hands together. Silence descended on the gathering. Like all priests, the man's head was clean-shaven, and his robes were of spotless white linen.

"Our tutor, Minthu."

At this brief introduction, a man of around thirty stood up. A senior member of faculty, he was one of Karnak's most respected teachers of holy law. Although discipline was harsh in Egyptian classrooms, Minthu rarely enforced corporal punishment. Instead, his boys were encouraged to participate in lively discussions. As a result, they were some of the most brilliant scholars in the land, and many were assembled at the meeting. He welcomed the group in a warm manner, and opened the floor to everyone.

Another man with short-cropped, white hair, rose from the table. Everyone recognised him as Ity, High Priest of Karnak.

"This meeting has been convened for the good of Amon." His rasp penetrated the hall like a lance of chillness. Instinctively, several acolytes pulled their robes closer about their shoulders. "Our king means to take a wife." He paused. "His most important wife. He intends to confer that honour on Lord Yuya's eldest daughter."

9

Shocked rumbling filled the hall. Wave upon wave of outrage continued for several minutes.

"This is by no means unheard of in our history," Minthu countered politely. "It is not imperative that Pharaoh wed a royal."

At these reasonable words, silence returned to the room.

"You are right," Ity agreed. "However, it will make the king's children bastards."

"That's going too far!" an army cadet shouted, leaping to his feet. "Amenhotep is a god. Egypt has never boasted a greater king!"

"No one is disputing that, Merimose," Minthu soothed. "Although it would be best for you to control yourself until the floor is open to more junior ones such as yourself."

"I agree with Merimose," another youngster spoke.

Ity glared at him, only to receive a cool stare. Standing in his place the boy regarded the assembly as if he was in charge.

"Lord Men," Minthu smiled, much to Ity's ire. "It is an honour to have such a distinguished artist with us."

"The honour is mine," was the smooth response. "I wish to convey my opinion of the king's divinity, on behalf of the workshops, which as we all know, are an important component of Egypt's economy. Without them our temples lose their prestige."

"We will remember your fine words when you become manager of the king's studio, but only when you're out of the nursery!" Ity mocked. Several young boys snickered and made comments.

"I *will* be in charge one day. You, however, face replacement as High Priest in my lifetime. The only reason you are all in an uproar is because His Majesty chose not to marry into a family which served Amon."

"We are agreed that both the priesthood and monarchy are of one accord," Minthu interjected hurriedly, without losing his courteous smile. "Naturally, those from a younger generation will replace others of us who are older. Welcome, Lord Men."

Safe in the knowledge he had not lost face, the artist bowed from the waist, and sat down. The boys stopped scoffing and viewed him with mounting curiosity. Ity's face, black as thunder, glowered for the remainder of the meeting.

***

TIYE

Later in the week I visited the palace again, escorted by Father. Many years later I discovered how my husband had gone to great lengths to persuade the mighty Lord Yuya to bring his only daughter to court. Father thought the king wished to add me to his harem.

Instead, I became Queen of Egypt.

***

AMENHOTEP III

I loved her at first sight. According to tradition I was to marry my sister, but she was only good for hair pulling. Tiye was for me. So, I swept away three thousand years of tradition and married her.

All Egypt loved my queen. She was one of *Kemet*'s people. And no one dared to attack my choice of chief consort.

(Shifts uncomfortably)

Not even the priests.

***

A glittering procession wound its way across smooth flagstones up to Amon's temple. Gaily painted in a variety of hues, it belied the sombre atmosphere inside, where priests waved censers and chanted ancient hymns. In one supple movement, bearers placed the king's litter on the ground. A sea of people cheered as Amenhotep alighted. Instinctively, Tiye, who was following behind, moved closer to her husband. Squeezing her hand affectionately, the king walked by her side into the temple.

11

Once inside, a rush of awe enveloped Tiye. The god's power was greater than she had imagined. Even as Pharaoh, her husband was dwarfed by it. A long hour passed before the couple emerged. Blinking in the clear sunlight at the temple entrance, they waved. Crowds, which had patiently waited all morning, roared their approval. This time, Amenhotep stood for several minutes, allowing his subjects to view him while he basked in their adoration.

Wondering at her husband's ability to remain congenial for extended periods of time, Tiye was aware of feeling positively irritated. Her sandals hurt, and the combination of incense, smoke, desert sand, and the sun's hot afternoon glare, made her dress cling stickily to her body. Despite her discomfort, however, she stood erect and queenly near her husband's shoulder. For his part, Amenhotep had never felt so complete. Both monarch and god, his human side had finally joined with the life partner he would take into eternity.

Eventually, it was time to depart. Tiye approached her litter with gratitude. Her parents had spent much time in the royal court, but nothing could acclimatise her to the publicity which she had been forced to endure over the past year. Before entering her litter, the new queen noticed her brother, Lord Ay, speaking to another soldier. Painfully lean, Ay was covered in taut, wiry muscles from years of soldiering. On a recent campaign he was hospitalised for sunstroke. He promptly changed his career from army commander to court adviser. Briefly, he turned in the direction of his sister. Tiye waved in response, but the latter abruptly turned his back and continued conversing. Thinking their pretty queen had acknowledged them, the crowd cheered.

Vaguely displeased with her sibling, Tiye collected herself. Taking her place in the wooden litter, embossed with gold medallions, and fringed with silver tassels, she allowed herself to be borne on the sturdy shoulders of her bearers as they began the long journey to Malkata Palace.

***

Pungent incense filled the air while perfumed lotus water spilled over Tiye's neck and shoulders. A lute player strummed a mellow tune softly in the background. Tension mounted in the bride's heart as female attendants dressed her in finely pleated linen. Now the coronation was over, her wedding night loomed before Tiye like a monster from her father's illustrated *Book of the Dead*. Involuntarily, she shuddered.

The girl's long tresses were washed in wild asses' milk by her bath attendants. Then they were raked across her narrow shoulders with a wide-toothed comb. Finally, the last touch of henna was applied to her hands and feet. Afterwards, the chief attendant departed with her beauticians, allowing Tiye to enjoy the privacy of her royal apartment.

Alone at last, the girl's first reaction was to abandon the indoors. Discarding her sandals, she stepped onto a verandah which overlooked the most magnificent garden she had ever seen. Running down its steps, and scrunching her white toes in the damp carpet of grass, Tiye sighed with delight at the green-and-red-breasted parrots which flew squawking overhead. Refreshing breezes swept off the Nile and rustled through the palm trees over her drying reddish-brown hair. Slowly, the Chief Consort to Amenhotep-the-Magnificent, Pharaoh of all Asia; living forever and ever, relaxed.

After savouring the freedom of wandering in solitude across the palace grounds, Tiye rested on the patio steps outside her room. She gazed in wonder across the manicured lawns filled with a riot of yellow, indigo, red, cerise, and blue. Monkeys scrambled happily up sycamore and palm trees, chasing each other, while stuffing their small, pink cheeks full of nuts left by afternoon groundsmen. Tiye's fingers plucked a sprig of jasmine from one of the twin pillars which stood at the bottom of the stairs. Her eyes travelled up one gaily painted column to an empty alabaster saucer sitting on its flat top. She noted the saucer was filled with small pieces of meat.

"Beautiful, isn't it?" The young woman whirled around to see her husband padding across the verandah's brightly painted ceramic tiles. His pleasant demeanour from their coronation was still in evidence. The king had changed his robes, and now wore the plainest of white kilts.

Only a tell-tale red waistband denoted his rank. "Have you met my falcon?" he asked, pointing ahead.

Tiye peered sharply into the surrounding trees. Suddenly, she became aware of a neat bundle of white-and-brown plumage glaring balefully at her from a hibiscus bush.

"Meet Imhotep," the king introduced.

"Wasn't that the name of King Djoser's main architect?"

"The very same. *Our* architect, Amenhotep-son-of-Hapu, gave me the falcon as a present. See how it stares!"

Tiye regarded the unblinking yellow eyes with trepidation.

"It looks annoyed," she observed.

"Oh no, my bird has a sweet temperament!"

Amenhotep's powerfully developed body moved lightly across the garden's clipped lawn. Removing a red-and-white kerchief from his belt, he wrapped it twice around his right arm, before flicking it out in a movement of grace and skill. Immediately, the bird settled onto his muscular forearm.

"How did you do that?"

"Imhotep is a subject who does Pharaoh's bidding."

"It looked more like a priestly magic trick from Heliopolis. Only more impressive."

Delighted at the compliment, Amenhotep swung round to his queen and bride. Screeching, the bird flapped strong wings as if to pounce.

"Just don't bring it over here," Tiye said, hastily moving up a step.

"Human and animal should live side by side. It preserves the harmony of nature."

Crooning softly, the king began to stroke his beloved pet's head with one bejewelled forefinger. Despite a mild headache, which had plagued Tiye throughout the day, she began to unwind. For the first time she dismissed her fear of the wedding night. Before his bird could protest, Amenhotep placed Imhotep neatly on a plinth next to them. With a ruffle of feathers, the falcon settled into a posture of arrogant surprise. Tiye covered her pearly white teeth and laughed. Imhotep lowered surly eyelids, and regarded the newcomer with mute antagonism.

"Has it eaten?" the queen ventured, looking up at the full dish of meat.

Smiling, her husband nodded, and stooped to swiftly kiss her. Without further ado, he positioned himself on the steps next to his bride and, lightly draping one arm over her shoulder, began talking. Towards sunset Amenhotep fell silent. Disinterested, his feathered friend flapped strong wings and fled into the purple evening shadows.

"Imhotep listened to you."

"I don't think so," was the quiet reply. "But it's nice you think that."

"He doesn't like *me*," Tiye said flatly.

"That's because Imhotep's female. Named after those unsmiling portraits of the architect whom she resembles. No doubt she's deeply jealous of my beautiful wife!"

Tiye shivered.

"I'm glad we won't have to meet Imhotep. They say he was a wizard who drank the blood of Pharaoh's wife one summer's solstice."

"You've been reading Me-Thoth's horror stories. He's a wonderful writer."

"So, you've heard of him," Tiye said. "I've never met anyone else who liked scary stories."

"They were more interesting than memorising Egypt's list of kings for my history tutor. But now," her husband said, pulling her to her feet, "we're expected at dinner."

***

The wedding banquet was the largest affair Tiye had ever attended. Tables groaned under weighty mounds of fruit, vegetables, and meat. Wine, both red and white, flowed in a never-ending supply. The dining hall was filled with courtiers, their wives, and families.

Outside, in the city streets, Egyptians feasted and rejoiced. Musicians played into the night, and scantily clad dancing girls performed for the pleasure of the king and his new bride.

Clapping in time with the dancers, while warmly greeting his guests, Amenhotep was able to eat and drink continuously into the early hours of the morning. Throughout, Tiye was a model of decorum. Sitting ramrod straight, she ate little and hardly spoke. As in-laws to the king, Yuya and Thuya were the guests of honour. Lavishing attention on his mother-in-law, Amenhotep chatted to her, while pointing out the most succulent meats. Meanwhile, slaves hovered anxiously over the royal pair, eager to fulfil their every whim. Several times during the meal Tiye caught sight of Ay. Impeccably dressed, he moved about the Great Hall, mingling with soldiers and aristocrats alike. Everything about him was genteel, and her heart swelled with sisterly pride. He was so like Father, she thought.

Later, the royal couple retired from the banquet to their bridal suite. Mildly inebriated, Amenhotep slipped off his starched kilt and stumbled towards the bed, grinning lopsidedly. His bride clutched her sheet. Lamps were snuffed out by unobtrusive hands. Tiye lay in the dark, still holding her sheet close to her chin. Moments passed. A chunky foot touched hers. She moved out of the way. Slight snoring indicated her husband was asleep. Moments passed. Finally, Amenhotep rolled onto his back, laughing out loud.

"You're awake," Tiye observed unnecessarily.

"I wanted everyone to go."

"I thought you were asleep."

"I wouldn't do that on our wedding night."

"This isn't our wedding night, it's morning."

The king snuggled close to his wife.

"You're so tiny," he murmured. "Like a little mouse."

He smooched her cheek. Realising he was content only to hold her, Tiye began to thaw.

"I have a headache," she explained.

Lightly, Amenhotep's calloused fingers stroked his wife's throbbing temples. Their dexterous movements sent Tiye into a slumber from which she did not emerge until the next day.

***

When Tiye awoke the sun was high in the sky. Momentarily disoriented, she realised two things; that she was queen of the most powerful nation in the world and, more importantly, she was neglecting her duties by rising late.

"Where is my husband?" she demanded of the staff.

"The king is hunting, ma'am," a Nubian serving girl replied timidly. "His Majesty left at dawn."

"Dress me," she ordered.

Towards the middle of the day, an irate First Lady of the Land emerged from her apartments. The court was empty. Only a lone guard patrolled the polished floors of the Great Hall. Since anyone of importance, including her brother, was at the hunt, Tiye had nothing to do except be mistress of the house. She decided on an official tour of inspection. During the hot, still hours of the afternoon, while Pharaoh hunted, his wife discovered that granaries, cellars, and kitchens yielded their secrets effortlessly under her penetrating eyes and astute observations.

Finally, satisfied that some of the day had been well spent, Tiye took leave of her stewards. Kicking off her sandals, she paced the gardens. Having become Amenhotep's primary wife, Tiye was now the most illustrious woman in the world. Pleased with the fact, she sat on her porch to contemplate the beauty around her. A flutter of wings spoiled her smug reverie.

"You're back," she curtly addressed the visitor.

In reply, the miniature falcon beat its wings, before settling down to stare at her. Tiye felt ill at ease until inspiration dawned. Clapping her hands imperiously, she summoned her servants. In no time, Imhotep was dining on small pieces of fresh meat. The bird even condescended to having one of her wings stroked.

***

2.

AMENHOTEP III

I was Egypt's richest and most beloved monarch. I built more temples and monuments than any Ramesside. In fact, Ramesses-the-Second, (called *Great* by himself), stole most of my monuments and remodelled my features into his likeness. Some even say he re-carved the Sphinx of Giza to resemble him. (It wouldn't surprise me. There is grandeur and godliness, and then Ramesses' overweening ego.)

But enough of the upstart. My Great Wife was also adored, and instead of expelling me from the throne for marrying outside the royal family, the priests had to toe the line while I built Egypt from the inside out. My mortuary temple – which employed countless artisans, priests, and even chefs – boasted silver floors, walls of gold, and an electrum ceiling. That was before an earthquake destroyed it.

I am peeved that two ruined, faceless statues are all that remain of my grand design, while Ramesses continues to haunt tourists from one end of the Nile to the other.

***

TIYE

The accursed priests of Amon owned two-thirds of Egypt's land in our time. Since their demands on Pharaoh's treasury was exorbitant, my husband devised a cunning scheme. He suggested building temples to the god's glory, and promptly constructed monuments to himself. He also ensured we used our money for us – before the priests could lay their hands on that, too. Amenhotep designed a magnificent palace at Malkata, with a private lake for me. Not content with that, my darling installed the world's first chariot racecourse outside our door.

We enjoyed ourselves immensely.

***

"Do you think I should build another palace in Akhmim?"

"I have no idea," the Great Wife snapped. "We are always at parades, or hunts, surrounded by people. I don't know what I think, anymore." Numbly, Amenhotep contemplated the ground. Tiye tossed her girdle on the floor. "At last I can breathe! As for these necklaces you're intent on festooning me with – Senta, take them off!"

The chief attendant hurried to remove the offending objects. Discreetly she swept away any other items into the chests which lined her mistress' dressing room. Nearby servants quickly retreated from the petulant queen. No one dared look at Pharaoh.

"Your opinion is valuable to me," he began.

"Bah!" Tiye continued as cosmetic pots were hurled about.

Her young husband returned to contemplating the floor in abject silence. Once, he glanced up in time to catch a commiserating look from Senta. Immediately the girl, who looked only a few years older than her bad-tempered mistress, blushed to the roots of her plaited hair and quickly turned away.

Realising any further discourse with his wife would prove fruitless, Amenhotep left the apartment. His security chief was waiting. Rapidly, he strode away with the man, down the large passageway leading from the Great Wife's apartments to the outside courtyard. In the distance he heard a shriek as some poor girl had her hair pulled.

Collecting himself, he turned to the security chief.

"Arath, I wish to walk."

Arathamon leapt into action. Several guards set out in the direction of the garden. Intelligence officers were installed at strategic vantage points in readiness for potential assassins. Meanwhile, a group of soldiers was summoned. While preparations were made, Amenhotep waited.

Senta's glance, unwarranted as it was, had intrigued him. Even if his wife threw tantrums, he realised that an entire harem of willing womanhood was at his disposal. He might visit it tonight.

Finally, the soldiers arrived to follow the main guards. They scurried out of the double doors and into the enormous park. Splitting into four separate sections at the entrance, the men dispersed into the trees.

Amenhotep turned to Arathamon.

"Do you know of a lady called Senta?"

"She is one of Her Majesty's attendants, sire."

"Chief attendant."

Following his master down a path lined with shrubs and flowers, the man kept a sharp lookout for his agents. At one point the king plucked a magenta rose. Raising it to his nostrils he inhaled deeply.

"Ask her to meet me here, after dinner."

Arathamon prostrated himself before joining the others in their mass invisibility.

***

Dinner was prolonged. Queen Tiye sulked. She ate little, drank less, and found fault with the service. Several waiters around her were replaced as she criticised their skills. Her spouse was quieter than usual, which added to Tiye's aggravation.

"Why are you being so moody?" she demanded querulously as dessert was served.

"I'm eating, that's all."

"And far too much!"

"After hunting all day, I need to re-fuel."

Raising a goblet to her lips, the Great Wife's eyes darted over Amenhotep's calm dissection of a duck.

"I suppose you caught that mallard yourself," she snorted derisively.

Leaning gently towards his wife the king lowered his voice.

"My darling," he whispered, "while I understand your first pregnancy is no easy thing, I assure you being Pharaoh has enough problems without being henpecked in front of my subjects."

He rinsed his fingers in the proffered water bowl.

"So I'm reminded a hundred times a day," was the heated retort. "But do you ever take a palace inventory? Thanks to me we've saved enough gold, which you were wasting, to buy another temple to your eternal glory."

At the shrill register in Tiye's voice several noblemen and their wives glanced at the royal table. Amenhotep smiled extraordinarily sweetly and leaned even closer to his wife.

"I jailed a man today for speaking out of turn," he whispered. "My vizier informs me I was too lenient. The next person who does so at Pharaoh's court will not be so lucky."

Amenhotep dabbed his lips with a napkin. Disappointed that the royals were doing no more than whispering sweet nothings in each other's ears, the curious nobles returned to their meal. Queen Tiye raised her alabaster wine glass. Her dark eyes contained a spark in their cantankerous depths, but she remained silent during the remainder of the formal state dinner. She would let her husband know her opinion of his mindless threats at a more appropriate time.

Late in the evening, when the moon was high in the sky, Amenhotep rose to his feet with the entire court, including Tiye, following his example.

"Pharaoh is pleased with your obedience," he grinned.

Unable to reply, Tiye contented herself with frosty silence. Her father would be furious to hear of Amenhotep's attempt to intimidate his daughter. Arranging her linen shawl across her shoulders, she followed her husband out of the hall. Courtiers dispersed to their lodgings for the night, and the royal couple returned to their apartments. Fond of sleeping together, the king and queen were still shocking the nation by sharing a common bedchamber, which only the poorest peasants were forced to do. Tonight, however, was different and at the familiar gold-plated wooden door Amenhotep halted.

"I have business to attend to," he announced brusquely.

Before Queen Tiye could enquire as to the reason, her husband vanished towards the southern end of the palace, walking with characteristically rapid steps. Irritated, but too tired to think after a day at court, the royal wife submitted to the ministrations of her faithful body-servants, and soon found herself attired for bed.

***

Oil lamps filled the darkened garden, bathing the surrounding trees with an incandescent glow.

"This is my favourite place, Senta" the king commented in his pleasant bass voice. "Look at the orchids!"

Despite her apprehension at finding herself in Pharaoh's presence, the girl blurted: "I thought they only grew in the jungle."

"They do, but I created false humidity with lots of water, so they flourish. An ancestor of mine, Tuthmosis-the-Great, brought back some cuttings from one of his campaigns."

Although accustomed to giving orders to staff directly beneath her, Senta found herself tongue-tied, and uncertain how to reply before the king whom she did not directly serve. After all, as the latest kitchen gossip would have it, Amenhotep (now called "the Magnificent") had recently imprisoned a subject for giving him the wrong answer to a question.

Lightly, the king's hand touched her shoulder, directing her to a seat in a nearby arbour. Feeling the girl's body tremble, he immediately retracted his hand. They sat side by side. Despite her innate misgivings, Senta could not ignore the young man's comeliness. Amenhotep, feeling vaguely nervous, nevertheless chatted on a variety of topics. Curiosity finally overcame the woman's shyness.

"How old are you?" she burst out impulsively.

"Seventeen."

"I'm nineteen."

"Are you married?"

"Not yet."

"Why?"

"I don't know." Senta thought for a moment. "I think it's because I work for Her Majesty."

A glint appeared in Amenhotep's eye.

"I suppose you're on call twenty-four hours of the day," he remarked casually.

"I have to ensure everything my girls do is correct." She glanced at him and then averted her eyes. "I apologise for this afternoon. Staring at your face directly was ... improper."

"It used to be punishable by death," Amenhotep said mischievously. "In truth, I wanted to thank your staff. It is no easy feat to endure Tiye's tirades."

The young woman did not answer. Instead, she surveyed her hands. They were small and dark. Palace rumour had it that the king's grandfather, Amenhotep-the-Second, had ruthlessly seduced many a hapless female servant in the grounds at the dead of night. Amenhotep-the-Second was also notable for his extraordinary bloodlust, which led him to club seven kings to death outside Amon's temple. It was widely held that his favourite wife, together with her child, had been sacrificed within his tomb in accordance with his final will and testament.

In his grandson, however, compassion stirred.

"I wish to apologise," the king said, rising unsteadily. "I should not have brought you here."

Immediately, Senta was on her feet, appearing more frightened than ever. Worse than seduction was a king who lost interest in his victim! It was not uncommon for monarchs to blithely incarcerate subjects they had no use for. Like the man who had spoken out of turn recently at court. The cooks whispered the unfortunate was only a messenger. Once he had delivered his missive from the front, which had created ire in His Majesty's heart, the supreme monarch had found an excuse to vent his displeasure.

"Have I offended Your Highness?" she asked.

"Oh no!" Amenhotep scratched his head covered in curly, dark locks, and flushed. Senta noticed the fullness of his red lips. She did not pull away her eyes in time. "Ah, I caught you again!" the king cried playfully, appearing like any other Egyptian boy, full of fun and laughter. "You see, I was embarrassed by my wife," he continued. "She was scolding me this afternoon in front of her maids, so I invented a ludicrous story about jailing a messenger for relaying unpleasant news." He turned to his new friend. "When I was co-regent girls used to constantly eye me. It seemed more natural than picking out a Babylonian princess with big teeth for treaty purposes. Do you think I'm agreeable to the eye?" he asked suddenly. It was Senta's turn to blush. "It pleased me when you looked at me that way this afternoon."

"I felt sorry for you," she blurted tactlessly.

"Ah, I misunderstood." Pharaoh fell silent.

Senta dropped her hands helplessly into her lap.

"May I be frank with you?"

"By all means."

"In this light you look like the god Your Majesty is, but you have also put me in an awkward position by inviting me here. I am not part of your harem. I am employed by Her Majesty, the Great Wife, and if she finds out about this ... dalliance, I shall surely be fired, or beheaded."

Surprised, Amenhotep took her arm gently and led her out of the arbour.

"Since we are being honest with one another, let me share a secret. I enjoy hunting. Choosing my prey is one of the rare times I'm allowed to make a decision. But I also enjoy being chosen. It's more real somehow. The female of the species, even in the animal kingdom, usually selects her mate." A peal of laughter floated through the trees. It was a hearty laugh, which invited one to become part of it. "Now, to solve your dilemma, I'll play the part of a supreme monarch, requesting your advice on some important matter – perhaps in relation to my queen. It would save a beheading."

Senta did not know whether to take the king, who looked so much like an ordinary (although uncommonly striking) boy, seriously or not.

However, Amenhotep was far away, and appeared to be hunting for caterpillars in a giant sycamore above them.

"I have an idea," she said after some thought. "Her Majesty finds the afternoon heat suffocating. It was the cause of her distemper earlier today. She wishes to ride on the Nile. You're a great architect. Why don't you recreate part of the Nile for her in the form of a lake here, in these grounds?"

"I was trying to think of something for my beloved along the lines of a large bath," the king said, his eyes shining. "An enormous tub filled with lotuses and soap, so none of her maids would ever find her, let alone her poor husband!" Forgetting herself, the girl began to laugh, and Amenhotep joined in. They were both wandering past a large rock pool glinting in the moonlight. When they reached the palace entrance Amenhotep hugged her in a brotherly embrace. "Don't worry," he said warmly, "the queen will keep you in her employment."

***

"Where did you go last night?"

The argumentative question hung in the air.

"I have a harem."

Amenhotep slowly drank his morning cup of honeyed water. In preparation for a bull hunt he was attired in a short, coarse linen kilt, and sported two daggers. Tiye stopped as if she had not taken this foray into account.

"I wish you had told me," she continued less irritably.

Her husband darted her a sideways glance. Tiye's diminutive shoulders had drooped.

"I'm lying," he amended. "I didn't visit. I'm building something."

The Great Wife brightened.

"Is it one of your temples?"

"A lake."

Frowning slightly, Tiye chewed her slice of bread. Unlike most noblewomen, she ate very little and was usually content with fruit, or bread for breakfast.

"I don't understand."

"For you." Amenhotep stood up and went to the large window next to them. "Do you see those gardens? Your lake is going to stretch from the eleventh arbour out. Measuring three thousand, seven hundred cubits long, and seven hundred cubits wide, it will cover one hundred and forty-eight acres."

"A lake?" the queen exclaimed. "But whatever for? We have the Nile!"

Amenhotep's eyes narrowed.

"I don't want you traipsing off to the river in your condition. Going for boat rides here, closer to the palace, will be accessible and private."

Tiye puckered her brow.

"I'm sure the baby will have arrived by then."

"Not all of them," the king replied blandly.

Overcome, Tiye threw her small arms around Amenhotep's swarthy frame and squeezed him affectionately.

"That's wonderful! I'll go every day," she promised.

***

Thickets and high grass surrounded the king. Nubian slaves, clad in loincloths, thrashed the underbrush. Bulls fled in all directions. A lion unexpectedly ran out, whipping its spiked tail from side to side. Amenhotep fixed an arrow to his bow and let it fly. The beast roared in pain and collapsed to the ground. Carcasses of animals piled up in tiers. After despatching two dozen, the king ordered a halt to the killing.

"That's enough for one day, Arath." He pulled off his blue helmet. Curly locks clung to his head in a wet mass. "Ensure the beef is distributed to the poor."

The security chief obeyed and ordered an end to the hunt. Pharaoh tapped his horses lightly and steered them to the banks of the Nile. Throwing himself into the shallows, he floated on his back, surveying the fronds of a sheltering palm tree.

"How high is the river this year?" he called out.

"It's over the normal limit, Your Majesty."

"Excellent!" Amenhotep trod water. "I'm going to take some of our Nile god, Hapi's reserves."

***

Excavations created an ever-growing pile of dirt in Malkata. Muddied workmen hauled large baskets of earth from the royal garden to the Nile.

Lord Yuya was visiting his daughter. Pursing her lips, Queen Tiye surveyed the activity from behind a latticed window.

"The hole in our back yard grows ever larger," she observed.

"It needs to be deep," her father replied logically, "if it's to be a lake."

"I just hope we don't dig into the other side of Geb," she stated acidly, referring to the earth god. "It would not do to meet the sky at the bottom of our garden."

Yuya shifted uneasily.

"When is the baby due?" he asked.

"In two months."

"The king will be pleased."

"Oh, blow the king!" Tiye exclaimed vehemently.

"Control yourself." Her father's face registered both fear and alarm as he looked about for evidence of spies. "Remember who you are," he chided.

"I am Queen of Egypt and the Great Wife. Perhaps you are the one who needs reminding."

Her father shook his head. His prominent nose was more pinched than ever.

"The youth of today are certainly freer with their thoughts —" he began.

"Rubbish!" Tiye turned away from the ugly sight of the gaping earthen hole. "My husband loves me, but I sometimes wonder about his actions. He hunts all day," she complained. "When he's not, he spends all our money on building."

"There are no wars to fight, my dear, and as for the money – it resides in Amon's coffers. Do you really want the priests to hoard it?"

"You're right," she admitted grudgingly.

"Does Amenhotep visit the harem?"

"Not yet."

"It seems to me then, that you are blessed with the perfect consort. You are carrying his child, possibly the heir, while he constructs monuments to you and forgoes the charms of other women." Her father selected a piece of fresh date from the sideboard next to him and popped it into his mouth. "No wonder he hunts all day."

"I just wish they'd get rid of that blasted hole," the pregnant queen declared moodily.

She felt an irrational desire to cry. Instead, she glared at her father.

***

Two months later ...

Moping by the earthen bank Amenhotep gazed sadly at the gaping abyss.

"What are you doing here?" Tiye asked, stumbling upon her husband.

"It's wrecked," he muttered.

"Your project has just begun." Amenhotep closed his eyes briefly. He re-opened them and sighed. "That eyesore will remain empty until you put some water into it," she pointed out.

"I can't."

Noting her husband's depression, Tiye joined him on the grass. Picking up a clod of earth, Pharaoh shaped it with powerful, stubby fingers. Tiye waved towards the river.

"All you have to do is run water from the Nile into this cavity through the earth. Or, better still, wait for the floods."

"I hoped there was a natural spring under the earth."

"Maybe there is. The other way is more practical." The queen rose. "Whatever you decide, please hurry darling, the baby is almost due."

Hope stirred in the king. Animated, he scrambled to his feet, losing a sandal in the process. Tiye waited patiently while her husband retrieved his footwear. Grinning shyly, he placed the gob of mud in her hand.

"It's an image of us. It'll guard the entrance to Amon's temple."

"Another temple?"

"Bigger than anything before."

The queen nodded. Picking up her skirts, she climbed up the bank.

"Just don't make me do this again. I am in no condition for hiking."

***

PART I:
Childhood

3.

AKHENATEN

I was born on the first of March. A normal baby, I chewed my toys, gurgled, screamed, and wet myself with gay abandon. There is another story: That I was found in a basket floating in the reeds.

Blinds. Shutters. Closed windows. Mother: Compressed lips and pale.

I never did find out the truth.

***

Pulling down scrolls, scribbling over pictures of Horus, and smashing ithyphallic sculptures of Min, Amenhotep Junior worked off his fury by amalgamating his destruction into one giant mud pie. No one knew why his latest nanny had to leave, but his father was in the Great Hall pleading with the woman to stay.

"I hate her!" the child explained tearfully as a perplexed Queen Tiye looked around her office. "I want my own Mummy to look after me."

Forgetting the disastrous condition of her workplace, Tiye scooped up her son and calmed him. Suddenly, Pharaoh stood in the doorway.

"This has to end immediately. We're running out of staff in the nursery."

Scowling he advanced towards his namesake.

"Don't," his wife pleaded.

Suddenly, the king stood rooted to the spot.

"Isn't this your study?" he asked, surprise replacing wrath.

"Yes, yes – now leave us alone."

Amenhotep Junior, eyes wide with terror, tried frantically to wriggle free. Finally, the queen put him down. Desperate to get away, the child scampered through the rubble. Passing his father, he glanced

31

momentarily at his face, before emitting a wail. Running down the hall-way, crying and ringing his hands, the unhappy prince disappeared into the living room, where he could still be heard.

"Is that boy all there?" Pharaoh asked.

"He's bright," was the gloomy rejoinder.

Unexpectedly, the floods of tears ceased. Both parents hurried down the corridor and put their heads around the living room door. At the end of the room, a handsome, bronzed child crouched before Amenhotep Junior. He offered the toddler a piece of sugar cane.

"Want a ride in my chariot?"

Amenhotep sucked the sweet fibres greedily and nodded.

"Thank Amon for Dhutmose!" Pharaoh exclaimed. His face creased in thought. "Perhaps we could replace the nannies with him."

"It's not a good idea," Tiye replied quickly. "Our eldest son needs to keep developing. A ride in the open air for the brothers will do."

Omitting to tell him their sons would be pulling each other's hair halfway through the chariot ride, Tiye returned to her study with her husband. Sitting gingerly on the edge of a tapestried couch, the king surveyed the ruins about him.

"That brat has an eye for composition."

He pointed to the mud pie with pieces of pottery and bronze frag-ments sticking at odd angles out of its rounded exterior.

***

Maya was building a sandcastle. Small, pudgy hands created mud turrets, holes for windows and a door so that "the evening couldn't get in." His mother, Lady Weret, who was as rotund as her son, beamed.

"Look at Maya building his fort," she observed proudly. "He'll be a great warrior someday."

"I doubt it," Queen Tiye pronounced unkindly.

Overlooking her guest's bullishness, the hostess turned to her with a bright smile.

"And how is handsome little Dhutmose, and Baby Amenhotep?"

"My sons hate each other," Tiye replied briefly, jangling her bracelets.

Lady Weret thought for a bit. She had been led to believe that the opposite was true, and the boys cared deeply for one another.

"Isn't Amenhotep at his terrible two stage?"

"He's five." The queen sighed. "Believe it or not, he's as good as gold. It's only when Dhutmose is around he acts up."

"If that's the case it might be because Baby is secure in his mother's love."

"I love my sons equally," Tiye lied.

She looked down irritably at Maya, who was tugging at his mother's skirts. Standing up, the queen made it clear that her house call was at an end. Seeing another visitor's angry stare, Maya burst into tears. It was not his fault he was plump. He simply did not know when to stop eating. Maya's stomach was a bottomless pit. Never full, or comfortable, it refused to let him know when he had consumed enough. It was as if there was no timer. Tears streamed down his cheeks and plopped onto his mud-encrusted stomach.

"There, there," his mother soothed, handing him a piece of sugar cane.

Soon he was quiet, and in a few moments the child was once again building his castle. Alone.

***

"Hello!" Amenhotep Junior waved cheerily to the boy at the top of the stairs. The obese child stepped back as if the newcomer was about to hit him. It was their first day at school and Maya was miserable. "I'm Amenhotep, but you can call me Junior," the prince continued, clambering up the steps with difficulty.

"I'm M-Maya," the younger child stuttered as the prince reached him.

Amenhotep draped his arm around the child's shoulder.

"We've got our writing lesson together. I saw our names on the list. You're sitting next to me."

That is how their friendship began. Every day the nobleman's son and the prince of Egypt sat next to each other at their lessons. Having an aversion to physical games, the pair huddled together during their lunch hour reading books, or playing *senet*, the Egyptian equivalent of chess. On weekends Queen Tiye suffered herself to visit Lady Weret, "for the good of the empire," as she put it.

"Why can't you mix with normal children?" she asked her son in frustration one day. "Dhutmose has nice friends."

"I'm not Dhutmose and I'm not normal!" Amenhotep yelled.

A few ladies-in-waiting simpered.

"That's right," Tiye said quickly. "You're extraordinary."

Amenhotep flattened his hair which was constantly sticking up at odd angles.

"Now if you've finished feeling sorry for me," he continued huffily, "I'm going to play with Abner."

"The Hebrew?" Tiye's voice did not carry disdain, but a note of anxiety.

Even while Amenhotep threw his mother a challenging glare, his sharp intelligence pinpointed the difference.

"Yes," he answered stubbornly. "The *Jew*."

"Alright," his mother surrendered.

Having expected a verbal sally, the prince self-consciously picked up his writing palette.

"Would you please bring out two bowls of water for our writing, Pawah?" he politely asked a guard.

Clunking flat-footedly out of the nursery in his papyrus sandals, Amenhotep made his way to the lotus pool outside his room. All the while he could feel his mother's eyes – no longer angry, but worried – following his footsteps.

"*What's wrong?*" the child asked himself.

He dipped his brush in a water bowl. Stirring it in his lamp soot cake, he began a hieroglyph. Despite being a budding poet, given to flights of fancy, the child in Amenhotep needed certainty from his elders. Accustomed to his mother's strength, he now felt as if his understanding of her had experienced a strange shift. Although he hated rules, the prince expected their existence and secretly wished Tiye would enforce them. It felt decidedly odd not to be stamping and screaming, until he was dragged off to the outer rooms of the harem to vent his temper on a variety of cushions and toys. Amenhotep Junior relished battling authority. Instead, he now sat dolefully by the pool in perfect freedom, writing.

A naked child splashed into the deep end, opposite him. Swimming across with strong, confident strokes the newcomer pulled himself out of the water.

"I'm here," the visitor announced happily, shaking water over prince and papyrus with equal abandon.

"Stop it, Abner!" Amenhotep barked. "Can't you see I'm composing?" Scrunching up the sheet of paper he began the laborious process of writing his poem all over again. "There's an extra bowl for you," he added. "Although you probably won't need it. You're covered in enough water to fill the Nile many times over."

"Where's my scribe's equipment?"

"You're supposed to bring your own. You *do* own a palette for school, don't you?"

"*You're* the royal host. Surely even a miser like you is rich enough to afford paper, especially since you invited me to a sissy poetry competition."

"Don't get on my nerves today, Abbie," Amenhotep warned. "And start. My mother's watching and she doesn't approve of Jews."

"Oh poop, the court's full of them, including yourself! I'm going back for a swim."

With that the boy executed a belly flop on the lily-covered pond.

"At least he's normal," Tiye remarked to Senta, who was standing by her at the study window. "A nice stroke too," she observed. "My son needs more athletes in his life." She picked up a sheaf of documents. "My work here is done. Make sure Abner has some lunch, and bring the boys up to my study when they've finished."

***

35

Lamps flickered in the shadows while Tiye wrote as if her life depended on it. Drafting a letter to the Canaanite Prince Abdi-Ashirta was not a task she would leave to her army of diplomats and scribes. She needed to keep the insolent Amurru vassal at bay. If he was not kept on a tight leash, the evil prince, who had united nomads and bandits in Syria, would demand gold.

A light tap woke her out of her reverie. Two children stood at the open door. Recognising Abner and her youngest son, she welcomed them. Amenhotep looked undecided, as if he did not know whether to be sullen, or conciliatory in his manner.

"Did you enjoy your afternoon?" the queen asked.

"It was wonderful," Abner replied boisterously, without a trace of shyness. "We swam, ate, and composed poetry."

"You swam; I composed," Amenhotep corrected haughtily. Having decided how to play out the interview, the prince took a chair. Legs dangling off the ebony seat, he peered down at Abner. "You can sit in front of my mother, but only if you prostrate yourself fifty times," he said smugly.

"Why fifty?" the latter asked, puzzled.

"Because that's how old she is," Amenhotep Junior explained with malicious glee.

Tiye indicated a small stool on which Abner seated himself.

"This is made for children," he noted happily. "Look Amenhotep, my feet touch the ground!"

"I have an adult's chair," was the proud retort. "Mummy says I can sit here, isn't that right?"

"You call your mother 'Mummy'?" Abner squealed. "Only babies do that!"

Tiye laughed with him, enjoying making her youngest suffer for the slight, however, inaccurate, about her age. The prince barely batted an eyelid. Instead, he descended into frosty silence.

"So, Abner, do you like poetry?" asked the queen.

"No," he replied candidly with a lop-sided grin.

Tiye's small, dark office, home to covert diplomatic exchanges, was illuminated for the first time. She realised what had brought this child to her attention. Both strong and beautiful, he was future court material.

"*I must find out more about his parentage,*" she thought.

"I do love shooting though," the boy was saying earnestly.

"Like my husband," the queen murmured.

Amenhotep rolled his eyes. For a whole hour he sat in his adult's chair, legs hanging high above the floor, clutching his sheet of poetry in one sweaty palm. No one asked about the piece he had composed, which was so advanced that even a palace scribe would have difficulty with the grammar; so lofty in its sentiments that even priests would never comprehend its spirituality. And still they talked, his mother and the friend he had liked, up until now.

"I have to go," the prince declared eventually. "I have important business to attend to."

He hopped down from his chair, losing both sandals in the process. Scrunching his composition even more tightly in one hand, he violently shoved them back on.

"What do you have there?" Tiye asked, stretching out one hand.

"It's nothing," the boy replied, dying to show off.

"You spent all afternoon writing. I want to see it."

His mother's imperious tone allowed the prince to give in without shame. Inwardly pleased, he feigned reluctance in handing over his paper.

"This is good," Tiye said.

She placed it on her desk and squinted in the lamplight. Amenhotep's gloating was only temporary as, with immense seriousness of purpose, his mother brought out her pen. In swift red slashes she ruined his masterpiece in seconds.

"There," she declared in a satisfied tone, handing it back to him. "That will give you a few useful pointers. Well, off you go on your important business. You don't mind if I keep talking to Abner, do you?"

"Not at all," the boy mumbled.

Crestfallen and infuriated he left the study.

"Close the door, dear," his mother called cheerily after him.

Heavy-hearted, her son obeyed. Once outside in the corridor he inhaled deeply to control his emotions. It was then he noticed the lack of security guards. Due to swap shifts, those about to go off-duty had retired to the end of the corridor. Their muffled voices floated down the passageway as they exchanged greetings with the new sentries. Furtively looking about, the boy reached up on tiptoe and gently slid the bolt across his mother's study door. When he heard it click into position Amenhotep gave a satisfied belch. Pulling up his kilt around his wide hips, he walked westward, whistling.

***

Pharaoh hastily put down his palace paper.

"Who locked the queen in her study, Aanen?"

"Your son," the butler answered.

"Dhutmose? That doesn't sound like him."

"No," the man replied in an aggrieved tone. "Amenhotep Junior."

"But he's only turned six!" his father protested. "He can't reach that high. As for my eldest, he would never do such a thing. You'll have to behead the guards."

"Your Majesty, the younger prince has already confessed."

"You make it sound like an inquisition. Now get me some pancakes. I have a hunt this morning."

"Queen Tiye extracted the truth," the manservant persisted.

"Aah! That makes all the difference." Amenhotep picked up his papyrus scroll, edged with gold, and continued reading the news of the day. Shortly, his Great Wife appeared. "How are you this morning, dearest?"

"Tired."

Tiye sat down at the breakfast table and ordered watermelon and grape juice.

"How's our son?"

"Grounded."

Laughing heartily, the king returned to his paper.

***

4.

Swinging a satchel filled with papyrus, palette, pumice blotters, pieces of *ostraca*, and two new reed pens, Maya made his way to Scribe School. He had forced Mesa, his charioteer, to drop him off at Magnificent Crescent, which was a block away from his destination.

Determined to lose weight, the child puffed along like a Nile boat rowed by strong Nubians. Meanwhile, Amenhotep Junior waited nervously at the school gate. His bodyguards had advised him several time to return indoors.

It was almost time for the first class, and he needed at least five minutes to get to Mathematics. Professor Me-an Strakthat would not be happy if any of his pupils were late. There would be no special treatment for the prince, and the boy's minders had strict instructions from his father to bring him home immediately after school. King Amenhotep had no intention of his son calculating pyramid measurements in detention again.

"Your Majesty, it's nearly eight o'clock," one of the guards pointed out.

"How many times do I have to tell you I'm waiting for my friend, Pawah? Now leave me alone before I put you on probation!"

The man regarded the prince with a look of compassion. It was a wonder Amenhotep Junior had any friends. Perhaps the boy was afraid of yet another offended nobleman's son avoiding him. It happened. First the children were sick, then they sneaked in the back entrance to school. In one extreme case, a boy asked to be moved down a class after Amenhotep struck the unfortunate with a particularly heavy scroll. Just as Pawah was about to suggest *he* wait for the prince's friend, Maya appeared, puffing and struggling valiantly up the tree-lined road of Garden Way.

"He's here!" Amenhotep shouted jubilantly. "See," he said, giving the bodyguard a withering look. "I told you he would come." The school gong rang. "Hurry up, Maya, it's eight o'clock!"

The latter glanced up, his face red and sweaty, to see the prince rushing to help him with his books.

"Who are these people?" the boy panted, finding himself surrounded by several large men, intent on relieving him of his well-deserved lunch. "Please don't touch that," he implored, watching his tasty pudding with syrupy sauce disappear into the hands of a six-foot Syrian.

"Why were you walking to school?" Amenhotep asked as they trudged up the stairs to class. "Chariot break down?"

Maya could hardly hear above the clanking spears and shields of the surrounding escort.

"I wanted the exercise," he explained. "You shouldn't have waited for me. Now we'll both be late."

"We won't be punished. You'll see – I'm Pharaoh's son!"

As the door swung open to reveal Professor Strakthat, the prince immediately realised how wrong he had been. Despite his rank, the teacher was waiting with his favourite switch to give the royal behind six of the best.

"I'm glad you could make it, Maya," the instructor said calmly. "Your latest test scored ninety-eight per cent – top of the class. Well done."

Whispers of admiration went up from his classmates while the boy squeezed himself into the back row and tried to disappear. Meanwhile, his friend was subjected to the oddest caning he had ever witnessed. Strakthat, not content to use an ordinary stick, brought out one dubbed Khufu's Might; a switch which had been shredded at the end for maximum effect. The fact that the tutor had bothered to name his instrument of torture demonstrated the extent of his sadism. Maya shuddered. It was his fault Amenhotep was late. Temporarily shutting his eyes, he tried to blot out the dreadful scene. He need not have bothered. Cries of: "How dare you?" and: "My father will be hearing about this!" floated from the front of the class. This behaviour only served to incense the teacher, and instead of six strokes, the prince received a shower of sharp thwacks about his head and shoulders.

At one point, Amenhotep who, despite his flabby frame, was accustomed to sparring with the athletic Dhutmose, grabbed the cane and hit his mentor. Being too short to reach the adult's head, he settled for strikes against the man's legs. Several students began to laugh, and shouts of: "Fight! Fight!" broke out. Soon the whole class was chanting. Finally, the insurgent found himself led to the principal's office by an ear which was rapidly turning into a cauliflower. Maya sank miserably into a mass of boys who immediately commenced throwing ink cakes and water pots about the unsupervised classroom.

***

"You are charged with inciting a riot," Principal De-ath said quietly. Short hair sticking up over his elongated skull, Amenhotep's jaw was set, his fists clenched. He refused to speak. "I must admit it's an exaggeration," the man conceded.

Still, the prince remained furiously silent. The room was pleasantly quiet and dim after the bright sunlight of a noisy classroom. Reserved for seeing students, the headmaster's front office was labelled the Chamber of Horrors. Amenhotep was shrewd enough to see that there did not appear to be anything remotely horrifying in it, apart from a ceremonial dagger bequeathed by his father to the school on its opening day a decade ago. In fact, he deduced correctly, the room smelled faintly of incense.

"Would you like a sweet?" Without waiting for a reply, De-ath pushed a bowl of amber-coloured sugar crystals towards the rebel. They were the boy's favourite. He licked his lips and involuntarily put out a small hand, before remembering his vow not to co-operate. Reluctantly, he drew it back. "I'm going to have one," the headmaster continued. "Professor Strakthat is always enough to sour my day."

"You're only being nice to me because my father is King," Amenhotep blurted out, unable to restrain himself any longer.

"On the contrary. I despatched a courier to Pharaoh requesting his advice on how to discipline Your Majesty, and he's in favour of a sound thrashing, followed by detention for a month."

"I don't believe it. You're just using scare tactics. Now, if you'll excuse me, I have a writing class to attend."

"You're very good at composing songs, aren't you?"

"Yes, I'm a genius."

"The Great Wife tells me you write. Is that true?"

"Mummy doesn't lie."

Amenhotep bit his lip, remembering Abner's scornful laughter at his title for the most powerful woman in the land.

"I want Your Highness to write me a poem."

"I have a lot to do." Amenhotep hopped off his chair. "You can leave your request for extra homework with my secretary, Pere. He'll attend to everything."

"You're not going anywhere," the headmaster said with an edge to his voice. He drew back the bowl of amber drops and stood up. Suddenly, Amenhotep was aware of the man's size. It was common knowledge that De-ath had been a wrestler once. "Your father wants me to deliver a poem from your tender hand to him by three o'clock this afternoon. If not, he'll punish you himself. Now, you're welcome to send your own messenger to the palace to ascertain whether I'm telling the truth or not, but if I were you, I wouldn't waste any time." Without further ado he shoved a piece of papyrus unceremoniously towards the royal trouble-maker. "You can use my scribe's palette if you wish. Now, do you want me to send a message to Malkata?"

Shaking his head Amenhotep picked up a reed pen and began to write. Satisfied, the headmaster surreptitiously placed the bowl of candy close to the boy's elbow and left the room.

***

"Has he always been like this, Professor Strakthat?"

"He's wilful," the embarrassed teacher replied. He had lost self-control which warranted demotion, or worse.

"Don't fret over your job," the headmaster said, as if reading his thoughts. "The boy's a brat. Thank God he's not the heir. Can you imagine a country ruled by that? He'd be a tyrant!" Professor Strakthat shivered involuntarily, recalling how many second sons became king. "Sometimes gifted children are worse than their retarded counterparts – take, for instance, the bumbling Maya."

"Please forgive me, sir, but Maya topped his math class this term."

"The fat kid who resembles a head of lettuce? Unbelievable!"

Professor Strakthat, who had been obese as a child, said nothing. Inside his head a clammy hand had taken grip. He was spun back to elementary school where a group of children had seized his lunch. Surrounding him, they threw the package to one another, calling him names and singing songs. Tears welled up in his fifty-one-year-old eyes. Excusing himself, he retired to his classroom to blow his nose on a monogrammed kerchief.

***

"Do you like *ostraca*?" Amenhotep Junior asked, lifting his head from an hour of frantic scribbling.

"I prefer writing on wax," Maya confided.

"So do I." The boy sat back, stylus in one hand. "Detention is beginning to bore me."

"I didn't think it was something we had a choice about."

"I can't speak for you, but I deliberately provoke those idiots so that I can have an hour's peace in which to compose my poetry."

"Why can't you do it at home?"

"Because I'm a prince," said Amenhotep haughtily. "I have duties, obligations – things you wouldn't understand."

"Mummy!" Maya's eyes twinkled.

"What?"

"I hear Queen Tiye corrects your work if you do it at home," the latter replied innocently.

Amenhotep's eyes narrowed.

"Occasionally," he assented.

"Abner says she spanks you for bad prose." A wet sponge caught the younger child's ear. "Thank you for the eraser," he said spiritedly. "I need it to correct a sum."

"Why don't you erase the whole lot and save our teacher the bother? Everyone knows you're only here to keep me company."

"But of course! What are friends for?"

***

King Amenhotep awoke one morning, alone in his bed, as Amon intended monarchs to sleep, and thought about his wife. Calling his dresser to bathe and robe him, he readied himself to walk through the shady porticos which led to the harem. A page boy was dispatched to deliver news of his imminent arrival, lest his queen be caught unawares. It was not unfashionable for first wives to sleep in late, or even take lovers, and he had often wondered how Amenhotep Junior had wound up so unlike him. But it was not for a civilised spouse to ask questions.

At half past ten his fanbearer announced the presence of Pharaoh Amenhotep: Nebmaatre; living forever and ever: Life! Health! Prosperity! The chief consort graciously received her husband, who was garbed in a dazzling sheath of gold and red. The richness of the damask, she reflected, indicated importation from Mitanni, a country from which his ancestors originated.

Tiye enquired after her husband's health, while a servant poured newly bottled white wine from her estate. The king took a sip from a gold cup. He enjoyed visiting his first wife. Not only was she efficient, but after ten years of marriage there remained much civility between them. Her apartment, so unlike his, was Spartan with its simple, brightly patterned rugs and drapes. Knowing her husband derived happiness from her company, Tiye made light conversation.

45

"Do we have enough for a party?" Amenhotep eventually asked. "Our youngest child has a friend." Pharaoh rattled his brains. "Maya."

"I know his mother. How much do you want?"

"Junior's bought the boy a chariot." Amenhotep drank a third of the wine.

"Gold-plated?"

"With a charioteer. Maya's only four. He's a bit small to be taking the reins on his own, even if we harness the carriage to ponies."

"Are we giving away ponies?"

Tiye noticed her husband's goblet was emptying rapidly.

"The reason I came to see you is because I want a bit of a celebration, too." Always careful not to encroach on her husband's personal decision, Tiye remained silent. "I want something cheery for Karnak."

The rest of the wine disappeared.

"You want to throw a party for the priests?"

Tiye could not help herself. It was like a poor relative trying to host a rich uncle.

"For the people." Steel entered Amenhotep's voice. "I think we need them on our side if we're going to assault the priesthood."

Folding her arms, the queen gave him her full attention.

"I'm listening."

***

"What do you want, Junior?"

Picking up his sceptre, Dhutmose fastidiously arranged his robes, and tried to ignore the brother capering around his ankles.

"Your presence at a party this afternoon."

"I'm attending Mass at the temple and so are you. We're to be in our pews by noon. Your nanny should have told you."

"I fired her."

"No wonder you're not dressed! Now hurry up. Today Dad is going to bring down the priesthood and he wants to walk up the aisle with all of Mum's kids."

"Why? I have important preparations to attend to."

"Because the priests have labelled us bastards."

"Ooh!" exclaimed Amenhotep Junior, leaping back. "That's a rude word! I'm telling!"

"It wasn't used in that sort of context. Besides, you'd better be nice to me if you want my presence at your silly party."

"I'll make a deal with you: I'll get dressed if you come to Maya's."

"You must be mistaken. Commoners come to us."

Unperturbed, Amenhotep handed his sibling a scrap of papyrus.

"That's the address. Be there at two p.m. and don't be late."

"How am I going to make a sacrifice, eat my lunch and turn up to ... Pyramid Way by two?"

"Do it. And bring some friends."

"Why do I bother listening to you? You're only seven."

"Six! Because I have charisma."

***

Tasselled cubes of purple and yellow flashed cheerily from flag-poles lining Karnak's avenues. Cobalt blue sky arched over thousands of people, who sensibly sheltered under light awnings where free beverages, from grape juice to beer, were served. Mid-morning brought added supplies of wine, normally reserved for the upper classes. Mounds of duck, quail, and pigeon were piled atop hundreds of trestles decked out in Pharaoh's colours of green, red, and white. Dancers whirled through streets to the rhythm of musicians beating drums and blowing fifes.

Humming to himself, Amenhotep Senior donned his shortest kilt. He was the only pharaoh in history to have women scream at him. Normally he covered himself in long robes out of deference to his Great Wife, who became distressed with the attention accorded him by the female populace on their public outings. Today, however, he was a god, and intended to show the priests the extent and power of his popularity. All the stops would be pulled out as, with the permission of his queen,

Amenhotep strutted his stuff and warned the clergy of his intention to appropriate more of their funds for his temples.

***

"Mum," interrupted Amenhotep Junior, his chubby arms full of toys. "May I take these to my wing?"

"Whose are they?" she asked, peering over her letters.

"No one's. I got them from Dad's fan club."

"Have you been in those mail bags again?"

"I'm economising," her son replied. "I won't ask for any more birthday gifts if you allow me to take these. Can I have them?"

"But they belong to your father. You must respect the concept of personal property."

Amenhotep let the toys fall onto the floor and placed tiny hands on his hips.

"He's the one who keeps nicking all my stuff!"

"It's all his. He's Pharaoh, remember."

"Maya's got a party. There are heaps of kids coming, and I don't want to blow the budget."

Tiye suppressed the urge to smile as she waved him away.

"Only make sure you're at the temple by midday."

"The priests banned me last June."

"Not today," Tiye said sharply. "Your father specifically commanded you be there."

"Alright, Mummy," said the child, picking up his loot. "If you say so."

***

Steam mingled with men's shouts, women's rapid talking, and the screeches of a maid being buffeted by her superior. The fragrance of baking bread and cakes mixed with the savoury aromas of duck, vegetable broth, bread, and humus. It made for a heady, chaotic environment in the palace kitchens.

Amenhotep Junior extended his arms outwards.

"I want a very big cake."

"Coming up right away, Your Majesty."

"And lots of different desserts."

"We're whisking eggs and flour."

Climbing onto a footstool, the child peered into a bubbling cauldron.

"For heaven's sakes' Junior, it's half past eleven!"

Whirling round at the sound of Dhutmose's voice, the prince almost upset his chair and disappeared into the vat. A cook deftly caught Amenhotep and placed him on his slippered feet. Without further ado, Dhutmose seized his younger brother and dragged him bodily along the flagstones, which was covered in traces of feathers, blood, and rinds. Too preoccupied to cry, Amenhotep rapidly calculated the food and gifts he would need to present to his very best friend at Pyramid Way.

"Senta!" Dhutmose roared, pushing open the gilt doors.

His eyes fell on an untidy pile of statuettes.

"Oh yes," his brother explained quickly, "that's from Dad's mail."

"But those bags are full of fertility statues!"

"And toys."

"They're not suitable for children."

"Maya won't notice. Besides, some of the pieces are quite nice."

On hearing her name, Tiye's trusted attendant came running out of the bathroom with a brush and comb. Prising Amenhotep Junior out of his brother's hands, she set to work.

"Do you know about this?" the heir queried hotly.

"Queen Tiye had me clear out the adult stuff. I suggest you get to the temple. I'll have Baby there on time."

Momentarily mollified, the older boy vacated the premises. A distant shriek came from his brother who was having his hair combed.

***

Women raked their cheeks. The screaming was so deafening the more nervous priests blocked their ears with linen and wax wads. Every

49

policeman and soldier in Egypt appeared to be on guard outside Karnak. To no avail they attempted to hold back the hysterical crowds, which were now inebriated. Gratitude for the free food and booze, mingled with the heat, music, and arrival of the god himself, turned the crowd insane.

"Dear Amon, my vest's ripped!" swore Dhutmose aggrievedly. "Why did you have to wear such a short kilt, Dad?"

"Hold your brother's hand," his father ordered.

"Where's Mummy?" Amenhotep Junior asked, clopping between them in sandals several sizes too big for him.

"She's arriving later," Pharaoh answered, waving brightly at a sobbing female overcome with lust. "It wouldn't be safe for her."

"It'd be a damned sight safer for us if she was here," retorted Dhutmose, jerking his head back from a screaming fan. "For one thing, it'd tone down the girls."

"Be grateful I'm not naked," the king replied in a flat voice. "It used to be the custom on celebration days."

A line of soldiers accidentally broke, causing several hundred people to fall forward on top of one another.

"Dad, we've got a riot on our hands," Dhutmose said in a quavering voice, his panic rising.

"Keep walking, we're almost there."

But worry had overtaken the heir. Alarmed, he swivelled his head around as police whacked people smartly over the head with batons.

"It'll stop once we reach the hall," a boy said behind them.

"Hump!" the stricken prince greeted his friend, Horemheb.

"If your father's mortuary temple doesn't get every penny, the populace will lynch the priests."

"Hopefully, I won't have to sink this low when I'm crowned," grumbled the prince.

"No need to worry, you don't have Dad's sex-appeal," a voice squeaked at waist level.

Dhutmose looked down at his brother's crescent of milk teeth with deep disdain.

***

Amenhotep-the-Magnificent pulled off his wig and ran one hand through his wet hair.

"That was a success," he said, with the satisfaction of one who had accomplished exactly what he set out to achieve.

"Very clever dear," Tiye responded in a chillier tone.

"Did you see that? I'm going to have a solid gold roof, columns of electrum, and over two feet of thick silver on the floors! No plated wooden stuff."

He laid back on a couch, his face suffused with bright pleasure.

"Not to mention several additions to your harem."

"Ha! Ha!" Amenhotep's head jerked up. "Thank you for helping me," he said. "It was very understanding of you."

Gazing at the perfect physique of her husband, Tiye reflected there was not an inch of fat over the powerfully developed muscles.

"You look fifteen," she said, remembering their courtship.

Amenhotep leapt up.

"Now for Junior's party. I'd better make sure the cooks produce a cake." Kissing his wife swiftly on the brow, the king temporarily halted. A romantic impulse swept over him and he kissed her again, this time lingeringly on the mouth. "I'd better go," he said finally, pulling away. "Otherwise, we'll be the only two partying."

***

"What does Amenhotep think he's doing?" thundered High Priest Ity.

"Building his temple," Minthu replied.

He broke off a piece of dry biscuit and dipped it in a mug of warm milk sweetened with honey. Ity clenched his fists in rage and paced around the cedar dining table at which Minthu was unsuccessfully trying to break his fast in peace.

"It's going to be HUGE. How much of our treasury is he planning to take with him?"

51

"I'm sure you'll get it back," Minthu said, alluding to rumours of tomb-robbing, in which priests played a part.

"It's that female cow, Tiye's fault. She's behind all this."

"I haven't seen His Majesty interfere in her husband's affairs. It's the secret of her success."

"Tiye's a commoner. I've never recognised her as the Great Wife. And those children of hers are bastards, every one of them."

"The only illegitimate offspring are the ones which keep appearing in Amon's nursery," replied Minthu, referring to the harem where priests visited the handmaidens of the temple.

"I'm beginning to wonder about you," remarked Ity, resting one glowing coal of an eye upon his head tutor. "Where do you stand in all this?"

"On the side of sanity. Our king is married to a brilliant woman who has brought the annual palace expenditure under budget ever since she ascended the throne. The royal couple never borrow from our temple. There has been no famine in Egypt during the reign of Amenhotep-the-Third. I say let him build a mortuary temple. We can charge at the door when he's dead and buried."

Ity's eyes slanted into dangerous slits.

"That's hardly amusing."

"It's sad because it's the truth." Minthu fixed him with a calm, steady gaze. "A downright tragedy that Amon, who is our supreme god, seeks to devour all the material wealth of our country."

"You are one mite away from blasphemy."

"On the contrary, I've been fasting and praying to the god all day." Minthu pushed back his hexagonal stool. "Now if you don't mind, I wish to walk the grounds in peace without your permission. You are not Pharaoh, yet."

The colour drained out of Ity's purple and pink complexion. His anger was so great that he sat down, unable to say another word.

***

Struggling out of his linen kilt, Maya folded it away. No one had come to his birthday party. Standing on tiptoe, he placed his wet loin-cloth on a shelf marked: "Washing". It was piled high with his laundry, and the last item upset the balance so that the entire lot tumbled onto his small head. Buried in an assortment of towels, shorts, underpants, kilts, gowns, and gloves, the toddler began to cry from shock and fear. Nanny Lamish hurried into his room. She pulled the boy out of the mess and sat him on her lap. Wiping his eyes, she commanded him to blow his nose into her clean handkerchief.

"It's your birthday. No one should cry on the day he brought joy to his mother's heart."

"But the clothes – I'll get into trouble."

"Hush! That shelf is too high. From now on you can put everything into a basket. How does that sound? And since you're so clean, we'll empty it twice a day."

Maya brightened. No one had ever suggested he had faultless standards of hygiene. He had always been painfully aware of needing to change more regularly than everyone else because he was continually drenched in perspiration. Without further ado, his nanny led him to the swimming-pool which was far nicer than a bath. Maya paddled at the shallow end, while Lamish pointed out the types of fish darting in and out of the lotus buds. Soon, he forgot about yet another failure to be normal, and began to splash happily in the shaded pool. After half an hour he called out to his nanny from the middle of the pond where he had caught a baby perch. Turning around to face her, he squealed as it jumped out of his slippery hands.

"That's not how you catch fish," a schoolboy's voice corrected.

"Amenhotep! What are you doing here?"

"It's your birthday, dummy. I brought presents."

"But my party finished hours ago, and no one was there."

Maya almost wailed at the memory.

"Do you want your gifts, or not?"

The child's eyes grew round at the sight of several boxes.

"Is there more than one?"

"If you get out of the pool, you'll find out." Amenhotep Junior sat on its edge and removed his wig. "I'm sorry I'm late," he apologised. "I was delayed."

But Maya was not listening. Small fingers, trembling with delight, opened an exquisitely painted wooden box set down before him. Inside, were two brindled bunnies which he pulled out with a shout of joy.

"I love rabbits!"

"Why do you think I got them for you? Don't take them out of the box," Amenhotep warned. "They'll run away."

The frightened bundles of fur merely huddled together with flattened ears. Slowly, they started to reach up and sniff the air. Nanny Lamish came to the rescue. Shoving the pets unceremoniously back into their container, she beamed widely at the royal visitor.

"They're fabulous," she declared. "I'll put them in a cage with some lettuce. Meanwhile, go inside and have dessert. We've got sticky pudding, date cake, and lots more."

Unable to resist sweetmeats, Amenhotep followed her into the house as if in a dream. Maya, who was feeling hungry again, puttered inside with them.

"I hope you don't mind if some of my friends join us," the prince said, devouring a date slice as the crunch of chariot wheels braked outside.

Maya was about to reply when Dhutmose burst into the hall, leading a group of children. Striding across the wooden floorboards, he hugged Maya and presented him with a gold locket. Lamish and the servants bustled about, bringing out the treats they had wanted to serve Maya's school chums several hours ago. Amenhotep's eye caught a glistening green jelly.

"Don't forget," he said, pointing a spoon at his brother, "Maya's *my* friend. Gold won't buy him." Turning to his gelatine surprise he dug in. "We'll have to get this at court," he muttered.

Maya gazed at the locket as if unable to believe it was for him. Dhutmose laughed heartily, and threw himself on the nearest divan.

"Oh, my goodness, it's Pharaoh's heir!" gasped Lady Weret from the rooftop where she was doing her afternoon needlework. Dropping her sewing and running downstairs, she called out to her husband who, like most of the household, was taking an afternoon nap. "Get up, Iawy, the king's sons are here!"

"Look, Mummy," cried Maya as Lady Weret, with her ladies-in-waiting, entered the dining hall. "Solid gold!"

"Yes, dear."

His mother immediately approached Prince Dhutmose, who bowed from the waist.

"Don't prostrate yourself," he implored as she tried to curtsey. "A woman as beautiful as Your Ladyship should never have to grovel."

Iawy, who was adjusting his robes behind his wife so as to look presentable, raised his eyebrows. Amenhotep Junior responded by crunching an apple as loudly as possible.

"I have another present for you," he declared, turning to Maya. "Come outside." Taking the wide, sweaty palm in his own chubby (and now sticky) one, the prince led his friend into the sunshine.

"Where are we going?" Maya wheezed.

"To the gate."

"But why? I'm not allowed out of the house, except to go to school. And you shouldn't go anywhere without your guards."

"Don't be silly. You have to do everything I say because I'm a prince and you're only an aristocrat."

"An aristo-what? You use such big words, Amenhotep. I can't understand you."

"Call me 'Akhy'."

"But why? It's not your name."

"'Akhy' is short for 'Akhenaten'." The boy lowered his voice. "It's my secret name for when I grow up and become a priest. For now, you have to use the code." They were at the gate. "Do you like it?"

With a flourish, Amenhotep extended his hands. Maya pushed his head through the wooden bars.

"I can only see chariots."

"Can you see yours?"

The boy shook his head and then he saw. Two beautiful white ponies stood next to a small blue-and-yellow chariot. A muscular, dark-haired man waved to him. Amenhotep rocked back and forth on the sycamore bars.

"He's yours. His name's Arktakthat."

"Ark-tak-what?"

"You can just say 'hey, come here.' That's all I ever do. It saves remembering names."

Maya stared dumbstruck, as Nanny Lamish appeared at his side.

"Come in, dear," she said, taking his hand. "We're missing the birthday boy and his best friend."

"LOOK what Akhy – I mean Amenhotep Junior – gave to me. My very own chariot with a *driver*."

The woman dropped her charge's hand, and raised both palms to cover her mouth. Amenhotep grinned. Slowly, Maya pushed the gate open with his small, strong body, and thumped along to where Arktakthat stood. The charioteer unfurled a canvas step to the blue-and-gold interior. Maya knew they were the colours of Amenhotep Junior. He held the rail as if in a dream and admired the beauty of the burnished carriage.

"Where to, my lord?"

"Anywhere," the child breathed.

"Anywhere it is."

Arktakthat flicked the reins and they were off, cantering down a tree-lined boulevard on a sunny afternoon of the best birthday of Maya's life.

***

5.

AKHENATEN

I remember the clay ... white and brown ... speeding, gliding under my child's hand; pulling itself up towards me ... sliding away.

The firm adult control of the studio head, whose kindness opened a new world for a delinquent child, and channelled energy from sheer bloody-mindedness into creativity.

(Laughs)

It only half-worked!

***

Amenhotep Junior skidded along the polished granite floor with his freshly waxed feet.

"Now you try," he dared Maya.

They were standing in an empty artist's studio among mounds of clay, jars of paint, brushes, and rags.

"I don't know," the worried child said. "I might go through the door."

"Hurry up, I'm a prince and you're keeping me waiting."

Taking a deep breath, Maya shut his eyes and tried to skate as he had seen Amenhotep do. Instead, he tripped into a forward roll and banged his head against the nearest pillar.

"I'm hurt," he whimpered.

"Stop crying," ordered Amenhotep, alarmed at the prospect of being found out.

"What's going on here?"

A tall man, arms on his hips, towered over the prince.

"Nothing. As a matter of fact, we were just leaving."

"Waxing your feet again, eh, Akhy? Why don't you learn to use my products for a useful purpose instead?"

"Do address me as 'Your Majesty'," Amenhotep sniffed.

"When you respect me, I'll respect you. Name's Men, by the way – head of the king's studios. How do you do?"

"I know what your name is."

"But you've never once used it, have you, you snotty little brat?"

Amenhotep was so stunned by the artist's manner, he gulped air, but no words came out. Before he knew what was happening, the man had gathered Maya up into his arms. At the same time, he propelled the prince to a potter's wheel.

"Now," Men directed, setting Maya down gently in order to pick Amenhotep up and dump him unceremoniously on a stool. "I reckon you owe me an hour to work off the cost of that wax. He grinned a gap-toothed smile. "At least, that's how long you normally stay down here before your nanny finds you, isn't that right?"

"You can't make me do this!" the prince protested.

"I thought you were an artist. You sit around writing all day, don't you?"

"This isn't composing," replied Amenhotep, vacating his chair. "It's pottery-making. Only the lower classes do that."

"Is that a fact?" The accomplished potter scratched his head. "I'll put it to you like this: If your father discovers that his younger son – and only second in line to the throne, mind you – comes down to the studios every Tuesday with the sole purpose of stealing His Majesty's wax, what do you reckon he'll do?"

"Nothing," replied Amenhotep bravely, while his lower lip trembled. "It's Dad's wax, after all."

"I believe your father, being a serious artist himself, would approve if you came down here and did something useful like making a pot, a wax head, or maybe a nice pottery hippo. It would take half an hour and I could turn my head to your graffiti-spraying and destruction of my property for the rest of the afternoon."

"How much is this going to cost?" asked Amenhotep, mustering his best worldly manner.

Before Men could give vent to a harsh reply, Maya squealed with joy.

"Look, I've made a crocodile!"

In his hand lay a small, patterned lizard. Men patted him on the head.

"Bravo! Would you like to paint it?" Maya nodded vigorously. He did not have to be asked twice to pick up various brushes laden with yellow, red, blue, and green pigment. With deep concentration he produced a flamboyant work.

Realising he was trapped, Amenhotep asked for clay and reluctantly resumed his seat.

"What do I do?"

"Hold on," commanded Men as he started the wheel.

***

Splashing Maya with water, Amenhotep was answered with a flick of paint. Soon clay and watercolour were flying around the studio with gay abandon, interspersed with giggling and screams of: "Don't!": "Wait till I catch you!" and: "Take that!"

"What's going on here?" Pharaoh asked mildly.

Men had swung open the door with a flourish, in order to show off his new pupils diligently decorating vases. Instead of receiving royal approbation, the renowned artist hung his head, while the king absorbed the scene of his wrecked studio.

"Is that you, Junior?" Amenhotep enquired of his son, who was covered in canary yellow.

"It is!" was the joyful reply as the boy wiped his eyes. "We were just making a pot for your *Opet* Festival."

"I apologise, Your Majesty," Men whispered. "Normally they're very good. I'll have this room tidied at once."

"Not immediately," the king demurred, tiptoeing delicately over a tafla lump. He picked up a piece of pottery covered in erratic marks. "Did you draw this?" he asked his namesake.

"Maya did – under my instructions, of course."

Pharaoh turned to face a terrified, overweight child still clutching a gob of clay.

"You're the mathematician," he said cheerfully. "And as a friend of the family, most welcome at the palace." Turning to his son the king suggested: "Why don't you boys get cleaned up and join me for morning tea?"

"Are there any sweets?" Amenhotep Junior asked shamelessly.

"There are always sweets, and you can also tell me all about your paint fight." The king held up the pottery piece with its sketch. "May I keep this, Maya?" he asked.

"Y-yes, Y-Your M-Majesty," he stuttered. "I c-can do a b-better one," he added quickly.

"No need: I like the expressive style." Whistling softly to himself, Amenhotep stepped over a large broken vase. "These sessions are going well, Men. See to it my son and his friend have weekly lessons." Relieved, the head of the studio tried to prostrate himself. "Don't bother," the king said. "You might cut yourself."

***

Inside the Great Hall, trays of red, orange, and yellow cakes stood piled high next to pitchers of milk, and grape juice. Freshly scoured, and wearing clean linen robes, the royal children padded through a vast colonnade to their meal.

"Ah, just what a thirsty artist needs after a hard morning's work!" Amenhotep Junior declared.

Selecting several titbits for his plate he sat down to eat with a hearty appetite. Meekly, Maya followed suit, but only took a single biscuit and half a glass of pomegranate juice. Glancing furtively at Pharaoh, the child squeezed into a seat furthest away from him.

"So, Maya," the king began pleasantly. "Is this your first visit?"

"N-no, Your M-Majesty," replied the guest, dropping his biscuit.

"He had a birthday last month," the younger Amenhotep said. "You knew that."

"I haven't seen you at court before," the king continued. "Is your father a nobleman?"

"He does all our taxes," Prince Amenhotep replied again, this time with an edge in his voice. "You know who he is, Dad!"

Maya's eyes widened at the prince's daring.

"Y-yes," the child responded, feeling as if he were visiting the palace on false pretences. "I've met Junior's mother – I mean Her Majesty – the Great Wife."

"Ah! And what did you think of my beloved wife?"

"Think?"

Maya was so baffled, every thought in his head disappeared. He stared impolitely at Pharaoh with his mouth open.

"She terrified him," Amenhotep said angrily. "Like you're doing now." Getting out of his tailor-made child's throne, the prince walked over to his friend and pressed his hand. "Don't worry," he reassured. Turning to his father the prince said crossly: "He's only *four*, Dad!"

"I know," the king replied hurriedly, hoping that no tears were about to be produced. "And from what I heard, likes horses. I was hoping you both might like to join me on a hunt."

***

In the palace stables Prince Amenhotep crammed a small blue war crown over his auburn locks, while a soldier attempted to squeeze Maya's head into a round, black helmet.

"No good," the soldier announced loudly. "We need a LARGER size."

Maya reddened as several ever-increasing sizes of helmets and belts were brought to fit him. Eventually, Amenhotep Junior picked up an adult's hat and stuffed it with rags. Cramming it onto Maya's head, the prince pulled the strap hard under his chin, and expertly double-looped it. Then, Amenhotep took a groomsman's waistband, stuck a couple of extra holes in it with his fishing hook, which he kept in a leather pouch slung around his wide hips, and clipped it around his friend.

61

"That's a safety tie," he explained to the wheezing child. "You can loosen or tighten it. Same with the belt."

Prince Dhutmose appeared with a whip and bridle. Maya stared in awe at the young boy with the perfect physique. Attired in a fresh kilt, the prince wore a blue war crown adorned with a gold cobra. Immaculate from his crowned head to his leather sandals, Dhutmose led a roan stallion from the stables to the compound. Maya gawked, and then rubbed his eyes, as if he had seen a vision.

"You admire him, don't you?" observed Amenhotep jealously.

"H-he's very regal."

"That's because he's an athlete. Wins every chariot race on our track."

"What's a 'track'?"

"Come and see. It's right outside our front door."

Amenhotep pulled his friend into the sunlight where scores of groomsmen and soldiers were assembled in the stadium for the morning hunt.

Snorting horses reared, whinnied and shook their manes, as chariots were cleaned and checked for loose axles and rusty cogs.

Maya gazed at the carriages, some of which were embossed with silver. Others shimmered with gold, and all were higher than he. Multi-coloured spokes whirled as charioteers tested them.

In one corner, he saw a small red-wheeled vehicle which stood alone.

"Whose is that?"

"*That* belongs to Hump, Dhutmose's best friend," Amenhotep explained. "He's a child-soldier. Recruited at our age, he was pulled out of bed one night and kidnapped by bandits, only to be rescued by the king's soldiers. His mother died, screaming like a stuck pig, and his father had all his privates removed before the family home was torched. Everyone in the village died," Amenhotep concluded. "Everyone, that is, except Hump. That's why his chariot sits there in the corner, all alone. He's an outcast."

Maya gulped.

"Is – is he very f-fierce?"

"You'll see him at the hunt."

At that moment a group of men in front of them moved away and Maya found himself gazing at the biggest open space he had ever seen.

"Let me show you the track," offered Amenhotep, pushing his friend into the middle of the wide, dusty arena. "All the charioteers line up in their carts at the south end of the stadium. We sit up there in the middle and they race round and round, doing laps. The first one across the line wins."

"Does he get anything?"

"The prize is supper with Dad and a dancing girl, or two." The prince dug Maya in the ribs.

"What do you mean?"

Instead of answering, Amenhotep tugged his friend's hand and headed for the exit.

"Come on. We're going to be late."

They ran across the field, out the wooden gates, and into Queen Tiye's belly.

"Be sure to stay with the others on the hunt today," was all she said. "And look out for Maya. I don't want him taken home in an ambulance."

"What's an 'ambulance'?" asked Maya breathlessly.

Suddenly he was heaved into a chariot by a burly chauffeur. Tying the boy in, Arktakthat smiled.

"It's a special chariot for when you're sick. The driver gallops through the streets and yells: 'Ambulance! Get out of the way!'"

Maya giggled.

"Does the chariot have red spokes?" he asked. "I saw one of those this morning."

"Don't worry, Maya. You're not going home in one. I'll take good care of you."

Appearing out of nowhere, Amenhotep Junior stood on tiptoe outside the blue-and-gold carriage. He handed his friend a miniature whip. It fitted Maya's hand perfectly.

A serious boy, no more than seven, strode towards them. Clad in a grey army kilt, he wore two daggers stuck in his belt on either side of his trim waist.

"Great day for the lions, Your Majesty," he intoned in a deep voice.

"Yes, it is, Hump," Amenhotep Junior replied.

The boy moved on.

"*That's* Hump?" Maya's eyes were round with wonder.

"His real name's Horemheb."

"Are we fighting lions?"

"Not fighting," corrected Amenhotep. "Hunting." The prince smacked the chariot sides. "Take him away, Arktakthat."

Maya stayed silent as they rumbled along. As if understanding his passenger's trepidation, the driver made small talk, pointing out the various chariot models, and ranks of personnel assembled in the paddock outside the king's stables.

"That's a Horus cart." Arktakthat pointed to a bronze carriage which sported a falcon in profile. "They have green wheels."

"What about the yellow ones?"

"We have two priests on board today, Maya."

"Do priests hunt?"

"These ones do!" the charioteer laughed.

It was a deep, husky sound. Maya instantly felt safe. He joined in with his high-pitched child's giggle, until his eye was caught by the small, red-wheeled chariot rolling past. In it the serious boy was expertly flicking his black ponies with a whip as they trundled to the front.

"Is Horemheb really an orphan?"

"The boy has parents, but his family aren't rich. He joined the army young."

"So, his mother wasn't stabbed?"

Arktakthat raised his eyebrows.

"His mother is my mother's washerwoman."

"And is his father alive?"

"He died in a fire. A band of Libyans torched his village three years ago." They rumbled towards a rocky outcrop containing several lions in cages. Pharaoh Amenhotep-the-Magnificent readied himself to fell them as they were released from their pens. "I suppose your royal friend told you something different."

"The prince told me porkies," replied Maya flatly.

***

6.

Holding his books limply in one arm, head bowed, Maya stood alone in the dark hallway. It was term break and he had been hunting for Prince Amenhotep. Everyone, including the king, was busy. Queen Tiye had not been approached. Secretly, he was afraid of the intelligent, harsh woman he now called 'aunty', and tried to avoid her whenever possible. Dhutmose was consumed with outdoor pursuits and, being an older boy, had little in common with a five-year-old. Only the younger prince, he realised, lit up the palace, which he now considered to be his second home. Maya shivered. He did not wish to return to his house where his father's bullying had become worse during school holidays. So, the child stood miserably by a papyrus-shaped pillar, killing time.

"Looking for someone?" Pharaoh's kindly face was inches from his own.

"N-no, Your M-Majesty."

"Skulking in the corridors? Very good then. As you were." Amenhotep wandered ahead, before changing his mind and turning back. "Would you like a walk, Maya? I'm going to Karnak to inspect its granaries."

"Oh, yes please!" cried the child, relieved not to be left in the dark passage.

Amenhotep took the boy's hand and they walked outside through the porticos. There were no visible bodyguards, although Maya knew they were everywhere. Lurking behind columns and walkways, they covered the royals with an invisible shield.

At the temple Pharaoh cut an imposing figure as he chatted easily with senior priests and acolytes. He even acknowledged the young dancing girls, who peeked out from corners, hopeful of catching a glimpse of their king.

"Are there any children here?" Maya piped up.

"Amon has a harem, so there must be a few." Amenhotep turned to him. "I'm very sorry for your sake that Akhy isn't around."

"Do you call him 'Akhy', too? But that's his secret name! He'll kill me when he finds out everyone knows."

Amenhotep gave a deep belly-laugh. Placing large chunky hands gently under the boy's armpits, he swung him into the air, and carried him through the hall of famous kings. Pointing out vivid walls painted in primary colours, Pharaoh read aloud the hieroglyphic inscriptions of his bygone ancestors. They walked to the far end of the complex and ventured into the section of Tuthmosis-the-Great. There was a lot of worship here, Pharaoh explained because Tuthmosis had conquered many lands and formed an empire on his own, for the glory of Amon. Wandering through the impressive pillared hall Amenhotep taught the fascinated child about the mighty rulers of his family.

At first, worried he weighed too much, Maya was tense. Eventually, however, he relaxed in the warm, tanned arms of this man who was physically much stronger than his own father. Feeling secure he began to ask questions. The king responded with clear, precise answers, rather like Queen Tiye, except in a more easy-going manner.

"I thought you only liked hunting," Maya commented as they reached the main granary.

"In other words, you're surprised I'm not a brainless action man."

"Oh no!" squeaked the child, flushing. "I d-didn't mean –"

"That's what comes of having an intelligent wife, I suppose," the king sighed.

"Do you love her?"

"With all my heart." They entered a huge room filled with grain. "Only marry someone you love, Maya, because marriage lasts until you die."

"That's a long time," gulped the boy, looking up at the largest wheat mountain he had ever seen.

The king put him down.

"This is where the priests keep the spare grain for the people of Egypt. It's only used for emergencies, to supplement poor harvests, or when there is famine."

"Shouldn't people get the reserves from you?"

"I'm a busy king, so our priests distribute it."

"But what if they didn't give people the food and kept it to themselves?"

Amenhotep scratched behind one ear.

"Why would they want to do that?"

"So they could sell it at a high price when there was a famine, and get more gold for their temples."

The king escorted Maya rapidly from the storeroom. On their way down Malkata Avenue he was ominously silent. Knowing he had somehow offended, Maya puffed alongside the king. The child's new sandals, worn specially for palace visits, cut between his toes. At last, Amenhotep became aware of stertorous breathing next to him. He awoke from his introspection.

"That was a long way for you," he observed compassionately, picking up Maya again. "You're tired. I'm sorry. It was very inconsiderate of me not to think of your legs."

"Oh, no!" the child protested. "I had a wonderful time."

The boy's linen kilt momentarily bunched around his waist. Pharaoh was about to pull it down to cover his legs, before noticing red streaks. Four cuts across the tiny lower legs stung his vision.

"I have an idea," he said, forcing down a surge of anger. "Would you like to stay with us at the palace?"

"In the harem?" asked Maya, quailing at the thought of spending any time with the Great Wife.

"You could share Akhy's – I mean Junior's – room. School is nearby, although you are welcome to be taught by private tutors, just like my son. I think he misses you since he was expelled last spring."

A cloud swept over Maya's face.

"Father would be angry."

"He wouldn't," Pharaoh responded quickly. "In fact, you could stay here, starting with tonight. In that way you wouldn't have to go back home. I could get your things and bring them back."

"Can I see my mother?"

"Whenever you want. She could stay for sleepovers in the harem. Would you like that?"

"And my father?"

"You can invite him," Pharaoh replied lightly.

"What if I didn't want him to come?"

"Then he would have to stay at home."

Maya brushed back his hair. A ray of hope swept over him. One small arm clasped the king's neck.

"Would you be my father?" he asked timidly.

Pharaoh pushed the plump bottom higher in the crook of his elbow.

"Your wish is my command, Maya. We can do lots of fun things together. I'll always be here for you," he added, kissing the sweaty brow.

***

"This is your bed." Amenhotep Junior pointed to one corner. Despite his haughty exterior, he was more excited than he had been in his whole life. Finally, he had a real friend and a brother close to his age. "Is it alright?" he added anxiously.

Maya, who was busy stroking the linen sheets, turned down a heavy brocade quilt.

"Oh, it's beautiful," he breathed. "Is this a puppy?" he asked, noticing a small black-and-white ball next to his pillow.

"He's six weeks old."

"For me?"

"He wouldn't be on your bed if he was mine." Amenhotep turned around and stretched out his arms. "This room needs re-arranging," he pronounced. "I'm going to get Bak."

"Who's Bak?"

"Men's son."

"Is he nice?"

"He's a great artist," the prince declared to his friend, who was none the wiser for the explanation.

***

It was afternoon. Lizards scurried past the royal bedrooms, flitting in and out of the shrubbery. Lotuses shone brightly on the ponds. Most members of the royal house were enjoying an afternoon nap, or a desultory game of Egypt's favourite board game, *senet*. A skinny, half-naked boy with thick, straight black hair stood in the middle of an enormous bedroom.

"What do you think?" Amenhotep Junior enquired.

Reclining on his bed, covered in its blue-and-gold coverlet, he waited patiently for the designs which would presently tumble forth from the visiting home decorator.

"I see white."

"That's not very original," replied the disappointed prince.

Bak took no notice, moving in a circle as he continued to survey the room.

"White will make this place appear brighter and larger. You'll need that effect with the two of you cooped up in here." He pointed to the windows. "Heavy rose-and-gold brocade curtains will keep the evening chill out. And plain wooden furniture."

"Not painted?"

"*Plain.*"

"Won't termites get to it?"

"Papa has some stuff which is toxic to insects. By the way, Maya's bed should come away from the outer wall. He'll catch cold otherwise."

"Then it's settled." Amenhotep swung his legs out and sat on the edge of the bed to put his red socks on. "I'll leave you both to get better acquainted."

"Where are you going?" Maya asked in a nervous tone.

"To see Mummy. I want to sing her my new song."

"Believe me – you don't want to hear that," said Bak with a smile.

Any unease Maya was experiencing with the new boy instantly evaporated.

"Alright," he said, his confidence returning, "but could you bring me back a snack, Junior? I'm starving."

"The butler's outside. Order one for yourself. That's what he's paid for."

The door clicked shut. Maya desperately searched his mind for a topic of conversation. The visitor sat cross-legged on a carpet in the sun and waited.

"I hear you're a mathematician," Bak eventually said.

"I like figures."

"They need accountants at court."

"Whoever said I was going to be an accountant?" Maya asked in surprise.

"We're all here for a reason. I, for instance, am the son of Men, our king's finest artist, so my life is cut out for me. We'll all be working together. Of course, you'll be a high-flown dignitary while I'll be a supervisor of sculptors in the king's studio."

"You're awfully sure of everything," remarked Maya, not knowing if he liked seeing his life unfolding before his eyes.

"I hear Pharaoh took you to the granaries yesterday."

"What of it?"

"You'll probably wind up being in charge."

"He was just taking me for a walk. I'd lost the prince."

Bak stretched lazily and stood up.

"I'd better be going and let you settle in." The dishevelled child walked towards the large gilt double doors. As if remembering something he turned around. "You'll find that everything here is planned."

The door clicked shut, leaving Maya to sit on his bed alone.

Losing interest in the idea of a sandwich, he decided to move to the floor where Bak had sat. It was sunny and he felt pleasantly warm.

The puppy bounced over and plumped itself into his lap. As it did, the cloud of loneliness over the boy dispersed.

Basking in the sunshine Maya marvelled at his new surroundings, trying to absorb the fact that he had been admitted into the world's greatest house.

"I shall call you Plump Lump," he addressed the dog, giving him a big squeeze.

***

7.

A flutter of wings awoke Maya, as he rolled to one side, in time to see a large peacock flee through the bedroom with Amenhotep Junior in hot pursuit. Reaching the closed double doors, leading to the corridor, the prince launched himself into a flying tackle.

"What on earth are you doing?"

"I want a new feather for my pen," Amenhotep gasped, scrambling from a pile of cushions which had broken his fall.

At that moment a large goose began to honk on the verandah. Maya's puppy squirmed out of his cocoon of blankets and bounded out of bed. The alarmed peacock shot through Amenhotep's small, solid legs, causing him to lose balance and fall face forward onto the cedar floor. The dog chased the bird onto the patio, which in turn, fleetingly tangled with the goose.

"*What* is going on here?"

Queen Tiye stood in the doorway while the prince clutched a grazed knee.

"Nothing Mummy," he lied. "Everything's under control."

"Good morning Maya," she nodded towards the bewildered boy. "I hope this doesn't put you off living with us. BREAKFAST!" she thundered at Amenhotep. "You're an hour late. The king wants to eat with his new son, even if you don't."

Having displayed her authority, the Great Wife returned to the dining hall.

"I'm sorry," the prince apologised, nursing his leg.

"Does your mother do that a lot?" asked Maya getting out of bed and pulling up the covers.

"Stop making your bed. Leave it for the servants." Amenhotep grabbed his hand. "Let's go!"

"But I'm still wearing pyjamas."

"So's Dad. We don't want to be late."

Running through the palace, hand in hand with his new brother, Maya felt a surge of exultation flood his soul. The excitement of belonging to a large, noisy, but above all, happy family, thrilled him to the core. Giggling, he panted to keep up. In the dining hall Pharaoh was pleased to see the unruly duo.

"Did you sleep well?" he asked mildly.

"Oh yes, Your Majesty!"

Maya scrambled onto a seat which had been reserved next to his new father.

"You can call me 'Dad'. Junior, are you going to cut up your brother's pastry, or shall I?"

Without waiting, the prince divided the pastry into pieces on Maya's plate.

"These are hot," exclaimed the surprised boy.

"They're fresh. Have some cold duck," urged the king. "It's very good. Junior, pass the salt."

His mouth full of porridge, the prince handed his father a silver shaker, while servants bustled around to no avail. Maya noticed Queen Tiye ate only fruit.

"Where's Prince Dhutmose?" he asked, moving closer to the king.

"Reciting a liturgy at the temple," Queen Tiye said tersely. "He wants to be a priest, like all my sons. If we get one pharaoh out of this brood, I'll be surprised."

"Akhy – I mean Junior –

wants to be a farmer," Maya quipped.

The king looked bemused. His wife spluttered into her drink.

"I must be excused," she announced, dabbing her lips with a napkin. "I have letters to write."

Pharaoh stood to his feet and made a half bow. Maya stared. He had never met such a polite adult male.

"Are we good then?" asked the king when their plates had been cleared.

The prince picked his teeth with a blue-and-gold toothpick.

"I'd like to sit for a while, Daddy," he said burping. "To digest this porridge."

"You can do that at the stadium."

Amenhotep Junior threw away his piece of wood which inadvertently struck his new brother in the eye.

"Come on Maya, we're going to the races."

***

At the venue pandemonium reigned as ushers, officials, and soldiers rushed about in a state of panic.

"Dear Amon, the imbeciles forgot my throne!" the king exclaimed.

Deciding it wise to leave, Amenhotep Junior joined Dhutmose in the pits where the charioteers were getting ready. Together they checked the bridles and harnesses of the spirited horses. Maya stayed with his new father.

"Useless!" the king stormed. "I should fire the whole lot of them."

The boy looked up anxiously.

"What does 'fire' mean?"

"To get rid of one's inefficient employees. The only problem is they'd turn into a pack of tomb robbers. Let's look at today's charioteers, instead. Do you know Horemheb?"

Pharaoh waved to a dour youth, hitching two magnificent black stallions to his red wagon. On spotting his sovereign, the boy immediately threw himself in the dust. Amenhotep Senior then introduced Maya to Horemheb. The latter shot the dumpy child a jealous look, but Maya only smiled.

"I like your carriage," he said shyly. "I heard you win all the time."

An unfamiliar warmth stole over the charioteer who had been consigned to soldiers' barracks since he was four. Without meaning to, Horemheb smiled back. Pharaoh moved on with his latest charge, to speak to the other drivers.

"Who's the kid, Dhutmose?" Horemheb asked.

75

The heir looked up from under his carriage.

"Our new brother. Hangs out with Junior. Bright – useless at sports."

"Where *is* Junior?"

"Talking to Nefertiti, as usual."

Horemheb shaded his eyes. Sure enough, Amenhotep Junior was locked in discussion with a girl who listened to him intently. Gazing in their direction for some time, the child soldier drank in the vision of the slim girl with high cheekbones, and long dark hair.

"Hump, I need you to hold this wheel. A spoke's come out."

Mildly irritated, Horemheb's army discipline nevertheless brought him to Dhutmose's side in an instant.

"You can't race," he declared.

"I didn't ask for your opinion. Just hold the jolly wheel," replied the prince, bending another wooden spoke expertly into place.

"Get another car. I don't want you to beat me today, but that's plain dangerous. You're not qualified to make repairs."

"And you worry too much. Now go back to your mark, Hump. We're about to start. And, believe it or not, I *am* going to beat you."

With a heavy heart Horemheb ascended his carriage. The starter ordered competitors to take their places. His eyes scanned the grounds, searching for Amenhotep Junior and Nefertiti, but they had vanished. No doubt they were in the audience, holding hands by now. Disappointed, he tried to focus on the task at hand. Staring ahead, the boy pulled back the reins, allowing his steeds to feel enough tension to know they were about to race.

A combination of the gong, his whip and the chariot's break from the pack, made for one perfectly timed moment. Horemheb, out in front from the beginning, wheeled around the track as effortlessly as he swam the Nile on troop manoeuvres. Everything was one fluid motion of arms, cramped buttocks, and steely legs. The red wagon he had trained in for the past three years had become part of his own body. The horses, accustomed to the familiar carriage and rider, swept to victory.

"You improve with each month," Dhutmose remarked cheerily, as his rear wheel wobbled dangerously to a halt behind Horemheb.

Although he loved to win, he resigned himself to taking second place to his friend's talent. The latter turned to see King Amenhotep striding towards them.

"Don't bow!" Pharaoh said quickly. "I'm going on a hunt. They can't find my throne."

"Normally he'd have to behead the lax attendants," Dhutmose pointed out.

"I'm hunting ostrich," his father said, staring directly at Horemheb. "Do you want to come?"

"I'm ready, Your Majesty." The boy leapt to the ground. "Is Maya riding with us, too?"

"He's in the stalls, playing with Plump Lump," the king confided.

***

A chubby hand waved from the crowded circuit.

"Hi, Nef!"

Blushing and hitching up his kilt, Amenhotep Junior materialised flat-footedly at his sweetheart's side. Ignoring the rivulets of sweat cascading over her admirer, Nefertiti bestowed her most radiant smile upon him.

"Hello Junior," she said fondly.

The boy blinked up at her for a moment. She was the most beautiful girl in the world. Without thinking, his tiny hand reached out to stroke her long hair which hung to her waist.

"So, there you are!" Dhutmose boomed.

"Go away," his brother ordered crossly, forgetting he was trying to make a good impression on the lovely girl.

"Dad wants to see you at the ostrich hunt," the older prince announced. He bowed courteously to Nefertiti, who giggled while ogling the handsome heir. "That's all," Dhutmose added. "You can go back to your girlfriend now."

Amenhotep Junior slitted evil eyes at his brother, as the latter swaggered away.

"Would you like to walk to the stables?" Nefertiti asked. "I want to see your horses."

"My horses?"

"You tamed some Arabian stallions, didn't you?"

"Er – oh yes!" Amenhotep Junior trotted alongside her happily, while her attendant placed a parasol over the pair. "Although that was for Maya's birthday. I *do* have some of my own," he countered quickly. "They have to be broken in before my seventh birthday and it's a bit hard for the groomsman, so I ... er, help."

"I don't want to watch the last race, do you?" Despite it being the grand final of the children's championship, the prince shook his head vigorously. No doubt his cradle-snatching brother wanted to show off for Nefertiti. Good grief, he was almost fourteen! "I hear not even Pharaoh could break them in," Nefertiti breathed, taking the boy's arm. Now Amenhotep Junior understood why his groom had looked so relieved at the end of their ride earlier that morning. "You have a special gift. I also hear you have a talking parrot."

"I like animals," Amenhotep replied dismissively.

"I'd love to see it sometime."

Under the rays of her unconditional acceptance, the boy had no desire to boast. A person he had never known existed within him was making his debut – a modest, unassuming person – someone he liked. Looking into her porcelain face the prince grinned happily, with just a hint of shyness.

"We shall," he promised.

***

By mid-morning the stadium milled with horses and riders. Chariots, dismantled wheels, and clattering reins – some embossed with silver and gold medallions – bewildered and excited Maya. Patting his dog, he gawked at the mass of gaily variegated plumes on the flowing manes of the spirited horses. Plump Lump barked happily in the stands and wagged his tail, overjoyed at the outing with his best friend. Amenhotep

78

Junior arrived from the pits and persuaded Maya to leave the dog with their nanny. They walked alongside one another, occasionally stopping to pat one of the horses. Finally, they spotted Pharaoh.

"Where's our car, Dad?"

"Next to mine, at the western exit."

Taking Maya's hand, the prince weaved his way through grooms-men, beaters, gruff bodyguards, and towering Nubian mercenaries. An electrum-plated carriage gleamed in the sun. Two white ponies neighed on seeing the youngest royal. He caressed their muzzles while they tossed their manes and pawed the ground. Next to his father's chariot stood a gold-plated one with roan stallions.

"Jump in, Maya," the prince ordered, cracking his small child's whip.

"But this is Dad's carriage."

"Don't you trust me?" Amenhotep Junior slapped his reins. "Giddy-up."

Pulling slowly away from the throng, the children ambled out of the stadium. Forgetting his initial trepidation Maya jumped up and down excitedly, clutching onto the wooden handrail. Sauntering up Malkata Avenue, towards the Nile, the hunting party was one of the largest the royal palace had staged. At first, Amenhotep Junior and Maya joined the rear of the parade. Not content with falling behind, however, the prince began to overtake the harem's caravan. All the palace children were driven by personal chauffeurs. Many gawked at their brother en-viously. Some pointed. A few girls cried with jealousy. Adjusting his sunhat, the prince cracked his whip above the stallions to show off his skill as a driver.

When they had reached the Nile, the party boarded a flotilla of barges and boats, which sailed to the opposite side of the river where the ostrich were being hunted. On the western bank the group stopped and waited for all the boats to dock. Maya noticed his new brother was becoming particularly motivated. Servants produced large hampers for his inspection. Wine jars were selected. At last, when everything was ar-ranged to his satisfaction, the prince sat with Maya on an oblong boulder and waited for the rest of the party. Suddenly Dhutmose, with his retinue which included Abner, loomed above the pair.

"So, what's Little Brother up to?"

"None of your beeswax. Go back to Dad. He must be missing his favourite already."

"Jealousy won't get you anywhere."

"Although it has in your brother's case," Abner commented. "To the back of the pack!"

Dhutmose joined in the ensuing laughter.

"Sucking up to the king again, Abbie," Amenhotep Junior said calmly. He threw a pebble into the clear water with unaccustomed force. "Still, I suppose I can afford to be generous. Dhutmose, being the heir, has no real friends."

"That's not fair," Abner began. "You were asked to join us, but you refused. You can't expect me to join women and children on your account."

"Why not? Maya has. It's what a loyal pal would do."

"Let's go, Abbie," Dhutmose said. "The only reason my brother joined the hunt was to steal Dad's chariot to show off his riding skills. You're in for a caning, Little Brother."

Abner laughed scornfully and kicked at the wet sand, which stubbornly refused to fly up. Amenhotep Junior twisted a pudgy palm in mid-air.

"Bye," he farewelled in a provocative tone.

Dhutmose and Abner scrambled up the bank, past the girls and nurses, back to their chariots.

Eventually, the younger prince moved his party out of the rolling green thickets, and into the desert.

"It's so hot!" exclaimed Maya, after they had cantered several miles.

Now in single file, the party wended its way through the large cliffs beyond which the ostrich waited. Suddenly, Amenhotep Junior veered down a steep bank.

"Where are we going?" asked his frightened passenger, gripping the wooden carriage rail as they bumped down the rocky incline.

Instead of answering, the prince tethered his dusty stallions to a tree by a fast-flowing brook. Then, he sat down in the grass.

They waited for the others to join them. Soon enough, the banks of the brook thronged with people. Horses were unhitched from their carriages and allowed to roam.

Rugs, sheets, and pillows were laid out by maids who chattered happily. Parasols were provided for everyone.

A spread of cold meats, including duck, pigeon, crane, and owl, were massed together with gravies, oily sauces, humus, and thin pancake bread. Waiters provided flasks of grape juice to the children, while the adults drank beer and wine.

"This is my first picnic!" Maya squealed with joy.

"Courtesy of me," replied his friend, struggling to unseal a pottery wine jug. "Sit down and taste this."

The mud seal crumbled. Widening the mouth of the jar, Amenhotep Junior sloshed some of the contents into two cups. He gave one to his friend.

"It's strong," Maya coughed.

"From the cellars of Tuthmosis-the-Great," announced the prince proudly.

"It must be worth at least two cauldrons of gold."

"Trust you to compute the price." Amenhotep Junior sat back against a flax hamper. Crossing one ankle over the other, he raised his cup. "Cheers!"

***

8.

Having escaped punishment for stealing the king's horses, Prince Amenhotep and his new brother retired early to their apartments. Doffing their papyrus sandals, they hurriedly washed in a gold hand basin and snuggled under their bedsheets before sunset. Not even Queen Tiye's visit, late in the evening, woke them. On being accosted by a barking puppy, (which suspiciously looked more like a jackal with each passing day), the Lady of the Two Lands decided it best to leave her questions until the morning. At dawn, however, the prince pleaded a prior engagement and left his companion to face breakfast alone.

Lifting the latch of the garden gate, Amenhotep Junior padded to a pond where a gorgeous, dark-haired girl awaited. It was just after sunrise, and both he and Nefertiti wore capes. Quietly they approached an old cottage on the outskirts of the palace grounds. Trampling through twigs and decayed ferns, they brushed the bark away from a battered door and, turning its squeaking handle, made their way inside.

"Blinky's over here," the prince whispered, moving to a cage draped with a tarpaulin. Muffled twittering emanated from under the cloth. Carefully, the boy balanced on tiptoe, and pulled it away as if he were a magician performing a conjuring trick. A large white parrot with a yellow beak stared at Nefertiti.

"HELLO," the parrot greeted, hopping closer to the wooden grill. Nefertiti shrieked.

"I taught him to say that," Amenhotep Junior said proudly.

"You?"

The girl was so breathless with excitement she would have believed anything her tiny guide told her.

"It's safe to pat him." The boy stuck one palm into the cage "Try it," he encouraged.

"I'm too scared."

Amenhotep tickled the bird. It nibbled the prince's fingers and drew closer, while Nefertiti's nervous titters transformed into delighted laughter. Eventually, her eyes turned from the cage and roved across the dark room crammed with old furniture. It was then that Amenhotep discovered the parrot had encircled one thumb with his talons and was biting down with its yellow beak on his finger. Continuing to coo, the prince attempted to extricate himself, but his feathered friend would not let go. Espying a piece of rope on the cage floor, he pulled it up with his free hand and dangled it in front of the bird. He hoped the parrot would take the bait, but its persistent attack on his finger was growing.

"What are you doing?" a voice from the gloom demanded.

Startled, Nefertiti inadvertently stepped on a pile of table legs which rolled across the floor and crashed against a far wall.

"Playing, Uni," said the prince, relieved to see the ancient manservant's scowling face.

"Blinky bites," the man noted sharply.

"He's friendly. Come over here and see for yourself." The servant lumbered towards the child who, smiling brightly through tears of pain, whispered hoarsely: "I can't get him off!"

"That's why I put a sign on it," replied the man, tapping the side of the cage.

By now the wily bird had leapt back onto his perch, the model of perfect decorum. Fluffing out his feathers, he contemplated the prince with a proud and pleased look.

"You little good-for-nothing," Amenhotep hissed. "That was a deliberate attack!"

By now the steward was picking up the furniture legs and, oblivious of the children's rank, scolding them indiscriminately for setting foot in the deserted cottage. Mortified, Nefertiti backed away. Quickly inspecting his fingers, Amenhotep spotted only the smallest of nicks. He took Nefertiti's hand.

"We're leaving," he announced haughtily.

The children departed, while Uni continued to rail about youth's irresponsibility, the long hours he had to work at a thankless job, and the state of His Majesty's dungeons.

***

Cotton sheets lined the walls as Bak stirred the first pail of pastel green.

"Junior, stop reading the paper and help me."

"No need. I trust you."

With that the child, who had scrubbed off the dirt from his garden foray, lay on his cloth-of-gold quilt for the remainder of the morning. Towards noon, Maya arrived. He stood uncertainly at the doorway, surveying the room which was piled high with furniture, paints, pots, and odds-and-ends. Bak waved him in with his brush, spattering a cotton sheet in the process.

"I thought we were going to have plain wooden furniture," Maya said, looking under the bed. "Come on, Plump Lump."

"Your father won't allow it," replied Bak. "I've applied a stripper. If you touch anything, wash your hands, or it'll rip your skin off."

"Why on earth won't Dad let you get new fittings?" the prince enquired. "We are, after all, a fashionable family."

"His Majesty is economising. My father can't even obtain a supply of diorite for the new monuments. He's expected to conjure images of Pharaoh out of thin air."

"Are you making fun of Dad?" the prince queried hotly. "No one from the lower classes can perform witchcraft, including conjuration, on the king."

"I'm pointing out the existence of a crisis. We can't build his funerary temple, which is supposed to be his house of eternity. Imagine being homeless for all time."

Bak went back to painting the skirting in silence.

"You may have a point," the prince muttered. "The priests can certainly afford to have a new wing added to their harem. *And* it's filled with solid gold tables and chairs."

84

"Ooh, really?" Maya's eyes were wide with delight. "Can we visit it?"

"No – not with me. I was expelled. But I do want my new hassock, Bak. Make sure it's finished by Dhutmose's birthday."

"You should know, Maya, that your new brother was expelled at two for insurgence," Bak explained from behind a coversheet. "I don't know why you want to one-up Dhutmose on his birthday, Junior. Your pursuit of trend is beyond me. Pharaoh is the same. If you lot don't have the latest fashion, you suffer anxiety attacks!"

"You're lucky to be in the middle of a delicate operation, otherwise I'd thump you," the prince rumbled belligerently.

Maya tickled his puppy under the chin.

"I'm taking Plump Lump outside," he announced. "It smells in here."

Wrapping the leather leash around his chubby fist for security, the child and his pet departed for the garden.

"And what does the news of the day say?" Bak asked.

"Oh nothing, it's just a palace newsletter. You know," confided Amenhotep Junior, "we are victims of propaganda in Malkata. This sort of rubbish certainly isn't peddled on the streets."

"What do you know of the streets?" Bak queried mildly

The prince gritted his teeth with annoyance.

"Lots. I'll have you know I go out all the time – incognito, of course." There was a giggle from the verandah. "Shut up, Maya!" A large pillow flew through the door. "And stop eavesdropping. As I was saying, Bak, they want us to believe in the superiority of Amon, and exhort us to greater acts of worship." The prince picked his nose absent-mindedly. "I don't think *he's* God." A crash from behind the makeshift curtain caused Maya and Plump Lump to rush back into their bedroom. "I wish you were less clumsy," whinged the prince, extricating the unfortunate artist from the folds of cloth in which he had become entangled. Green paint ran across the cedar floor.

"Oh! Oh!" squeaked Maya, mopping frenziedly with anything that came to hand.

"Stop that!" ordered Amenhotep.

"But it'll ruin the floorboards."

"Leave it. What do you think, Bak?"

The children stood over the spreading pool of green.

"It could work."

"That settles it. We'll have a green floor to mirror the grass outside. I want a couple of painted plants, and ducks flapping about."

"There's enough flapping in here of a morning," said a peeved Maya.

***

9.

Amenhotep Junior turned the plaster cast in his hands. It was of his mother and nearly finished. Pulling out a larger cast from the stack between the table and wall, he placed it on the floor, and sat down in its concave interior. Stretching out to his full length the boy discovered that, although slightly uncomfortable, it accommodated the length of his body. Sporting a pleasing oval interior, it might have depicted half an egg.

With an effort, he pushed its bulk out of the studio, and up the hallway in the direction of his digs. Puffing slightly, he returned to collect another cast of roughly the same size. Making his final visit to the studio, the prince closed the door. He climbed onto a footrest to reach the tool bench where, carefully selecting a small saw, he began to cut out pieces of wood to precise specifications.

***

"What are those, Junior?"

"Plaster casts."

"But what are you doing with them?" Maya was anxious. "And why are you carrying planks of wood?"

"I've invented a method of transportation faster than the chariot. We must test it out."

Tacking his shaped boards onto the bottom of the casts Amenhotep Junior fitted their tongues into small grooves cut around the inside of the plaster. Hooks on the ends of the moulds were threaded through with strong rope. Maya followed his friend, dragging his U-shaped piece of plaster through the palace until they reached the empty dining room. Morning sun flooded the space, which had been cleared of all furniture. Placing his cast at the doorway, the prince lay on his stomach and, before Maya could ask any more annoying questions, pushed himself off along the gentle incline of the wooden floor. He swept down to the opposite end in one flowing movement.

"That looks like fun!" Maya exclaimed, clapping his hands.

Without waiting for encouragement, or orders from his friend, he body-surfed down the room.

"Let's have a race," the prince suggested.

In no time they were tobogganing down the hall with screams of delight.

"Oh, how wonderful!" panted Maya, red-faced. "Let's go really fast."

They took their positions. Amenhotep threw off his kilt so that he was clad only in his royal underwear.

"Right: Take your marks. One, two, three – GO!"

The casts rumbled ominously along the floor. Picking up speed, Maya felt rushing wind tearing his hair back. Unable to see the rapidly approaching far wall, he closed his eyes tight. Suddenly there was a crash of two carts as they simultaneously hit the frescoed wall. Amenhotep was the first to speak.

"Are you dead yet?"

"Let's do it again," was the muffled response.

***

SLAM!

"Ow, my head!"

"Why don't you wear a helmet, Maya?"

"It's all very well for you to talk, you've got Dhutmose's war crown."

Panting from their tobogganing exertions, the two boys pulled their plaster casts back several metres up the gently sloping wooden floor-boards. Suddenly, the double doors swung open.

"Where in Amon's name is my battle headdress?"

Amenhotep Junior peered from under the outsize leather helmet. In two swift strides Dhutmose retrieved his personal property.

"How am I going to protect myself now?"

"You're lucky I don't give you a hiding," Dhutmose retorted.

"We're experimenting," Maya broke in.

"That's right," his partner-in-crime affirmed. "We're trying to break the sound barrier."

"There's no such thing. Do you realise I'm half an hour late for my co-regent's function? Dad's going to flay me alive."

"Then I'll inherit your headgear."

Dhutmose raised his fist.

"Don't provoke him," Maya whispered as the doors slammed shut behind the angry heir.

"He won't hurt me," Amenhotep said, secretly breathing a sigh of relief. "The palace doctors have told my family that I'm sick on account of my funny wide hips and elongated skull."

"You should be more polite to Dhutmose. He's going to be Pharaoh someday, whether you like it or not, and he knows you're as healthy as a horse."

The prince stepped into his souped-up toboggan. It had recently acquired a rounded nose for added speed.

"Don't forget, he needs friends to manage his empire." So saying, he sped off down the floor, to crash into a newly painted column with a resounding thud. "I think we're getting faster."

Paint flaked off a bas-relief of Pharaoh Amenhotep-the-Magnificent. Maya looked up at the severely damaged portrait of the man he had come to know as his father.

"Don't you think it's about time we started to behave?"

His friend puckered his brow and pushed himself upright.

"I'm sure I don't know what you mean."

***

Candles flickered against the blue-and-gold hangings in Tiye's study. She and her husband had sat together for half an hour without saying a word. It was clear the king was in a towering rage. Out of respect for his wife, he had refrained from venting the multitude of expletives roaring through his overheated brain. Instead, the king inhaled deeply. The ambassadors of Syria and Mitanni rose in his memory, together with the painfully late Dhutmose. With each passing day his family was aggravating him, with one exception – the queen. When he had calmed down, Tiye opened the conversation.

"Our youngest son passed his exams."

"With honours," Pharaoh responded gloomily.

"He took our views on religion a step further." She was unable to conceal the pride in her voice. "Minthu was impressed."

"I've had enough of religion."

"At least he hasn't caused any incidents lately."

"That's true."

A candle sputtered and died. Tiye drew a taper from her bookshelf and attempted to light an oil lamp.

"Let me do it," her husband offered. "Everything at court went wrong today," he moaned, lighting the lamp and shaking the taper's flame to extinguishment. "The ambassadors were asking to make marriage alliances with my daughters – imagine that! Never since the beginning of time has such a request been made of the King of Egypt. Marry their daughters? Humph! On top of that, I welcomed the Prince of Crete into our new living room, which is looking suspiciously shoddy."

"Senta says the floor polish is scraped. I'm looking into it."

"Don't bother." Something akin to a glint appeared in Pharaoh's eye. "I'm going to surprise the vandals."

***

Screaming with glee, the children skidded up and down the floorboards. Their vehicles had acquired rails, sleek sandpapered exteriors – all in the name of added speed. Sitting in the back of the darkened living room, piled high with tables and chairs, which had yet to be placed in the newest hall for visitors, the king did not know whether to be angry, or proud.

While his sons' new toys appealed to Pharaoh's sense of adventure, damage to the expensive decor offended his interior decorator's eye. Not since the days of the pyramids had there been a king who had built so many monuments or palaces. Amenhotep Senior's vision was unmatched, even by the imagination of his architect, whom he allowed to take all the praise.

His younger son, far from being sickly, was as robust as any of his horses. The peculiarly wide hips, and elongated skull were obviously just part of his makeup. Leaning forward, the supreme ruler saw much of Tiye in the long angular face covered in puppy fat, and wreathed in smiles. Maya, too, was becoming more confident. He kept up with the prince in their car racing. Once, when he won, the king had to keep his applause in check.

At midday, the two boys responded to the lunch bell by hiding their equipment under a leather hood, before disappearing down the hallway. Their father slowly made his way out of his hiding place. Hurrying over to the protective covering he raised it, and inspected the strange carts. The clank of a spear to his right made him spin round, hand clasped to the short sword which he always wore girded about his hips.

"Your Majesty!" a guard exclaimed prostrating himself rapidly.

"Do you know what these are, Pawah?"

"The prince's carts, Your Highness," the man replied, rising from the polished wooden floor.

"Are you guarding them while they play?"

"I always protect them."

Spotting two dark objects in the toboggans the king pulled out the child-size helmets.

"Did you give them these?"

"I had them made. The children's heads were suffering bumps."

"As are my statues and columns." Not knowing what to say, the man stayed silent. "These are excellent," the king continued, inspecting the helmets' padded interiors. "You obviously care about my children, Pawah. I'm promoting you to Security Chief of the Royal Nursery."

"Thank you, Your Majesty, but —"

"But what?"

"I thought you knew."

Pharaoh shook his head.

"Those two told me they were studying. The only reason I'm not beheading you is because I know what gifted liars all my children are." Amenhotep Senior carefully replaced the helmets in the painted plaster carts. "They say my second son is not normal, but today has changed my opinion of him. You obviously knew that he was just a boisterous child looking for an outlet. I thank you from the bottom of my father's heart."

"It was no trouble, Your Highness," Pawah protested, wishing he had done more.

"Watch over my youngest. One day he will do something out of the ordinary."

***

A figure stirred from the annex of the long living room.

"Dad!"

Amenhotep Junior dropped his toboggan, while Maya scuttled behind the nearest plinth.

"What are you doing?"

"As you can see."

Choosing a live demonstration over a verbal explanation, the prince confidently placed his vehicle at the end of the hall. Lying face down on his stomach, he pulled his leather helmet over his eyes, and stretched out his arms before him.

"I know what you're attempting," his father said anxiously, "but I don't think it's safe."

"Too late!" squeaked Maya from behind a vase as the prince, determined to impress his father, swept past at top speed. Avoiding colliding with a portrait of Pharaoh, the boy pulled on one side of the ropes threaded through the nose of his vehicle, and skidded round to a halt. "Hooray, you did it!" Maya shouted, throwing up his arms in ecstasy.

Flushed with triumph, the prince straightened and pulled his helmet off.

"What do you think, Dad?"

"What's wrong with your chariot?"

"This is faster."

"And more dangerous."

"More dangerous than hunting lions?"

"Without a doubt." Unable to contain his curiosity, the king approached his son's strange vehicle. "Did you make this?" he asked, crouching next to it and running his hands across the sides.

"All by myself."

"Out of plaster casts," Maya explained, before clapping his hands over his mouth.

"By yourself?"

"Of course, Daddy," said the prince. "I'm a genius. Do you want to see me do it again?"

His father rose.

"Yes, but this time both of you."

***

The doors burst open revealing an exceptionally ill-tempered queen of the realm.

"What on EARTH is going on here?" Tiye demanded. "I can't study with this infernal racket."

"Darling!" Her husband waved from the end of the room. "Come and look at this. Our sons have made their own vehicles."

"They look suspiciously like my missing portrait casts. Only yesterday that ghastly Men had to cover me in plaster and rags again."

"Aren't our boys clever?" the king enthused. "Maya and Junior are so inventive and original. I'm very proud of them."

Tiye squinted as the rays from the setting sun struck the far windows. Suddenly, she was seized with a terrible foreboding.

"Have you attended to the affairs of state this morning?"

"I always do," Pharaoh responded.

"Yet you have been missing all afternoon. None of you turned up for your midday meal."

"Dhutmose's brigade eats more than enough for all of us," Amenhotep Junior said, to the delight of his father, who joined in the children's laughter.

"So, you lot have been in here for six hours?" Taking a low stool by the double doors, Tiye fixed a basilisk eye on her husband. "Show me what you've been doing," she ordered.

***

"Mummy doesn't approve," Amenhotep Junior commented sadly, after a demonstration which had ripped up half the Persian rug.

A butler appeared with refreshments. The prince's father smoothed the neck of his son's crisp linen vest.

"Your mother doesn't like me hunting either."

"But you still do."

"Actually, I'm going to stop."

"But why? You love the chase!"

"Because Mummy's right. I could get killed and then where would we all be?"

"You can't die, Dad. You're invincible."

"We saw you hunting last week," Maya said. He was eating a large flat scone smothered in humus. "You were strong and fast, just like us."

"I promised to stop in two years' time, Junior."

"So, I'll give up tobogganing in two years."

"You have to now, before you kill yourselves. Remember, Mummy cares about you."

The prince pouted.

"She doesn't care about anything except spoiling our fun!"

"That's right," Maya agreed. "She's always yelling."

"Your mother knows those carts could have put you both in the infirmary." Amenhotep patted his namesake's head, trying to slick down his jutting spikes of hair. It was useless. His youngest son was destined to look as prickly as his personality. "Let's go into dinner," the king said, taking both children's hands. "And try to behave – for me."

Maya looked up at Amenhotep Senior with adoration, quite sure there was no more perfect father in the world.

***

10.

Pharaoh and the Great Wife were not sure whether to feel aghast, or laugh. Their youngest son approached his child's throne with the most garish hassock anyone had ever seen. The servants were brushed aside as he placed it under his flat feet.

"What is *that*?" asked Prince Dhutmose loudly.

Aggrieved that the attention was slipping from him to his younger brother on his birthday, the older boy's temper was frayed to breaking point.

"An ocean of colour. Bak's latest."

"You have no right to hire him. He's *my* artist."

"He's *my* friend."

Clambering onto his throne, Amenhotep Junior placed his hands in his lap, and viewed the ambassadors from Mitanni with interest.

"Is this the latest fashion, dear?" Pharaoh asked of his wife, ever fearful of being left behind.

"In the nursery," replied Tiye with a straight face. "There's no need to be jealous." They listened to the ambassadors for an interminable hour, while Dhutmose and their youngest pulled faces at each other. At the interview's conclusion, she turned to her husband. "Don't forget about Heliopolis, darling."

Patting his arm, Tiye left to attend to her diplomatic correspondence.

***

KER

  THUNK!

    THUNK!

      THUNK!

A diminutive body rolled down the palace's main staircase.

"Are you alright?" Running to the prince's side, Maya grasped a limp hand. "Oh, no!" he blubbered, pulling away the helmet from his friend's pallid complexion.

Suddenly the prince shook himself awake.

"Don't worry – just a spell of unconsciousness – an experiment."

Picking himself up, the boy brushed off stray pieces of lint.

"B-but, did you do that on purpose?"

"I enjoy spells of nothingness. Great inspiration comes to mind from God during those interludes."

"Or brain damage," his father's voice boomed above them.

Clattering down the steps in his leather armour, which he had donned for his afternoon hunt, Pharaoh picked up his youngest son.

"The mind resides in the heart, not the head," the child giggled, snuggling into the warmth of his father's suede-covered arms.

"Don't be ridiculous. When I'm mummified, they're going to preserve my grey matter."

Holding the edge of the king's kilt, Maya put his thumb in his mouth and followed him up the steps. Their father kissed Junior's plump cheeks, which instantly became ruddy once more.

"You're too precious for me to lose. Do me a favour, try to stay alive until manhood." The king lowered his reckless son onto a couch at the top of the stairs. Picking up Maya, he perched him on hard-muscled thighs. "Would you two like to go to Heliopolis for the summer? You could live in a turret full of books and bother the priests with your unceasing questions. They have a ninety-foot staircase winding around the outside of the tower. You could both get fresh air and exercise, away from my rules and regulations, and your mother could have a break."

"Yes, yes, it'll be fun!" Maya agreed, jumping up and down on the king's knee.

"How would you know, Maya?" Amenhotep Junior asked. "You haven't been."

"Abner has, and he says they have real magic classes, where the students chop off geese heads, and then put them together again, good as new."

"Ooh!" the prince exclaimed, clapping his hands with macabre glee. "Can we go soon, Dad?"

"Of course, but to study. Settle down, Maya, I'm not a horse!"

***

A month later, flying down the Heliopolitan school banister at top speed, Amenhotep Junior reflected on how he would court Nefertiti. Arriving at the bottom of the stairs with a thud, he arranged his crumpled gown, embroidered with hundreds of gold-and-blue beaded stars.

"Morning," said Abner brightly at his right shoulder.

"I have no time," was the terse reply.

"Got a date with your girlfriend? I have a girl too. Her name's Rachel. I'm meeting her for lunch."

"Lunch?" Amenhotep squinted through the windows at the sun dial in the large courtyard. "I thought it was morning."

"It is, and you have a class in ten minutes, or don't you remember?"

"But it's six o'clock!"

"Nearly seven. You overslept. As for me, I have five hours in which to get ready for my date."

At that moment Maya appeared through the swinging saloon door in front of them.

"Where are your books?" he asked his brother. "We have classes on Saturdays."

"I'm not going," Amenhotep announced. "I know everything, anyway."

Thrusting out his jaw with determination, the prince sauntered through the doors, his head held high, only to be quickly ejected by a disgruntled steward who was in the process of cleaning up.

"I was the last to leave," Maya explained, rubbing the bridge of his nose. "Don't worry, I've got some *shat-bat* in my pocket."

"I'll see you two later," Abner said as a raven-haired girl waved to him from the courtyard.

"Where does he think he's going?" asked Amenhotep, his voice rising.

"All students above the age of seven get weekends off. Rachel is keen to fill in time before their official date. That's when the parents turn up," Maya added with relish.

"Give me the bread," the prince ordered, sticking out his hand.

"Aren't you going to class?"

"I'm meeting Nefertiti now. We're going horse riding." Maya handed his friend the flat, sweet bread which he had been keeping for his afternoon snack, and which had flattened even further in his pocket. "This is more like a cracker than a cake," the prince grumbled.

"The cowherds are still plying their trade behind the Old Hall. If you're lucky, you might cadge a cup of milk from one of them."

Amenhotep Junior checked his wallet.

"Have gold – will trade. I'll bring you back a scarf."

Maya's eyes gleamed. Heliopolitan scarves were of a linen so fine they resembled a butterfly's gossamer wings. Highly colourful, they were a fashion statement created to stir envy and desire in men and women alike. Whistling happily, the nobleman's son clutched the banister his friend had lately slid down, and climbed the cold stone steps to his lesson.

***

"Ahoy!"

Waving frantically in windmill fashion, Amenhotep Junior caught Nefertiti's attention from the turret.

"What are you doing up there?" she called.

"Studying."

"Isn't that library reserved for priests?"

The prince, intent on cutting the image of a serious scholar, emerged loaded down with scrolls, and a satchel full of writing instruments.

"You can help me if you like," he said, running down the staircase with "borrowed" books to meet his love.

At the bottom of the steps, he puffed and wheezed with the physical effort, as much as the excitement of seeing his girlfriend.

"Where's your valet?" asked Nefertiti, taking a few scrolls from the top.

"Don't need one. I'm not a pampered royal."

A tall priest, dressed in a Greek robe, stepped into view. Amenhotep Junior swallowed convulsively.

"Where do you think you're going with those?" the newcomer demanded.

"I'm helping with a lesson, Orestes. The lecturer is teaching Hebrew history. This is Nefertiti."

As the boy had hoped, Orestes was disarmed by the beautiful girl.

"It's very good of you to be helping," Orestes smiled. "Do you read?"

"Every day."

"How interesting. I suppose your boyfriend teaches you."

"Now and then, but my father, Lord Ay, is my real teacher."

Orestes started.

"You are Lord Ay's daughter?'

"I am."

"Queen Tiye's niece?"

"The same."

Colour rose in the man's cheeks.

"Your father reported you missing over two hours ago. The city is crawling with military police in search of you." Turning to the hapless prince, his instructor barked: "Get to class immediately, and leave those books here! When you've finished this afternoon, you are to report to my office, do you understand?"

Flushing with humiliation, the boy placed the scrolls in a neat pile on the stairs, but unable to resist, he answered in the most chilling tones he could muster: "Remember, Orestes, I am from the royal house of Thebes. When I'm governor, or perhaps even Pharaoh, I won't forget this."

"Threatening Heliopolis, are we?" sneered his infuriated teacher.

"I'll make you sorry," the boy promised with uncanny calm. "Nefertiti is my future wife, as surely as you will be sent down."

"The only brat to be sent anywhere is you. You're expelled! Get your things and leave immediately."

"Very well, but my father shall be hearing about this."

"Pharaoh has no power over the priesthood," growled Orestes, to an ensuing gasp from Nefertiti. "Now GO!"

***

Tiptoeing into his room Amenhotep Junior quietly closed the door behind him. One of the drapes was open, providing a glimmer of light. He walked towards his bed and accidentally kicked the sharp, bronze-tipped corner of a wooden chest. Cursing profusely, the prince hobbled to his mattress, and eased himself onto it. A soft stirring from the opposite side of the room was accompanied by the whine of an animal awakened. Before he could resist, Amenhotep was assaulted by a dog as big as himself, barking joyfully, while simultaneously covering him in kisses.

"Junior, you're back! What were the pyramids like?"

"White."

"Is your leg alright?"

"I'm bleeding like a stuck pig, Maya, and your jolly cur's licking my wounds. I'll be dead of gangrene by morning."

Maya struggled amid his embroidered cushions. Leaning on one elbow he struck a flint and lit a small oil lamp. Rubbing his eyes, the boy pulled aside the sheets, hauled himself out of his luxurious bed and placed the light on a trunk at the foot of the prince's cot.

"The nursery's chief of security is now your valet," he said, yawning. "Pawah brought your luggage in here this morning, with strict instructions not to unpack. By the way, Queen Tiye thinks Plump Lump's a jackal."

"What does Mummy know? The valet should have stacked the suitcases properly. I'll have him fired."

"You can't. Pawah's on your Dad's payroll, not yours. Besides, you like him."

"Do not," muttered the prince, fossicking in his bedside cupboard. Pulling out salve and cotton wads, he dabbed the scratch. Amenhotep Junior, together with his mother, had decided early in life that first

101

aid kits were a necessity if he was to live past the age of three. His knowledge of medicine, together with his collection of bottles, potions, herbs – not to mention bandages for every cut, wound, bruise, and even cracked ribs – made him popular with the boys in his household. And he always charged for his services. (No royal child had a better art gallery than Amenhotep Junior. Even Queen Tiye admired his collection of glass grapes and faience cups.) "You know, Maya, those monuments were built thousands of years ago. Yet, they look brand new."

"Are they large? Daddy says they're bigger than anything in the world."

"They're big," the prince admitted, placing a clean wad over the surface nick, and deftly winding a piece of fine linen around his ankle. "You know, Maya," he said, easing himself between scented, fresh sheets, "unlike other monuments in our country, they have no inscriptions on them."

"Daddy says they look like stars."

"When the sun strikes them at an angle, they throw shadows out, and then they *do* look like stars. It's an astronomer's delight. You'd love it." Yawning, Amenhotep pushed his ebony headrest out of the way and placed his hands behind his head. "Whoever built them didn't worship our gods."

Before Maya could ask questions, his brother had fallen into a deep sleep.

***

11.

A friendly croak sounded in Maya's ear. He rolled over and pulled the covers above his head. Something dry and rubbery moved up his left leg. Throwing off his bedclothes with a yelp of fright, he was struck dumb. Green and white frogs covered the room. Sitting on chairs they belched from the belfry, hung over lampstands, and hopped across mattresses with gay abandon. Unwilling to leave his warm bed, (and half-wondering if he was dreaming), Maya lay perfectly still. Amenhotep wandered in from the patio reading a book.

"Is this real?"

"I'm afraid so, Maya. Got my spells mixed up. I'm trying out the chapter marked 'Plagues'."

"This isn't much good."

"You're telling me. I can't get the blasted things back into their box!"

Maya brushed back his floppy hair to no avail.

"That's not what I mean. Everyone knows frogs are good luck. Send them to the pond. If you want to make a plague, try locusts."

With that, he tucked himself back into bed. Amenhotep Junior lifted his wand – a hickory stick he had pinched from the teacher's desk in the nursery – and pointed to the web-footed amphibians.

"Away to the pond," he commanded. Immediately, the frogs hopped outside and dived into the water. Instantly, Amenhotep lost control of the piece of wood as, shaking like a jelly, it leapt from his hand. "Snake!" he shouted, leaping out of the way as a large cobra slithered across the floor.

Maya sat bolt upright.

"What now?"

"There's a snake in here."

"No frogs, though!" Maya clapped his hands. "They can't have been real."

As if to contradict him, Plump Lump walked in from the verandah with one hanging from his jaws. He began to devour it under a table. Suddenly, Bak appeared, carrying several pails of paints.

"We have a snake," Maya explained.

Splotches of blue, white, and green splashed onto the bedspreads as earthenware pots crashed to the floor.

"Stay where you are, Bak," Amenhotep commanded.

"Are you nuts? I'm leaving!"

The double doors flung open as a sentry announced:

"The Great Wife, Queen Tiye."

"How many times do I have to tell you not to be late for breakfast?"

Bak froze in his tracks.

"Mummy," explained Maya patiently. "We have a snake."

"So, do I," the queen replied. "My last birthday gift from your brother. Is this a new design?" She looked at the paint-splattered bedspreads. Turning to Amenhotep, who was engaged in a pantomime of putting one finger to his lips, Tiye scowled. "Be quick, the Nubian ambassador is expected today." Turning to leave she sniffed the air. "Better get the maid in – it smells like rat droppings in here."

"Has anyone seen my mice?" asked Dhutmose, careening into his mother on her way out.

"No, but we have a cobra," Bak said.

Dhutmose caught sight of the coils.

"It's only a python. You'll be alright, they don't bite. Hey, I like the paint splatters! Is this the latest thing, Akhy?"

"Um – it's quite the trend," his brother replied, crawling under his bed.

"I'm surprised the dog hasn't attacked your snake," Dhutmose remarked.

"It's eating a frog," Bak explained.

The younger prince emerged from under his bed with a scroll.

"I've got it," he declared. "Stand back, everybody." Leaning over the serpent he intoned, *"Doody Kamza!"*

"That helped a lot," responded Dhutmose sarcastically. He tried to pick up the snake. "You know, Junior, sometimes animals just need to be handled authoritatively."

The younger prince slapped his brother's hand away from the reptile which now had several stomach bulges.

"Those are your mice," Maya deduced.

"That's it," Dhutmose rumbled menacingly. "I'm cutting it open! I don't care whose pet it is."

"It isn't a pet, it's a magic wand," Maya explained.

Suddenly exhausted, he flopped back into bed. The youngest prince leafed frantically through his book.

"Why don't you just say the opposite of what you said to the frogs?" a muffled voice suggested.

"Good idea, Maya. Come back wand!"

Suddenly, the prince was holding a hickory stick.

"There are my mice!"

The heir scurried after two small creatures which fled outside.

Bak sat down, heavily.

"You're a real magician!" he exclaimed.

"I'm going to beat those Heliopolis idiots," the prince beamed.

Maya threw back the bedclothes.

"I wonder. If these rehearsals are anything to go by, we're all doomed."

"I've lost them," Dhutmose lamented. He climbed through the large open window which ran along the side of his brother's apartment. "My pets are now part of your wildlife park, Junior."

***

Pharaoh Amenhotep-the-Magnificent was enjoying an elephant ride. The Nubian ambassador had brought ten pachyderms as a tribute for His Majesty, the all-conquering King of Egypt. They covered Malkata Park, with the ambassador evincing polite interest in the variety of shrubs, which his host insisted on describing in botanical detail.

Nubia, always a troublesome spot, had been ruthlessly conquered down to Napata by Pharaoh's great-grandfather, Tuthmosis-the-Great. The latter, who had enjoyed such varied pastimes as painting vases, had also brought back flora and fauna from his campaigns, examples of which dotted the rambling gardens.

As the party took their ease atop their elephantine transport, they were able to savour a blend of fragrant smells, view rare flowers, and delight in the antics of monkeys, and brightly coloured birds. It was the perfect diplomatic visit.

***

"Your mice are still alive," Maya remarked casually to Prince Dhutmose.

He was grooming his hair in readiness for the day. The other children craned their heads towards the garden in time to see several elephants trumpeting and rearing in the distance.

"Why are elephants stampeding through the park?" Bak asked in a puzzled tone.

"They've seen the mice," explained Maya combing his floppy hair with Greek olive oil.

"He's right," Dhutmose gasped. "Whatever you do, Junior, don't breathe a word of this."

"By Amon's beard, isn't that Dad?"

A mystified Amenhotep Junior pointed towards the disappearing figure of Pharaoh as the herd galloped for the Nile.

***

A sad party of elders tried in vain to solve their problem.

"We've lost Nubia," the king commented sadly.

"Whose idea was it to go elephant riding?" Ay queried acerbically.

"Mine."

A silence descended over the mournful group.

"Elephants don't become wild unless they eat too many berries," Tiye stated logically, breaking the silence after a while.

"These ones did," the king replied with vehemence. "I reckon that wog from the jungle deliberately made a gift of wild animals, so I'd be ripped limb from limb!"

"Nonsense," his wife retorted. "He was riding with you, wasn't he?"

"Nobody presents Pharaoh with killer elephants. It's suicide," Ay pointed out. "Anyway, something has to provoke those animals before they lose control."

"Pardon me for feeling paranoid."

Looking injured, Pharaoh pulled his woollen cape close around his shoulders.

"Oh well," Tiye shrugged. "I suppose it's war then."

"Which is a stupid idea after they decided to bring you a peace offering," Ay added.

"What do you suggest I do?" asked the king.

"Let it go," his brother-in-law advised. "You beat Nubia to a pulp in your fifth year on the throne. Your monuments will testify to that victory for all time."

"Are you implying we'll lose?"

"I'm saying you have a fulltime job with those children of yours," Ay snapped.

***

It was almost eleven o'clock in the morning and the sun was about to turn the coolness of the day into searing heat. Merimose was inspecting his barley. It had been a good crop this year, and he and his family were looking forward to a bountiful harvest. Nebetah, his wife, was organising a group of harvesters in a clearing between the wheat and barley.

A low hum started in the distance. Their son, Iuty, shaded his eyes. He was seven and shouldered his reed basket with the others. It seemed to him that the horizon line between green fields and bright blue sky had darkened.

"Locusts!" Merimose yelled to his men.

They flattened themselves to the ground while fluttering wings stormed above them. In a few moments all was peaceful. Cautiously, the farmer rose. He groaned. Nebetah, however, was waving from afar.

"The wheat's alright!" she called jubilantly.

***

Hundreds of disgruntled lords and ladies pushed away their goblets. Pharaoh had declared a toast of imported Greek wine, which was unfortunately as red as the bloodied water, filling every waterway and spring from Memphis to Karnak.

"Am I about to be assassinated?" he whispered anxiously to his wife. "Why aren't they following my lead?"

"Darling, try *white* wine instead," Tiye encouraged.

She did not allow her spouse to see the fear and anger which had knotted her stomach during the tense evening.

"To Egypt!" declared the king, after the foreign beverage was speedily replaced.

Immediately, his court followed suit. Lyres played, and a troupe of dancing acrobats tumbled past the throngs of finely dressed lords and ladies.

"Remind me to hang our youngest son by his thumbs," Amenhotep whispered to his wife.

***

12.

It was school holidays and another morning at court. To ensure proceedings ran smoothly, King Amenhotep ordered his entire family to be present. Tiye took a long, hard look at her husband's latest garb, her sons' clashing footstools, and the depressed, undernourished figure of Bak seated next to Maya's portly frame.

"I think," she said in clipped tones. "This family does not present a prepossessing sight to its subjects."

"I feel very prepossessed," said Amenhotep Junior. "How about you, Dad?"

"I had an excellent breakfast and felt a wonderful sense of well-being." He looked crossly at his wife. "Until now."

Bak shrank under the Great Wife's appraisal. Maya was in the middle of a mental sum set by the heir. His mouth moved silently as he computed vast sums in his brain which, fuelled by food, was speeding unnaturally quickly.

"I've got it," he said at last, addressing Dhutmose. "It's one million, two hundred and one – if you subtract the ratio of the circumference of a circle to its diameter."

"How on earth did you do that? It took me an hour to calculate. You've done it in seconds without writing materials!"

"A gift," replied the child without pride.

"Watch out," Amenhotep Junior addressed his brother. "My friends will take over the highest court positions someday."

"You forget yourself," his brother rejoined hotly. "They will have to go through the selection process. And, don't forget, you didn't make the grade at Heliopolis!"

"They have. And I'm a genius. Despite our eccentricities we are the brightest and the best." Amenhotep Junior leapt over to pat his brother's arm solicitously. "Perhaps it's time you stopped exercising your body and used your brain instead."

109

"If we weren't at court, I'd deck you."

"I have decked you – verbally. Try it. It's fun."

"Your idea of fun isn't mine."

"There you go," his brother said cheerily. "Verbal annihilation. You're doing it!"

"Ssh!" Tiye glared at her sons.

Pharaoh patted his namesake's head in case the temperamental child began to cry, and consequently ruin the morning's audience.

"Look at the ambassador from Mitanni," he whispered. "If you can remember three things about his speech, I'll excuse you after lunch so that you and your friends can finish decorating your rooms."

"Slurring, colloquialisms, and glottal stops."

Pharaoh was surprised. His son had not missed a beat. Suddenly, a lunch gong sounded from the dining room. The Royal Audience Hall emptied with alacrity.

As usual, everyone ate their fill except for the Great Wife. Instead, Tiye surveyed the boys with mute hostility.

"How's the room progressing?" she asked finally, as dessert was served.

"There's nothing like it in the palace," Amenhotep Junior replied, pulling a banana from its bunch.

Bak said nothing. Maya pretended to be busy eating. It did not protect him from the Great Wife's glare.

"Did you know your father's economising, Junior?"

"For the life of me I can't see why – we're rich!"

"You don't know anything about our finances."

"I do," he countered. "The priests are taking more and more of our gold and land. One day they'll rob Pharaoh and the people."

Instead of replying, Tiye turned to her wine steward.

"I'll be inspecting the cellars this afternoon." Turning back to her son, she warned: "Amenhotep Junior, you can only use one coat on your bedroom walls, otherwise you will be severely reprimanded. Do you understand?"

"Yes, Mother."

"One coat?" Bak was almost apoplectic. "You need a primer and at least *three* topcoats!"

"Especially if you want ducks," added Maya.

"Don't worry, I have a plan," Amenhotep Junior placated.

He was carrying what appeared to be the contents of the entire fruit bowl from lunch. When the boys reached his apartments, he carefully locked the doors from the inside, and handed out apples and pomegranates.

"What are you doing?" Bak queried. "The wet paint needs air in order to dry!"

The prince crunched an apple and began tapping a gold appliquéd wall situated behind his bed. Maya watched with interest. He gasped as part of it swung back, revealing a door to another room. Lighting a silver oil lamp, Amenhotep led his friends into the most cluttered storeroom they had ever seen.

"It looks as if you've smuggled the entire contents of Karnak's library in here," Bak noted, wading through a mountain of papyrus.

"I'll have to return those scrolls. They're for kids, anyway. Won't be missed."

"Kids?" Maya flicked rapidly through a book. "These are sacred writings!"

"In praise of an idol. You know Amon is invisible because he doesn't exist." Bak cleared his throat, while Amenhotep Junior chuckled to himself as if he had said something particularly witty. Diving into a wooden chest he began giving orders. "I'm going to hand stuff out to you," he said.

Amenhotep gave Maya several dusty boxes inscribed with rough hieroglyphs in a child's uncertain hand. Bak, in turn, placed them carefully in tiers outside the door. The prince climbed out of the chest, slid back the lid, and led his friends into the daylight. Shutting the door, so that it became part of the wall, he opened the first box.

"It's still good," he said prodding the green compound.

"That's malachite," Bak observed, excitement mounting. "Enough for decorating the entire harem!"

"I'm a bit of a magpie," Amenhotep confessed. "But you should find all the paint you need here."

***

Queen Tiye's mouth fell open. The walls glistened with lotuses, papyrus thickets, small gazelles, and bucking calves. A floor of ducks, fish, and flowers nodding in the breeze, gazed up at her.

"I specifically said ONE coat."

"It is," lied the prince. "You can check the records. Nothing's missing from Men's studio."

"There are at least four on this dresser alone." Tiye scrutinised the walls. "Junior, have you a fixation with ducks?"

"Everything's an extension of creation."

"Did Bak do all this?"

"I helped."

A telltale giggle from the corner of the room alerted Tiye to the truth.

"Do you like it, Maya?" she asked pleasantly.

"Oh, it's wonderful – a real child's room," he enthused.

"Yes, it is" Tiye said agreeably. She stepped onto the patio. "AKHY!" she roared.

***

"He's put in a pathway," the Great Wife fumed, "*and* a lake!"

The king nervously drummed his fingers on his desk.

"It's not a lake, it's a pond."

"We don't have the resources. Where did he get the gold to build it?"

"The boy's a genius. He landscaped it all by himself. And he told me to remind you that the name 'Akhy' is a secret."

Tiye raised her hands in the air.

"No one doubts his gifts, but that that child's impossible. His secret name frightens me. He told Maya he was going to call himself

112

'Akhenaten'. It means 'He who works for Aten'! What if our son really does confront the priests of Amon when he's an adult, and starts worshipping Aten? I want to send him to boarding school but you won't let me. Why is every mother in Egypt allowed to get rid of her sons except me?"

"I thought our youngest son was your favourite."

"I have no favourites. He is more like me when his nose is in his books than Dhutmose, who takes after you in his love of architecture, and the chase."

"I'm an architect, but I have to confess that today I've been topped by a little bookworm. Dhutmose would never have that kind of vision, even though he's twice Akhy's – I mean Junior's – age."

Tiye sighed.

"I don't think the landscaping is *that* good."

"He explained it all to me."

"So, you *know*? How are we going to justify this expenditure to the priests?"

"We won't." Pharaoh ceased drumming his fingers. "To tell you the truth, my dear, I intend to take a stand."

"For the love of Amon, don't get expelled from the temple like your son."

"My child should never have been made to feel unwelcome at the priests' school." A cloud passed over Amenhotep's brow. "Our youngest is still a baby, and sometimes babies can't control their own actions."

"You're telling me!" Tiye smiled. "Actually, the garden never looked better."

"I was stunned," the king agreed proudly. "Look, dear," he said, taking his wife's dainty hand in his. "Our son is trying to make things nice for his new brother. Junior is lonely, but in these past few weeks, I've never seen him happier."

"He's more tractable during his lessons, too."

"That's because he doesn't go to school anymore!"

The couple laughed.

"They're both lonely boys," Tiye commented shrewdly. "And I think Maya might not only be bright, but also endowed with integrity. It will serve the empire well when he's an adult."

"He's still very timid." The cloud returned to Amenhotep's countenance. "I wanted to flog his father and cast him into prison."

"Parents should discipline their children. Goodness knows, ours need more of it."

"Maya wasn't disciplined, he was abused. He needs love, not the stick."

"Junior told me about Maya's father last summer, but I didn't take it seriously. I suppose that's why you're the sovereign, darling. Wise decisions are your domain." As her husband's chest inflated, Tiye brushed his arm. "Promise me you'll be careful with the priests."

"I will, but make no mistake: Amon's gold is going right back into our coffers."

***

Bak and Maya were sailing model boats on a pond filled with ducks, cranes, and flamingos. Amenhotep Junior patted Plump Lump absent-mindedly, while reading his morning paper. It was another newsletter printed on expensive papyrus informing him of the week's palace news, the next race, and Horemheb's new status as junior chariot champion.

It was a perfect morning, all things considered. His friends, pets, and creative impulses had all met with approval and success. Even Dhutmose swam in the new pond. He was also privy to his father's confidences. Dad was at the temple this morning, battling Amon. In the last two weeks, Amenhotep-the-Magnificent had appropriated several coffers. He was also forcing the priests to sign over granary rights to Pharaoh in case of famine. Amenhotep Junior thought the king should go all the way and personally disperse food to the peasants.

However, he was still a child, the morning was filled with bright sunshine, and he had a poem to write.

***

13

"Lights off. It's way past your bedtime."

Amenhotep Junior clambered off his bed, where half a dozen friends sat strumming their musical instruments.

"Dad, we're in the middle of a composition."

"It's half past eleven. You have school in the morning."

"But I'm two terms ahead! Besides, I'm back from Heliopolis, and we're celebrating." Several teenage women passed the open door. On glimpsing Pharaoh, they drew their veils across their faces. Others flashed him toothy smiles. Blushing, the king turned back to his son, who was craning his small head forward. "Dad, are you having a party?"

The older Amenhotep shifted his weight awkwardly from one foot to another.

"In a couple of hours."

"Can I come?"

"It wouldn't be suitable. Now lights off."

"I'm having a party, too." As if struck by inspiration, the boy rushed to his snack table and held up a small cake. "And you're invited!"

Not wishing to enforce his will, the king glanced at the children. Truly it had been fine with him all along. He approved of his son's gatherings. Visitors from the *Kap*, noblemen's heirs, and even Dhutmose's friends all attended. It was educational, too. They wrote poems and plays, and composed beautiful music for the harem.

"Make me a promise. Keep it down for your mother's sake."

***

Saffron and incense filled the air. Over a hundred foreign women, arrayed in costumes of their country, filled the king's apartments and spilled out onto the patio and lawns below. Wine flowed while nubile maidens handed out platters of meat, vegetables, and sweetmeats.

Musicians strummed their lyres and whistled tunefully on bronze and reed pipes.

Pharaoh, dressed in a magnificent tunic of blue and gold, beamed from ear to ear. Mixing with his guests was no easy feat. The entire female audience was intent on obtaining that sole, prized interview with His Majesty. Occasionally, the monarch raised his glass. It was only then that his smile faded. For his faithful manservant Aanen, it was easy to detect melancholy and a hint of anger in the royal eyes.

Meanwhile, Amenhotep Junior tapped his fingers on his windowsill. His party had finished hours ago.

"You know what, Maya," he said. "I'm going to exert vengeance on Dad."

"Whatever for?"

"He's engaged in immoral revelry."

"He's a *king*, and has a harem. I thought of all people, you would understand."

Amenhotep Junior flicked a piece of papyrus off the ledge into the garden below.

"Then he should go to the harem. I'm writing."

"Your mother's studying over there. The racket would disturb her."

"I hadn't thought of that."

Pushing back the bedclothes, Maya draped a shawl around himself. Why the Malkata household felt obliged to keep all the windows open at night was beyond him. Apparently, they were obsessed with fresh air, although mosquitoes whizzing about one's head was scarcely healthy. He settled next to his friend. The pair watched the all-female gathering sipping wine and laughing under the lamplight. Finally, Maya put one arm around the prince's shoulders.

"What did you have in mind?" he asked.

***

Never since the days of Tuthmosis-the-Great had a butler seen the sovereign of Egypt so distraught. It was as if a campaign to Canaan was imminent.

"Where are my carp?" the angry king asked.

Frantic for an explanation, Aanen began talking so he could marshal his thoughts.

"Your Majesty must remember that of late, much angling has taken place. The stocks in the main pond are depleted."

"Balderdash!" Amenhotep picked his teeth ruminatively. "Have it checked out," he said. "We have a thief."

***

THWACK!

A cry of pain, followed by a thud in the darkness, reminded Amenhotep Junior that he was an excellent marksman.

"Are you keeping a lookout, Maya?"

"Definitely. You scored!"

Squinting with determination, Amenhotep strung his child's bow and let fly a volley of blunt wooden arrows. The garden was uncannily silent. Disappointed, the boy shaded his eyes.

"There must have only been one."

Sighing, he lit an oil lamp and drew the drapes. On the lawn Arathamon observed the moonlit sky from the flat of his back. Finding the culprit was proving easier than he thought. But what was one to do with a thief who provided security measures over his stolen property? The royal household was indeed a combination of mayhem and madness. The entire family was filled with geniuses and criminals. Overhead, the morning star shone brightly, winking as if to personally signal him.

"I must get a promotion, or I'll be dead by thirty."

As if in acknowledgment Venus glowed even more brightly in the night sky.

***

"Look out!"

A sixty-foot wall of water rose behind the prince's apartment. Using great presence of mind, Maya burrowed under his bed and clambered into the nearest wooden chest. Pushing down the linen garments, he pulled the engraved lid over his head.

Amenhotep Junior rushed for the double doors, and unlatched them as a waterfall cascaded over the balcony and into the bedroom. Clutching onto the door for dear life, he purposely jammed his arm behind the huge gold-plated wooden latch. As the avalanche roared down the corridor, he heard yelling from the alarmed sentries, followed by a huge Nubian, swimming valiantly up the flooded bedroom in search of his charges. Spotting the prince swinging from the door, and gulping helplessly in the tide, he seized the child around his waist.

"Don't pull," Amenhotep gurgled. "I'm stuck!"

"Allow me to assist, Your Majesty."

Gently, but firmly, disengaging the bruised arm, the guard held the boy aloft and waded into the corridor.

"Maya's still in there!" the boy bellowed above the roar of the flood.

The Nubian placed his master on a table, and returned to the room. Suddenly, the water disappeared. Swimming one moment in ten feet of it, the guard unexpectedly crashed onto his belly.

"That would have to hurt," Maya noted, crawling out from under the bed.

"Sire, you're dry!"

"Is the prince alright, Duban?"

"He's safe."

The man looked about him in amazement. A variety of perch, carp, and even *tilapia nilotica*, lay strewn about the room. Amenhotep Junior, who had vacated the safety of his table, peered around the doors.

"Fish for dinner, anyone?"

***

"AKHY!"

"Oh, my goodness!" Maya fell off a high chair which had been his lookout. "He's coming! Quick – hide!"

Frantically, the prince bolted the front door of his room, rushed out the exit, and climbed over his balcony railing. Running around his landscaped pond he looked up, only to discover his father had somehow negated to choose the orthodox method of entry to his son's rooms, and was looming threateningly above him. Sheer panic struck the boy's stomach. Although never disciplined with corporal punishment, the prince turned tail and ran.

"Come back!" Pharaoh cried in hot pursuit.

Although he scurried as fast as his legs could carry him, the boy found himself swaying in mid-air before he could hide under the wooden garden seat near his verandah.

WHACK! WHACK!

Two large shovel-hands descended on his backside as Pharaoh, finally exhausted, slumped into the seat and placed his namesake next to him.

"That's for stealing my property."

Amenhotep Junior nursed his behind. Aware his father's hands had made more sound than impact, he was nevertheless stunned. In all his years of delinquency the king had never raised a hand to him. He gazed with anguish into his father's eyes, and knew immediately: Mother made him do it. The supreme monarch of Asia looked cowed, frightened, apologetic, and anxious. All at once. Relieved, Amenhotep Junior opened his mouth and bawled at the top of his lungs.

"Oh, for goodness' sakes, I hardly touched you," his father fussed, arranging his son's kilt so that it once again hung correctly.

"That's not the point," the child said, suddenly self-contained. "It was the intent. WAH!"

"Shush! We don't want Maya to think he's got another father like his."

That did it. The delinquent dried his eyes.

"Alright then, let's negotiate."

"We're negotiating nothing," Pharaoh hissed. "You're the baby, I'm the adult."

"I'm *not* a baby."

"You behave like one."

Not knowing what to say, the prince pursed his lips and folded his arms.

"I'm tired of this," his father continued. "I'm not surprised the Heliopolitan priests threw you out." New injury replaced the sullen expression on the child's face. "Here," said the king, drawing out two flattened pastries from his waistband. "If we're going to negotiate, you'd better learn that the first lesson of diplomacy is always carried out over tasty delicacies."

Forgetting his own point of view, the boy's eyes glowed as he accepted his favourite type of honey-laced cake.

"I think we could come to some kind of arrangement," he said in his best adult manner.

Inside the prince's room, behind the window, Maya drooled.

***

14.

Wiping sweaty palms on his thighs, Amenhotep Junior controlled his wavering voice.

"Mummy, can I go for a chariot ride?"

"With your stallions?" The boy nodded. "I suppose so. Make sure your father watches you."

"Don't worry," he whispered, suddenly shy.

"I don't mind supervising you," the king said, putting down his papyrus scroll filled with the daily events of the empire. "My hunt isn't until noon."

"Maybe Dhutmose could keep an eye on his brother," suggested Tiye, noting her son's downcast head.

The king reached for his glass of milk and downed it.

"Dhutmose is hunting. I'm meeting him after his first kill."

"I swear all the males in this family have a death wish." Tiye looked at her son again. "I'll come with you," she offered.

"You?" the king said in surprise.

"I'm not only good for books," she rejoined huffily.

***

"Mummy, you can go back now," said Amenhotep Junior, who had described two circuits of the racetrack with his perfectly be-haved horses.

Tiye's hawk-like eyes penetrated the arena. After several minutes, she spotted what she was looking for in the shape of a dark-haired girl sitting in the stands, watching the prince.

"Alright," she acquiesced, much to her son's surprise. Instead of departing the stadium, however, Tiye sat in a shady corner on a comfortable, suede-upholstered seat. "This I have to see," she muttered to herself.

"Hi!" the prince called to Nefertiti, moments later. Pulling hard on the horses, he made them whinny. Night bucked slightly and shook his mane. "Sorry, boy," Amenhotep apologised. Clambering out of the carriage, he rushed over to pat the horse with one hand. The other searched for a stick of sugar cane, which he soon produced, to his steed's delight.

"So that's how he does it," muttered Tiye.

"They're beautiful." Nefertiti moved out from the awning and into the compound. "And you're such a good charioteer!"

"I am," agreed the prince, who was concentrating on appeasing his horses. At eleven o'clock he was starting to feel the glare of the sun. "Like a ride?"

"Why do you think I've been waiting here all morning?"

Wishing to hurry, Amenhotep Junior looped the reins deftly over his wrists. Allowing the girl to climb into the chariot first, he followed, scrambling over the top step, which was still too high for him. Slowly, they made their way around the outside of the track, where Pharaoh had thoughtfully planted shade in the form of leafy trees.

"It's a lovely day," Nefertiti commented.

"Uh, huh," replied the prince, whose temper tended to climb with the heat of the day. Although he desperately wanted Nefertiti to enjoy the ride, he was over an hour late for their appointment. The horses needed to be near water and so did he. "Would you mind if we went to the temple?" he asked. "After I put Night and Morning away?"

"Are you allowed?" asked Nefertiti, disappointed not to be seen in a fine car with her princely boyfriend.

"Any time I feel like it. I want to go for a swim."

"Ah!" responded the girl archly.

***

Doffing his kilt, the boy threw himself into Karnak's pool with a shout.

"I don't swim," said Nefertiti.

"I don't care," was the surprising response. Amenhotep Junior stuck his spiky auburn hair under the water. "That's better," he announced.

"So, you really were hot."

"Terribly," the prince puffed as he performed a windmill version of the backstroke. "You see, as much as I love the sun, I have to be careful."

"I understand," replied Nefertiti who, for the sake of her feminine appearance, was hardly ever allowed outdoors.

She cast a glance over her shoulder at the clergy who were gathering for prayers. In the midst of Karnak's white priestly robes, she detected a hint of royal blue. Perhaps the striking Prince Dhutmose was doing the rounds. She looked down fondly at her chubby, naked friend gurgling among the lotuses.

"Look," he called. "A goldfish! Come and see!"

In spite of herself, the girl threw caution to the winds and dived in. Something akin to a gasp shuddered through the columned halls of Karnak as Queen Tiye's eyes slowly rounded.

***

Pharaoh scoffed a sandwich while listening to his waspish wife. They were expected at a parade shortly to present themselves as the perfect royal couple.

"Oh, come on, dear," he said at last. "They're only children having a little fun."

"That's not the point. The girl is shameless."

"She's just a child."

"Women should be indoors."

"And women shouldn't read, let alone own, vast libraries." Amenhotep put down his half-eaten beef and cucumber wrap. "Darling, if I didn't know better, I'd say you were jealous."

"Don't be preposterous! Of what, may I ask?"

"Your son is growing up. At seven he has a girlfriend; at twelve they'll marry; and come his sixteenth birthday you'll be a grandmother."

"I'm worried because Nefertiti is Lord Ay's daughter," Tiye responded in measured tones.

"Why didn't you tell me it was Nefertiti?"

The king wiped his mouth on a napkin and adjusted his *nemes* headdress. He needed the Great Wife at his side during the parade and it would not do to sour her mood.

"I'm still attending," she said, as if able to read his mind. "But I'll change my clothes only after you promise to speak to your son."

"Don't worry, I'll cane those shameless buttocks he's been flashing all over town."

***

"Oh Dad, stop poking your nose into my love life!"

Unsure whether to laugh or be angry, Amenhotep Senior jolted back at the adult tone.

"Junior!" he remonstrated. "What sort of parents would we be if we didn't care?"

"Enlightened?"

"You know what your mother's like."

"A nosy old killjoy."

A flush of anger reddened Pharaoh's cheeks.

"Sorry," the prince amended quickly. "But I like Nefertiti. We were just riding, that's all."

"What about the pool?"

"I get hot. It was eleven o'clock. I would have been riding at nine if you and Mum hadn't been fighting over who was to supervise me. I'm not a baby, you know."

"I know." The king, who was always ill at ease with disciplining his children, fidgeted. "I never told you this before, but I was a co-regent at twelve."

"Everyone knows that."

"I also fell in love with your mother as a youngster."

"When?"

"Not at seven – a bit older, but I knew then, I wanted her to be my girlfriend ... and wife."

"So, there you are, Dad!" Amenhotep Junior extended his hands. "You understand." Unable to control his feelings, he hugged his father warmly. "We're related after all!"

The king melted. Patting the outrageous spikes, he kissed his son's head.

"You have a good heart, my son," he said. "Now I have to go to town and be a god."

***

Litter bearers hoisted the royal pair onto their shoulders.

"Did you speak to him?" the Great Wife asked.

"I always do what you want."

"And?"

"He promises not to swim."

Tiye stared straight ahead at the cheering crowds. Over the years she had managed to block them out while thinking other thoughts. Content her son would no longer be spied on by gossiping priests at Karnak's temple, she sat back in her throne. Things were going to work out perfectly.

***

125

PART II:
Adolescence and Scientists

15.

Gazing dreamily at the cloud-covered mountain tops of Mitanni, Prince Amenhotep drew a fleece around his shoulders. Sipping a cup of vegetable soup through chattering teeth, he tried to concentrate on the letters strewn across his bed.

"Have you answered your father, Junior?"

"Bak, I can barely lift my fingers to drink this broth."

"I know what you mean," mumbled his friend from a bearskin couch. Drawing a blanket up to his chin, he screwed a suede bonnet over his head. "Why doesn't King What's-His-Name heat the place?"

"I demanded no special treatment."

"I'll never be able to sculpt again. My fingers are numb."

"My fingers are blue." The prince shakily set down his soup. "There's a curse in this country called frostbite."

"I would normally pretend to care. But I'm trying to survive over here."

"There's another option," Amenhotep suggested, blowing on his hands to keep them warm. "We could share this bed."

"I'd rather die."

"You will if you stay on that couch tonight with one blanket."

"If it was daylight, I'd think about making a run for the Syrian border." Peering out of his coverlet through the window, Bak shivered. "The clouds are smudged. This place is full of evil witchcraft."

"That's rain up there on the range, not witchcraft."

"How can you tell?"

"That smudging is water. Hump told me. Do you know who would do well out here?" asked the prince, smiling despite his suffering.

"Maya!"

"We should write to him. What *are* you doing?" Bak, hobbling under the weight of blankets and sheepskin slippers, flopped like an exhausted eel next to Amenhotep. Paper scattered everywhere. "Watch it!" the prince exclaimed irritably, trying to retrieve his letters.

"The only thing those letters are good for is wrapping round your legs as extra protection against the cold." Glimpsing a view from the window, Bak pointed. "By Thoth's beard!" he exclaimed. "Is that snow?"

Amenhotep craned his long neck towards the window. Rapidly he closed the wooden shutters, slid into bed and pulled up the sheepskin duvet.

"Get in," he prompted Bak. "That's an order."

***

In an international research centre, a group of scientists studied ancient Egypt. They all approached the subject from different angles. A time machine was what they craved. Their boss, Walter Zars, a serious man of fifty, was getting closer to their goal.

"Has anyone seen Walt?" asked Tom Wahlberg, as he entered the main research facility. A senior researcher, he was one of the Americans making progress on the study of Akhenaten. Only the sound of computers greeted his query. The English academic from Cambridge, Ernest Jones, shrugged, while Karen Smith, from the University of Manchester, remained invisible behind a stack of papers. "Does anyone object to me accessing his workstation?"

Again silence. Before anybody could object, Tom sat down in the professor's vacant chair, flipped on the monitor switch and logged in on Walter Zars' password. What happened next became a source of controversy, discussed by researchers in their cafeteria for years to come. A purple and pink cloud, resembling a galactic dust-swirl, flew out of the twelve-inch screen and unseated Tom.

Karen saw a blue and white flash atop her stack of work, and thanked the powers-that-be for its thick-papered protection. Goodness knows, she could have been burnt to a crisp. Not one to trust computers, she always printed out her pages after typing, and consequently sat behind a wall of groundbreaking research. Half the lab leapt out of their seats and fled to the end of the hall. The other half sat, awestruck, at their workstations.

A door at the southern end swung slowly open to a collective gasp as Walter appeared, delicately balancing two doughnuts on top of a large coffee. How he managed to dig up such luxuries in Egypt, nobody knew, although it was rumoured he flew them in with French champagne and caviar. Oblivious to the uproar, the professor made his way to his desk.

Noticing his computer was flickering, he mumbled: "I must have forgotten to switch it off." He pulled up a chair. "And I must have forgotten to *log* off. Well, well – senility has finally set in." Opening the plastic lid off his Frappuccino he mixed in raw sugar crystals. "Sorry, guys: I've compromised security. The Russian mafia from Hurghada will be halfway to Mount Nebo to dig up Moses' bones!" Just then, he noticed the empty desks. Karen was glaring accusingly at him from her corner while she put out a small fire which had caught one of her papyrus scrolls. "Anything the matter?" he asked.

"We've lost Tom."

"He's missing?"

"He was sitting at your desk," Ernest began shakily.

"Why?"

"He was trying to log in."

"On my code?"

"I don't know. A large pink cloud took him out."

"He was sucked into the computer." Karl Dacek said.

As usual, the Austrian geologist was looking for something healthy to eat, but his supplies had dissipated throughout the room. Macadamias, cashews, roasted peanuts, and almonds were scattered across keyboards, drowned in water, tucked in seats, and even wedged securely in the more elaborate hairstyles of his female colleagues.

"What's the date?" asked Walter, wiping froth from his moustache.

"What do you mean?" Ernest waved his arms in exasperation. "Haven't you been listening? You're responsible for Tom's death!"

"April the first," Karl replied in an amused tone, gazing longingly at his secretary's coif in which a particularly large nut rested.

"Tom's not dead," Karen said. "How do you know he didn't get up and go back to his office? You all ran away so quickly it was hard to know what happened."

"If he disappeared, he won't have gone far," Walter said calmly. "I suggest you all get back to work."

***

"How did you sleep, Amenhotep?" the crown prince of Mitanni smirked.

"Like a log."

Their host contemplated a dishevelled and bleary-eyed Bak with a cool eye.

"So I hear."

"What's for breakfast?" asked the Egyptian prince, pulling apart the pot covers spread before him.

"It's a buffet. Everyone pitches in – without servants."

Their host smiled, looking forward to an imminent fit of pique for which Amenhotep was famous.

"Excellent!" Picking up an ostrich egg, Amenhotep proceeded to smother it with sauces, while helping himself to a spinach-and-rosemary pie. "Years of doing this at Dad's court makes me feel quite at home," he continued to the Mitannian prince's disappointment. "Fork, Bak?"

Dumbly, his tired friend nodded.

"You're not serving him, too?"

"It's called manners." Amenhotep deftly shovelled the outsize egg onto Bak's plate. "Something which separates the Egyptian court from its barbaric neighbours."

Picking up a bowl of goat casserole from the sideboard, Amenhotep tore a hunk of bread and began eating.

***

130

"I'm not impressed," Tiye declared coldly. She placed the ruby in its tray. "I want something more expensive."

The king knitted his brows in vexation.

"Isn't it enough that I build you temples, lakes, and palaces?"

"This is supposed to be a gift for Egypt's *queen*. It wouldn't serve as a trifle for one of your concubines."

"It's worth more than anything else you're wearing," he responded.

"I'm not wearing jewellery."

"You're *covered* in it, my dear. Perhaps you are bored."

"I am," Tiye agreed vigorously. "And tired of being spurned in favour of younger flesh. Why, only last week the Princess of Mitanni received twelve emeralds set in gold for a single night of passion."

"Since when do you care what gifts I give to my other wives?" her husband enquired heatedly.

"Since you treated the Queen of Egypt like a harem girl." Tiye rose to her full height of five feet. "I shall be in my apartments. You will probably not visit me since I'm redundant."

Amenhotep swore softly in low tones and picked up the jewel. He held it to the light.

"Nefer," he addressed one of his viziers. "Isn't this a stone worthy of a queen?"

"In truth, Your Majesty, yes – but perhaps not the *chief* queen."

"The problem is I can't see anything these days," Amenhotep muttered. "Everything is so difficult. Even getting up in the morning is a major headache for me."

"To His Majesty: Life! Health! Prosperity!" his minister intoned.

"Yes, yes." The king rolled the glimmering ruby between pudgy fingers. "I still love her," he remarked wistfully. "It just seems that she is more difficult to please now. When we were teenagers, I gave her a small chalcedony piece personally fashioned for her. It was roughly hewn and out of proportion, but she held onto it for years. I don't know what became of it." He stared down gloomily at the offending rock. "This is badly cut. Have it repolished."

***

Amenhotep Junior scrutinised his colleague with a pained expression. They had been arguing for the better part of an hour, with Bak becoming bolder by the minute, and taking liberties with his tongue which he would never have done within the confines of Malkata Palace.

"I don't know what you're talking about," the Egyptian prince finally said, throwing back his head haughtily. "My father loves me."

Normally such disdain would have put a noble in his place. It was never wise for a commoner to provoke a royal, however close to the inner circle. But Amenhotep's companion was made of sterner stuff than the court flatterers. Whether it was the freezing conditions, or sleepless nights which had emboldened Bak, it was hard to say. What was abundantly clear was that the young artist was as irritable and phlegmatic as the spoiled prince.

"We've been here over a month and learned nothing, Junior. And I'm not sure whether your father wants us to learn anything."

"That's a harsh thing to say."

"Haven't you thought it strange that you're always travelling? Most royals have these blasted foreigners come to them. Take the *Children of the Kap* organisation for instance. No one need ever visit Kush while those foreign kids are on your doorstep. That's the way it should be – learning about barbarians captured in war, and groomed in the ways of the mighty Egyptian royal court."

"Who branded our brothers and sisters barbarians?" Amenhotep was suddenly animated. "We Egyptians have far too parochial a vision of earth! God made all peoples."

Bak sighed.

"Whatever you say, but I haven't learned a word of Mitannian and, frankly, I don't think these savages warrant my diligent study of their weird ways."

"Fret not, I've learned enough for both of us." Amenhotep turned to the fire burning merrily in the hearth. Having put aside his original desire to be treated like everyone else, the prince had ordered heating. "It's not *that* cold."

By way of reply, Bak stubbornly pulled up the collar of his leopard-skin coat.

"We could sculpt if you wish," his friend offered, changing the subject. "It'll beat learning the language. Did you know King Shuttarna transformed the second storey into a studio?" Bak made no reply, but Amenhotep fancied his eyes sparked with his old zeal. "Let's have a look."

"Not on your life! This is the only warm room in the house."

"In that case you'll have to put up with Mitannians invading your privacy. You know how they hate to see people alone."

Picking up the hem of his woollen robe, the prince of Egypt unlatched the door of their study. Grumbling, Bak followed. He dreaded being left alone anywhere in that strange castle. Having minimal grasp of the native tongue, he was frightened of being accosted, especially by one of the pretty harem girls who often stopped to chat. In fact, he thought morosely, as vapour breathed from his nose while they travelled the icy passageway, he had only mastered: "Leave me alone!" and: "Naff off!"

Ascending the stone stairwell, Amenhotep hummed a song he had composed. Not wishing to converse with the glowering Bak, his mind wandered from music to art, and then on to God. Pale grey shafts of light shone down from narrow, oblong windows. The mountain air agreed with them, the prince thought happily. Always the optimist, he had battled the freezing conditions as best he could. Yesterday, when he could finally stand it no longer, servants had been politely entreated for extra fires, which were lit with pleasing alacrity. Furthermore, he had struck up a friendship with Prince Tushratta who, like him, was second in line to the throne. Gifted with a quick wit, the boy who was roughly the same age as Amenhotep, had granted the royal guest's every wish, and had even anticipated his whims.

"Amon, this is enormous!" exclaimed Bak, visibly impressed.

They stood in the middle of a room which stretched the length of the palace. Filled with pottery wheels, a variety of paints, and stone for sculpting, it represented a smorgasbord of delights to the frustrated artist.

"It's better than what we have in Egypt." Amenhotep rubbed his hands together with pleasure. Bak was not listening.

Instead, he floated from one artist's dream to the next. There were so many materials in the room, he could have spent a year moulding, sculpting, glazing, and painting.

Overcome, he eventually sat down at a wheel and began fashioning a pot. The prince was content to settle by the blazing hearth with a resident lap dog.

"Do you want to pick up a brush?" Bak called after an hour's bliss. "The paints are so bright, they're fluorescent!"

"Not at the moment."

"I've just figured out why you like travelling so much. It's an excuse to do nothing!"

"Utterly untrue. I'm thinking."

Bak shrugged, picked up a brush and flicked its bristles. Soon he was pounding the end of the reed to obtain a finer brushstroke. Using crayon, he outlined several hieroglyphs on a piece of granite. Then he applied the rich, warm colours set before him. Different from Egyptian compounds, the paints presented a challenge of application which he found exhilarating. He mixed and created effects which absorbed his busy mind for most of the morning.

At midday, a stupefied Amenhotep and his dog awoke from their heat-induced doze. Picking up the fluffy ginger pup, so unlike the large, lean breeds he was accustomed to in his native *Kemet*, the prince strolled the length of the room, inspecting its contents before stopping at Bak's work.

"We'll have to do something about art in Egypt."

He seized a piece of charcoal and, using a fragment of pottery, drew a face in several expert sweeps.

"That's damned ugly," Bak commented genially.

"You don't understand – it's the *style*. When we get back home, I'm going to train you. I want something modern for the court, something bright and colourful. Art should express the joy of life. There is so much joy in living," the prince murmured, half to himself. "We should express it in the arts. It gives glory to God."

"Joy? I've never been so miserable in my life!"

"Then you're not looking. This light, so unlike our own, is liberating. And what about this magnificent studio? Have you ever seen anything like it? Father will be green with jealousy!"

"I wouldn't tell him," Bak warned. "He'll send us back here. He seems to take pleasure in banishing you from Malkata on an annual basis."

"And what about the *girls,"* Amenhotep continued, a light sparkling in his dark eyes. "There are so many beautiful women accosting us – mainly you. Stop complaining, Bak. You're only young once! I wish I was as good-looking as you," he added wistfully.

"You're a prince, and next in line to the world's greatest throne. I have only my looks."

"So, you're saying I'm ugly?"

"No," Bak said in a slow, deliberate voice. "I'm saying those tarts don't speak my language."

"Who needs words for the language of love? Really, you do worry me at times!"

"I have a betrothed, Neferure, in Egypt."

Amenhotep turned his attention to the puppy. It wagged its tail with excitement.

"And what do you think of this wet blanket, mister?"

"You should take a good look at yourself, Junior. Only the lonely and mentally unstable talk to animals."

"On the contrary, it takes enlightenment and openness to the Creator to have rapport with his furred and feathered creations."

Having had enough activity for one morning, Amenhotep returned to his spot by the hearth, where he snoozed until the lunch bell.

***

A misty envelope surrounded Tom. Unable to see anything, he remained stock still.

"I wonder if I'm dead," he thought.

"You're not dead – only visiting."

A slight individual, clad in an unusual robe, stepped into view. From the creases in his brow, Tom gathered he was extremely displeased.

"I'm sorry, I didn't mean to come here," the scientist apologised.

"Good, because I was expecting someone else."

The two men regarded each other for several moments.

"You look familiar," Tom remarked after a while.

"Why don't you go back?" the stranger suggested uncharitably.

"If it were possible, I would have done so already."

The latter exhaled an exaggerated sigh as if he was dealing with a slow-witted child.

"Allow me," he said, pushing Tom to one side. It was then the scientist noticed a bench gleaming with an array of silver and gold knobs and elegant handles. "Top lever goes back: Bottom lever sends you to hell." The man bared his teeth, which were large and well-formed. "Take it from me – I've been here a long time."

"What's your name?" asked Tom quickly, already knowing the answer.

"King Akhenaten."

Knocked off his feet, Tom felt a dizzy spell, not unlike last week when he had imbibed Walter's champagne at a researchers' function. A split second later he found himself in the privacy of his study.

"No one has to know about this," he cautioned the room, completely forgetting the hordes he had dismayed earlier that morning.

The books sat impassively on their shelves making no comment.

***

136

16.

"My casserole's cold, Bak," the prince complained, trying not to look disappointed.

"That should be the least of your problems. Your father hasn't spoken to you since we arrived."

"We're at court. He can't afford to show emotion."

"What's to afford?" Bak muttered. "He's your *father*! He's supposed to greet you with open arms. Instead, he hasn't bothered to look once in this direction."

"What bugs me is that Mummy hasn't even acknowledged my presence. We've been away for months."

"It's me."

"Don't be ridiculous."

The prince shot a glance at his mother, who continued to stare impassively ahead. Suddenly, an impish desire swept over him and he began to wave.

"Stop it!" Bak admonished. "Your father's addressing the Syrian consul."

Ignoring him, Amenhotep's right hand motioned his mother as he smiled at her with dazzling white teeth. A high-pitched giggle erupted behind them.

"Hello, Maya!" Amenhotep Junior grinned.

"You resemble an ostrich about to take off," the rotund nobleman observed.

"Perhaps that's why His Majesty has not recognised his own son," Bak said sarcastically.

The court had grown quiet watching Amenhotep's antics, and the artist's last words drifted softly, but stunningly clearly, through the pillared hall.

Instead of responding, Tiye continued to sit as still as a statue.

Pharaoh momentarily took his eyes off the ambassador to scowl at his second son. Undeterred, Amenhotep Junior began to use both arms to stir the currents around him.

Prince Dhutmose, standing directly behind the king's throne, covered his grin with one hand. Encouraged, his brother leaned back on his chair and promptly crashed to the floor.

Several people leapt up to assist the royal jester to his feet. Bak noted with horror that the ivory throne he had spent meticulously decorating last summer had turned to matchwood.

The king continued to receive visitors as though nothing had happened. His face, however, was a dangerous shade of purple.

***

The family gathered in the living room to welcome the youngest prince back from his travels.

"What on earth did you think you were doing?" Tiye exploded.

"Trying to catch your attention."

"You must stop misbehaving!"

"It's his prerogative as the youngest," a voice answered from the gloom.

Dhutmose, who had entered the room, grasped his brother in a vice-like embrace. Leaving him winded, he turned to Bak.

"Rubbing noses will do," the latter said nervously.

Clasping him around his shoulders, the older prince rubbed noses with the boy in a traditional Egyptian greeting, before turning to collapse next to his mother on the sofa.

"So, what's happening out in Mitanni, Bak?" he asked. "I must say, you were very brave to accompany our delinquent on tour."

"Nothing. It was horrid."

"Nonsense," Amenhotep Junior countered. "All the girls wanted to kiss him."

Dhutmose laughed with delight.

"Were they pretty?"

"Utterly smashing," his brother said. "But this one here refused them all."

"So, Mum's right," Dhutmose smirked. The Great Wife slapped his hand. "Ow, that stung!"

"Bak was studying, weren't you?" she said.

"It was too cold to do anything."

"You were warm enough," Amenhotep Junior interrupted. "After all, we shared the same covers!"

Tiye fixed her youngest with an odd look.

"And what is the state of the kingdom?" she asked, changing the subject. "Did you speak to the king – exchange diplomatic confidences?"

"We painted," her son replied.

"*I* painted," Bak corrected. "This one lazed by the fire all day with his pet Persian."

"Please tell me it's a girl," Dhutmose implored.

"Which reminds me." Amenhotep Junior pushed a cane basket towards his mother. "These are for you."

Gingerly, the queen lifted the wicker lid. A smile of pleasure creased her face.

"They're cats!" she pronounced in disbelief.

"They look like slippers," Dhutmose laughed, picking up a black-and-white ball of fur. Opening its eyes of unimaginable blue, the kitten yawned with a tiny pink mouth. "Have you ever seen eyes like lapis lazuli?" he gasped.

But Tiye was absorbed with a grey bundle before her. Slowly uncurling itself, the creature opened wide, leaf-green eyes, the size of saucers.

Gazing up at the queen, it placed a tiny paw on her hand. In an instant the years of strain and worry disappeared. Tiye could no longer hear the young men conversing at the top of their voices.

The tiny fluffball captivated her heart as none of her husband's jewellery had in recent months.

Reaching out with her other hand she gently touched the tiny paw. The kitten extended the pink pads of its sole over the queen's fingers. It did not let go.

***

"Junior, you're a genius!" Bak exclaimed. Together they looked around the sumptuously decorated room. "New ebony furniture, fresh flowers, and wine – what more could you ask for? Do you know your mother had these rooms refurbished after receiving those ridiculous beasts?" Bak threw open a shutter to let in the afternoon light. "You're a brilliant manipulator. Look at all this food!"

Mutton, ibis, duck, and an assortment of pastries, desserts stood on the table close to the window.

"I gave Mummy those gorgeous cats because I love her and knew she would appreciate them." The prince searched in vain for a fireplace. "I didn't know she was going to react this generously, if at all."

"She did look happy." Bak tucked into lamb shanks. "I've never seen the queen look pleased about anything!"

"You're right. And Mummy must have been beautiful once. I never noticed until today."

***

Arranged on the carpeted floor, with an assortment of photographs and notes, the chief researcher, Melissa Simpson, sat with her group, chewing pretzels and drinking tea from large, cracked mugs. With the exception of Ernest.

He had ordered *ahwa* and was savouring the strong Turkish coffee which reminded him of the good stuff he missed from home. He noticed, with vague distaste, that a New Zealander, Abel Curry, was quaffing beer straight from the bottle. Although he desperately wanted to show his disdain for the antipodean, the latter's six-foot-three hulking frame prevented him from doing so. In fact, Ernest reflected ruefully, he himself had personally contributed little to the conversation except for the occasional grunt, oddly akin to a squeak, which emanated from his corner.

"I've never seen those images," Karen said, nibbling on a salty bread stick. "Except on Walter's computer."

"What is it with that computer?" Abel swigged his Heineken. "It shows stuff which no one's ever seen, then mysteriously goes on the blink when anyone tries to access it."

"No one should be accessing Walter's files without his permission," Ernest pointed out in a superior tone.

The Kiwi turned his enormous shoulders towards the speaker.

"Guess that's why I saw you there at lunchtime, eh, Ernie?" he winked.

Overcome, the researcher adjusted his glasses and smiled wanly.

"I've tried," Melissa confessed.

"So have I," Karen added to everyone's surprise.

"Aren't you supposed to be writing a huge thesis?"

The distinctive American accent cut across the crunching, slurping and note-shuffling. Blushing, Karen giggled coquettishly. Much to Ernest's consternation, she unfolded her long legs and batted her eyelashes.

"Karen's not all work and no play," Melissa cut in. "And stop flirting, George, you're married."

"Fortunately for Karen, you're misinformed," George Miller laughed, revealing a swathe of enamel normally associated with commercials.

"Let's have a vote," Melissa suggested in a businesslike tone. "Who thinks Theodore Davis discovered Akhenaten's body?"

The American lifted his hand.

"How could you?" Karen asked reproachfully, putting away her legs.

"What's up, mate?" Abel asked. "Do you know something we don't?"

"Reason?" Melissa poised her fountain pen above the blank notepad on her knees.

"The mummy resembles the dead pharaoh."

"Or Smenkhare," Ernest butted in waspishly. "Akhenaten had sons."

"That's enough, Ernest," Melissa remonstrated sharply. "Any other reason?"

"Sure," George added lazily, picking up a green-and-white flying saucer from a Spacies packet, and popping it into his mouth. "A fellow countryman unearthed his bones. It's pure patriotism on my part."

"You could be right," Abel said. "Many scientists held off declaring Akhenaten's body was found in cache fifty-five because the mummy seemed young. Now, however," he said, opening another beer bottle with his Swiss knife, "modern Egyptologists have scientifically deduced the corpse belongs to a thirty-year-old. I reckon before the decade's out our Joe Doe will be forty and displayed in the Cairo Museum's mummy room as the great Pharaoh Akhy himself."

"And there you have your reason," George smiled, swallowing the last saucer and staring deliberately at Karen with fun-filled eyes.

"That's a good reason," Melissa commented. "Does anyone want chocolate mousse? I had it flown in from Hurghada."

"I'm still sceptical," Ernest blurted, not quite knowing why he differed with the others, except that he had taken an extreme dislike to the two large, good-looking foreigners, one of whom was ogling his girl.

"Why?" Melissa stabbed her pad.

"No one in this day and age is going to say that body belongs to Akhenaten."

"Why not?" Abel's eyes were cool. He was clearly not as genial as his American counterpart. Regretting having started a fight he might not win, Ernest's mouth twitched.

"I'm not saying your theory isn't logical, but Akhenaten clearly stated on every monument and stela that he wanted to be buried in his city. Don't forget, the remains of a burned mummy were found on the floor around his sarcophagus at Amarna."

"After the locals fought over the discovery in the early part of the twentieth century – I remember reading about it," Karen said. "Very good, Ernest!"

Melissa finished taking notes to her satisfaction. This brainstorming session was working a treat.

"Yeah, okay," Abel said. "But what man in Egyptian history looks like a woman? Akhenaten. What male mummy in Egypt looks like a woman, and yet is a man? The clown in cache number fifty-five. He was found in the wrappings of Akhenaten for goodness' sakes!"

"But he was discovered with a shrine of Tiye," Melissa added, forgetting that she was only supposed to be writing. "And the mummy had only *one* arm crossed over its chest in a traditional queen's pose."

"In fact, the wooden sarcophagus belonged to Lady Kia, King Tut's Mum," Karen said, looking for more food. "Confused? You will be!"

The New Zealander waved his bottle.

"There you go. It's all a crock."

"Not necessarily." Ernest straightened his slight frame to appear taller. "If there is one mummy which resembles a woman, but is in fact a man, with the same blood type and antigen as Tutankhamen, it's safe to assume that Akhenaten *was* depicting himself and members of his family truthfully with their pendulous stomachs and elongated skulls. That's got to be worth something."

"I like the Moses theory," Karen said, changing the subject.

"You would – you're writing a biblical dissertation," Melissa rejoined.

"Who said that?" Karen asked, surprised.

"Everyone," Abel replied. "It's no use gawking at her, George. The girl's got religion."

"There's nothing wrong with that. I come from the Bible belt myself."

"Evidence!" Melissa fluted. "Why is Akhenaten Moses?"

She poured Ernest another cup of coffee which he accepted gratefully.

"Moses' body was never discovered," Karen reminded the team. "I'd like to believe Akhenaten's wasn't, either."

"And that's the reason why some don't want to admit those bones belong to the heretical pharaoh," Abel concluded.

George glanced at Abel. He had lived in New Zealand while studying at college and was familiar with their legendary love of rugby and beer. Rather like Australians. Not that he would ever express his opinion. He had discovered the difference between the two nations in an

English pub, where he made the near fatal mistake of confusing one nation with the other.

"Are you saying scientists want to believe Akhenaten was Moses?" he asked, shifting his long blue-jeaned legs closer to Karen's frame.

"I think academics want to keep Akhenaten in the shadows," Abel said belligerently. "He threatens their preconceived notions, perhaps even their religious upbringing."

"You've had one too many," George grinned.

"Listen mate, they should have his bones jammed right up alongside Ramesses-the-Great in the Cairo Museum's mummy room. Face facts – Akhenaten affected the way we think today. Ramesses is just a dead tyrant."

"Not anymore." Karen had discovered a croissant next to Ernest. "Ramesses is loved and adored these days."

Ernest drained his cup. Melissa shot him a warm glance. Instinctively, she gathered, he felt out of his depth with the two warring giants. Now, however, he felt special with her attention, and subsequently more confident. He cleared his throat.

"Today Akhenaten is at best a maverick king who worshipped the sun, and at worst, a notorious ogre who destroyed his empire."

"True," agreed Karen, who was too busy eating to say much.

"That's a bit over the top," criticised Abel. "These Egyptologists are so extreme. They all have opinions – none of them correct – and nobody wants to use questions as tools to discover the truth."

"I disagree," said George, still with good humour. Having decided he liked the people he was with, (although finding it arduous to understand their accents), he had no desire to turn the evening into anything but a pleasant exchange of ideas.

"Why?" Abel asked. "I haven't made a single untrue statement."

"Some Egyptologists, like myself, do ask questions."

"You haven't asked one jolly question all night." Abel leaned closer towards Karen. "He's saving that one for asking you out."

"Order, order," fluted Melissa automatically. "What about showing us your photos, George."

"Oh, yeah." Lazily, a great hand covered in blond fuzz, picked up a black-and-white photograph. "I nearly forgot. I downloaded this off Walt's computer. What do you think, Abel?"

Abel held the picture in the flat of his palm.

"Cripes, it's a mummy! It's got to be Akhy. Look at those lips – rubber – like Jagger."

"How did you get this?" Melissa asked, dropping her report.

Karen snatched it away from her.

"It shouldn't exist. You know, if I wasn't afraid of being labelled a crank, I'd swear Walter was some kind of wizard."

"Or else he's playing us for fools." Ernest said darkly.

"Could be." Abel stared at the photograph. "I do think Akhenaten's bones should be put in the mummy room, though. May I have another drink?"

***

King Amenhotep-the-Magnificent sat in the empty hall on his throne. His son, who had finished prostrating himself, lifted his face. Pharaoh frowned at the emaciated figure.

"Let's go to my office. It's less formal."

Obediently, the wraith-like Amenhotep Junior trotted at the heels of his stocky father, who led the way to a small room in the west wing. Removing his crown, the king placed it on a side table of solid gold. His son noticed two white streaks in his father's otherwise thick, dark hair.

"Is Hatti polite?" Pharaoh asked.

"The king is well-disposed towards Egypt."

"And Mitanni?"

"A firm ally."

Silently, the monarch stared into space for a few minutes. Amenhotep Junior waited. It had been Queen Tiye's painful duty to inform her son of the latest developments in his father's health. In the last six months His Majesty had suffered a litany of complaints, including an abscessed jaw, dizziness, and alarming forgetfulness.

"Did you paint?" the king suddenly asked.

"A bit."

"That's not what I heard. The Mitannian castle spent a week clearing out their second storey of art supplies!"

"I don't see how – I brought back most of their equipment."

Amenhotep Senior chuckled.

"You always were precocious. Well, that'll be all."

Swallowing, his son rose. Having wanted to discuss the trip in detail, the prince instead found himself concluding the interview by fumbling with the latch of the office door. He wondered whether he should apologise for his previous behaviour at court, or simply exit before his father's failing memory recalled the incident. He pushed the door to one side. It squeaked.

"One more thing."

"Yes, Father?"

"Don't ever embarrass us like that again. I had to gift the Syrian ambassador ten chariots so he wouldn't spread rumours that my son was an epileptic." Pharaoh laughed. "In reality, I didn't give him a single nut or bolt. Dirty, bearded ... never mind." He waved one arm in a gesture of dismissal. "You can have them. Your mother and I laughed ourselves silly – in private, of course. We haven't done that in months: Welcome home, Junior!" he boomed.

*****

Seated on his favourite chair, next to a table laden with vases of fresh flowers, and a tray of macadamia nuts, Ay was enjoying a free afternoon.

Slowly, he savoured the age-old story of the peasant Bata and his brush with royalty. He was about to reach the chapter of the hero's transformation into a bull by a wicked queen – something the priests at Heliopolis were still rumoured to be capable of – when his peace was shattered by shouting.

"Sergeant Horemheb to see Lord Ay, Counsellor and Adviser to His Majesty, Queen Tiye. He has an appointment," the man added apologetically.

"Send him in, Ramose," Ay said, collecting himself.

Soon, a ruddy-faced youth stood before him. In his teens, Horemheb scarcely made a suitable afternoon visitor for the worldly courtier, but Ay bobbed his head in welcome.

"Where's the king?" asked Horemheb without preliminaries.

"Cruising down the Nile, I expect. Now that His Majesty can no longer hunt, he sails."

"Why doesn't he fight? Aren't kings supposed to make war?"

"We don't need to."

"Since when did Egypt not need to fight? I tell you, Ay, it's jolly frustrating being a soldier these days."

"Aren't our neighbours at peace with us?" the older man asked, amused at the youth's intensity.

"They're never at peace. Tuthmosis-the-Great campaigned up until the end of his life. You didn't see him put up his feet and go paddling up the Nile."

Ay looked distinctly ill at ease. Rolling up his papyrus scroll he beckoned the boy to sit opposite him.

"You need to relax." He offered macadamias from the silver tray. "Amenhotep would make war if it was necessary. Dhutmose is a great warrior, but has not been well recently. It would do to keep your options open." With a casual air, Ay crunched a nut in the powerful jaws of a silver clipper designed for the purpose. Horemheb used the pommel of his miniature bronze dagger, and nothing but the strength of his wrists. "You know, Amenhotep is only second in line to the throne, although he has to grow up." Ay smiled gently. "Like you."

A nut snapped suddenly, spraying macadamia and shell in equal portions across the room.

"There is a rumour that Amenhotep Junior had been sent over-seas on diplomatic missions due to his brother's ailing health. If Egypt has an old king and unfit heir, we need a strong army. Our neighbours will attack."

Having studied Horemheb for years, Ay realised his intelligence would create a powerful ally for any future king.

"I cannot say whether the rumour is true or not. I personally think that you are right, Horemheb. Egypt needs to flex her muscles. But, without diplomacy, the economy cannot flourish. Nowadays we are prosperous and respected by all our allies."

"That's because of Queen Tiye." Ay blinked at the perspicacious reply. "She's up all night composing letters to the Syrians, Libyans, and even those surly Hittites. It frees up that useless husband of hers so that he can build. I mean to say," Horemheb began to laugh at the thought of the oddly shaped Prince Amenhotep, "he hasn't even been good at siring heirs. If Dhutmose goes, we're all in trouble with Junior."

"On the contrary, the king has sired many heirs. It's just that he favours the Great Wife, my sister, and will therefore choose one of her sons to rule the ancient land of *Kemet*."

"I forget," blustered Horemheb. "Queen Tiye is your sister. Please forgive me. I'm still young and have much to learn."

"You speak well of her. There is no harm done."

The youth, unused to sitting for extended periods, flexed his bronzed limbs.

"In fact, there is much to admire in Amenhotep Junior if he inherits the throne. I think he'll wage war on Egypt's enemies." Rising from the gold brocade cushion, he stretched his legs. "Please give my regards to Nefertiti."

Before departing, he deposited a small ivory box on the table next to Ay. Intricately worked, it cost a month's salary. Exhaling a long breath, the vizier placed it in a wooden chest with Horemheb's other gifts, and returned to his scroll.

His daughter had never set eyes on them, and her father was unsure of what to do with the collection of precious love tokens.

***

Tiye was laughing behind one bejewelled hand. With the other she caressed one of her new cats.

"How can you take anything Horemheb says seriously?"

"He has potential. He's going places."

"It's your job to mingle with these whippersnappers when they have achieved stations worthy of their ambition. How do you know who will make it and who won't? You could be wasting valuable time."

"Did you know Amenhotep Junior has selected his cabinet, just in case he becomes king?"

"That was my work. You've been in my papers."

"Your son isn't blind to his brother's medical condition, and he is preparing for a takeover. Why do you think he spends so much time at Bak's studio? Junior is contemplating building creations to outdo those of his father."

"I'd like to see that," Tiye responded, genuinely surprised that her poet-son bore any similarity to her husband of thirty years. "He's like me – he enjoys a good book."

"Bak is his choice of sculptor for his reign. Amenhotep Junior is currently instructing him."

"My son is a teacher, I know."

149

"He is also interested in architecture. If the younger Amenhotep works for Dhutmose, we might see him build vast palaces. However, now that he's contemplating becoming Egypt's future pharaoh, he's delegated the task to someone else."

"You are well-informed," Tiye remarked sharply. "Perhaps we should give you a raise. And what does Horemheb think? Is he suggesting my son thinks what I dare not articulate?"

"The boy had an interesting slant on Junior's attitude to war. Am I correct in assuming that if he ascended the Horus throne, his reign might differ from his father's?"

Tiye's eyes glazed over.

"Possibly," she acknowledged. "Which reminds me: I need to interview that boy alone."

***

Entering the gloomy annex, the prince felt oddly afraid. His mother was nowhere to be seen. As he was about to leave, a light suddenly flickered in the dim recesses of the outer hall. The queen whooshed past him, apologising for her lateness.

"Where are your guards, Mummy?"

"Stop fretting, they're on their way. Now come in and tell me about your trip."

Amenhotep Junior joined his mother on her divan. They sat at opposite ends of a dark blue couch which was covered in leopard skin pillows.

"I met the Hittite king," her son said, launching into Tiye's favourite topic of politics, "and he expressed both his respect for Egypt and its monarch. In Mitanni I spoke to King Shuttarna." The boy pulled out a small package from inside his robe. "This is for you from His Majesty."

"It's a letter." Tiye pulled open the leather-bound package. In doing so, her face lost all displeasure. "With a book!"

"His Majesty has the highest regard for you." The prince's lips twitched. "Apparently you two write to each other all the time."

"We correspond. I'll read it later." His mother placed it on her desk. "Now, what about social activities? Did you attend dances? Hunts? I forgot – you don't hunt." Tiye exhaled a short, disappointed breath.

Amenhotep interlocked his bony fingers.

"I know what you're asking, Mother. I met a lot of people, but I have also been praying and fasting."

"If you're shy, just say so. We can arrange a marriage."

"Bak, on the other hand, hooked all the girls."

"I didn't know he liked them."

"And I am in love with a lady," her son announced quietly. "An exquisitely lovely one."

"Excellent! Who is she?"

Amenhotep scrunched his fingers into a knot.

"I don't know if you'd like her."

"Is she royal?" Tiye queried, recalling rumours of her son's late-night forays with the serving girls in the palace kitchens. ("He likes a good soup, that's all," Pharaoh would protest, trying to mollify his wife in one of her more unsettled moments.)

"She is of noble birth."

"Well, that's a start," declared his mother, visibly relieved. She placed one hand on his knee. "You don't have to tell me until you're ready." Her eyes darted to the letter.

"The king of Mitanni doesn't know about it either," continued her son, aware of her thoughts.

The queen's face clouded as she withdrew the warmth of her hand.

"I hope you are not taking advantage of our vassal's daughters without proper overtures," she lectured, her voice rising dangerously. "I don't care if we have to build a new wing for the harem, but I won't have you bringing disgrace on this household. You're Egypt's royal ambassador, Amenhotep Junior, whether you like it or not."

A fragile nerve snapped in the youth.

"By Amon's beard, Mother!" he swore. "I wasn't even announced in the Great Hall yesterday. All I ever do is run from one end of Egypt to the other to keep out of Father's way, although what I've done wrong, I'll never know."

"You're rude, wilful, and obnoxious."

The words, spoken with icy calm, stung like a slap across the prince's face.

"I THINK!" he exploded. "I have more brains in my little finger than all the bloated bodies of our fat priests!"

"Why are you screaming at me?" his mother asked. "You get your intelligence from my side of the family." She rubbed her tired eyes. "No one's disputing you're brilliant, but you constantly cross authority – like you're doing now. I am the Great Wife, Queen of Egypt. I am your *mother*."

Amenhotep lowered his blazing eyes.

"I'm tired of keeping out of everyone's way."

"No one's ashamed of you –"

"They are! I don't look, or sound like anyone else. I'm brilliant and capable, but you all fawn over Dhutmose because he's the heir and bulges muscles on every inch of his torso."

"Pull yourself together."

"I'm tired of all this tiptoeing around," Amenhotep Junior declared flatly. "The woman I am in love with is Nefertiti."

"Ay's daughter? Your old flame?"

"Did it ever occur to you I might simply like to stay at home and marry the girl next door?"

"She's not the girl next door." The queen's mind was racing. This was a good match. The pair even looked alike. And the girl was beautiful with her porcelain skin and rosy cheeks. "Have you informed your Uncle Ay?"

All rage left her son. He sank into the fur pillows.

"Of course not," he muttered. "And don't tell him, either."

A wave of exultation swept over his mother.

"Only when you're ready," she reassured. "Now you must be tired. We'll pick up this conversation tomorrow on our afternoon boat ride."

***

Pharaoh had never seen his wife so excited.

"She's gorgeous *and* intelligent," Tiye was saying. "Nefertiti *reads*."

"Like you."

"Our son needs a partner on his wavelength. He's lonely."

The king enveloped his wife in his enormous arms.

"The way I was before I met you," he whispered, nuzzling her neck. Tiye patted his cheek.

"Stop that, we have work to do."

Reluctantly, the king released her.

"You should talk to Ay," he said, downing his morning glass of milk and contemplating the park he would shortly go riding in. "Knowing our son, he's liable to blurt the whole thing out in one of his pious rages."

***

Lord Ay was sad.

"It's the second son."

"It's still a royal union," Tee consoled.

Her husband shook his head.

"Dhutmose would have been the match of my dreams. What's the use of working all day and night for preferment for an obscure marriage? You do know that once Dhutmose has heirs, Amenhotep Junior will cease to be a contender for the throne?"

"Your work has borne fruit," his wife said firmly. "You can't honestly expect the future king to marry anyone but his sister Sitamon."

"Those two hate each other. They'll certainly never have any children."

"But Nefertiti suits the younger Amenhotep, dear. He adores her."

"That's news to me!"

"Oh darling, you must go around with your eyes shut! Haven't you seen the way they look at each other?"

153

"I rather suspected this to be a diplomatic marriage concocted by the king and queen. Now you speak of love!" Ay put a fist to his brow. "I just remembered – Horemheb."

Tee was nonplussed.

"The army officer? What's he got to do with anything?"

"Never mind," her husband soothed, swiftly kissing her cheek and slipping on his sandals. "I'm going out to walk off my excitement."

***

Ay wiped his nose with the back of his hand. It had been a long ride to the barracks and the tiny dormitory was freezing.

"I don't want you courting my daughter anymore."

Horemheb's heart shattered into fragments. His military training, however, kept him standing as erect as a soldier on parade.

"As Your Lordship wishes."

Ay's facial muscles constricted. While Horemheb mooned over Nefertiti, the wily official had seized the opportunity to ingratiate himself with the next generation of Egypt's all-powerful military wing, which rivalled even the priests' authority.

He had prepared the remorseful little speech which would invariably follow a public announcement of his daughter's engagement.

There would be no hard feelings and Lord Ay's alliance with the army would stand firm. Now, however, he hesitated.

"I still value our afternoon talks. But I have Nefertiti's future to consider."

"I understand."

When the adviser had departed the soldier's knees gave out. Sitting on his narrow pallet, with its single grey blanket, Horemheb cried until dawn.

***

Tee had been waiting for her husband to speak for the last hour at dinner. Watermelon was served for dessert. He did not touch the fruit.

"You're quiet."

"I made a diplomatic blunder," Ay replied. His jaw set as if he was hardening himself against his emotions.

"Do you want to talk about it?"

"Horemheb has afternoon chats with me. The boy is lower class of course," he lied, "but a brilliant soldier and a member of the new generation's innermost circle. Even Amenhotep Junior likes him."

"And he's in love with our Nef."

"How did you know?"

"You mentioned him yesterday morning in the same breath as our daughter's engagement."

"It is essential that the up-and-coming members of court are united. This could cause permanent damage."

"Dhutmose will be king. You can still invite Horemheb to our home."

"I suppose so."

"Don't worry about this marriage," his wife counselled. "You have been wise. Now be patient. Amenhotep Junior is the right choice for our daughter, and he will be influential, even if he does not become king."

Selecting a piece of watermelon Ay began to eat in carefully measured bites.

***

18.

Moving past hundreds of guests in the congested dining hall, Bak found his way to the young royals' table. Having saved the artist a seat for over an hour, Amenhotep Junior made him especially welcome. The court glittered with an assortment of jewels as people turned out in their colourful best for the engagement of the year. Pharaoh and his Great Wife sat together, holding hands, locked in conversation. Several times the king kissed his wife's neck and stroked her tiny shoulders.

"Your parents are behaving like newly-weds, Junior."

Bak squeezed himself next to Maya, who was intent on occupying two seats.

"Dad's in a good mood. He gave me ten chariots last week."

The young sculptor dropped his napkin.

"I don't believe it. That's a fortune!"

"How do you think I came by my gold-plated car for visits to Nefertiti?"

"I thought Pharaoh was angry about the ruckus you caused in the Royal Audience Hall."

"Possibly, but he was madder than a hatter with the Syrian ambassador."

"I hope you don't mind me saying this, but I think you should be careful of your Dad. He's becoming unpredictable of late."

The prince dug a fork into his pigeon pie.

"He's gone grey, that's all."

"I hear you're redecorating," Maya said, breaking into the conversation, and addressing Bak.

"It's a fulltime job."

Scarcely able to breathe in the confined space between Maya's portly frame and Amenhotep's elbow, the artist gave up trying to eat.

"Prince Dhutmose commissioned Bak to refurbish his apartments," Amenhotep Junior announced proudly. "It made the palace paper."

Liquid perfume from the wax cone on Maya's head trickled down his wig and into one eye. He dabbed his face, momentarily causing Bak to stop breathing.

"I was wondering if you'd like to look at my humble establishment," Maya said, offering the painter a future commission.

"He'll be busy for at least six months," the prince cut in airily. "Royals are very particular."

Maya hardly noticed the rebuff.

"Maybe you'd care to come over to my house at noon tomorrow, Bak. Meryt is a wonderful hostess," he said, referring to his wife of six months. "And Neferure will be there."

Clearing a space for himself by asserting his bodily presence, Bak dug into braised duck.

***

Karen pulled her silk shawl close about her shoulders.

"Do you surf?"

George laughed.

"No, but I rock climb."

"So does Abel."

"Yeah, he told me. You like him, don't you?"

"Not in that way. I do think you two have a lot in common. Everyone at the lab calls you Tweedledum and Tweedledee."

"With emphasis on the last syllables, no doubt," replied George, finding them a seat in the park. They sat next to each other under a palm tree. "I do miss America," he said at last.

"I miss England."

"I miss real coffee."

"Abel misses ice-cream."

"He should. I've been to his country. They make the best ice-cream in the world. It's like cream. I put on two stone in a place called Christchurch."

"That probably wouldn't show up on you."

"I'm all muscle," he jested.

"So, you don't surf. Do you like cars?"

"I own a Bentley, or two."

Karen's eyes widened.

"You must be rich!"

"I guess."

"Mind you, Americans are," Karen said, not quite knowing why she was prattling on about something as personal as money. She did know she was having difficulty in keeping her eyes off the powerfully developed thighs clad in their casual blue denims. "You're a professor, aren't you?"

"I'm not sure why. I spent most of my time travelling, instead of teaching."

"Like now."

"I'm writing a book."

"About cache number fifty-five, no doubt."

"It's more like a Mills and Boon romance." They both giggled. "The heroine's a bit like you," he said seriously, locking eyes with his new friend.

"Oh." Karen looked at her hands. She wore spectacles for heaven's sakes. "Are you married?" she asked suddenly.

"Me? No. Why do you ask?"

"Everyone says so. With an attitude like that I thought you were from the West Coast."

They rose from the seat and continued walking around the museum grounds.

"I'm from Missouri, as a matter of fact."

"Don't you teach at Berkeley?"

"I used to."

Karen put her hand over her mouth.

"You're not the professor from Yale everyone's talking about?"

"I'm based in California, although I tutored at Harvard for a while."

"That's the holy grail of American institutions!"

"Only if you do law," was the modest response. George kicked a stone along the dusty path as they rounded the Cairo Museum one last time. "Which I did for a bit, before losing interest."

"My youngest brother read there," Karen said.

"You see? I always pick the smart ones! It's nice to know your family is as bright as you."

George stopped. Quickly, he assessed the steps to the museum, the glass doors, the metal body detectors for humans and baggage alike - all protected by militia. And inside. What a mess! He had never seen so much stone cramming corridors to capacity. Hardly any statues were cordoned off. He himself had been guilty of bodging stone tablets which he had only read about as an Egypt-crazed teenager.

The Cairo Museum's contrasts of poverty and wealth hit home to George several years ago. While looking at Queen Hetepheres' catafalque, he noticed her bed and chair had been set up in a glass case with bracelets she had once owned. The Egyptian guide had informed his group that the various sizes of bangles, ranging from small to large, showed how fat the mother of Cheops must have been in old age. George reflected how small her wrists must have been at any stage of her life, when his foot accidentally clunked a pail. He leapt out of the way of two women mopping the floor with ragged towels appended to broom handles. Wearing hijabs with their work clothes, they shrank from his bulk. For the first time in his life, the handsome American felt ashamed. Of his wealth, his education – of being over-nourished.

Having smoked too much apple tobacco during lunch, the Egyptologist had dragged everyone away from the treasures of Tutankhamen to the basement to spin yarns on some ghastly, obscure mummies. George's opinion of him was not the highest. However, faced with the badly equipped cleaning staff, the man courteously allowed the women room. George's eyes had been fixed on the rags.

"They can't even afford a mop," he thought. *"How the heck are they going to look after any more treasures?"*

***

Playing with the hem of his tasselled gown, Bak watched the chariot races without interest. Newly married, he wished to be in the embraces of his wife, or developing his career. He longed to be back in his studio where he and Amenhotep Junior had advanced several steps in their new art. Now, the prince sat in the stands looking as bored as his friend. Or, so Bak imagined. At half-time he noticed his friend standing on tiptoe, desperately craning his head towards Ay's family group.

"Are you going to tell Nefertiti you're in love with her, or wait for your brother to snap her up?"

"What do you mean?" the prince's eyes narrowed into jealous slits.

"So, you *are* in love!" Bak caught sight of a red chariot rumbling past the royal box. He waved at the serious youth, who promptly ignored him. "You've obviously made a move without telling me. Horemheb looks dreadfully put out."

"I don't know what you're talking about."

"At least he made his intentions known to Lord Ay, which is more than you've done. Did you know that by refusing our soldier friend as a suitor, the Lord Chancellor has cleared the playing field for you?"

"I'm nervous."

The prince sat down on his courtside seat, a bundle of nail-biting misery.

"You may be blue-blooded, but courtesy to a future father-in-law never went amiss. Ay knows how you feel. He's just waiting for you to approach him."

"You don't understand, Bak. As much as I love my uncle, he's a different person when it comes to his daughter."

"For one thing, he'll expect you to make the proper overtures." Bak tugged at his friend's elbow. "You forget – you're a prince. Any girl would be pleased to marry you."

"Not me personally," Amenhotep Junior rejoined bitterly. "To do that, the royal groom would have to be Dhutmose."

"Why do you compare yourself to your brother and father when you're more intelligent than both of them put together?"

Laughing shortly, the youth blew his nose on a handkerchief embroidered in his personal colours of blue and gold.

"Get up," Bak encouraged, and not quite knowing why he felt so brave, pushed the prince out of his comfortable seat. "Make way!"

Climbing up two tiers of stands, Bak and the prince arrived, flushed and sweating, in the royal box. Heedless of protocol, they banged past Pharaoh's legs. The latter, who was chatting to his wife, cheerfully pushed them through. Ay welcomed the boys pleasantly, as if he was half-expecting their company, but for the first time in his life, Amenhotep Junior was tongue-tied. Furtively glancing at Nefertiti, he noticed her eyes were wide with a mixture of apprehension and curiosity. Bak thumped the prince's shoulder blades.

"His Majesty wishes the pleasure of your daughter's company, sire," he announced.

"We would be honoured," replied the courtier, as if he was expecting the bold request. "Nefertiti, hurry up. The semi-final is about to begin."

Soon, the dazed prince found himself clasping his girlfriend's hand while watching the most exciting race of the day. He was certain Pharaoh had nudged him in the ribs a couple of times, too.

"They look good together," Tiye commented as applause for the champion charioteer broke out.

Horemheb crossed the line, a clear winner. Reining in his lathered horses, he saluted before clattering up the wooden steps to the throne. Officials placed lotus garlands over his neck and shoulders. The king rose to present him with a lion skin from a beast he had personally slain. Beaming with success, the champion bowed to his monarch and family. It was Horemheb's proudest career moment to date. Not only had he been promoted to Major that week, but he was now the top sportsman of his country in the pastime it loved best – charioteering.

Then, the young soldier caught sight of Nefertiti. It was as if a bolt struck him in the head and chest. Inwardly he wilted, but his army training propelled him into the stables, where he tethered his steeds and readied himself for the evening's festivities.

***

Darkness fell across Malkata as the first palace lamps sputtered into life. In the streets, citizens swarmed to rickety tables set under leafy trees on pavements strewn with sandalwood, leading up to the auditorium. While the masses celebrated Egypt's chariot racing week, a lone figure streaked across the palace grounds under a new moon to the soldier's barracks.

"Hurry up, Hump, the king's waiting."

"What are you doing here, Dhutmose?"

"Checking up on you. Is that wine on your breath?"

"Wheat juice."

"Dear Amon, can you walk?"

"I haven't tried."

"Why are you so miserable, Hump? You just defeated me – the royal heir – in our final race for this year. You're Egypt's greatest charioteer. You're famous!"

Horemheb raised himself on his pallet and fell back.

"Guards!" Dhutmose called. Immediately, two sentries appeared. "Towels and poultices, now!"

As they fled to do his bidding, the prince filled an empty pottery jug with ice-cold water from a bucket parked next to the foot of his friend's bed, and without warning, tipped it over him.

"By Ra!" Horemheb exclaimed, leaping from his bed in a single bound. "What did you do that for?"

"You're capable of walking," Dhutmose said coolly, throwing him a towel. "We need you sober at the king's table. This is your big night, Hump. You're going to become a general soon."

***

"What, in Amon's name, is up with him?" Dhutmose asked, tearing apart a piece of flat bread, and dipping it into his bowl of green oily sauce.

162

A plump individual looked up from his casserole.

"Are you talking to me?"

"I always talk to myself in public," the prince replied sarcastically. "Of course, I'm talking to you, Maya – you're Hump's best mate, aren't you?"

"I hardly know him," was the self-satisfied denial. "I'm part of Junior's brat pack."

"Is *anyone* Horemheb's friend?"

"He works all the time," explained Maya, slurping his bean soup. "But it's common knowledge he's pining for Nefertiti."

"Nef?" Dhutmose regarded the girl, sitting on Amenhotep Junior's right, with new interest. He observed his younger brother dotingly feeding her marinated morsels of fish from his own plate.

"Enlightenment dawns in the morning with great joy," Maya quipped from an ancient saying.

"You really are most peculiar," Dhutmose remarked. "It's a wonder I never noticed before."

"What did you expect of one of Junior's cronies?" the latter replied in a conspiratorial whisper. "We're all subversives planted here in the palace by the royal truant himself for the sole purpose of upsetting the establishment."

Laughing heartily, Dhutmose took a draught of beer, and handed Maya the cucumber salad.

***

Sitting at a basalt stone-table, in the enormous park which Pharaoh had landscaped twenty years previously, Dhutmose and Horemheb conversed over leftovers and cold beer.

"Listen Hump, I know it's hard, but there are other women. You're still young with plenty of time to fall in love."

"Nefertiti's not royal," the officer said sourly. "I wasn't asking for the moon."

"She wants my brother."

"Even though I'm ten times better looking than that pompous boor." Not knowing what to say, Dhutmose rubbed his stubbled jaw-line. What with running after his brother, mother, and Horemheb, he had scarcely slept in the last forty-eight hours. "Everyone says I'm lower class," Horemheb continued vehemently. "That's not true. My family were aristocrats. My only crime is that they were killed in a fire. I had to become a soldier."

"No one's saying you're lower class," retorted Dhutmose hotly. "You're at the royal court for heaven's sakes. You're my *friend*."

Horemheb's upper lip curled with contempt.

"I don't want to be a snivelling cur, accepting crumbs of legitimacy from your friendship. I want to hold my own."

"Which brings me to another matter," responded Dhutmose, ignoring the diatribe, "you must be more pleasant to my brother."

"That woman-shaped wimp!" Horemheb exclaimed, referring to the prince's increasingly odd physique. "He's the rudest person I've ever met. I don't know why the king doesn't exile him permanently."

"It's his temperament."

"He's insufferable – and those friends – dear Ra!" Horemheb pushed himself back from the table, unable to contain himself. "All flabby, fat, and weird!"

"Abner's not like that."

"Abner's a *Jew*."

Dhutmose blinked at the bitter outburst. He continued calmly: "We need to keep the peace if you want to advance in life, and that means forgetting about Nefertiti."

"I'm not speaking to Amenhotep Junior ever again."

"You'll have to." Dhutmose's voice hardened. "Things are not as they seem."

***

Tiye pushed her single lamp across the desk at which she was working.

"Have you spoken to Horemheb?"

"This afternoon, in the park, Mother." Dhutmose dabbed his brow with a handkerchief. "I'm fed up of all this bickering."

"That boy unnerves me. Do you think he'll get over this?"

"Horemheb can have any woman he wants. In fact, I've fixed him up with a pretty damsel for Saturday night."

"Good." The Great Wife added her seal to a letter she had composed to Shuttarna of Mitanni. "Keep an eye on him."

***

Amenhotep Junior was shaking in his gold-embossed sandals. His entourage waited patiently. Bak wanted to roll his eyes, but curbed his impatience.

"I know you fancy my daughter," Lord Ay was saying, a shade exasperated. "But what are your intentions?"

The boy's mind was blank. Not wishing to state the obvious, Ay glanced uncomfortably at his wife. Bak dug his friend furiously in the ribs.

"I'm here to take her for a chariot ride," the prince explained lamely. "But only for an hour."

"Your Lordship must excuse His Majesty," the artist interrupted boldly, addressing Ay. "Prince Amenhotep was at Horemheb's private victory party until the early hours and is not himself."

"Ah, yes!" Ay breathed, relieved to have a worthy excuse. "The celebrations for Egypt's champion charioteer always last for two days, do they not?" Waving to an attendant he ordered: "Bring Nefertiti."

Taking his wife's hand, the courtier climbed the stairs to his villa.

"What's happened to your brain?" Bak fumed.

"I want to take my girl for a ride. Surely a prince can do that."

"You don't simply show up to her father's house! What were you thinking?"

"It's a modern approach and I'm a modern man."

165

"We all know how you like to change things, but when a prince of Egypt turns up to his girlfriend's parents, it's to ask for her hand in marriage, not to ride around the blasted block!"

Ignoring his friend's vituperation, Amenhotep adjusted a blue plume on one of his stallion's heads.

"Do you think my horses look presentable?"

"They're fine, but mark my words, Ay is going to consult with your father and, from what I hear, the king is subject to horrifying rages these days."

"Dad's reportedly unstable, although I haven't seen any evidence. I think people are just realising he's more like me than they could have possibly imagined. How do I look?"

"You're not listening." Bak dusted the prince's red jacket. "And you look fine."

On cue, Nefertiti appeared. Pushing aside Bak, the prince moved quickly towards the vision of loveliness. She descended the villa's whitewashed steps in a swathe of draperies and perfume. Extending his hand, Amenhotep Junior led her to his waiting chariot.

"I *do* like your carriage," she said, visibly impressed with its gold exterior. Amenhotep puffed out his chest.

Waving imperiously to his entourage, he ushered his fiancée into their car. Seizing the reins he swiftly kissed her, and they trotted along the avenues of Malkata in the morning sun. Left behind, an agitated Bak sat on Lord Ay's steps to wait.

***

"What is it?" asked Tee, unable to contain her joy.

"Wait a minute, I'm opening the gift."

Her husband pulled off the layers of papyrus and gold thread.

"It's a wooden chest, worth a fortune! Quick, open the other package."

"You know what this means," Ay said, carefully folding the wrapping paper. "Our future son-in-law has rediscovered his manners."

"I don't think Amenhotep Junior means to be rude," said Tee, lifting an exquisitely worked alabaster lamp to the light. "He's eccentric, that's all."

"How reassuring for us!"

"Oh darling, this is the beginning of an engagement – let's enjoy it."

***

"What's our son doing?"

The king's mouth was full of healing berries as he hovered at his wife's study door. He carried a bowl in one hand.

"Courting."

Tiye was trying to edit her letter to King Shuttarna, but kept getting interrupted. First, it had been the servants with their demand for a pay rise; then her son had stopped by to discuss a gift with which he wanted to impress his girlfriend. Now, her husband was at her door. Tiye invited him in with a resigned air.

The king tiptoed respectfully around towers of books and papers. Sitting at the opposite end of his wife's desk, he briefly knocked knees with her.

Setting down the bowl he was carrying, he spat the berries into it.

"By Thoth's beard, those doctors want to plug me up like a mummy before I'm dead," he grumbled. The queen contented herself with shuffling through her papers. She was in search of a misplaced paragraph, containing the key to a tactful conclusion of her letter. "Our son," the king continued, "has been visiting Lord Ay's house."

"As you did with my father."

"No!" Pharaoh's voice rose. His wife placed her papers in a sheaf and regarded him gravely. "He does not make proper overtures," Amenhotep explained. "And his behaviour is embarrassing our household. He's *your* son. You should speak to him."

Tiye flinched. Whenever they argued, it seemed, Junior was suddenly her responsibility.

167

"My dear, our son sent engagement gifts this morning. Don't worry, he's only nervous like you were."

"There's nothing timid about that boy. Furthermore, I resent the comparison. I courted you correctly, and out of the deepest respect and love."

"Well, our son's in love and keeps forgetting himself."

"That's no excuse."

"I'm not saying it is." Tiye looked longingly at her letter. "Anyway, turning up on my father's doorstep was hardly proper. Papa thought you wanted to turn me into a harem girl."

"That's absurd."

The king's ire evaporated, and a wounded look appeared in its place. Reaching across his wife's desk, Amenhotep's pudgy hands began to tidy her scrolls. Tiye refrained from ordering him to desist.

"I have spoken to our son and Lord Ay," she said. "The formal engagement will take place next week."

"Excellent." Her husband lifted a scrap of papyrus covered in hieratic scrawl. "I believe this is what you were looking for."

***

168

19.

Sickness pervades the palace. People rushing everywhere. Some care. Some worry about jobs lost if they do not. One person fears beheading; another flagellation.

"Dhutmose is ill."

"The heir is ailing."

"He vomited twice last night."

"That brother of his cracked his skull."

"It was deliberate."

"Amenhotep Junior always wanted the throne."

***

"The doctors say he's purged himself twenty-four times in as many hours." Pharaoh rubbed his brow. "I thought you said it was a stomach bug, Tiye."

"Our daughters, Sitamon and Nekhbet suffered in exactly the same way last week."

Amenhotep twisted his fingers.

"It's not ... poison?" he asked anxiously.

"The tasters have been doubled around Dhutmose since he was declared regent last month."

The queen glanced at her husband, who was feeling more helpless with each passing moment. Regarding her nails, Tiye decided a manicure was in order.

"Bring me a beautician," she commanded a young female servant. Bowing quickly, the girl hurried away. Amenhotep's eyes followed her. "I see you're cheering up," the queen observed drily. Startled, her husband whipped around with a sheepish grin. "We must keep a close watch on the heir," she continued.

The beautician entered the room. Offering her right hand to the woman, Tiye chatted with her husband. She spoke in carefully crafted dialogue, designed to pass the time, and lull the worried couple's state of mind. While she talked and Amenhotep listened, the Great Wife had time to reflect that her beloved, who never missed a day's work had, nevertheless, cancelled all his appointments in order to be available for his ailing son. His stocky body stayed completely inert. The queen had her fingers clipped, then her hands were moisturised, and finally smeared with henna.

Eventually, the sun sank behind the palm trees. Attempting to restore circulation, the queen shifted on her fleece-lined stool. She continued to expound on administrative matters, briefing the king on current events. Evening fell over the land, and oil lamps were lit in the darkened palatial chambers. At the stroke of seven, the couple joined the rest of their court for a meal in the Great Hall. While they dined the heir coughed blood into a bronze-plated bowl.

Deciding it was too hot to spend the night in his chamber, Amenhotep Junior slept peacefully on the roof, surrounded by Nubian servants who fanned his slight body with ostrich feathers.

***

Dawn broke over the sound of wailing. Women gnashed their teeth, and rent their garments, as they poured dust over their freshly shaved heads. Dhutmose's body was as cold as the stone monuments which would have recorded his reign forever. Dry-eyed for most of the morning, his mother made funeral arrangements. Lord Ay, with other high-ranking court officials, visited her several times.

In his private apartments, the young Amenhotep wept with uninhibited passion, while his father stared in silent shock out of his studio window overlooking the palace grounds. Egypt had lost its heir. While it was not the end of his illustrious dynasty, Pharaoh felt a profound sense of loss. Of all his children Dhutmose was not only the one most

170

akin to him in spirit, but also the one who would most likely have made a great king.

At mid-morning his queen entered the studio where her husband drafted most of his architectural plans.

"We have to make a joint appearance in the hall," she announced brusquely.

The king did not move. Tiye stepped closer to him. In one fluid movement, he turned to clasp his wife around her tiny waist. Burying his face in her soft stomach, he began to cry. Tiye stretched out a perfectly manicured hand to stroke her husband's head. Loud sobs were muffled in her womb. Ruffling his greying hair, Tiye searched her mind for comforting words, but found none.

****

AMENHOTEP JUNIOR

I'm alone in darkness, having lost a brother who treated me as his equal. When no one wanted to play, or spar with me, Dhutmose took me under his imperial wing.

Some courtiers say I'm not Pharaoh's heir, but a Jewish boy. Others say I'm Mummy's illegitimate offspring. Although my physique does not resemble Dad's, I try to be a good son.

There are times when I wonder about the truth.

****

A blue war crown was fitted over the prince's elongated skull. Part of the difficulty with the fitting lay in his auburn spikes, which refused to flatten. Clothed in several layers of linen to camouflage his pear-shaped physique, Amenhotep Junior faced his father.

Pouring libations of water and oil at Pharaoh's feet, the prince served him the dry white wine. As Amenhotep-the-Magnificent: Nebmaatre held out his faience-inlaid goblet, artists rushed to record the event. Tiye compressed her lips, watching her men with ill-concealed pride.

"The hour has come," Pharaoh announced. Kissing his son's cheeks, he clasped him in a warm embrace. The court applauded while sistrums rattled, and drums were beaten. "Be seated Son of the Sun, my heir, Neferkheprure: Amenhotep-the-Fourth."

Amenhotep Junior's attenuated fingers trembled as he straightened the heavy leather helmet. Since Dhutmose's death he had changed. His robust confidence was replaced with anxiety which manifested itself in occasional stammering.

In an attempt to be sympathetic, the king rallied his diplomatic skills.

"How is the studio? Do you need a bigger one?"

"N-no, th-thank you, F-Father."

"I could have a larger one built. You have your own school now." The co-regent nodded and swallowed again. "I'm sorry," his father apologised unexpectedly, pressing his son's hand. "We are so different in our sensibilities, you and I – although that's a very good thing for Egypt."

"Maybe you're right," replied Amenhotep Junior, casting a distracted eye over the gathering.

"I *am* right. Your mother and I have never agreed on anything, yet we have successfully ruled the wealthiest country in history. It has also made for richly satisfying connubial bliss."

"Father!"

Hundreds of gilded cedar tables laden with food were crammed into the hall, already packed with hundreds of people. Haunches of ox, hippopotamus, venison, and ibex towered over neatly stacked layers of pigeon, flamingo, and duck. Carafes of Memphis wine rubbed shoulders with ewers of Mycenaean red. Boldly patterned Cretan drinking horns matched Egyptian alabaster goblets. Plain grape juice flasks stood proudly against small yellow-and-blue bottles containing imported beers from Syria, Palestine, and Turkey.

Courtiers and businessmen, together with servants and village headmen, lined both sides of the enormous coronation chamber.

At its head King Amenhotep and his co-regent were enthroned behind ceremonial tables, piled high with traditional offerings of fruit and flowers.

"Unfortunately, the doctors have put me on a diet," the older king mumbled, as his son started on a full plate. "As for my needs, give me real food and a dancing girl." Amenhotep Junior glanced at his father. "I apologise for my earthiness. You really would make a fine monk, these days. Despite once being a brattish child, you constantly make me feel guilty."

"I'm not conservative," replied his son, carefully avoiding any beverage that looked faintly Greek, and choosing fresh lime juice instead, "but I believe in love."

"Of course you do." Pharaoh bit into a peach.

"It descends from the Creator who is in all things – animals, birds, and humans. I'm writing a poem about it."

"I hope you're not confusing us all into a soup."

"Don't you think it's wonderful? Life begins from love and starts as a tiny seed which sprouts into wheat; or an egg, which turns into a chick –"

"Or a little girl who turns into a nubile maiden, ripe for the royal lap." Finishing his fruit, Pharaoh raised his goblet. "You need to get married."

"What are you two talking about?" Tiye asked, joining in the conversation.

"Our youngest here will need a well-stocked harem when I'm gone." Waving aside his son's protestations, the king selected a piece of pomegranate from the silverware. "Death, too, is a part of life. Stick that in your great poem and ask the Creator why." He turned to his queen. "Our boy is fully conversant with the facts of life. He can't wait to experience Pharaoh's pleasures."

"I find that hard to believe when he's shut up in his studio all day."

"Let me hasten to reassure you that he has talked of nothing but the birds and the bees all evening."

Tiye noticed a familiar light in her husband's eye.

"I'm getting too old to bear children," she remarked, a trifle more loudly than intended, nevertheless cupping her auburn hair flirtatiously with one hand. The king winked.

"Now look what you have done, Junior!"

Unable to think of a suitable rejoinder, the prince finished his lime juice in what he hoped was a telling silence.

***

20.

AMENHOTEP JUNIOR

I won't worship him, God of death, God of war. He's not the Creator.

I feel stifled.

*****

TIYE

My son is either inspired, or mad. In part, he follows my dream and those of pharaohs before him. There must be a solution to Amon's meteoric rise to power. The sinister god swallows Egypt like a python with its prey.

He would stuff the throne whole down his throat too, if he could.

*****

Arrogantly tossing a schist carving of Horus aside, the co-regent stalked through his father's workshop.

"What do these bird-headed statues really mean, anyway?"

"Sire, these craftsmen have a quota to fulfil," Abner whispered. "If you keep breaking things, your father's project will be delayed."

Amenhotep Junior rounded on his companion.

"Surely, you jest? Our entire country's revenue is spent on a never-ending supply of stone animals, which we are supposed to worship as beings greater than ourselves." Pointing to a figure of Amon in the form of a ram, the new king sneered: "And here he is, the omnipotent god of Karnak himself!"

"Please, Your Highness," the courtier feebly protested.

"It's a *sheep*, Abner." Smiling maliciously, the prince rounded on his friend. "Jews sacrifice such a one to their god, don't they?"

Gasps caught in the throats of the surrounding artisans.

"I believe sacrifices to gods are made in all cultures," responded the ashen-faced Abner.

"You're not wrong."

The tour continued. In half an hour the co-regent had completed his task of insulting the royal workshop. Once outside the complex, Amenhotep paused in an open portico. Choosing a cedar chair, he sat down. Mopping his brow, Abner leaned against a pillar.

"What's the matter?" his employer queried provocatively.

The new adviser to His Majesty, the future Amenhotep-the-Fourth: Neferkheprure, Co-Regent of all Asia, rapidly straightened his defeated posture.

"It's only the mid-morning heat."

"In which case you should sit down and rally your flagging energies."

Choosing a fig from the fruit bowl, set next to him by a hovering servant, the prince consumed the fruit in swift, decisive bites.

"I must say," Abner began tentatively, "as your friend and a Hebrew, I heartily condone all you believe in, but –"

"You're afraid." Amenhotep Junior snorted contemptuously. He finished his fig, and wiped his fingers on his white kilt. "You're the same boy who chose my powerful mother over me. You buttered up Dhutmose, too. Well, now you work for someone who doesn't care what people think. Embarrassed?"

Abner's temples throbbed with mounting ire.

"I never said you embarrassed me."

"Why are you scared?"

"I'm not!"

"You're lying. You must always tell the truth. The Creator is truth. He expects us to live by a standard no less high than His own." The co-regent picked up a large bunch of grapes. He had finished his temple fast two days ago and was ravenous. "And try to remember to address me by my title."

"Yes, Your Majesty." Abner stared miserably at the multicoloured tiles of the workshop portico. Presently, he drew up his head. "In that case, I have something to tell you," he said resolutely. "You must fast more."

Amenhotep's eyes rounded in surprise.

"What do you mean?"

Unwavering, Abner met his stare.

"You're too fat to be Pharaoh."

"How dare you? I'm not some baby you can torment any more. I'm about to become king of the entire world!"

A flock of crows flew upwards out of their palm trees. Abner's upper lip twitched.

"Even so, Your Majesty, as you can see, I am trying."

Annoyance transformed to hearty giggles as the co-regent considered his friend's words.

"Indeed!" he proclaimed, wiping his eyes. "You can be Prime Minister when I ascend the throne."

"I would be honoured."

Amenhotep Junior regarded him quizzically.

"Are you sure?"

"I'm telling the truth. Who wouldn't be?"

***

177

21.

Members of Walter's research team were seated at their computers. They were on a morning tea break, which was rapidly becoming heated as a debate began.

"What I find amusing, Tom," said Karen, crackling her potato chip packet, "is that Freud was an admirer of both Moses and Akhenaten."

"Why is that funny?" Ernest asked crabbily. "You *are* a weird girl."

"Moses was the one person our great psychoanalyst was originally hero-worshipping before he struck pay dirt with Akhenaten," Melissa added.

"Who says he struck anything but dirt?" Ernest rumbled. "The guy was a quack. Whoever heard of boys wanting to marry their mothers, and girls their fathers? The truth is Freud had a secret affair with his niece, and spent his whole life transmuting his inherent sense of Jewish guilt through his work, trying to justify his lust. It's almost as if he was saying: 'I can't help it – it's psychological'! Not only that, but he also dragged the entire human race down to his level by accusing us of being as neurotic as he. The guy was a pervert who should have been locked up in prison, not lauded as a saviour of the human mind."

"Don't his actions prove his theory?" Melissa asked. "And he wasn't the only one. Lots of uncles seduce their nieces. Furthermore, his guilt had nothing to do with being Jewish."

"Heck!" Tom sat down, pulling his tie open sideways. "All I want is Akhenaten. Look, Walt, you yourself said the Bible was accurate. Exodus says nothing about Akhy, as you like to call him. It does state the Hebrews built the Ramesside cities of Pithom and Per Ramses. That puts Moses clearly in the Ramesside period. Now all we need do is choose our Pharaoh. Which one drowned, or is missing from his casket?"

"Avaris already existed on the site of Per Ramses for centuries," Walter explained patiently. "Who is to say that a writer living in the time of Ramesses, didn't recap Moses' life, calling the old city of Avaris by its new name of Per Ramses?"

"I'm not convinced," Melissa said.

"Who else could Akhenaten be but Moses?" Walter challenged. "Don't you find it strangely coincidental that two princes of Egypt decide to worship one god and create mayhem in the process?"

"Moses defeated Pharaoh," Ernest said. "The reason there is an historical gap is because no Egyptian king would want the world to know about it, much less carve the fact into monuments as a record for all time!"

"How come Ramesses-the-Great was quite happy to broadcast his defeat at the Battle of Kadesh?" Karen asked. "It's plastered over more monuments than you can count."

"There you go," Walter said triumphantly. "Karen's right. In the same manner Tuthmosis-the-Great records his defeat, as well as his victory, at Megiddo."

"That's true!" Tom brightened. "He speaks of the failure of his men to be disciplined in taking the city, and of their greed in looting the gold and silver on the plain, while escaping enemy soldiers were hauled up into the citadel, and the gates securely closed against the advancing Egyptian army. In the same way Ramesses records his outrageous bravery at Kadesh. And although he was courageous, Ramesses was defeated."

"Neither incident was recorded as a failure," Ernest countered. "Tuthmosis took Megiddo. Ramesses said he won Kadesh, and later set up a successful treaty with the Hittites. He's Egypt's most famous king. Why, even today Egyptians venerate him!"

"Still, Walt has a point," said Melissa thoughtfully. "It is possible to trace Egyptian writers presenting both sides of a story, as far back as the Sixth Dynasty, when there was a revolution in the time of Phiops I. It was a matter of public record. Incredible, when one tends to think of pharaohs as tyrants."

"I was reading about that last night," Tom said, visibly brightening.

"Then we are agreed," Walter stated. "Moses was a royal in line for the throne. So was Akhenaten. Moses believed in one god. So did Akhenaten. Moses created a revolution, so did –"

"You know," Karen broke in brightly, "Moses' commandments were Egyptian laws, already in practice."

"Some of them," Walter agreed, irritated on being interrupted.

"Has anyone noticed the prophet behaved like a pharaoh?" Melissa asked. "It's the main reason the Old Testament is so full of terrifying authority."

"You will do this or die." Karen investigated her chip packet for scraps. Disappointed, she discarded it into the wastepaper basket next to her desk. "I heartily concur."

"I'm still not convinced that Akhenaten and Moses are the same individual," Tom stated. "I'm intrigued, however," he added quickly, noticing the glares. "But I don't feel it in my gut."

"Neither did Theodore Davis when he discovered Akhenaten," Ernest said. "And he was wrong."

"If Theodore Davis' discovery in cache number fifty-five was Akhenaten's body, then Akhenaten cannot be Moses," Tom pointed out logically. He stood up. "The most important thing for this team to discover is whether or not we have Akhenaten's body. If we don't, we might have found Moses."

"But, if we do, I think we still have him," said Walter. "In my view Moses was more than one person. I also think Akhenaten gave history a shove in the right direction. He is the first and only historical equivalent of the Jewish prophet. The more I learn about him, the more I am convinced he is our man. In which case, guys, we need to get cracking and let everyone know."

"I think Akhenaten was greater than Moses," Melissa ventured. "He had a personal love-relationship with God, and addressed Him as 'Father'."

"That's why they call him the first Christian." Karen was smiling at the red-headed research co-ordinator for the first time.

"He was also an authoritarian bastard," Ernest interjected. "The entire army was ordered to guard his city of Akhet-Aten to make sure no one could get out."

"I thought it was used to protect its citizens," Karen said.

"Why do you think no one opposed Akhenaten? He was nuts, but he got away with stripping the priesthood of its money without being assassinated. He controlled the army with an iron hand."

"Please excuse me." Karl, who was sitting in the back row, deposited his ever-present bag of dried nuts and fruits to one side. "I am only a geologist, but it seems to me that you have overlooked a major point."

"Go ahead," Tom encouraged, remembering the furore Karl's team had caused in dating the sphinx.

"Tuthmosis and Ramesses were both kings, ruling their country and fighting battles. However, taking on the priesthood seems to have been quite another thing. It seems to me that when the *priests* were challenged, their opponents were erased from any records. It is why there was no obvious trace of Akhenaten in history until we really looked."

"We're Egyptologists. We all know this," Walter responded grumpily.

"Then know this – to challenge the Egyptian religion was not considered battle – it was *heresy*. Akhenaten was declared a heretic. Every trace of him was stamped out. We have only rediscovered him recently. He was obliterated from the memory of Egypt, and the world, for thousands of years. Herodotus didn't know of his existence, or Strabo, or Jesus or Mohammed."

"Although if Akhenaten really was Moses, he would have been revealed to Jesus on the Mount of Transfiguration," Karen could not resist. "So Jesus would have known him, and perhaps mentioned that he was an Egyptian king."

"What's your point, Karl?" Walter asked.

"That you are right when you state pharaohs recorded their failures to rule, or fight. Religion was another matter entirely. To question it was unthinkable. Akhenaten and Moses were not only consigned to the shadows of Egyptian history – it was as if they never existed. And that, ladies and gentlemen, is the reason you do not find any trace of the great contest between Moses and Pharaoh in Egyptian records, or any mention of the plagues. Your mistake was to assume Moses was battling the king, but unlike confrontations at Megiddo, or Kadesh, this was not a political battle, but a religious one. Kings could be questioned, but not gods, or the priesthood. Both Akhenaten and Moses did this. Both were eradicated from Egyptian history."

"You seem to think they were two different people," Tom noted.

"That's my assessment. It doesn't change the fact Akhenaten was important. It is perfectly possible for Moses to be a composite of several people. What Akhenaten is, and sadly Moses is not, is an historical figure whom we can establish has having existed."

"History labels Akhenaten a failure," Walter pronounced sarcastically.

"History is clear on that point. Akhenaten engineered a revolution, but he and his family were purged. If he isn't Moses, he failed in the world's view, but not in mine."

"Karl's right about the lack of detail on Moses in Egyptian history," Melissa remarked, causing several of her colleagues to bristle. "I think Akhenaten was an unbelievable success. Nobody can convince me that billions of people worshipping one god, thirty-one centuries later is anything but a success. It's extraordinary, stellar – one of history's truly outstanding legacies. And the reason, you now see Karen sitting over there writing a Biblical thesis!"

"I'm inclined to think the two were one and the same person," Tom said. He shut his folder. "Man, I wish that if aliens had visited our planet two thousand years ago, they'd have taken photographs!"

"They did," Walter said mysteriously.

***

22.

AMENHOTEP JUNIOR

My imagination is black and white compared to this ... a creation beyond my dreams ... Aten-inspired.

I see a new art.

I must give it to the world.

***

Walking across the freshly polished floor of the Great Hall, the new regent was again locked in discussion with his boyhood friend.

"It occurs to me, Bak, that the priests of Amon have blasphemed. Originally, the first point of Creation belonged to Heliopolis. Now they have usurped that right."

On entering their workshop, Bak sat on the rough floor and began to knead clay.

"Junior, I love you as a brother," he said, shifting his thin buttocks on the cold limestone floor. "I don't want to lose you in some vicious plot."

But his friend was not listening.

"There was no reason for my brother, Dhutmose, to die," he mused. "He was conservative. So, perhaps a revolutionary will survive. We can't live in fear,"

The co-regent glanced at his friend, who had assumed one of his contortionist positions.

"I have a headache."

"Maybe you should stop lying on cold stone floors, Bak."

"Or stop listening to you."

Bak belched loudly and contemplated the ceiling. Picking up a lump of wet clay, Amenhotep Junior hurled it at his friend.

"Prepare yourself, my faithful follower. They're going to stone us for this!"

***

AMENHOTEP JUNIOR

Mummy's patronising me again. I know she means well, but she thinks if I worship Aten in the courtyard of an Amon temple, my vision will be contained.

She wants compromise. I want the truth. There must be a way to make her see.

***

"I believe in Aten."

"So does your father, so do I," Queen Tiye replied.

"You also worship Amon."

"I should think it was a foregone conclusion in the god's city."

Amenhotep Junior bit his stylus.

"I believe in one god."

Bile rose in Tiye's gore.

"Is that such a problem?" she asked, controlling herself with an effort. "Most of us have a favourite deity."

"That's not what I mean, Mother, and you know it. God is one. Multiple gods with animal heads are figments of people's overwrought imaginations. You must also know there are many who follow my beliefs."

"I have no doubt your administration will be suited to your dictates. You are to be king. They're obliged to follow you."

"I'm not interested in the kingdom. I am talking about God; the Creator; the One who made all life."

Queen Tiye's arms jangled their gold bracelets.

"Enough! Your brother demonstrated religious zeal, but at least he was practical. This obsession with Aten ..." She paused, choosing her words. "… is leading to madness. Whoever heard of only one god? You cannot expect Egyptians to embrace a single deity to the exclusion of all others. It will cause unrest."

"That's precisely what I intend to do – establish the worship of a sole god over this land! It pleases me that you understand my plan."

"I am frightened to comprehend its meaning," Tiye replied, straightening her wig. "Now I am going to the Hall of Administration to see what we can do to appease Amon's High Priest. I mean to say, you built a temple to Aten in Amon's courtyard!"

"I have to be true to my father in heaven," the prince persisted stubbornly. "Besides, I can't be expected to pray to Amon at sunrise and sunset. Those times belong to my god."

"And we're going to use that explanation for your rudeness. Really, my dear, if you were younger –"

"You'd put me over your knee?"

"I'd send you back to where you came from."

With her parting shot, Tiye left her son to ponder the story whispered in the harem: *A basket in the reeds … a baby drawn from the water.* Before the old depression of abandonment and adoption overwhelmed him, Amenhotep Junior drew himself to his full height.

"Bah!" he muttered. "They just don't understand." He strolled onto the patio where a breeze stirred in the persea trees. Restless discontent seized him. *"I will heed Abner's advice and fast more,"* he thought. *"If my god is to reign supreme, I must seek his strength."*

Fortified with the knowledge that he alone would discover and execute the will of his heavenly father, Amenhotep brightened. Humming, he retired to his rooms for a well-deserved siesta.

***

In the marketplace Major Horemheb was fanning his fat friend to prevent overheating, and perhaps even death.

"You don't know him," Maya wheezed as they drew into the shade of a tavern. "Amenhotep Junior knows a lot about Tuthmosis-the-Great

185

and the battles he fought. If you think the heir is a pacifist, you're wrong, Hump."

"Indeed," the newly appointed Major replied. Pushing his companion behind a trestle he ordered cold beer. "This isn't two centuries ago." Horemheb seized one of the pottery mugs of chilled liquid set before them. "Our problems are different. Now stop talking and drink up before you expire of heatstroke."

A chariot clattered by, scattering peasants and livestock in its wake.

Driven by a man with a child passenger, they were both clad in military garb. Indignant roosters crowed and flapped their tawny wings, fluttering out of the way of the chariot.

The waggling of crests and wattles caught Maya's eye.

"Remind me to buy some things for dinner before we go," he said. "My wife gave me a list for this week's shopping." Gulping down the thick, sweet beverage, his complexion slowly reduced from bright crimson to pink. "All I'm saying," he continued, returning to the original discussion, "is that our future pharaoh is interested in more than the god, Aten."

"That," responded Horemheb, stabbing the air vehemently with one forefinger, "is another worry. He's built a temple to a ... disk. His god doesn't even have a face!"

"So, what's wrong with building a temple to Aten, other than your personal dislike of the deity?"

"He's erected one in *Amon*'s courtyard and the priests are seeing red. There isn't a day when I don't get some bald, holy man complaining in my ear. If I didn't know better, I'd swear they wanted me to personally enlist our army to pull it down!"

"They do, but the Gempaaten temple, as it is called, is not intruding on the inner sanctuary. Mark my words, if you approached Amenhotep-the-Magnificent and Queen Tiye about it, your career would run faster down the drain than water out of Abner's brand-new flush toilet." Thoughtfully, Maya took another draught of date beer. "It would be hard not to be in Amon's shadow, Hump. There is so little room for diversity in Karnak."

"Next thing you'll be telling me you want to move upriver with the king. He's leaving this city – do you know that?"

A glint appeared in the treasurer's eye as he wiped his mouth.

"I've heard Akhenaten, I mean Amenhotep," he corrected, as Horemheb looked wildly about for spies, "is designing a new capital. It's a rumour, although I do love sailing up and down the Nile."

Another wheeled vehicle rattled past. This time it was a donkey-drawn cart with oversize wooden wheels.

The two courtiers instinctively shielded themselves from a cloud of dust thrown up by its passage.

"You should accompany me on campaign if you like travelling so much," said Horemheb.

"I'm content to sail on the Malkata lake, although the wide, open spaces of the Nile are my personal favourite. It's wonderful sitting under the stars at night on the riverbank."

"Until an asp bites you in the behind. I know all about the riverbank," concluded Horemheb grimly.

"However," Maya said, eyeing roast duck in a passing waitress' hands, "together we'd see foreign cities and peoples. I'd enjoy that."

"If you ever desire a Syrian vista, you are most welcome to join me next week."

"You sound lonely, Hump."

"It always is at the top." Swigging his beer, Horemheb regarded the tavern clientele moodily. "You must experience that in your lofty position as Chief Treasurer."

"I do my job and go home."

"I envy you. For me all I can do is eat, sleep, and drink the army."

"There's more at stake in your profession," was the diplomatic reply.

"If Egypt's cashflow isn't her single greatest stake, I don't know what is." The officer lifted his head. "I smell duck."

"They always serve it here." Maya downed the dregs of his delicious beverage. "It's time to celebrate your promotion to 'Major'."

***

23.

TIYE

My son wants to revolutionise our empire. The downward curve of his stubborn mouth, so like mine, told me that this morning. Every mother enjoys seeing herself mirrored in her progeny.

There's a hitch. No one wants to change what's perfect. Despite Amon's obscene pre-eminence, the country is at peace.

Still, my son could make a difference.

***

In the unbearable heat of midday Amenhotep-the-Magnificent sent for his chief wife on a romantic whim.

"I don't want children," Tiye stated emphatically, on entering his boudoir.

"Are you refusing me?"

"I'm informing you of the Great Wife's pleasure."

"Which is?"

"Peace." Tiye flopped on her favourite pillow. "No more offspring to disturb me, or this country. I am beginning to think that we do not make good fruit."

"Perhaps I should summon the Princess of Mitanni."

King Amenhotep made no move.

"Or the Princess of Babylon."

"I don't like her – too many teeth."

They laughed together. Tiye patted her cushion.

"Lie beside me," she invited bossily. Happy to oblige, her husband curled up next to her.

"You were always my favourite mouse," he murmured, caressing her greying auburn hair.

"Do you call others by my pet name?"

"I do have names for them," Pharaoh sighed. "None, repeatable."

Tiye moulded her slight body into the generous curves of her husband's.

"I would like a boy. A duplicate of you."

"You'd like to replace our future Amenhotep-the-Fourth?"

"He's a thorn in the side of Amon, which I approve of, but he's a fanatic, which makes him a pricklebush for us."

"I'm still King. We can moderate his stance."

"I wish Dhutmose had lived."

"And I wish we had chosen another heir, but there isn't one – at least not from our bodies."

Eyes closed, Tiye rubbed her husband's pot belly with a faint smile.

"I'm going to drift off."

"Why do women always do that?"

"Do what, dear?" she murmured.

"Fall asleep when one gets close to them. Every time I want to consummate my marriages for the sake of the empire, I am surrounded by snoozing females. No wonder I can't make heirs!"

"You just don't understand women. Snuggling is conducive to sleep. Right now, I feel like a little girl, tucked up, warm and relaxed. If you want romance, you need to create an active atmosphere. It's rather like staging a bull hunt."

"That's interesting." Pharaoh yawned. "However, the mood has passed."

Eyes glazed, fanbearers cooled the dozing couple as they forgot the dark cloud looming above their nation.

***

AMENHOTEP JUNIOR

My head fell into both hands after the coronation. However, building a city is infinitely more exhausting than becoming a king.

I have a vision. I follow God, not my own impulse. I do His will. Nefertiti understands, but even she did not wish to come to Akhet-Aten. Aten persuaded her.

Now she sees.

***

The regent disappeared around a corner leading to Tiye's apartments. His wife followed, hurtling down the maze of adjoining rooms and passageways. Startled house staff scampered out of her way. As she rushed past a niche, covered in paintings of the new royal couple's wedding, one slender hand emerged from the shadows to grasp her elbow.

"This is hardly dignified," Amenhotep Junior whispered, half-laughing.

"Let go!" Nefertiti pulled her arm away. The king rapidly released it to prevent bruising. "Why won't you discuss this?" she asked hotly. "My entire family lives in Thebes. I don't want to leave."

"God revealed his purpose to me in a dream. Besides," her husband added authoritatively, "I am Pharaoh. My word is LAW."

"You're a human being," Nefertiti objected loudly.

"Don't raise your voice. I can hear you perfectly well."

As Amenhotep smiled, an effulgence rose in his face. Nefertiti was momentarily transfixed.

"This is a decision to be made between a husband and wife," she scolded, returning to earth. "If you want to leave our home, that's fine, but I don't want to be stuck in the middle of a desert, miles away from my family."

"God spoke to me."

"Which god? Abner's or ours?"

"The Creator. There is only one."

"You take your religious infatuation too far!"

Picking up her skirts, she attempted to flounce away, but Amenhotep Junior stepped in front of his irate wife.

"If we stay here, the priests will rule," he reasoned. "Eventually, they will kill us. They are already saying I am an illegitimate Jew in order to discredit me. In Akhet-Aten, *we* will reign. Think about it, Nef. I've always promised you more power than any queen."

His wife's ruby lips trembled. Minutes passed.

"I would like to see the plans for your new city," she finally conceded. An audible breath escaped her husband's lips.

"I'll give them to you this afternoon," he promised happily.

"I want to take my parents with us."

"Mother wants Lord Ay to remain in Thebes, although I'll see what I can do."

Chewing her lips meditatively, the young woman added: "The temples should be open-air."

"They will be."

"The priesthood," Nefertiti whispered urgently, "has to be destroyed. It's no use simply moving."

"I'm not having anything to do with the destruction of Heliopolis. I studied there, and many of my beliefs are grounded in that city's ancient teachings."

"I have no objection to Ra's priests."

"Then we are of one accord on our national policy." Amenhotep Junior rubbed his brow. "I would love to discuss this with you further, but I need to see Mother. She requested my company half an hour ago."

Nefertiti kissed her husband before walking back to her chamber.

"You look downhearted. Perhaps there is something I can do," a familiar voice said. The queen started as the figure of her father loomed before her. "May I come in?"

"You are always welcome, Papa," his daughter replied coldly, brushing past him to enter her room. "Aren't you supposed to be in court?"

She sank onto the nearest couch and poured herself a cold cup of water.

"Queen Tiye adjourned early."

"In order to see her son, which is why you are here."

"Well, yes," Ay confessed, laughing pleasantly.

"Do you ever embark on an action which isn't premeditated?"

"You would never have been born if I hadn't carefully calculated stealing your mother away from that prissy priest of Ptah."

"I don't believe that old story anymore," Nefertiti said yawning. "What brings you here, Papa?"

"I'm wondering if you and your revolutionary husband intend to run away."

"Leave, yes; run, no."

"Would you like to clarify your position?"

"I'm sworn to secrecy."

"You're not in any danger, are you?"

"I don't know." A disturbance swept briefly across the finely chiselled features. "My husband won't listen to me, although he does give me freedom to rule."

Ay pricked up his ears.

"He hasn't assumed full control of the throne yet."

"We have plans."

"His, or yours?"

"Mine would need to be ... implemented."

"So, you're the dangerous one," Ay mused softly. "I thought as much."

A flash of haughty anger struck crossed his daughter's face.

"I believe that certain administrative branches need to be curtailed. It's the only way to maintain power!"

"You're too young to know the ways of power."

"No one's too young to die," she commented in reference to her husband's dead brother.

Reaching out one bony hand, Ay placed it on his daughter's shoulder.

"It would be best if I served your husband. No ruler can be everywhere at once."

"I want you at my side," Nefertiti admitted grudgingly. "It is my other half who is intent on doing everything by himself."

Ay retracted his hand.

"You must persuade him."

Almost immediately the young queen brightened and nodded.

***

Ay rubbed his forehead.

"I've been over these plans twice already."

Tee hovered anxiously in the doorway. It was midnight and her husband had been up since early morning. High cheekbones protruded from his wan face, and his deep-set eyes reminded her of a living skull.

"More grape juice?" she asked tentatively.

"Something stronger, perhaps."

As his wife disappeared in a rustle of skirts, the exhausted courtier sat back, folded his arms and closed his eyes. The drawings percolated through his overworked brain. Homes and wide streets, with a palace and nearby temples dedicated to the worship of Aten, populated the empty desert in brilliant detail. Having dispensed with his father's architects, the new king had designed his own city. Encompassed by a circle of hills and cliffs, Ay could not help noticing the city resembled a diagram of the sun.

"The city is seventeen miles square," he said when Tee returned with an ewer of wine and two goblets.

"Memphis should be the capital instead of Thebes. Nefertiti thinks the new city of Akhet-Aten is in the middle of nowhere, and she has a point. If her husband wants to abandon Thebes as the capital, it would be better to set it up in an established city."

"Our young king is making a statement." Ay sipped his drink thoughtfully. "His city, Akhet-Aten, 'The Horizon of the Aten', is a calculated political move to place the reigning monarch in the centre of Egypt. It shows that he, and not the priests, rule this country."

"True. It will also be good for your career," concluded Tee on a practical note. "You will have more influence in Akhet-Aten than here."

Ay pored over the architectural plans.

"It's not apparent from these preliminary sketches," he said at last, "but we are going to be worshipping in open-air temples."

"How exciting!"

Lotus scent wafted across his shoulder as Tee leaned closer to inspect the ink sketches.

"Our daughter is going to fret about her complexion," Ay said drily. "She takes great pride in that pale skin of hers." Placing the papyrus on his ivory desk, he stifled a yawn. "I promised Queen Tiye I'd go with them to keep an eye on things."

Tee shook her head.

"It's still hard to realise we're leaving. What on earth did the priests say to make our king so angry?"

The Divine Father exhaled a long breath.

"They wanted more control than he was prepared to give. The king doesn't refer to the problem, except as 'it'. Whatever 'it' is, there is now division between the monarchy and the priests. Queen Tiye will continue to exert her moderating influence in Thebes, while I attempt to contain her son's excesses out 'in the middle of nowhere', as our daughter so aptly describes Akhet-Aten."

Tee drained her goblet.

"Whatever you do, darling, don't upset the future Amenhotep-the-Fourth. He's a fanatic."

"Which reminds me: We have to accustom ourselves to calling him 'Akhenaten'."

***

24.

Yellow desert spread out in all directions. Queen Tiye shifted uneasily, while Horemheb rubbed his nose, and Maya coughed in the dusty air. Meanwhile, her son, now called Akhenaten, or He Who Works for Aten, prattled with unabated fervour.

Close to tears, the dowager pinched herself, struggling to remember that Akhenaten's father, too, had visualised statues and architecture. For some reason this felt different, and the queen could not shake off a feeling of foreboding she had experienced since they had departed Thebes.

"I have no idea how the king's going to carry this out," Maya whispered to Horemheb.

"He's built the models in Thebes, according to Ay."

The sweating nobleman looked about at the smug faces of courtiers, most of whom he had never seen before. Pharaoh wiped perspiration from his forehead, while his mother, as rigid as one of Hathor's statues in whose temple she worshipped, made no comment.

"We should retire to the boat," she suggested fruitily, having stood for nearly an hour under her parasol in the blazing noonday heat.

"I haven't finished yet, Mother."

"I have."

Turning abruptly, she walked to their barque moored at a jetty which was still undergoing construction. Her son had no option but to cancel his sightseeing plans. Once on board, the queen called for refreshment. Sipping the cool wine, she hoped her son would follow her example. The significance of her action was not lost on any member of the court, except the future king. Buildings, plazas, and temples, all etched in his keen memory, poured forth in a torrent of word-pictures like a never-ending waterfall.

As the craft pulled away from the city of Akhet-Aten, Tiye rose to her feet and crossed the deck to its opposite side, in order to escape the endless monologue. Her son, wrapped in his creative flow, pursued her to the handrail. Away from the nobles of the court, the queen assumed her most pleasant expression, and leaned closer to her son.

"Enough!" she hissed.

Turning away to the Nile, she drained her goblet.

"But I-I thought you w-would be interested," the young king or stammered.

"I'm sorry to hurt your feelings, but I have my own to consider," she rejoined flatly.

***

Back in Thebes, Queen Tiye burst into her husband's bedchamber.

"I must speak to you." He lifted feverish eyes. Momentarily put off by his appearance, his wife hesitated. "I forgot you weren't well. Would you prefer to consult a physician?"

"I would prefer almost anything to being interrupted," he responded belligerently.

Content that the king was fit enough to roar, Tiye perched herself on the edge of a chair.

"We need to talk."

"About what?"

"Our son. He's dangerous."

"All kings are dangerous," Pharaoh rumbled ominously.

"This is different. Let me explain. Amenhotep Junior changed his name to Akhenaten. It's a direct threat to Amon."

At that moment, the heir appeared at his parents' doorway. Having returned from his city, he had bathed and exchanged his dusty clothes for white linen.

Tiye rubbed noses in greeting. Pharaoh muttered indistinctly. His speech, directed at the prince, gathered momentum.

"He's talking about the guards," Tiye explained.

Pharaoh gesticulated, before suddenly clutching his jaw and doubling over in pain. Tiye rushed to the aid of her husband. Several attendants swiftly eased him back onto his bed. They applied herbal poultices to his forehead and body. Ashen-faced, the prince stood rooted to the spot.

"It's becoming a common occurrence," Tiye said, retrieving her wig, which had fallen off.

"How?" the co-regent asked angrily, recovering from the initial shock of seeing his father collapse. "It's the first time I've ever seen Dad like this. Doesn't he have doctors?"

An avalanche of nurses and aides pushed the prince out of the way. He left, and it was only towards evening that the co-regent, cape in hand, managed to gain admittance to his father.

Accustoming his eyes to the dimly lit room, he approached Egypt's sedated monarch, who was sleeping surrounded by servants and physicians.

"Has he a specialist?"

A young medic of his age gestured towards a panel of doctors standing around the royal bed. An older man cleared his throat.

"Naturally, Your Highness, we are trying to make the king comfortable as possible."

"What is the nature of my father's condition?"

"His Majesty is susceptible to fainting fits caused by melancholia."

"I understand." The co-regent threw his blue-and-gold cape over his shoulders. "See to it that he improves by sundown."

***

AY

He never did.

My sister cried for weeks. My son-in-law was devastated. When it came time to support his mother at the funeral procession, however, Akhenaten was a tower of strength.

A million Egyptians crammed into Karnak's temple for Mass. The roadways were blocked; the Nile was jammed with boats overflowing with the faithful; and the desert highways were filled with humans instead of jackals.

Amenhotep-the-Magnificent ruled a prosperous Egypt for nearly forty years, but not even Tiye counted on the Two Lands' outpouring of grief.

It assaulted our eardrums on that ghastly morning as we walked out of the palace, and shattered them all the way to the Valley-of-the-Kings.

Egypt will never spawn another sovereign like the magnificent one. He was my friend, a masculine man who encouraged his wife to be the greatest scholar in Egypt, and, despite its inherent danger, carved a path for his genius son to walk.

You don't think Akhenaten: Moses did it alone, do you?

***

PART III:
Exodus

25.

Dishevelled and perspiring, Maya leapt out of his chariot and fled up the barracks' steps. Bursting into the officers' mess, where General Horemheb was eating with Ramesses, he hurried to their table.

"Care to join us?" Horemheb asked. "It's camp gruel – your favourite."

Maya took several deep breaths and sat down at the long table.

"Listen to me. You have to change your name."

"I never did care for 'Hump'."

Ramesses excused himself and rapidly exited the dining hall.

"You know," remarked Maya, "he resembles that charioteer with the kid we saw in the pub last summer. By the way, congratulations on yet another promotion."

"My career is taking off. Ramesses' boy's name is Seti. Precocious mite. His father treats him like a regular little addition to the squadron." Horemheb finished his porridge, and pushed the bowl away from him. "Now, what are you in such a hurry to see me about?'

"It's the king – there's been a coup, and military police are swarming all over the palace."

"Is His Majesty alright?" Horemeheb rose.

"Sit down. The king's the instigator of it."

"But who's he deposing?"

"Amon."

"He can't depose a god!"

"Well, our friend has," Maya replied, pushing his wig to one side. "When he changed his name from Amenhotep to Akhenaten, it should have been a clue. Both His Majesty and Amon's High Priest will call for you." Maya clutched his friend's arm and looked desperately into his eyes. "Go with the king," he said so seriously that Horemheb nodded. "Akhenaten's planned all this from the beginning. Do you remember that *heb-sed* festival three years into his reign?"

"It was strange. Most kings celebrate it after thirty years, but then it made sense because Akhenaten was declaring the supremacy of Aten."

"Right, and he's been building a city in the middle of Egypt all this time. Now that it's ready, His Majesty has suddenly decided the priests of Amon have insulted him and his family, so he's shifting."

"Are you going?"

"We all are."

"I'd rather stay away from the madness."

"This is a matter of life and death. Akhenaten's furious. He's going to leave, setting fire to everything in his wake – and not just Thebes – the whole of Egypt!"

"Raze Egypt to the ground?" Horemheb scratched his head.

"He'll aim for her temples."

"What about Heliopolis? They don't worship Amon there."

Maya exhaled a long breath, and pulled off his wig.

"You just don't get it, do you? Akhenaten doesn't want any major god, aside from the Aten, to exist in Egypt."

"He'll provoke a national revolt. People won't stand for it."

"Oh yes, they will," Maya said firmly. "You see, the king will allow the people to have their minor deities like Bes. The general populace has never cared much for Amon, or Ra, unless it was a feast day of drunkenness and revelry."

Horemheb snorted.

"Pharaoh's a clever man," he mused. "Ruthless, too."

"Listen, Akhenaten is going to rename you Pa-aten-em-heb. Have you got that?"

"Pa-aten-em-heb – yes, I think so."

"Ramesses is Parnefer. Don't forget it, and warn your comrade to behave as though nothing had happened, especially in front of Pharaoh. Now ..." Maya rustled around in his linen pockets. "Take these."

"What are they?" Horemheb asked, surveying the square shapes of clay shoved into his hand by Maya's sweaty fist.

"Tickets to admit you and Ram on the boat to Akhet-Aten. It leaves at nine o'clock tomorrow morning, one hour after the king and his family vacate the city, and two before it goes up in flames. Don't forget your new names. They're printed on the back of the stubs."

"I'm not leaving. Neither is Ramesses. What's going to happen to my army? Akhenaten isn't contemplating a purge, is he?"

"He needs soldiers, which is why he's going to summon you this afternoon. I suggest both you and Ramesses get the regiments training on the front lawn – make it look good for you and the troops."

"I can do that." Horemheb paused. "Who, in Amon's name, are these military police? I didn't authorise them."

"Do you remember the upstarts at Akhet-Aten?"

"You said you didn't recognise the faces. And Thebes is to be destroyed?"

"The temples are going up in smoke, but Queen Tiye is staying."

"Then it's settled: I'm not moving."

"Please, Hump," Maya beseeched, tugging his arm and almost weeping with hysteria. "Akhenaten's crazy. The new desert-ranger Mazoi police are thugs, and the court's full of flatterers who'd sell their grandmothers. Even Ay's going – in fact, Queen Tiye forced him. He told me this afternoon."

"So, he'll be a double agent," Horemheb chuckled.

"I'm taking you, Hump, whether you like it or not. That Jew, Abner, is behind all this," he added darkly.

"Rubbish! Abner's sane. He's had to put up with Akhenaten since they were kids and he's got many a tale to tell, I can assure you."

"I grew up with the king, too."

"You didn't know him after pre-school."

"He outgrew me – went travelling with Bak – although we always remained friends." Maya looked up at the general with sad, blue-grey eyes. "I've known our king since I was four, Hump. That's why I know what he's capable of." Heaving himself out of his chair with difficulty, the accountant hitched his damp kilt about him and re-fitted his wig. "I expect you and Ram on the nine o'clock boat, and don't forget this afternoon's preparations if you want to help your country."

***

Akhenaten strode through Malkata Palace surrounded by his bodyguards. Overnight, half the Amon regiment had defected to the new Aten corps. Others had disappeared, having fled, or been incarcerated in Pharaoh's dungeons.

"Pa-aten-em-heb and Parnefer are here to see Your Majesty," Abner said, referring to Horemheb and Ramesses by their new names.

In the throne room, the military duo prostrated themselves at Akhenaten's feet.

"I assume your allegiance is with me?" the king queried without preliminaries.

"The army is at your service, Your Majesty," Horemheb said.

"As it has always been."

Horemheb thought it wise to prostrate himself again. Unsure of himself, Ramesses waited, trying to look as calm as possible. The palace was filled with the clattering of sandalled soldiers' feet; snatches of perfunctory orders and the screams of hapless victims – mainly the kitchen staff – who were being bullied into packing.

Akhenaten turned to Ramesses.

"Captain Parnefer, you were exercising Ptah's chariot division in the main compound of the king's barracks when you were summoned to the palace this afternoon?"

"It is my duty to keep my royal master's cavalry in prime condition."

Akhenaten pursed his lips.

"And you, Pa-aten-em-heb, were seen to be conducting archery practice with the Horus regiment, an hour before, in the same place."

"My aim is to keep Your Majesty's army in prime condition."

"Aren't these two disciplines normally conducted behind the main stable area?"

"Not these days, Your Majesty."

Fortunately for Horemheb, the king was smiling. His henchmen, as the general noticed, were grinning hideously. Most had yellow teeth.

"In that case we will see you in Akhet-Aten. I take it you are both coming."

"Pharaoh's wish is our command," Horemheb replied, feeling more grateful for Maya's visit with each passing moment.

***

In a spacious office, overlooking his mother's lake, Akhenaten was transported with delight. He gazed brightly into space as if in a trance.

"It's going to be the most glorious moment in history, Ay."

"I trust all the boats are loaded and ready for their trip down the Nile."

The king continued to commune with the open space in front of him. His father-in-law surreptitiously surveyed the chamber. Filled with scrolls, it contained little more than a few chairs. The king's personal palette and styluses lay next to a papyrus he was working on. Ay noticed odd cartoons, peeping out of boxes of papyri. A few hieroglyphs designated the monarch's purpose for the new city. The mission statement was incomplete, fitting in with the bare, whitewashed newness of the room.

"This office is uncluttered, but familiar" Ay remarked. "What was it before it became Your Majesty's private study?"

"Dad's trophy room. It was chock full of bulls' horns and lions' paws."

"I remember it," the latter responded, not wishing to enquire as to what had become of the late King Amenhotep's prized possessions. "When do you sail?"

"Tomorrow at dawn."

"You will be able to worship Aten as He is rising."

"And at sundown at the original point of Creation," Akhenaten beamed.

***

Gold-tipped prows pulled away from Karnak's jetty. In the metallic dawn Lord Ay stood to attention on the wharf, wondering what would become of him and the abandoned capital.

A stocky figure, clad in a freshly laundered kilt, sauntered up to join the dismal farewell party. Ay drew a cape over his shoulders against the chill of the morning air.

"Welcome to a club of history-makers, General Horemheb. Our careers are now forever interlocked."

"I trust we will be good for Egypt."

"I hear you and Ramesses will stay on to supervise the destruction of Egypt's idols."

"That's the plan."

The adviser searched the face of the man he had known since the latter was a child, but found no clue as to Horemheb's real thoughts. Was the youngest general in Egypt someone he could work with, or take into his confidence? If not, the ancient land of *Kemet* was doomed.

Meanwhile, Akhenaten and Nefertiti waved joyfully from their royal barque. The dowager, ensconced under the shelter of a small pavilion onshore, glowered silently.

Horemheb noted the family resemblance between the aged queen and her brother. Truly, their family had waxed powerful. He scanned the sycamore decks for Maya. As the second boat's stern followed the first, he recognised a portly figure on board. Automatically, Horemheb waved.

Thinking his superior was initiating a ceremonial salute, Ramesses followed suit with his battalion.

"What are they doing?" Meryt asked her husband as a great shout erupted from the crowd on the jetty.

"Ramesses has committed a *faux pas*," the little courtier giggled.

Waving extravagantly back, he was joined by others on board the departing fleet of boats. On the shore a crowd, which had gathered despite the hour, roared a cheery farewell. Unmoved by the high-spirited gathering, Ay and Horemheb turned back to the shore with heavy hearts.

***

26.

Twilight descended on the city as Queen Tiye and one of her oldest friends, Lady Perh-maat, strolled through Malkata's spacious gardens. Strangely empty without her husband, or sons, the grounds were eerily silent.

For decades Tiye had always juggled her administrative concerns with those of her family. Now everyone she loved had departed for Akhet-Aten, or was dead. Only she remained in the city adored by her husband and despised by her son.

She wondered at what the priests might have said to Akhenaten. The little boy she had once dandled on her knee always forgave his teachers' slights in the excitement of a new prank. Or had he? Pondering on how well she knew her own flesh and blood was fruitless. Akhenaten was a complex fabric of contradictions. Artistic and ruthless; happy and remote, it suddenly occurred to her that she never really knew what he was thinking. Maybe the fracas with Amon was not rooted in the past, but in a more recent snub.

Evening fell, and although there was no perceptible sound, Tiye, with her sharp nostrils, detected a trace of acrid smoke. A shudder ran through her, but she kept up the cheery front with her companion. They were about to inspect the throne room. It would be hard enough for Tiye to hold court without her beloved husband by her side. Hard enough without worrying about her son and the empire. She would deal with the fire later. Who knew, she might enlist the army to help her douse the flames? In any case, there was enough ahead of her.

"Weren't the troops smartly kitted out?" Tiye remarked. "As I grow older the young men become more appealing."

"That's inevitable," Lady Perh-maat replied. "I must be a hundred-and-ten, but I swear Ramesses is the handsomest man in the realm."

"My niece has a crush on young General Horemheb," Tiye confided. "I'll never get used to calling him Pa-aten-em-heb."

"A more handsome man in Egypt does not exist, except for Lord Ay."

"You are a flatterer! Didn't you just say Ramesses was the handsomest man in the realm?"

"And did you see your brother at the pier? He is forty, but carries not an ounce of fat, not a wrinkle."

"There are lines around those black eyes of his."

"The Divine Father's body is in perfect condition. He must be harbouring some mysterious secret."

"The secret is to exercise and not to give birth."

The pair giggled wickedly as they approached the throne room. Tiye paused to compose herself. Although it was crammed with her followers, she had always entered this chamber in the company of her late husband. She need not have worried. In one fluid movement, the nobles and ladies of the court rose to salute their queen. Many were weeping openly. Tiye's eyes scanned the array of black wigs, gold ribbons, stunning jewellery – a legacy of the Eighteenth Dynasty's refinement – and drew breath.

Taking Lady Perh-maat's arm she began walking down the aisle to a single throne set upon a dais. Eventually she let go, allowing her friend to join her family in the audience. Bracing herself, the petite, middle-aged lady continued to march along the polished granite floor, holding her head high as she had always done with her husband of thirty years. Row upon row of courtiers fell to their faces in full prostration as Egypt's queen took her seat.

"All rise," a clear bass voice sounded by her shoulder.

Gratefully, Tiye turned to acknowledge the service of a court officer, only to recognise Egypt's newly appointed general standing stiffly to attention in full military regalia. If she harboured any doubts towards Horemheb, they were dissolved in that moment. Then the audience did something unimaginable. It cheered. Like a tide of crashing breakers, the sound washed over the dowager queen in a roar until her eardrums burst, and tears coursed silently down her lined face.

***

A CITIZEN

We walked all night long to escape the conflagration. Never have I seen so many dispossessed women and children wandering aimlessly through these streets.

Is this what our king had in mind?

***

Flames licked black granite statues, while the hall metamorphosed from gloom to a white haze. Priests ran coughing through temple chambers, attempting to rescue items of value. Many succumbed to fumes and lay where they fell. Minthu crouched by a large outdoor pond watching the conflagration.

"Now I can sleep."

"Do you mean to commit ritual suicide?" a student enquired timidly.

"Not yet," Minthu laughed. "I never realised how many temples we owned. No wonder I was always exhausted!" He inclined his head towards another bald man in full temple regalia, standing silently in the sunlight near the granary. "Ity takes everything too seriously. Dressed in all that finery, he'll be dead within a fortnight." Tightening his loincloth, the esteemed tutor picked up his bundle of belongings. "Let's go. We will return in a month's time."

***

"Food for my baby," a woman begged.

Ay pushed past, shouting hysterically for his horses. Trapped in the marketplace he was stranded in chaos. Everyone was running helter-skelter through rickety cane stands piled high with melons, oranges, figs, tomatoes, and bread. Finally, Ay spotted the whirling manes of his distressed white stallions.

Ducking under the awnings of the shops, he crossed a small alley and came up behind the horses. They were rearing and whinnying, twisting his chariot back and forth. Jumping into the back of the car, the Divine Father pulled on the reins. As the horses continued to buck and snort, he pulled away from the curb. Ay guided them through a series of dusty lanes, which, he reflected, were the very same that General Horemheb had used, when pursued by ardent female admirers.

At the palace the courtier stormed into Queen Tiye's apartments. Engrossed in the board game of *senet*, she frowned.

"Even brothers should ask permission to see the Dowager Queen."

Ay loosened his necklace and sank onto one of her large pouffes.

"I can't breathe! The city's going up in smoke. Where are your soldiers?"

"Sailing up the Nile with my son."

Tiye moved a white pawn to the centre of her ebony gaming board.

"Are you playing alone?"

"No one wants to defeat me," she replied, glancing accusingly at her servants, who were huddled in a corner pretending to be absorbed in polishing the furniture. Ay stretched out one arm. Commandeering her pawns, took his own piece to the end of the board. "I have nowhere to go, but this water square," his sister complained.

"Game's over," Ay declared in two moves. He sat back, sweating profusely. "This bodes evil, Tiye, playing while your city burns."

"It isn't going to be destroyed." The queen set up the board again. "We bribed the town water-carriers to douse the temples at night."

"But the palace is commissioned to burn the houses of Amon!"

"And I'm commissioning an end to this senseless destruction."

Ay shook his head.

"You're engaging in a dangerous game. The palace is filled with Mazoi agents."

"I reserve my games for the board." Sideswiping three of her brother's pieces, Tiye landed triumphantly on a winning square. "Do you know why all of Egypt loves me?"

"I wasn't aware it did."

"Let me assure you it does, Baby Brother. Firstly, the mighty Great Wife to our late king, is a commoner. People relate to that. I am also completely without fear, which is why I can light fires with one hand, and put them out with another. So, what if we don't like the priests? It's no excuse for destroying perfectly good architecture."

"You're playing both sides of the fence."

"Which means you're not the only one," was the arch reply. "By the way, I believe I'm winning."

Regarding the board, Ay smoothly knocked down several white pieces. Tiye grimaced.

"I came to tell you, sister, that one of us has to go to Akhet-Aten to keep an eye on the revolution."

"As you can see, I'm preoccupied."

Ay rubbed his brow.

"A woman stopped me in the marketplace."

"One of your spies, I presume."

"She was a peasant clutching her baby. They were starving."

A *senet* piece dropped to the floor.

"No one in my city is going to starve while I'm on the throne!"

Ay shifted rapidly out of the way as his indignant sister bustled through the nearest exit.

"Senta!" she called shrilly. "Please inform Tutu that the Dowager Queen requests an audience with His Lordship immediately. You can come if you like," she added to her brother.

The hallway was filled with smoke. Guiding himself by touch against warm granite walls, Ay followed his sister down the hazy corridor into the throne room.

"It's empty," he observed sadly.

"That's because no one's here." Tiye felt a lump rise to her throat.

For a lifetime she had stood by her husband in that room, overseeing a country blessed by prosperity and peace.

"If only I had not rescued that little sod in the basket," she thought angrily.

Tiye climbed the stairs to her throne. Ay settled on the lower step while the loyal chief attendant Senta, hovered nearby.

Eventually, Tutu entered the chamber. Palpable arrogance emanated from the man. Instantly, Ay knew he had been hired by Akhenaten.

"How is the destruction of Amon's temples progressing?" Tiye asked.

"Your Majesty," the fawning voice replied, "I am pleased to report that the house of Amon is in ruins."

She swallowed, remembering her husband's contribution to its construction.

"We need to distribute the temple's grain to the citizens. Has General Horemheb left for Akhet-Aten?"

"Not yet, Your Majesty."

"Put him in charge of the operation, and bring him to me this evening."

***

"Dowager Queen Tiye is made of iron," Horemheb commented admiringly. "I don't know how she escapes being suffocated in that palace."

A faintly concerned expression crossed Ay's face.

"My sister is suffering from shock."

"She supports Pharaoh, surely."

"She does not condone this wholesale destruction."

"Neither do I."

"Nor I."

The pair stared at each other in disbelief.

"Why didn't one of us stop the king?" the general asked.

Ay shrugged. A shrewd gleam appeared in his eyes.

"We should bring this civil war to an end. Tiye's doing her best to drown the fires your soldiers are lighting." He leaned closer to Horemheb. "Might I suggest you place the fires *around* the temples instead of inside them?"

The general did not bat an eyelid.

"I assure you they are strategically placed," he replied.

"The wholesale slaughter of priests must also end."

"It was curtailed in the early stages of the conflict."

"This is a most peculiar revolution," Ay remarked, grasping his ebony cane. "It appears that no one agrees with, or even implements, it. By the way, how is our mutual friend, Maya?"

"As you know, he's with the king, and won't be returning to Thebes."

"A wise decision. With his sensibilities he'd wax hysterical at its burned buildings."

Horemheb bowed stiffly as the powerful aristocrat took his leave.

****

"Ramesses, go to Akhet-Aten and ensure our king knows that the destruction of Amon is proceeding smoothly. Also inform him that his mother is well, and that I will be in Pharaoh's new city within three weeks."

Ramesses shifted his weight from one foot to another. He cleared his throat.

"Pardon me sir, but is it true that half our troops are lighting fires, while the rest put them out? My captains are confused about their orders."

"There are things happening in Karnak which, as a member of the armed forces, one must not question."

Baffled, Ramesses saluted, straightened his dagger-belt and departed to do his master's bidding.

****

27.

AY

Eyes darting; glinting ... unfathomable.

Akhenaten is obsessed with his Creator.

I have a more practical purpose. Control of power is ruthless. One hand must take, the other retain.

Amon's destruction was my idea.

***

TIYE

Surely my son cannot know what is going on.

Grey-and-blue mist fills the valley. Blackened obelisks mount to the skies. The sun flushes pink and vermilion. Egypt is burning ...

***

AKHENATEN

Stone shatters. Pylons break. Tyrant heads scatter. Arguably my forefathers' images cast in Amon's likeness. Freedom to them.

***

Looking entirely made of marble, Akhenaten sat on his throne. He was in profile, slouching slightly, and clearly displeased. His slender figure, encased in a long flowing robe, gave him an aura of majestic authority. In his left hand he held a slackened leash to which was tethered a small plesiosaur.

"I don't care," he was saying. "Just fix it, Walter."

"But no one is going to believe me."

"Why not?"

"We're still trying to prove the theory, of course, but –"

"You're taking far too long!"

Akhenaten's brow creased, and he sank a little further into his great stone chair. His reptile opened her red mouth wide and hissed. Despite the transmitter between them, Walter jumped back.

"Try to understand," he said, collecting himself, "people don't want to believe you're Moses."

"I don't care what they *want* to believe," Akhenaten snapped, holding out a palm full of crushed seaweed to his pet. "If I had left my people to their own devices, they would still be worshipping idols and performing orgiastic rites in their temples."

"They did – for several thousand years after your death." The scientist rubbed his eyes. He was utterly exhausted. "You're *Pharaoh*," he reasoned. "The Bible isn't exactly flattering in its portrayal of Egypt's monarchs."

"You can't expect it to be, but the fact remains the Jews got all their good ideas from us. Or maybe it was the other way around if you wish to think I was Jewish. Velikovsky certainly had the axe out for me because he thought I wasn't!"

"Which brings me to another point: Do you ever get confused about your national identity?"

"National identity was never the primary reason for the revolution. God was. Now get to work and drum something up. Goodness knows I'm deeply sick of my memory being erased – or worse."

"I understand."

"No, you don't!" Akhenaten turned to face the archaeologist. "I can't tell you how heartily sick I am of being labelled everything from a weak king to a Nazi. It's all nonsense." Walter noticed a flush rising up the dead king's neck. "I loved my father, as I did my wife and children. If I wanted to give Nefertiti the Double Crown and treat her like an equal, pardon me for being light years ahead! Your depraved minds even spread lies that I was having an affair with my son, Smenkhare. Yes, I hugged him occasionally. You hug your son, don't you, Walter?"

"Of course I do, but –"

Unable to continue, Akhenaten waved an imperial hand in disgust.

"But nothing!"

"But you aren't Moses," Walter persisted, trying to steer them back to the original subject.

"I beg your pardon?"

"Every second king in your family is either an Ah-moses, or Tuthmosis, but you aren't. You're an Amenhotep."

Akhenaten appeared stunned.

"All members of my dynasty were named Amenhotep *and* Tuthmosis. And, what other king of Egypt said there was only one god?"

"No one," Walter admitted sheepishly.

"That's right, and you can tell those idiots of your time that only an Egyptian could have written the Mosaic law. We had forty-three books of Thoth, you know, the god of wisdom you replaced with the archangel Michael. Have you ever read the Ten Commandments? They are Egyptian laws. The Pentateuch is a body of *law*. Those books of Thoth were brought out to settle legal disputes." He leaned forward as if talking to a weak-minded child. "Like the Pentateuch."

Walter swallowed. He felt as if his very soul was grazed by the fire of authority which had suddenly manifested itself in the hitherto cynical and remote figure.

"Perhaps the God of the Old Testament is explained after all," he muttered.

"Speak up!"

"Moses was very pharaonic, wasn't he?"

"You mean tyrannical?" Akhenaten's mouth swept upwards into a contemptuous curve. "I suppose you could say that, but you live in a soft and cosseted world. In our day there wasn't even a proper dentist. If you ate too much honey you wound up with a toothache, which could eventually kill. And in every other way we were closer to death than you could possibly imagine."

"I don't see what that has to do with an unkind god."

"So, you think He was unkind?"

"I think Freud was right. Whatever was on Mount Sinai was more reminiscent of an evil spirit than God."

"I see." Akhenaten was silent.

"And you, or whoever Moses was, was simply a clever and terrifying magician."

"Possibly, but your type of people terrify easily."

Having digested the last of her seaweed, the dinosaur heaved an enormous sigh and flopped full-length onto the marble dais. Placing one flipper over the other, she closed her eyes and shut out the world.

"I need proof," Walter said doggedly. "Lucky for you, no one thinks the body in cache fifty-five is yours."

Akhenaten winced.

"What happened to my family ... was an unavoidable tragedy."

"I had forgotten that Moses abandoned all those who loved him."

"Not at all. I loved my family." Akhenaten appeared to ease under the flow of argumentative discussion. Indeed, Walter observed cannily, he thrived under it, not unlike a barrister. "I *was* dictatorial," the king admitted candidly. "But pharaohs and other world leaders were in those days. There was no other type of leader but a supreme one. Democracy came with the Greeks. Anyway," he said with a flicker of amusement, "your type of democracy in America is bought with money, I believe."

"That's rich coming from you."

Akhenaten laughed.

"I *was* rich. A lot of your historians keep mumbling on about how I lost the empire. Balderdash! They should look to Ramesses-the-Great for that. I was the wealthiest king in history, after I took back what was legally mine. Your historians never mention that. They prefer to see me as old, blind, and sick. Do you know why that is? I'll tell you. It's because I appeared half woman in my statues, and it prejudiced my case in the eyes of the male historians. You never thought I might be ill. You couldn't bear for me to be Moses. LOOK AT HIM, was the cry! That's what you've all been saying for the last two centuries. Apart from anything else, your xenophobic hatred of Egyptians keeps you from the truth." Akhenaten's face had turned away from Walter. He was observing something in mid-distance. "Do you know how lonely Moses would have been?" he asked. "A Jew at Pharaoh's court was not the problem. To be Egyptian among the Jews – now there was the rub!" He rose to his feet and stretched slim, heavily bangled arms before him. "Whenever I get lonely, I think of Jesus. He was a Jew, rejected by Jews. He was embraced by the Gentiles, but you transformed him into a white man. If someone his colour walks into your Sunday congregation you treat him as you do the inferior races."

"There are no inferior races."

Akhenaten smiled wanly.

"I declared that truth thirty-one centuries ago in my great poem." Abruptly he turned to Walter. "Incidentally, since you mentioned cache number fifty-five, did you like the little verse under the feet of my beloved wife?"

"I'm having more trouble explaining the contents of cache fifty-five than my whereabouts to my own wife on any given day of the week."

A grin split the face of the king. It was a beautiful smile of dazzling white. In that moment Walter realised how charismatic this man must have been with his elongated face, sloe eyes, and porcelain skin. At least it looked porcelain in this black-and-white world of monitors and goodness-knows-what-dimension.

"It's not my fault your scientists botched up their tomb invasions and can't work out who's who in my family. Besides, it's not important. I think you should concentrate on proving that I'm Moses. It'd help a lot of people."

That high self-esteem could only come from Akhenaten, thought Walter. Aloud he said: "I'm trying. I need a few more clues to add to the evidence." But Akhenaten's back was facing him as he encouraged the plesiosaur to budge from her comfort zone. "Another thing, Your Majesty," the scientist called out. "Before you go."

"Yes?" Akhenaten turned to face him, winding the leash around his hand as his pet growled and wiped her eyes.

“Why do you own a dinosaur? They didn't live in your day.”

“You wanted a clue. Come on, girl.”

Without another word, he walked the elephantine creature off their dais.

“Of course – the Leviathan from Psalm One Hundred and Four. Have a nice swim, Bessie!”

As if in response, a great screech emitted from the creature just before the monitor went dead.

***

28.

AKHENATEN

This city is like no other. I take my horses, Lightning and Thunder, around its outskirts with my beautiful wife, and sometimes one or two of our daughters. Egypt has never worshipped one true god. Now it will.

For all time.

***

NEFERTITI

I love the city. Egypt's heart beats at its core. As Aten's globe irradiates the land, so Akhet-Aten is the molten core of the Creator's will on earth. My husband and daughters are its arms.

... I long for a son.

***

A white melting orb climbed Akhet-Aten's firmament. City roads, swept clear as the dawn sky which hovered overhead, were hastily fumigated with limestone-dust, natron, and pumice. The central garbage dump had been set alight the day before, sending thousands of rats scurrying into the desert hills. Garlands hung over fence posts along the royal route. Priests and peasants alike, lined the main thoroughfare, considered to be the longest stretch of road in the modern world.

A parade for the king and queen marked their official arrival in their city. Waiting patiently for several hours, much of the crowd had taken to purchasing food and drink from a series of stalls set up along the processional route. Others amused themselves in small talk, while children played in makeshift creches.

Slowly, the first floats of the parade swam into view. A fleet of carriages, crammed with Mazoi police, accompanied a host of priests, chanting a new hymn written by the king. Children arrayed in colourful robes, and bearing red and blue pennants, sang happily in the bright morning sunshine. Soon the king and queen would sweep past in a spectacle which threatened to outdo those of the late Amenhotep-the-Magnificent. Waiting with a group, Horemheb scuffed the dust.

"Please don't do that," Maya implored, fastidiously, shaking the dirt off his sandals.

"Fancy footwear," the general commented, noting the intricate beadwork on his friend's leather uppers.

"They're new. I could procure you a pair."

"Standard army issue suits me fine."

Horemheb smirked to himself, before suddenly catching the eye of a girl in the crowd. She was about his age and standing nearby with her family. A comely maiden's interest was not new to the officer, but open disdain was uncommon. He turned away rapidly. Akhenaten's chariot descended on them.

The new king waved to the crowd, his face as radiant as the sun he worshipped. Arms clasped around her husband's waist, Nefertiti seemed transported to another world.

"Let's go," Horemheb said shortly. "We've seen enough."

"I want lunch."

"There's a place in the city I know. It serves the spicy meat you enjoy."

Maya's face was instantly illuminated at the thought of sustenance. Abruptly, he caught sight of an aristocratic group next to them.

"That young lady wants to speak to you, Hump," he said, nudging his friend.

"What lady?"

Maya nodded towards the teenager standing close to Horemheb. To the latter's horror, Maya turned to her.

"This is my colleague, General Horemheb. He's the brightest star in *Kemet*'s army. General, meet Armenia. She is her parents' only daughter."

Horemheb smiled faintly, but fear emanated from his eyes. The maiden inclined her head.

"I've heard much about you. None of it good."

Turning away, she rejoined her parents, who were conversing with Ay and his wife. Maya was aghast.

"How rude! I'm sorry. She's normally never like this, I assure you."

"Lord Maya!" Ay's clipped tones were unmistakable. "It's wonderful to see you, and the redoubtable Horemheb." He beamed warmly at the general, taking him into a bone-breaking hug. "Congratulations on your safe arrival last night. May I introduce our youngest daughter, Mutnodjmet?"

Horemheb greeted the child with a polite nod. Resuming his conversation with her proud father, they chatted for several minutes, before the older statesman moved away to mingle with other officials and dignitaries.

"He chewed the fat with you for a while," commented Maya, visibly impressed.

"I spent a fortune on Nefertiti."

"So, Lord Maya." Armenia was suddenly upon them, her eyes filled with mockery. "Is it going to be your godfatherly habit to introduce army boors to me in place of respectable suitors?"

The general was horrified.

"You're her *godfather*?"

"As you can see," a flustered Maya replied, "he is an aristocrat and a close friend of the Divine Father Ay."

"So is my father." The girl was now eating grapes from a passing hawker's display. "Care for some?" Unexpectedly, she thrust the bunch towards Horemheb.

"N-no," he stuttered, his mouth dry from anger.

"I will," Maya offered, sampling the ripe fruit with gusto. "We must go," he announced, his taste buds aroused. "Horemheb and I have to be somewhere."

***

The cramped inn was dingy and dark, but it was clear the general felt at home. Several soldiers greeted him with deep respect. Female musicians flirted openly, and dancers exercised their seduction techniques on their regular customer.

The proprietor immediately sent complimentary drinks of foaming beer to the rough trestle, where the general and Maya were seated.

Wiping an index finger across the plain acacia table, the latter inspected it for dust and found none. A topless girl approached them, smiling widely.

"I'll have the usual." Horemheb glanced at his companion. "Mega-helpings today, with yoghurt and all the sauces."

Ignoring the girl's fluttering eyelashes, he resumed conversing with his friend. Maya, on the other hand, gazed at her agog, and tried not to spill his beer.

"You frequent this place on a regular basis, I see," the gossipy courtier observed, adjusting his low-slung body on his stool.

"Army swill isn't the best form of nourishment. Besides, I like the service."

"And it likes you," his friend concurred, a sparkle in his eye.

Shortly, steaming meat platters with condiments, loaves of freshly baked bread, and even a pitcher of wine which they had not requested, arrived. Clean cutlery, napkins, and cheap, chunky goblets were added to the feast. Devouring the repast in silence, Maya was suffused with a warm glow. Wiping his fingers on a napkin, he helped himself to the carafe of sweet, white Memphis wine. Although he preferred Pharaoh's dry vintages, Maya imbibed it with lip-smacking satisfaction. Horemheb ripped apart his flat pancake of bread.

"You can thank the king for making free enterprise the order of the day, Maya."

"Every undertaking Akhenaten embarks on is without precedent."

"But I do enjoy the liberty at Thebes," the general stated, wiping beer froth from his upper lip. "Unlike you, I can do what I please."

"Ah, but unlike Thebes, it's relaxed at the court of Akhet-Aten. There is plenty of room for advancement for those young and bright enough to secure Akhenaten's favour. With respect to Queen Tiye, it's time you moved from the old city and made your permanent home up here."

Placing a hunk of coarse gritty bread on his sideboard, the general swigged his beer, before ordering another.

"I'm a soldier," he belched. "Pharaoh promotes me, and I don't have to make court appearances."

"You're more than a soldier. Think of all the friends you've made while still young. Most senior courtiers would happily trade half their gold for an audience with our Divine Father, Ay. Today he clasped you to his bosom and conversed with you at length."

"That snake!" Horemheb scoffed, attacking his gums with a duck bone. "Knowing people like Ay makes having enemies redundant." He grew suddenly serious. "I do have friends in respectable circles, but I don't seek them out for political ends. For reasons best known to himself, Pharaoh keeps advancing my station without ever granting me an interview. In Lord Ay's case, I wanted to wed his daughter, but nothing came of it." Sighing, he pushed his chair back, and loosened the gold-plated Horus buckle around his stomach. "Now all I desire is to preserve Egypt's borders from her foreign foes."

Maya sipped his wine and gazed into space. It occurred to him that Horemheb had never made overtures to any woman, apart from Nefertiti. It must have been true love, he reflected. No wonder the general preferred to remain in Thebes!

They listened in silence to an Egyptian love-song rendered by a female singer at the front of the bar. Perhaps Akhenaten, being a poet, understood the extent of Horemheb's feelings for the queen who could never be his. In sharing the same love, maybe he wished to somehow compensate. And possibly, Maya thought, stroking his chin thoughtfully, the same reasoning lay behind the king's refusal to grant an audience to one of his most distinguished servants.

"You and Ramesses – that is to say, Parnefer – are increasingly close, I hear," Maya said at the conclusion of the performance.

"We're like brothers," Horemheb shouted above the applause. "Always competing on the battlefield, in the study hall – always striving to reach a higher level of accomplishment. Ram's a brilliant soldier, too."

The singer began another lay in a sonorous voice. The inn quietened while she wailed in a strangely mournful key.

"It's good to befriend someone with common interests," Maya agreed, leisurely sampling a dessert of hot cream and nuts. "I think you should come to court – say Thursday, after chariot riding? Bring Ram, too."

***

Multicoloured mudbrick columns soared into the lapis firmament. Light filled every chamber. Open sky supplanted the roofs of courtyards and apartments in the bright, spacious temple complex. Every gaily painted mural celebrated life and movement. At the palace, the naturalistic style of the walkways and outer courtyard gave way to an unusual, even distorted, rendering of the king and his family.

Although forewarned, Ramesses gazed at the art, deeply perplexed.

"Some of these were painted by Pharaoh himself," said Maya, vainly attempting to make conversation with the dour brigadier. The latter glanced helplessly at Horemheb, who was trying not to laugh.

"Thank you for inviting me," the guest managed.

"It was no bother, believe me," replied Maya, whose hands fluttered nervously over his freshly pressed robes. They reached a large hall where a familiar figure sat on a dais at the far end. "Over here," he directed, adjusting his cape.

"It's Akhenaten." Ramesses looked to Horemheb for support. "I don't recognise him. He's changed."

It was true. The king of Egypt, positioned in the morning sun, appeared so dazzling in his cloak of white-and-gold, he resembled a luminescent being rather than a human.

"It's only the sun," Horemheb reassured. "You'll find Akhenaten refreshingly informal these days."

Taking no chances, the visitor fell face forward in prostration. Noticing Horemheb's ease in the presence of Pharaoh, his colleague forced himself to relax. Akhenaten leaned forward. His expression was benign and interested.

"Welcome! We already know our general intimately. It will be good to acquaint ourselves better with his greatest friend."

He exchanged understanding looks with Nefertiti, whom Ramesses suddenly noticed. Could it be, he wondered, that Pharaoh's presence was so charismatic that all surroundings paled in comparison to him? Regardless of the sun, the energy around Akhenaten was so searingly powerful, he almost appeared to be radiating light. While the brigadier pondered the godship of kings, Nefertiti arose with a group of her ladies-in-waiting.

"You must come with me," she invited, taking the officer's elbow. "I'll show you the palace. He's a handsome one too!"

She laughingly directed her last remark to her husband, who immediately joined in with her.

"Don't be too long," he called. "Otherwise I might send out a search party!"

Shaken by the royal couple's familiarity, so different from the public formality of Amenhotep and Queen Tiye, Ramesses followed the vision of loveliness and her handmaidens. While Nefertiti conversed in a lilting tongue, he gazed at her. Occasionally nodding, he scarcely registered a word she was saying. No wonder Horemheb was still in love with her.

At last Nefertiti reached a light blue door. She pushed it ajar. Her lodger gazed blankly around at the room covered in blue flying ducks.

"This room is yours for the duration of your stay. We assume you're on annual leave."

"I am, madam."

"I'm pleased," she laughed. "Otherwise Akhenaten would be forced to pry you away from the barracks!"

She followed his eyes to the paintings.

"They're delightful, aren't they? This is Smenkhare's room. Our eldest boy is in Thebes for the summer holidays. I'm sure he would love to have you here."

Smiling prettily, the Great Wife picked up her flowing pink diaphanous gown, and departed with her trail of lovely women. Ramesses sat down heavily on the edge of the heir's bed.

"What have I done to deserve this?" he addressed the wall.

***

As their first week in the new city ended, Horemheb found an increasing freedom in their stay. Ever the gracious hosts, Akhenaten and Nefertiti left their guests to their own devices. Although their every whim was attended to, the soldiers had time to swim, fish, and unwind. Ramesses, however, seemed gloomy and introspective.

One afternoon, as Horemheb merrily splashed among the lotuses of their private pond, his friend suddenly expressed his true feelings.

"I hate those ducks!" he exclaimed vehemently, throwing a pebble into the water and narrowly missing his superior. "In fact, I hate ALL the paintings in this wretched house, don't you?"

Cautiously, Horemheb emerged from the watery depths. He wiped a piece of lotus leaf from his eyes.

"Take it easy, Ram. You'll be going back to Thebes soon enough. In the meantime, enjoy yourself. It's not every day the king of Egypt takes a personal interest in one of his subjects."

"The only place I want to be is at my home in the Delta with my family," Ramesses affirmed. "You're good to me," he added in a different tone. "Bringing me to court. Most people would hog the honour to themselves, but not you."

"I forget you're married," Horemheb replied quietly. "How is Seti, by the way?"

On hearing his son's name mentioned, the proud father's eyes lit up.

"Bursting with health! Such a brilliant little chap, too. Do you know what he said to me the other day? 'Papa' he said, and mind you he's only three ..."

A small curve appeared on Horemheb's face. He waded to where his friend was seated, and hauled himself out of the pool. Drying himself with a linen towel, he listened for the remainder of the afternoon.

*∗∗

29.

AKHENATEN

We have been here for a month. The land slips away to the sea. Houses hurtle skywards in a frenzy of building activity.

My Chief Minister, Abner, is happy. He can worship a single god in peace. I wonder if there is more to God.

And whether he knows it.

***

NEFERTITI

Exhaustion sighs from the Nile. The pace is unrelenting. With my husband's ingenuity, we are building a city faster than anything that has gone before. Workers carry small bricks under their arms. There is less backbreaking struggle to build monuments than in King Amenhotep's time. However, I *do* wish whitewash would come.

The children are playing in the noonday heat. Nanny Tee has taken our eldest, Meritaten, for a walk. I'm minding Meketaten and little Ankhsenpaaten. (Our third daughter is heartbreakingly lovely.)

Lady Kia, a Mitannian princess, bore sons for us – two boys. Smenkhare, her first-born, is playing his flute, gifted to him by his grandmother. Discordant notes are hurting my sire's ears. The famous Lord Ay would never bear a moment's disharmony from anyone else. Instead, the doting grandfather places a white kerchief over throbbing temples and hopes the little heir will someday improve.

***

AKHENATEN

My wife is laughing as if she heard an amusing joke. We smile into each other's eyes. A breeze floats up from the Nile and rustles my heavy draperies. Children play at our feet.

In the distance I hear a flute.

***

At last all the children were crammed into the artist's studio. The smell of wet clay and fresh paint wafted through the spacious room which overflowed with portrait busts, wooden frames, and brushes.

"Get the royal daughters together," the master sculptor Tuthmosis ordered crisply.

Apprentices rapidly obeyed, stacking unfinished sculptures and sketches to one side as they made room for the family. Pharaoh gazed down at his queen, and kissed her tenderly on the forehead. Euphoric at being in his favourite environment of an art studio, Akhenaten barely noticed the discomfort experienced by various members of his court and family. Draping an arm around his beloved wife, he hummed blissfully to himself. She, in turn, nuzzled his neck and closed her eyes.

"I'm going to be sick," Horemheb muttered to Maya as they sat in a far corner, awaiting their turn to be recorded for posterity.

"Jealousy won't get you anywhere," said the accountant, waving at the noisy princesses.

To his delight, Ankhsenpaaten waved back, while the youngest, Setepenre, gurgled and steadfastly refused to co-operate with anyone.

"Are the artists really going to record this?" the general grumbled, fussing with his shift, which was becoming more crumpled with each passing hour. "It looks as though the circus came to town. There is no order anywhere."

"This is *art*."

"Everywhere I go I see the most awful pictures of Pharaoh's wife and daughters."

Horemheb eyed Setepenre, as if acknowledging a fellow soul in torment.

"Our king wants his subjects to know what he and his family truly look like, Hump."

"Rubbish! Nefertiti is the most gorgeous woman in the world, and they depict her as a deformed goblin. I sincerely hope they don't portray me in that manner."

"Or me," Maya smiled.

***

30.

AKHENATEN

Nile breezes blow across our balcony during the hot afternoon. Surfacing hippos regard me with round, black eyes. They twitch their abnormally small ears and submerge. I enjoy watching them. It is as though they are regarding me with intelligence ... apprehending ... thinking. This afternoon, however, I am in a black mood.

The priests killed my brother. I never told anyone what I thought, but they knew. They say Dhutmose had TB. They say I killed him, either accidentally in a fight, or deliberately to gain the throne. (One story says I saw him strike a Jew, so I killed him and hid the body in the sand.) They even say I am a foreigner.

It's all lies. Some Egyptians are jealous. I *hire* foreigners. I have a Jewish chief minister, although these idiots seem to forget that Jews, like any other race in Egypt, are considered to be Egyptian. We are all part of the same melting pot. My brother was a victim, and not of me. He's the reason I fought Amon. No one else in my family was going to die. That's why I shifted capital.

I grip the balcony rails overlooking the Nile. They gleam in the afterglow of sunset. If I have blood on my hands it is justified.

I had to save the monarchy.

***

Horemheb stamped his foot irritably, while Maya adjusted a black ceremonial wig over his sweating scalp. Having survived the portrait sitting in Akhet-Aten, the duo was now trapped in the longest meeting of their careers in Thebes.

The king's men were discussing the authority of the temple. So carefully circumscribed were the limits of power, that several weighty papyrus tomes, containing more legal jargon than the Books of Thoth, had been consulted for half the day. Witnesses of the Truth were summoned for advice. Religious ambassadors for Akhenaten, were deliberating the significance of each word.

"I'm tired of waiting," Horemheb snapped.

"Do calm down," Maya murmured plaintively.

He glanced at a row of priests who were viewing the pair with interest.

"How can I? I'm general of an unemployed army!"

"You're giving yourself airs."

"At least I'm not the one behaving like an effeminate pudding."

Glaring at the priests, Horemheb made several blush and avert their eyes.

"Now that you've given vent to your ill temper, not to mention corresponding manners, let me tell you this." Maya waved a pudgy index finger. "Your army *is* being used. Pharaoh has fought and won a battle with the gods of Egypt. No one in history has ever instituted the worship of one god. Aten needs to be established, and for that to happen, we need the full co-operation of the armed forces."

"What about my battles? It's all very well for you to talk. You were built to sit and wait. I'm primed for action."

"Let me tell you, mathematics is a very active mode of being."

"Akhenaten appoints capable people to spend all year staring at the walls." The muscular form leaned forward. "I'm going completely mad."

Maya squeaked and adjusted his wig.

"Learn to be patient, Hump."

"Akhenaten is the hump. On my back! I feel like a camel with two hundredweight of food and water, and no desert in which to roam."

"Then you're a lucky camel. You won't run out of provisions."

As the meeting ended, the weary pair made their way to a palace dinner. Trestles piled high with platters of meat, vegetables, and fruit was a welcome conclusion to the meeting.

The courtiers took their places. Their families were already seated, surrounded by strangers and friends alike. Oil lamps were lit, and incense kept mosquitoes at bay.

A girl timidly touched Meryt's arm.

"Who's that man?"

"Maya, Chief Treasurer."

"I don't mean the fat one, but the god seated next to him."

"I'm glad," Meryt laughed. "The generously proportioned man is my husband. The other is Horemheb, leader of our armies. He's extremely grumpy. Pharaoh's men are taking far too much of his time approving our by-laws!"

"He's handsome," the admirer replied, drinking in the visage of the military man with greedy eyes.

"I can arrange an introduction, Armenia."

"Oh no!" She shrank back. "I wouldn't know what to say."

"You can start with 'good evening'." Meryt rose. "I need to see my husband, anyway. He'll be shopping once we we're finished here. Nobody chooses cuts of meat like my darling."

Grasping Armenia's hand, the noblewoman propelled her into an empty seat beside the general. Then, pleased with her efforts at matchmaking, Meryt squeezed into a space next to her spouse. Maya kissed her enthusiastically. Murmuring sweet nothings, they held hands and tittered like schoolchildren.

Armenia remained silent, wondering what to do, while Horemheb glowered into space, refusing to participate in meaningless pleasantries. Eventually, Meryt tore herself away from her husband. Noting the awkward silence between the young people, opened the conversation.

"I believe congratulations are in order," she addressed Horemheb, while smiling encouragingly at Armenia.

"It's beyond me why the court even bothered. At least as a lowly foot soldier I had no expectation of my station."

"Were you a foot soldier?"

The general folded his arms and compressed his lips.

"I was a famous charioteer." He glanced at the female who had the temerity to address him directly. "Before your time."

"You look so young," she blurted.

Meryt laughed kindly. Armenia flushed.

"I'm not." Horemheb smiled despite his mood. "My twenty-third birthday was last month.

"I'm sixteen."

"It's high time you were married."

Having lost interest, the general resumed his silent brooding. In an hour's time he was meant to take a walk with Maya. Having never seen the portly treasurer walk anywhere, Horemheb was intrigued. It was sunset and he knew they had to hurry if they were to enjoy the hour at dusk.

Eventually, the little courtier kissed Meryt farewell, adjusted his wig and rose from his comfortable cushioned chair. He made a sign to Horemheb, and the pair departed the banqueting hall into the fresh desert air of Thebes.

***

Ambling through the perseas which lined the mortuary temple of the late King Amenhotep-the-Magnificent, Maya and Horemheb enjoyed a glorious sunset of mashed pink and gold. It was the accountant's favourite time of day and he loved the peace of the west bank. Passionate about architecture, his spirits soared in this place which contained several houses of eternity, including Hatshepsut's extraordinary temple. No one mentioned the queen who dared to be Pharaoh, although Maya felt it was hard to forget such a grand lady when her memory was preserved in the classic lines of a temple built for her by her lover, Senenmut. So striking was the building, it even distracted passersby from the stupendous wealth of Amenhotep's mortuary temple.

Now the friends, who were chatting amiably, approached a gold-plated fence leading to the late king's fabulous complex.

"You know, Hump, there's more to life than an army career," said Maya, swinging open the main gate.

"The army is my entire life. I didn't have your advantages."

"I see," Maya replied diplomatically, knowing full well his friend was descended from nobility. Despite the various stories circulated about Horemheb's life, the accountant knew the truth. It had only taken one afternoon in the Hall of Records. Every detail was recorded for posterity: The military lineage, the aristocratic father, and the mother who had died when her only son was three. No doubt, Horemheb had never forgiven his father for dumping him in a tough army boarding school, and leaving for the sandy shores of Crete, never to be seen again.

Approaching the mortuary temple of King Amenhotep, the pair entered through the ornate double-doors, and found themselves strolling on floors of solid silver. Horemheb stopped to gaze about him.

"We are surrounded by columns of gold," Maya explained in his best tour-guide manner. "The ceiling's electrum. I come here to think." Ignoring a flock of curious monks, the treasurer sat on the base of a gleaming column. "By allowing me to concentrate on higher things, I am able to put my life into focus."

"A logical pre-requisite to counting Pharaoh's silver and gold."

"Throw all the barbs you want," Maya responded. "As I was saying, Lady Armenia is a catch. You should take her out."

"That whippersnapper? I remember her now from the town square at Akhet-Aten – your goddaughter, no less. You should have taught her some manners when she was a baby. Now it's too late. She's missed out on a husband."

"Let me put it another way." Maya gazed up at a bas-relief which depicted Pharaoh and his wife locked in a formal embrace. "You are head of the army. What's the next step?"

"War."

"Marriage."

"She's not even good-looking," Horemheb objected.

"Clearly you didn't pay a scrap of attention to the lady, otherwise you would have realised that she's stunning. Her skin, alone, is exquisite." Maya kissed his fingers.

"One of us obviously noticed. Why don't *you* date her?"

"I am not only happily married, but my heart is for my wife alone. In short, I am in love."

Horemheb's laughter echoed in the high metallic chamber.

"Meryt is a wonderful woman. Are you sure she feels the same way about you?" he teased.

Maya nodded vigorously.

"Love makes everything worthwhile. It's the perfume of life."

"And you reek of it! Fine," Horemheb added soothingly, "I will date your nymph, but mind, if she bores me, I will send the trollop packing."

***

31

LORD AY

Stratospheric rise.

Appointed Commander-of-the-Horse and Divine Father, I am the king's most trusted friend. More honour is paid to me than anyone in the realm.

Naturally, I have detractors. I pay no heed. They usually disappear within the week.

As the beloved queen's father, my status is obvious. My only serious rival is Horemheb.

***

A huge shout erupted as the populace of Akhet-Aten roared its homage to the king who had released grain from Karnak. The priests had tried to burn it as part of a strategy to starve the new city of supplies. Fuelled by their hatred of Akhenaten, the holy men attempted to turn the tables on him, to no avail. With Queen Tiye in Thebes, the plot had failed miserably.

Flour and grain had been distributed since early morning. Together with his mother, Akhenaten had shipped grain from the priests' silos to his city, which was now under heavy guard. Oblivious to their nation's crisis, children played stick ball among the dusty legs of the citizens, who swilled beer, and ate kebabs on their day off.

Removed from the jostling masses, Horemheb and Maya found themselves a shady area for their friends, families, and other members of their burgeoning retinues.

"Where's Lord Ay?" Maya asked in his high-pitched voice.

"The King's father-in-law is due to arrive at Akhet-Aten next month." The general peeled an apple with his exquisitely decorated bronze dagger. "When it's completed," he added with a sly grin.

"He keeps trundling back and forth like you," commented Maya. "No doubt the Divine Father's busy in Thebes." He proceeded to fan himself with a palm frond. "My word, it's hot! Even in the morning this desert boils my blood."

"What are you talking about? It's full of trees."

"Not enough of them."

Horemheb turned his attention to a small group of children.

"Whose are those?"

"Mine," was the succinct response.

Maya's shoulders slumped as he realised his extra bodily activity was causing more sweat to exude from his pores. A personal fanbearer attended to the treasurer with vigour.

"I thought they looked familiar. Why are they running wild?"

"New law. Pharaoh thinks it's healthy for everyone to be natural, including children. It certainly relieves me of the responsibility of keeping them quiet."

The general lifted his brows.

"I would suggest ten days at the Syrian border for drumming discipline into the urchins!"

"That's why you don't have children. God would feel obliged to reassign them."

"Discipline is important. Now I realise why, not only your children, but also Akhenaten's, are an unruly lot."

Maya chuckled.

"Princess Meritaten is the worst. She's supposed to be the eldest, but I see very little good example being shown to the others."

"Ankhsenpaaten is my favourite. She's quiet. And very beautiful."

"Don't mention that within her parents' hearing. Everybody's trying to marry her off."

"There's plenty of time. She will mature, I suspect, like a fine wine."

"Speaking of fine wines, how's Armenia?"

"Adjusting to a warrior's lifestyle. Army wives must learn how to adapt."

"No doubt," Maya affirmed politely.

The crowds began to get noisier as the royal couple swept into view. They soon disappeared on their way to inspect the grain.

"Come to my house for a beer," Maya offered. "Or wine. We are making our own. It's a bit new, like everything else in this city, but has a reasonable bouquet."

"I should be delighted."

Beckoning his officers, Horemheb moved through the throngs of noblemen, who parted to make way. Collecting his family, it took Maya considerably longer than his friend.

Eventually, their individual parties gathered on the roof of his mansion where they spent the remainder of a sweltering afternoon sampling beverages from the accountant's well-stocked cellar.

***

In Thebes, the distracted dowager rotated her gold bracelets on her wrists. She was trying to think, but it was the middle of summer, and she was painfully aware the summons from Akhet-Aten meant a journey into a city of blazing heat.

Approached by yet another messenger she reflected it was becoming a regular occurrence. It was as if her son wanted his mother by his side. In the wake of her husband's death it was not a bad idea. Tiye reflected she could have a greater influence over the empire if she was close to the king. Nefertiti, however, was now the Great Wife. Akhenaten listened to her. Like her father Ay, Nefertiti was ambitious. Outwardly the epitome of femininity, Tiye reflected she was cannier and more ruthless than anyone in the family. It was one reason Tiye would heed the call to Akhet-Aten. Aware it was a good excuse to speak sense to her son, she knew it would also not bode well for her, or Thebes, should she refuse.

Meantime, the household was in disarray as the servants packed for both her and Beketaten. The youngest child of Amenhotep-the-Magnificent, Beketaten had been born a few months after her father's death. Tiye was secretly disappointed the newcomer had not been a boy.

However, the child surprised her. The little girl's wit and humour reminded the older woman of herself when she was young.

Already Beketaten was reading and enjoying history. During the afternoons she left the nursery to sit in her mother's study, while the aging queen wrote. At first, the nurse had been at her wits' end, thinking she would be punished. But Tiye acquiesced to the child's needs, and a new daily routine emerged.

After lunch, Beketaten joined her mother. In fact, the child was often in her company for most of the day, sitting at meals, watching her at court, and writing with a child's stylus and palette in her study. It brought great comfort to the elder stateswoman in what was rapidly becoming a chaotic time.

"Let's move. Beketaten, are you ready?"

"Since dawn, Mother."

"Why does everyone take so long to do anything here? Kares, pack this basket and take it to the mules. Aanen, the bedding should have gone by now."

"*My* stuff's gone."

"Before your mother's? This could classify as treason! Perhaps I should flay someone alive. Who will it be, Bekky? Shall we pick on Kares? He's very old and has too much skin, anyway."

Beketaten giggled.

"Oh Mummy – don't! Look at him!"

The dowager noticed her butler drop a roll of bedding.

"I might order him to commit ritual suicide on my ruined mattress." Tiye turned away to allow her shamefaced manservant to retrieve her goods. "No matter – let's go. We'll wait by the lake. At this rate we might reach Akhet-Aten next year."

***

NEFERTITI

Gold, carnelian, chalcedony. Showering subjects with gifts. How many more collarettes can my husband fit around Lord Ay's neck?

240

Today is a great day.

***

Crowds thronged hot, white pavements. Vast pyramidal pylons soared into a cloudless cobalt sky. Cooling breezes from the Nile swept across the palace grounds where Pharaoh's subjects awaited his appearance. Noblemen stood silently in the front row. Wondering how much favour they might receive from the king, and whether any one of them would receive more than the others, they were an uncommonly quiet bunch.

Behind them, sentinels from the Mazoi stood in serried lines to keep order. Small town officials, artisans, and peasants formed the expectant horde of breathless humanity. The air hummed with the newness of a mission. All had abandoned their life in Karnak to follow the charismatic leader of Aten. Many had joined Akhenaten's family out of mere curiosity. Some did not have a reason. They came, that was all.

As the twelfth hour of the morning registered on the town sun dial, two slender figures, sheathed in transparent linen, stepped onto the balcony. Spontaneous cheering from the masses greeted the king's informal waving. His wife followed his example more stiffly. Akhenaten's radiance transmitted itself to all, including Lord Ay and Lady Tee standing before him.

Horemheb nudged Maya.

"Two guesses as to who receives the gold collarette."

But neither was prepared for the extent of wreaths and gold necklaces which dropped from their sovereign's hand to his in-laws. Weighed down with gold, Ay's prostrations appeared more pious than he intended.

"Lady Tee," the king finally announced, beckoning to the nurse. "For services to the royal house."

"Now I know you didn't predict *that*," Maya whispered in Horemheb's ear. "No woman has ever received such an honour."

The general blinked in the hot sunlight.

"Our king is full of surprises," he replied dourly.

Abandoning her royal hauteur, Nefertiti beamed in delight at her mother. Confused and overcome, the latter continued to prostrate herself. Eventually, the honoured in-laws were ushered into the main palace. Their ornaments were removed for comfort and the pair were led into the Great Hall to dine with Pharaoh and his family. Outside, food and beer were dispersed to the general populace. Rejoicing in the form of music and dancing carried on into the evening. Since little work was going to be done on the morrow, a holiday for two days had been declared.

***

"I have to confess I'm tired," Akhenaten admitted cheerfully.

Nefertiti took his face in her hands.

"You have made the Great Wife happy by honouring her parents today."

"It was my pleasure. Impossible to do in our old haunt." Kissing her tenderly, Akhenaten sat down on a comfortable settee. "Have you realised how easy everything is now?"

"It's wonderful," agreed Nefertiti. "The city is perfect, the palace magnificent. We're finally happy."

Akhenaten took her onto his lap and clasped her close to his slender frame.

"I have never felt like this," he murmured, kissing the top of her head. "We can finally worship the Aten in freedom."

"And rule," she added.

***

Ay slumped into a large cushion, flung on the sitting room floor.

"What a day," he muttered.

"It was overwhelming," his wife agreed.

242

"Everything is surreal." Pharaoh's father-in-law rubbed his face. Faint stubble cut reassuringly into his trembling palm. "It's as if my son-in-law is living in a world of his own."

"I hope you're not suffering from heatstroke."

"I've been a soldier for many years. I know what it is to sleep on the hard ground, among the reeds – even in the jungle."

Ay recounted places and activities, as if he needed to reassure himself of concrete reality again. The day's celebrations had left him feeling as if he was no longer centred.

"I need to get ready to babysit Beketaten," Tee interjected, changing the subject. "I'll pack a few things."

"Bekky? But she's at Thebes!"

"Queen Tiye arrives tomorrow morning. You had better get to bed," Tee suggested, noticing bags under her husband's eyes.

Before he could move Ay, dazed with the combination of the day's heat and strain, fell soundly asleep.

***

"When is my mother due, Abbie?" Akhenaten asked excitedly.

"This afternoon. Her Majesty wishes to be escorted from the barque to her apartment, after which she is to be served dinner, followed by a night's rest."

"So, she won't be worshipping with us at sunset," Akhenaten responded sadly.

"Not today, although she is content to fit in with Your Majesty's plans during the week." Abner set down his papyrus which contained the dowager's instructions. "I would suggest your mother is simply requesting a concession due her age. It is unlikely she would snub her favourite son whom she has travelled so far to visit."

"Indeed." Akhenaten seemed far away. "I suggest to you she has come on an errand, Abbie, and wishes to be ready to deliver Karnak's message in full possession of her faculties." Abner did not reply. "I need a walk," Pharaoh declared. "I'm writing a hymn to God's glory."

Row upon row of vines trailed over pergolas as the king and queen strolled under the trellis' shade. Eventually, sitting by his favourite pool, Akhenaten contemplated its waters broken by pink-and-blue lotuses. The afternoon was still as the Aten beat down with its relentless heat on the city's inhabitants in the grip of their afternoon siesta.

Gracefully, Akhenaten lowered his fragile fingers into the ice chill of the pond. Running his hand through the water, he scattered a nearby lily pad with pearly drops.

Insistent croaking heralded a frog's activity in one corner of the artificial tank, and several lime-green bodies splashed through the depths. The king watched their strong legs, breast-stroking under the shimmering, dappled water. He turned to Nefertiti.

"I have a song."

"May I hear it?"

"It opens with: 'O Aten, how manifold art thy works." He giggled. "It's very posh!"

"The poem's language is loftier than what you normally use."

"It has to be," Akhenaten pointed out reasonably. "God is high above us. His praises require the appropriate medium."

"I'll duet with you when it's finished."

"You have a marvellous voice. It will complement a great hymn which will last from generation to generation."

***

32.

Bright sunshine flooded a garden overflowing with flowers and humming insects. Akhenaten sat at his easel, clad in a loincloth. His taut, sinewy body was burned deep brown by the sun. A vaguely contemptuous expression swept across his face as a diffident man in a blue suit approached.

"Go away, I'm painting."

"You invited me, remember?"

The king wiped a square sponge across an emulsion of paint, crayon, and charcoal.

"You're smaller than when we last met," his guest observed.

"You're not used to seeing me old and naked."

Dipping his sponge into a yellow plastic bucket, the artist squeezed it dry and picked up a brush.

"Nevertheless," Walter continued, eyeing the emaciated legs, "you're exceedingly thin."

"My stomach's still in evidence."

"It's the way you're built."

"What do you think?" the king asked, appraising his painting.

"I can't understand why your work is so jolly ugly."

A low chuckle erupted.

"That's what Maya and Tutankhamen thought. Eventually, my son prettified art again. I can forgive him. He was beautiful." Flicking paint spots, Akhenaten produced the desired stippled effect on blades of grass in his landscape painting. "A regular little angel," he murmured. "Never cried as a baby. Such a *good* boy, you know. No wonder he thought the world a lovely place. We only paint from ourselves."

"That's not true."

"No?" Akhenaten sighed. "Then I must have been mistaken for the last three thousand, five hundred years."

"I came to tell you about a Muslim writer's theory on you," Walter said, changing the subject. "Ahmed Osman thinks you're Moses."

"An enlightened writer who honours my memory."

"Anyway, Psalm One Hundred and Four is traditionally credited to Moses, and we all know you wrote it."

Just then a splash of something monstrously large caught Walter's eye.

"I saw two dinosaurs running into the bushes," he said, drawing closer to Akhenaten.

"Bessie has a boyfriend."

"I didn't know *plesiosaurs* lived on land."

"They don't."

Unwilling to ask any further questions, Walter kept his eye on the bushes next to the pond, which were rustling with great momentum. A sound, eerily like a human laugh, rippled across the hot afternoon air.

Suddenly, a behemoth Walter recognised as Akhenaten's pet, leapt out of the bracken. Hunching herself into a ball, Bessie pounced on a shadow near the pool. Moments later, she was followed by an even larger version of herself who, after scant deliberation, landed belly-first on her back.

They slid in unison straight into the water, where they executed a series of dives to rival each other in height and width of splash.

The archaeologist shaded his eyes. He goggled with awe at the lavender monster with canary splotches and an orange head.

"The male is very brightly coloured."

"I created him from a design by Bak."

Akhenaten shut the easel.

"Doesn't that need to dry?"

"It's already dry." His host wiped gnarled hands on a black woollen towel, streaked with colours of the rainbow. "Tea?"

"No thanks."

"I forget you're not English. Come inside and have a drink of lemonade. Better still, I could pour you a martini."

Inside, Walter removed his jacket and accepted a cold drink.

"I don't see why you're blaming me for everything."

"I'm angry. It's as if I was never a king, never a prophet. Imagine if someone desecrated the graves of your presidents. Simply because I lived a long time ago doesn't give you the right to dishonour me."

"With due respect, scientific research justifies our tomb invasions, if that's what you mean."

"Nonsense! My son was exposed to the world, naked in death. Separate parts of him were displayed in front of a film camera, before some kind soul put him back together, and placed him back in his coffin. If I'd known this was going to happen, I'd have requested cremation for us all."

"I'm sorry," the scientist mumbled. He stepped into the cool marble interior of Akhenaten's main living room.

"Here is where I entertain."

"It's wonderfully cool! I never knew the fourth dimension could be so hot."

"Whoever said you were in the fourth dimension?" asked the surprised king.

"Ouspensky." Walter ripped his collar open. "You don't mind, do you?" he asked, removing his tie.

"I would prescribe a loincloth, but I know how prudish your world is. By the way, Ouspensky was wrong. There is no fourth dimension. So, Walt, what have you got for me?"

"It's not so much what I have for Your Majesty, as what you can do for me." To avoid a royal frown, he continued: "I'm wondering about your father."

"You're not going to write a book on *him*," exclaimed Akhenaten plaintively. "Goodness knows, he was better looking than me ... and a better builder."

"That's it, you see – he was a builder. People must have died during the construction of his monuments."

"Not that I can recall."

"And you both created differently. He had men groaning at the ropes, pulling his megaliths along, while you had people carrying those three-foot stones, called *talatat* bricks."

Pharaoh's eyes crinkled.

"I had to get my city built in a hurry."

"And there's an old story about your father, fulfilling an oracle's prophesy in order to claim the throne. He allegedly put the Jewish people in chains, until the oracle admitted his evil, leaving the door open for a repentant pharaoh to free them."

"I am who I say I am. You just have to look."

Abruptly the set vanished. Walter rubbed his eyes.

"You okay there, mate?" Abel asked with cheery consternation.

"You're a bit peaky," added George. "Do you need to lie down?"

"I'm fine," Walter muttered. "Where am I?"

"Where we've been since six o'clock this evening," George laughed. "At Karen's!"

The sleepy scientist looked at his wristwatch. It was quarter past two in the morning.

"I'd better be going. I have a big day ahead."

"Let's give you a lift home," Abel offered.

Karen regarded him quizzically.

"I think he'll be fine walking. Shall I escort you out?"

"Thanks," acknowledged Walter, relieved to get away from the bright lights. "How many people were there?" he asked as they approached the vestibule.

"About forty." Karen lowered her voice. "Did you black out?"

"Sort of."

She opened the main door. Walter realised how chilly the desert air was in comparison to his recent experience in Akhenaten's sauna-like world.

Karen, who was carrying the dazed man's overcoat, slipped it over his shivering shoulders.

"I didn't do anything stupid, did I?" he asked.

"You dozed off, that's all."

"I don't even remember coming here," Walter shuddered.

"Did you speak with *him*?" she asked timidly.

"I had an encounter with a crabby artist and a dinosaur."

Walter stepped into the Cairo night and breathed deeply. A man pushing a donkey-load of rotting oranges, passed him, beating the exhausted beast as they climbed uphill.

Tourist brochures glossed over the poverty of what had once been history's greatest superpower. A fate which probably lay in store for America one day, he mulled gloomily.

***

33.

My son does not realise the significance of his foolhardy actions. He has locked himself in a beautiful city of his own making.

***

Holding her son's hand, Tiye made every appearance of enjoying the strange temple. Akhenaten pointed to the altar.

"What do you think, Mother? Everything is open-air so that we can communicate with God."

"Who resembles Ra in his manifestations."

"After a fashion."

He guided her past throngs of bowing priests.

"I hope you don't have too many of those," Tiye remarked with dry humour. "Remember what happened last time."

"These priests serve God, not an idol."

"Everyone knows you worship the sun in its noonday form."

"Or Adonai," was the mysterious reply.

"Adonai, dear boy, is not the sun." Tiye beckoned to a fan bearer. "I need to rest. These old legs are incapable of holding me up any longer."

"My temple is on par with Karnak. We have been touring this complex for over an hour, Mother."

"Don't I know it," the dowager muttered under her breath.

"The artisans are over there," Pharaoh pointed, "recording your visit."

"I can only assume they caught my best side." Tiye glimpsed a padded seat in an alcove and hurried towards it, pulling along half her entourage. "That's so much better," she sighed happily, sinking into its purple cushion. "By the way, whose chair is this? It's designed in the old style."

"Lord Maya's."

"The mathematician?" Tiye's eyes crinkled in a similar manner to her brother's. "I recommended him for your cabinet. How is he faring?" She regarded the gilt arms. "This chair's as expensive as a throne."

"He's fine, and it was originally a throne." Akhenaten smiled mischievously. "From Thebes. Maya added a cushion for comfort."

"If memory serves me, I recall Maya carrying ample cushions."

"Mother!"

As the tour of the temple concluded, Pharaoh guided his visitor towards her litter. Shading her eyes from the glare, the diminutive queen stepped into its comfort. She glanced about her, before stabbing the air in outrage with one index finger.

"What, in Amon's name, is that?"

A colossal naked statue of the king, sporting elongated features, a sagging belly, and full hips without genitalia, affronted her eyes.

"One of my pylons."

"It's the living end!" Tiye exclaimed.

"It combines both the masculine and feminine components of God, which are manifested through me, His representative on earth."

"By Aten's disk, you look more like a woman than Nefertiti!"

Nearby noblemen muffled their laughter.

"It's an artistic device," the king responded coldly. "Are you comfortable?"

Realising he was about to be rid of her, Tiye glowered at Pharaoh, who raised his hand in farewell. Her litter bearers hoisted her onto their broad shoulders, and walked slowly towards the palace.

"*I* think they're beautiful." Nefertiti materialised close to her husband's elbow. He squeezed her hand affectionately.

"Let's take a chariot ride tonight after worship."

"Won't you be neglecting your mother?"

"She's had enough of the outdoors for one day," Akhenaten stated. "And I've had enough of her!"

Pushing aside the single sheet, Horemheb sat up. Outside, under the cover of darkness, crickets sang lustily in their nocturnal courtship. In the distance, the Nile waters lapped rhythmically against the shore.

Throwing a regulation cloak, bearing the insignia of a general's gold star over his shoulders, he stepped outside. Clanking of metal, and the rustle of starched linen alerted him to the guards, who were hastily straightening their posture.

Ignoring them, Horemheb sauntered past the shale wall of his barracks. Aware that unseen security troops followed his every step, he cautiously approached the Nile's banks. One could never be too safe in Thebes, where daily pillaging and murder was the norm.

The general exhaled a long-suffering breath. Although he desperately craved privacy, it would not do to banish his bodyguards, as he might have done in younger days.

"It's a lovely night," he declared aloud, aware of eyes trailing him from the palms.

An incline dipped to the flat, muddy shore. He chose a well-worn path, and skidded down to the river's edge.

"I agree," a voice close to him replied. Startled, Horemheb's hand reached for the short dagger around his hips. Then he saw him – a bald figure sitting on a boulder, his white priest's robes fluttering in a cool evening breeze. "Sit down." The stranger's kind tone allayed any fears in the military man's breast. He sat on the ground. "That's better."

Horemheb glanced up at the shrubbery, filled with his soldiers, expecting them to advance, but the trees were as silent as the empty beach.

"Who are you?"

"Ity, once High Priest of Karnak, now a lowly monk of the insignificant temple you pass by every day on your way to work."

The stranger stretched one arm to draw his hood more closely about his shoulders. The radiance of his white garb, gleaming in the moonlight, gave the illusion of him being from another world.

"I thought it was deserted."

"My room faces the west wing of your soldiers' barracks. I come down here when it's hard to sleep, which happens a lot these days, I'm afraid."

"I take it you do not follow the edicts of Pharaoh."

"Heresies," the man replied, with ill-concealed contempt.

They sat in silence. A thread of cloud obscured the moon for an instant.

"I'm General Horemheb," the younger man stated, expecting an alarmed response from the stranger.

Instead, Ity continued to contemplate the dark Nile waters glistening under the night sky.

"I'm fond of moonlight," he finally remarked. "Its silent beauty brings one close to the divine." He rose and dusted his palms. "General Horemheb, if you ever have need of me, I shall be at the temple of my god, Amon."

***

34.

AKHENATEN AND BABY TUTANKHATEN

Holding the sweet-smelling flesh for the first time, I smoothed his brow. I always kiss my beautiful children, but with Tutankhaten I also blessed him.

"May you be forever young," I wished, removing withered lips from his cheek.

***

Flickering through glistening waters, spangled fish kicked up brown and white ripples. A five-year-old boy in ankle-deep water stabbed enthusiastically with his spear. Finally catching a fish, Tutankhaten triumphantly held it aloft, while feminine laughter greeted his victory. Skilfully he removed his catch, and plopped it into the reed basket with the others.

Ankhsenpaaten sat in the shade with her mother and grandmother. Unfortunately, her father was attending to the affairs of state, otherwise he would have joined them. Shyly, the little princess glanced at Nefertiti. The latter was engrossed in a conversation with the elderly Tiye. During state visits everyone was deferential to the widow of Amenhotep-the-Magnificent. It gave nobody much time for anything else.

Young Tut and Ankhsy had used this knowledge more than once to their advantage. The culprits responsible for raiding Ay's orchard had never been found. Ankhsenpaaten had experienced her first kiss and, more importantly, speared several fish for dinner. Now she was content to watch the exploits of her companion while passing out advice.

"A wonderful catch," Nefertiti enthused.

"I believe his style could do with some improvement," the old queen remarked sharply.

Her eyes, so much like Ay's, darted over the sleek-limbed boy at the pond's edge. For his part, Tut was enjoying himself hugely. No one was freer than the young prince, and at Akhet-Aten the children roamed about and did what they liked. All his nieces and half-sisters ate and drank as much as they wished and were smothered with love from both parents. In short, Akhet-Aten was heaven on earth.

At noon Tutankhaten sat on the riverbank, his basket full. He was tired, and the sun's scorching heat was something even he avoided. Sprawled on the grassy bank, the boy reflected that he had only performed for Ankhsenpaaten's delight. He had desperately wanted her to join him, but it was considered unfeminine for a girl to fish or hunt. They would have to bide their time until they were free of adults.

Absent-mindedly, he lolled on the riverbank, picking his teeth with a reed. The midday meal would be announced soon, and they would be summoned indoors, where he would be required to bathe and dress in clean clothes. It had been a good morning. Tutankhaten had spent the better part of the day exercising, which he always preferred to studying hieroglyphs. He felt sorry for Ankhsy having to listen to the boring conversation of both queens. He observed even Nefertiti's eyes were dull and glazed.

The domineering spouse of the late Amenhotep-the-Magnificent caused Akhenaten's wife much pain. A will of iron, coupled with a penchant for court intrigue, was an overpowering combination. No wonder his father made a break with Thebes! Ostensibly over religion, there was probably a deeper and more homespun truth to the story of Akhenaten's self-imposed exile from his father's capital.

"I approve of what you've done with the pond," Tiye remarked. "Of course, my husband's lake was larger."

"We are pleased with it," Nefertiti replied. "It amuses the children."

"It's healthy to swim, although boat rides are more dignified."

The younger queen said nothing. Instead, she smoothed her pleated skirt, wondering miserably when lunch would be announced. Tutankhaten grinned and waved at them.

"I've caught a hundred fish, Aunty!" he yelled.

Nefertiti fixed him with a dazzling smile.

"You must be a greater fisherman than Pharaoh," she called back. Her voice floated prettily across the trees to the boy's glee.

"Greater!"

Queen Tiye gasped at the boy's informality with a person of rank. As Lady Kia's son, he was beneath Nefertiti, who was not his mother.

"Come here at once," she ordered sternly. Nefertiti glanced at the woman. Akhet-Aten was a city dedicated to peace. No punishment, which included scolding, was allowed within family circles. As the little boy obeyed, clambering up the bank, his half-sister squeaked with fear. Standing before Tiye he continued to beam at her. The older lady's face softened. Licking the tips of her fingers she rubbed the boy's face. "You have a spot just there," she said tenderly. "There's no need to be a grub."

Kissing him swiftly on the cheek, she pulled him onto her lap. Ankhsenpaaten gurgled with delighted laughter, and rushed towards Nefertiti's skirts. The children reached out and slapped their hands together.

"I don't know what we are going to do with these two," Tiye commented. She glared at Tutankhaten, who pulled her face towards his mouth for a firm kiss.

"They'll probably get married someday."

"Or rob the granaries."

Tiye picked up her grandson and tucked him under one arm. Ordering her servants to gather his fish basket, the group retired indoors.

***

Kneeling in the Hypostyle Hall, Minthu prayed. Morning sun filtered through the columns, transforming into a blinding, yet suffused, light.

The priest's clean-shaven head and hairless body was clad in ragged vestments. For generations, the hall had existed. At interludes, its columns were infilled with stones of disgraced or forgotten pharaohs. An entire temple of Senwoseret had been carefully dismantled and recycled

256

into part of the entire, seemingly unbroken construction of stones. But this fact, like many others, was veiled from the dedicated priest.

Minthu was completely alone. He prayed deeply and fervently. There still existed devotees like him and, during the dark days, more returned to prayer. Stripped of their staggering wealth and power, they had nothing else. Some brave souls conspired to bring down Pharaoh, only to meet their demise. Most had gone into hiding. Minthu, however, continued to worship in the place he loved and knew as his home.

Every morning he diligently swept his section of the temple as he had always done. Towards dusk, he chanted the ancient prayers memorised from boyhood. At night he lit oil lamps for the hall's illumination.

No one bothered him anymore. At first Akhenaten's troops had killed as many of Amon's priests as was humanly possible, but since the heretic had moved the capital upstream, the fervour of his crazy movement had died.

It was common knowledge that Queen Tiye had disapproved of her son's actions. She continued to make public appearances, and even worshipped at the Temple of Hathor as she had in her husband's reign. Her son had declined to reprimand her, but she was unable to help the House of Amon. Perhaps even she did not dare.

At last, Minthu rose from his worship. Everything was as it had always been. The darkness of the hall balanced with a light which caused pylons to disappear, creating an atmosphere in which an ineffable mystery lived. As he gazed up, the white sunlight turned into celestial fingertips of bluish hue. The priest shivered, remembering Akhenaten's deity. Under the rebel king the sun was represented as a disc without human attributes, except minute hands tapering at the ends of its rays. The royal uraeus, firmly stamped at its centre, sent the adherents of every faith a clear warning. From now on all the wealth of Egypt and its ownership, including its temples, belonged to the king. Never again would the country be torn asunder by two rivals, namely the priesthood and monarchy.

The holy man sighed. It was true that most of his cohorts had enjoyed their temple girls more than their vespers. He had not been of their ilk. Perhaps that is why Amon had allowed him to survive. The fact that no one disturbed Minthu's everyday existence was nothing short of a miracle. Exhausted from his labours, he perched himself on the base of a column and dozed.

The voices were faint at first, then louder. Alarmed, the priest turned his wiry body to face the southern end of the complex. He could hear horses neighing and men's shouts. Instead of flitting away like a shadow, Minthu bravely maintained his post. He heard the unmistakable tread of soldiers' feet.

"The infidel is here," one man stated. "Look at him. Sitting on his throne as if he owned the place!"

Another laughed coarsely. The party of men grew. Suddenly, they parted for a handsome man of medium height, who marched through their ranks. At the sight of the stranger, Minthu's being experienced a palpable glow. A spark of hope ignited in his soul. Before he knew what he was doing, he fell on the rough stone floor in full prostration.

"Arise, holy priest of Karnak," an authoritative voice commanded. The latter scrambled to his feet. "I am General Horemheb," the stranger introduced himself in a rich bass voice. "There is no need to bow before me. I am not a king."

The priest found himself tongue-tied. His palms were tightly joined together in supplication.

"Perhaps he is pleading for his life," a wiseacre jeered.

The general turned sharply on the jester and glared at him. Satisfied with the ensuing silence, he turned back to Minthu.

"Is this a convenient time for an audience?" The priest regarded the visitor with puzzlement. Politeness from the powerful was not a rarity – it was unheard of. "Are you able to speak?"

The visitor's face registered concern as he leaned forward to inspect the man's eyes. After all, many adherents of Amon had been tortured in unimaginable ways. To lose a tongue was not uncommon.

"I am, sire," Minthu blurted out at last.

"Speak up," a thin, hook-nosed man ordered brusquely. "The general cannot hear you."

Horemheb turned to the man.

"*I* can hear him, Ramesses." Whipping one tightly muscled arm in a gesture of dismissal, he commanded: "Leave us alone."

His voice was unemotional, but Ramesses and his men instantly scuttled to the furthest corner of the temple.

"I apologise for the intrusion."

Horemheb lapsed into silence and looked about him. Having become accustomed to the luxury of the palaces of Akhet-Aten and Malkata, the neglected temple, stripped of its finery, distressed him. The man before him was clearly half-starved, and his robe bore more darned holes than a soldier's tent.

"Before you arrived, I had just finished my prayers," Minthu indicated the base of a column. "Please sit down."

Crossing his legs under him, the general gazed up at the ceiling. Every visitor did. The vertical columns leading into the light were designed to pull one's spirit to a higher level.

"I used to come here as a boy."

Minthu stroked his whiskers.

"I remember you," he said, refraining from mentioning details of worship in which Horemheb sang as loudly as any of Amon's singers. The general was suddenly abashed. Noting his discomfort, the older man decided to encourage his guest. "I am at your service, General. Speak."

"I have been told that you live here." Faint terror pulsated through Minthu. Horemheb instantly reached out a hand, as if to reassure him. It stayed in mid-air. "I need to ask some questions." The hand was retracted. Minthu was instantly on guard.

"What sort?" he asked warily.

"I'm not here to arrest you. If you need anything, please do not hesitate to ask."

"Are you here on behalf of the dowager queen?"

It was clear that the general knew little of polite conversation. In many ways he was like a holy man, comfortable on the hard stone, but not in the art of diplomacy. Minthu began to warm to him.

"I'm not here on royal business." Horemheb contemplated the ceiling again, while the priest wracked his brains. Minthu could hear the clanking of spears and guffaws of manly laughter in the halls. His guest turned towards the noise. "Are there any women here?" he asked suddenly.

"They fled long ago."

Horemheb relaxed.

"My men are highly disciplined," he explained, "but one can't always ... prevent things from happening."

His eyes roved the hall, as if surveying his troops for errant behaviour.

"Thank you for paying this temple honour," Minthu began. "Perhaps you wish to speak," he continued, licking his cracked lips, "but lack a politician's art. Please understand, I'm only a humble caretaker."

Startled, Horemheb turned his head towards the man, once renowned as a great teacher. However, noting Minthu's sincerity, he cleared his throat and began.

"High Priest Ity, your eminent colleague, lives below my barracks. He gives holy blessings to my soldiers, and has been doing this for months without my knowledge."

"But the penalty for Amon's blessings is death!"

"Not on my watch."

"I have not conversed with Ity for over a decade."

"Yet he is the reason for my visit. I wish to arrange a meeting between the pair of you. My soldiers will be here shortly after dawn. Is that too early?"

"Priests wake before sunrise, sire."

Minthu was about to express his fear of the soldiers, but hesitated.

"Not all my men serve Aten," Horemheb added, as if reading the priest's mind. "Be assured, the surly ones will stay at home." The general placed a cricket of lapis lazuli on the base of the column. "This should pay for incense."

He rubbed his hands together as if relieved that a difficult task had been accomplished. Emaciated fingers brushed his arm.

"Please, sire, I have sufficient." Minthu appeared awkward, almost fearful. To return the semi-precious stone was an insult. "If you wish to help, please bring sweepers. As you can see, one man is not enough." Noting their leader had concluded his interview, Horemheb's party of soldiers approached them. The general awkwardly retrieved his gift. "I do not mean any disrespect," Minthu added, pressing his trembling hands together.

"I need to ask you some important questions," Horemheb whispered. "Will you allow me to visit you tonight?"

Taken aback, Minthu, nevertheless, collected himself quickly.

"It would be my privilege."

As soldiers engulfed them, he closed his eyes to block out the sight of their rattling spears. When Minthu reopened them, the men had gone, and with them, the stranger who resembled a god. Lifting his arms, the holy man intoned a prayer.

"O great God, I give you thanks!" he cried. "Here is proof that you reward faith. Please take care of General Horemheb. Bless him and keep him from harm so that he might fulfil your purpose." He glanced furtively around the empty temple. "And may he make Egypt great again."

Minthu's thin arms fell to their sides. A surge of strength flowed through his wasted limbs. Picking up a broom, the man who had once been Karnak's finest tutor, began to sweep with bold, energetic strokes.

***

35.

TUTANKHATEN

Down by the river, egrets pick delicately at tiny shellfish. Slices of blue sky lie in pools of mud. I splash through one. Birds fly up. I'm left plucking reeds among patches of heaven.

***

Hunched in a thicket, both children were giggling. Several fat fish lay in a woven basket next to Tut. His half-sister Ankhsenpaaten was peering through a hole in the bushes. Distraught, her nanny Tee was calling desperately for her charge. Unwilling to face Nefertiti without the missing princess, the old lady did not dare leave the garden, and instead wrung her hands, while weeping inconsolably.

"Tutankhaten!" The boy looked up in dismay. His older brother, Smenkhare held two branches above his head. "Come out at once!" he ordered. Meekly, the child obeyed. His half-sister followed.

"Stop it! That hurts!" the little boy cried as his brother beat him.

Tutankhaten began to sob so noisily that half a dozen guards, and a harried Tee, ran over to see who was assaulting the young prince. Catching sight of Ankhsenpaaten, her nanny let out a loud cry. Taking the dishevelled, mud-encrusted child into her arms, she wept with relief.

"You're such a baby." Smenkhare threw the sticks away.

"There's no need to hit me!" Tut's eyes were streaming.

"You've taken up enough of the palace's time with your silly game of hide-and-seek." Smenkhare nodded towards Tee. "Your irresponsibility could have cost someone's job – or life."

Instead of eliciting an empathetic response, Smenkhare found himself the target of a furious glare from Tee. Quick to capitalise on a good thing, Tutankhaten bawled pitifully, fuelling his elder brother's decision to leave the scene as rapidly as his dignity would allow.

Once in the palace the children were bathed, clad in new raiment and seated near their father, Pharaoh Akhenaten. It was lunchtime, and all the family were expected to dine together. They managed to do so before the last stroke of the electrum gong sounded out across the peaceful palace gardens.

Ankhsenpaaten had a hearty appetite, her father observed. She and Tutankhaten were always smiling at each other, too. He became thoughtful.

"Did you have a productive morning?" Pharaoh addressed Smenkhare after the first course.

The heir was suddenly fawning.

"I achieved a great deal, Your Majesty."

Tutankhaten contorted his face behind his brother's back.

"Have you seen Meritaten?" Akhenaten enquired casually.

"I haven't had the pleasure today, but I'm hoping to visit her this afternoon. She was busy this morning."

Tutankhaten stuck his tongue out. Unable to contain herself, Ankhsenpaaten laughed so much, she spilled her fruit juice. Queen Nefertiti frowned. Leaning over, she whispered an admonition into her daughter's ear.

"And you, our youngest," the king smiled benevolently at Tutankhaten. "What have you been doing this sunny morning?"

"Studying, Your Majesty," the boy lied.

Ankhesenpaaten held her breath.

"That's good." His father reached for a piece of meat. He took it up delicately between spidery fingers. "I hear you have a gift for multiplication."

"Today my lesson was about fish."

Smenkhare's colour rose. He pursed his mouth, while his eyes grew wide with restrained rage. Ankhsenpaaten stuck a piece of her long sash between her teeth and sucked it. Nefertiti motioned silently for a servant to remove her youngest from the table. Her husband pretended not to notice, but ever watchful of his wife's movements, squeezed her hand.

"Exercises with fish? Good! It helps to have a picture in one's mind to speed up the mental processes. I, too, once had an education in the ways of our watery friends."

A faint smile played on the king's upper lip as he broke off a duck's wing. Tutankhaten bowed his head while his father spoke to other members of the family. When they were almost finished, the prince boldly faced Pharaoh and asked:

"What is Your Majesty's ruling on violence?"

A hush fell over the family. Akhenaten grew solemn.

"Violence is wrong if it is wrought on innocent people. But if it is against oppression, it is the right, and sometimes the only, way."

"I have an oppressor." A look of horror spread on his older brother's face. "He's seated at Your Highness' table."

The little boy pointed to Smenkhare, who had frozen in his chair. Akhenaten turned from one brother to the other. Already having been informed of the morning's events, he held out his arms to his favourite child. Tutankhaten ran into the embrace of his beloved father. Having finished his scanty meal, Akhenaten rose, clasping him close to his breast.

"I guess we should give Smenkhare a good flogging," Pharaoh reflected aloud.

Indulgent laughter from the courtiers echoed through the hall. Even Nefertiti, who secretly disliked the arrogant successor, smiled.

She chucked Tutankhaten under the chin. Sickened at the attention his brat of a brother was receiving, and not knowing where to look, Smenkhare turned away. He caught Meritaten's eyes watching him sympathetically from across the gathering.

Seizing the opportunity to escape, the youth bowed, pleading his courtship of her as an excuse to leave the family luncheon.

"It wouldn't do to spank the next king of Egypt," Nefertiti remarked.

"He isn't king yet," Tutankhaten said.

"His time will come." Akhenaten gently kissed the top of the child's head. "But it is better to stop violence than to spread it. I will make sure Smenkhare never strikes you again."

Comforted, Tutankhaten firmly clutched the king's bosom. As they moved into the outer courtyard, he fell asleep.

Handing the prince to Tee, who always hovered close to her small charges, Akhenaten took his wife's hand, and moved into a rose-covered arbour.

"He's a beautiful child," Nefertiti said.

"And very loud!" They both laughed together. Alone at last, Akhenaten took his queen's face in his hands and tenderly kissed her. "You're still as beautiful as the day I first laid eyes on you," he whispered.

***

Ay was incredulous.

"Horemheb's giving *gold* to the priests of Amon?"

Meryre, Overseer of the Treasury, bowed gravely.

"So it would seem, sire."

"But he's one of Pharaoh Akhenaten's generals. This is treason!"

Meryre deigned not to answer. Ay shifted in his chair as he searched his memory for facts he had painstakingly gathered on the general.

Recruited at an early age, the boy had grown up in the royal barracks. For reasons unknown to him, there were a thousand stories abounding on Horemheb's ancestry.

One thing was for certain: In all the time Ay had known the man, he had never exhibited any characteristics other than outstanding discipline and a remoteness of character, which even the king's father-in-law found distinctly chilly at times.

"He has also sent a team of cleaners to the main temple. Under that iron exterior, he has a compassionate heart, sire."

"I never took Horemheb for a fool."

"You may rest assured that he is not that."

Ay looked directly at his chief spy.

"You sound certain."

"I am."

"Explain yourself, and don't take all day. I have to be at the treasury soon."

"It is my belief that, as others have, the general intends to give his full support to Amon. However, this is not as contradictory a set of intentions as one might, at first, presume." He glanced at Ay, who tapped his fingers impatiently against his chair's gilt armrest. Licking his lips, the man concluded swiftly: "I think he wishes to serve only Pharaoh, but the priesthood has – shall we say – noticed his talents."

Ay threw up his hands.

"What talents? Horemheb's a lumbering soldier who drinks thirstily, eats as if he's never seen food in his life, and is more inarticulate than one of my mares!"

"That may be so," Meryre conceded, realising the Divine Father always disparaged the man he most feared. "But if the priests are wooing him, it might be wise to recognise the fact."

"You're right," Ay agreed reluctantly. "Thank you for your informative assessment. And now, I must be excused."

The snoop bowed with reverence. Then, he glided across the polished granite floor, out of the audience chamber.

Ay did not hurry to move. His eyes squinted thoughtfully.

***

36.

ANKHSENPAATEN

In the upper courtyard Meritaten sleeps. I crawl past her window, trying not to sneeze amid the exotic plants. Tutankhaten is in the nursery.

I hear him spinning a top. He was put to bed for his afternoon nap earlier than the rest of us, but now the little chap is wide awake, driving his nurse mad.

I see him intent on spinning the multicoloured wooden toy. Striped like a bee, it is chased in yellow and black bands.

Peeping through a rectangular white window, I whistle before ducking. Lifting my head, I notice Tut looking from left to right.

His attention is focused towards the uppermost corners of the room, where tiny stone grates allow birdsong, and sometimes birds, in.

Suddenly two strong arms whisk me up out of the garden and into the cool, clean mudbrick room.

"And why isn't this princess in bed?" Tee asks.

Tutankhaten is rocking back and forth, his infectious laughter piercing the high-ceilinged room. Triumph flows through my veins and I squeal with delight.

"Between the two of you, the entire palace will wake," my nanny declares.

Vaguely I perceive a twitch in the corner of her mouth. The afternoons are lonely for Lord Ay's wife, although she loves her job. During siesta time no one is about. Once I saw her roaming a corridor during that silent time of day. She looked sad. Lord Ay must have been studying. All through my childhood I never saw Lord Ay asleep!

***

Maya rested puffy hands on his knees. A thick papyrus sheet, covered in figures, fell to the floor in front of him.

"You're quiet tonight, Maya."

"Our treasury contents are not what they used to be, Meryt."

"Depletion is natural in the face of huge spending."

"This is different. I know there's an extra coffer in Karnak, but I'm unable to access it."

"Maybe someone else in authority has the keys."

"Our Divine Father." Maya rubbed his eyes. "I can't understand it. A decade ago Egypt was the greatest nation in the world. Now I'm scrounging to make ends meet."

"We aren't giving gold away like we did in Amenhotep's reign, are we?"

"Akhenaten doesn't answer such requests."

"A sensible king! I remember Tiye was constantly chastising her husband for overspending."

Maya looked directly at his wife.

"Akhenaten isn't well."

"Nonsense! He fasts a lot. Like most intellectuals, he spends too much time in that head of his, but his family takes his mind off his religious excesses. He makes much of Prince Smenkhare these days, too, showering him with gifts. Have you noticed how much like Kia that boy is?"

"No, but it surely can't help matters between His Majesty and the Great Wife Nefertiti."

"Nefertiti has always accepted the Lady Kia, together with his other wives. It changes nothing – Akhenaten has loved Nefertiti all his life. She must know that, surely!"

"The tragedy is our king had to marry Kia for sons. It's caused a lot of jealousy between the women."

Meryt leaned against her husband. She peered into his soft, sad eyes.

"Apart from the accounts, and Akhenaten's wives, is everything alright at court?"

"The accounts *are* the court – at least for me. It's an unending nightmare."

"I know the king still mourns the loss of his brother and father," Meryt continued, picking up her husband's papyrus, "but he's achieved what no other king has – freedom for Egypt."

"We're in bondage. Our money matters are in a terrible mess, and the State Department's going crazy. I mean look at us – when was the last time you took a vacation?"

With a subdued manner, Meryt poured herbal tea, which the couple found soothing last thing before bed.

"If you want us to retire in Thebes, we have a small house. I don't need these trappings," she said.

Impulsively, Maya took his wife's face in his hands, and kissed her cheek.

"You are the most excellent of women," he declared, his tenor voice cracking, "but we can't jump ship now."

Picking up his papyrus, he scowled with stern concentration.

***

MAYA

The money has run out. How do I know? I am Chief Treasurer. The empire's purse strings are supposedly in my hands. If only it were true. As it is, I have committed fraud a thousand times over.

It is time to pack. Aten falls dreamlike behind the western hills. Soon the earth will be covered in darkness. A tabby cat sleeps at my feet.

"Up, Senenmut," I order gently.

He opens surprised eyes. The day has passed and he was only beginning to enjoy his slumbers. We stroll across warm desert sand to my chariot. Wearily, I strap a few tablets to its floor. In one lithe movement my cat leaps up to perch upon a rail. Clucking my tongue, I call out.

"Hut-a-hut!"

The horses bolt forward. Ears flattened against his brown and grey skull, Senenmut holds on grimly for dear life.

*****

In the royal treasury, a battle of wills was taking place.

"My guidelines require me to count all silver this month," Maya objected. "I cannot part with any."

Ay bristled.

"I have Pharaoh's *seal*."

"I cannot allow any silver to go out without it first being counted."

"And how long do you need to do this?"

Maya ticked off his fingers.

"Today, tomorrow, and the day after."

"And then may I collect?"

"Certainly, with an up-to-date seal."

Muttering to himself, the Divine Father vanished through the treasury's low portal and into the hot sunshine, where his chariot awaited.

"You were brave, Lord Maya" a young accountant commented from among the gold bars.

"Most authoritative," another piped up from a stack of lapis lazuli blocks.

"I'm sick of that man," another pronounced vehemently, pushing aside a mound of silver pots. "He's nothing but a common thief."

"Three cheers for our treasurer!" a young boy suddenly proclaimed.

Outside, Ay swivelled about.

"What's that noise?" he enquired of the courtier nearest to him.

"I can't hear anything."

Faint shouts rang across the plain. Ay's mouth set as his eyes narrowed.

"Let us repair to the palace."

He set off briskly, trailing a group of noblemen after him.

In the Great Hall, the king appeared perplexed during the afternoon audience. Fanbearers kept the last phase of the sun's heat at bay with ostrich fans.

"He's flouting your authority," Ay complained.

"Maya? But he's part of the family!"

A pained expression flitted across the councillor's face.

"I'm your uncle."

"I'm not well," Akhenaten muttered.

Almost imperceptibly, the Divine Father's chest inflated but, unnoticed by the others, a canny light sparked in one of the king's downcast eyes.

Abner, who was standing by Akhenaten, used the silence as an opportunity to speak up.

"Our esteemed treasurer has been misunderstood," he stated smoothly. "It is Lord Maya's wish that he might finish counting the grain, wine, and gold as Your Majesty decreed. Then he will furnish Lord Ay with his order. Maya only asks for a seal to be placed with the records. Otherwise such transactions would be illegal, and the treasury might be susceptible to charges of fraud."

"Profound thanks for spelling out what we already know," Ay responded in a flat voice.

"Am I a money lender?" Akhenaten muttered.

He turned from one to the other.

"You need to remunerate the courtiers," Ay said. "It was the king's wish that everyone be paid bonuses this month."

"Did I say that? It must be true. The Divine Father remembers everything I say."

Abner cast a horrified glance at Pharaoh, hardly noticing Ay's mouth curving in triumph.

***

A messenger stood in the doorway of the royal treasury.

"General Horemheb has a request for fifty talents."

Maya looked up from a pile of gold wine goblets. His wig had flopped to one side.

"Horemheb knows we're counting," he replied faintly. "Does he have a requisition order from the palace?"

"I don't think so. He's arrived from Thebes and told me to come to you personally and order fifty talents." The emissary handed Maya a small clay tablet. "This is an army invoice."

"I can't supply chariot wheels, or silver, or gold." Maya handed the tablet back. "Tell the general I am sorry, but not even Pharaoh is getting any gold for his employees until the end of the week when I've counted his wheat and turquoise."

The soldier did not move.

"I have to take back my requisition."

A dry cough sounded behind the man.

"Pharaoh Akhenaten does require his silver, and that without delay," Ay declared unpleasantly. "This is his personal stamp. He has further requested your presence for a private afternoon audience, Maya. I believe he wishes to review your position."

"My position is here," the treasurer declared robustly. A collective intake of breath from Maya's assistants reverberated through the cool, dark room. Taking the tablet from Ay he scrutinised it. "Fine," he conceded, noting the impression of a ring which Akhenaten kept on his fourth finger. "Merthat and Paaten, see to it that our Divine Father has all he needs."

A smirk appeared on Ay's lips.

"I need my money," the soldier interjected with renewed stubbornness.

"You require Pharaoh's *seal*," Ay snapped, rounding on the messenger. "No soldier, let alone a general, would commission you to approach his counting house without one. Now begone before I have you flogged."

Terrified, the soldier took to his heels. Several of the accountants stared at the vizier. Maya appraised the silver, while taking note of the exact amount. "It's all there. My helpers will load it onto your chariots."

"I have my own." Ay clapped his hands. Several burly Nubians materialised to cart the money away. "It's been a pleasure doing business with you."

***

It was refreshingly cool in Pharaoh's bank, and Abner admired the precise work which was being undertaken by scribes, and accountants as they conducted the annual stocktake. Maya shot his visitor a suspicious glance. Abner only nodded pleasantly.

"Apparently some courtiers are to receive bonuses, Maya."

"I didn't know."

"Ay informed us that Pharaoh had given permission for them to be paid in silver."

"It was gold last month."

"Did you know what it was for?"

"Is this an inquisition?" Maya asked testily.

"You must forgive my rudeness, Your Lordship, but I've perhaps been misunderstood. It appeared to me, as Chief Minister, that Pharaoh had no recollection of ordering any valuables to leave the treasury for any purpose whatsoever."

Maya froze.

"Am I at fault?" he asked, his voice beginning to waver.

"Not at all. Please allow me to speak plainly."

"If you must, but be quick about it, I have a lot of work to do."

"I'm not in charge of the king's coffers, but if the Divine Father is asking for money, its end use would seem vague."

"I'm not a policeman, Abner-el. If Ay has a royal seal, I distribute funds. If you had one, I would accept them. Will that be all?" he asked.

A slow smile crept over the powerful Chief Minister's face.

"For now. Please pass on my regards to your wife, the lovely Lady Meryt."

***

273

"I can't breathe," Maya gasped.

"Relax. *Try*." His wife rubbed his back. Slowly, the courtier began to take deep, even breaths.

"I may be imprisoned for embezzlement," Maya groaned, hyperventilating again.

"Tell me in logical steps if you can. What is happening at the palace?"

"Ay is stealing from Pharaoh's bank, and Abner's filching from Ay in order to return the loot to His Majesty's coffers. Oddly enough, the Chief Minister does not replace the full balance, but it's better than nothing."

"So, you have a problem with the figures?" Maya looked up at his wife. She began to laugh, eliciting a wan smile from him. "Come," she said. "The whole of Egypt knows the Divine Father is a crook. Pharaoh's such an idiot we'll be bankrupt in a few years. Abner is a good man, though. So don't worry, you'll be around for a long time yet." She kissed his head.

"It's Horemheb too," Maya wailed. "He arrived from Thebes this morning, and sent a soldier to ask for a number of things without the king's permission."

"Are you sure? Did you check?"

"I didn't," her husband admitted. "But if it hadn't been for Ay, the soldier would have fought me for it, I'm sure."

"So, the old dog was there to protect the money he was going to later abscond with!" Meryt laughed. "Are there any more robbers?"

"I think that about covers it."

"Has Abner returned Ay's money?"

"Not yet."

His wife was overcome.

"He's probably run off to the Delta with the loot! Perhaps Pharaoh will come calling one day and then what will you do?"

"I'll lock him in the treasury while I go on permanent vacation. There'll be enough gaps for Akhenaten to set up a few tables and chairs."

Maya lay back on the pillows, which his wife had arranged on the living room floor, and stretched his arms above his head. Her merriment had rolled away the black cloud which had been hanging over him all afternoon.

"It's not that bad, darling. At least you have friends."

"When Ay comes to your defence, it's more dangerous than cavorting with a rattlesnake. I wish we could leave," Maya ended sadly.

"Now you're behaving like Pharaoh. He fled Thebes, and look where it's got him. An unbearably hot city, and possible loss of his empire."

"He looks so ill and alone."

"Nefertiti said he fasted for nearly twenty days last month."

"It's grief. His father's death was a great blow. Nobody in Egypt wants to worship one god, and he's wondering what the revolution was for."

"Don't take on everyone's burdens," Meryt advised sensibly. "Concentrate on those figures, and be grateful when Abner comes calling."

***

Maya tore his eyes from the scroll he was reading. Horemheb stood in the crowded counting house.

"I came as soon as I could," he said.

"For the gold?"

"To explain."

The accountant gestured about him.

"As you can see, we are very busy."

Pain registered in Horemheb's dark eyes.

"I need to speak to you in private."

"Let's go outside."

Maya put down his scroll, and the pair exited the treasury.

"I thought you would supply me on the basis of our friendship," Horemheb reasoned, blinking in the strong sunlight.

"Do you know what position that puts me in? I need an emblem of royal approval for the records. What if Pharaoh makes a surprise inspection? Lord Ay is waiting for me to trip up."

"That dung beetle threatened my messenger," Horemheb remarked grimly.

"He reprimanded a man who had no proof of who he was!"

"We have trouble on our borders, Maya. Pharaoh won't deal with it –"

"Is that my problem?"

"I need to fight our enemies. For that I require chariots and payment for the troops."

"Your troops *are* paid, General."

"Listen, do you want to live in a peaceful country, or one overrun by Hittites?"

"How am I to believe you?"

"We've been friends for years. You know how honest I am."

"Do you realise what sort of pressure I'm under? All morning we have been inundated with requests from court – ask me what for."

"Gold?"

"Precisely, and do you think anyone has Akhenaten's permission?"

"Ay would."

"He's robbing Pharaoh blind."

Horemheb started.

"It's true," the accountant wagged his head vehemently. "Stealing! I've been in a quandary over my career for the past week. I can't sleep, can't eat – I can't even breathe."

Horemheb dithered sadly.

"I can't ask Pharaoh for war equipment. He would turn me down flat."

"You might be able to ask Ay. He wants Egypt strong again. I'm sure he could cream off some extra funds from his surplus for your soldiers."

The clattering of chariots behind them made the treasurer jump.

"I'll wait until you're finished with Abner's guard," said Horemheb, recognising the gold crests as the horses drew up beside the pair.

"Your Lordship, Maya," said one of Abner's men, glancing at Horemheb, "please take this."

Maya perused the scrap of gold-edged papyrus, and beckoned the man into the darkened chambers of the treasury.

"If you're going to wait," the nobleman said, in parting to Horemheb, "you may as well make yourself useful. Position your troops to look out for Ay."

Happy to oblige, the general began giving orders to several of his men who were idling by their chariots.

Maya returned to the treasury.

"Pardon us, sir," a clerk interrupted him timidly, as the accountant removed bags of gold dust from their shelves, "but Lord Ay's horses are bearing down on us."

Tearing outside, Maya gesticulated wildly at Horemheb.

"Hump!" he yelled. "You'll get your equipment for the war effort so long as you do me a favour."

"Anything."

"If you want me to trust you with gold, you have to trust me on the silver Abner's men will be installing in my counting house. Make your troops form a line against Ay's party. Inform them it's tribute from Mitanni. If you're making border raids, he'll believe you."

"So, you're making a profit, are you?" Horemheb chuckled.

"Believe me, I'm just trying to break even," muttered the harried treasurer breathlessly, as he picked up his skirts and ran inside.

***

The Divine Father alighted from his chariot.

"What is the meaning of this barricade, General Horemheb?"

"I've recently exacted tribute from the King of Mitanni. It will take a few more moments to fill the coffers with our booty."

"I will wait as long as it takes," replied Ay courteously, visions of gold dancing in his head. "What did you receive as gifts?"

"The usual," Horemheb replied vaguely.

"Ah!" The king's father-in-law tapped his cane in a chariot rut, noticing that there was no more level ground outside the treasury. "I am aware Mitanni has been an ally of ours for many years. Is there any reason we are raiding them?"

"Your Lordship understands our foreign policy, but this is tribute. I did not conduct a border raid ... merely extracted the appropriate funds which were sadly overdue."

"I understand perfectly. There is no need to explain. Good work."

***

"Hurry up," Maya muttered more to himself than to his staff, who were working as fast as they could.

"Do you want us to continue counting?" a flustered scribe asked.

The Chief Treasurer's wig bobbed in affirmation.

"Let me do the worrying. So long as you're accurate, it's all I ask."

"It's just that we are finding it difficult, Your Lordship."

"Difficult? Why?"

"We count products, which then go missing, after which they then mysteriously re-appear."

"I am aware of the situation, and am sure you're doing your best to keep the ledgers balanced."

"The silver is our main issue at present."

"Concentrate on the gold dust bags, and blocks of lapis. And while you're about it, Me-aten, count at least five hundred chariot wheels and put them aside. I'll speak to you about it after these men go."

***

278

Flopping among the cushions, Maya resembled a fish gasping for air. Distressed at her husband's condition, Meryt gestured violently towards a nearby servant.

"Wine!" she commanded. Hovering over Maya, she removed his palace wig. "Your head is sopping! Take a bath, darling. We'll put you in the sun for a few minutes to regulate your temperature."

"I hope Akhenaten dies," replied the accountant, kicking off his sandals, and accepting an aloe vera compress. One of their children gasped in horror. "I'm sorry, Maya Junior," he apologised.

Meryt patted the boy's head.

"Your father didn't mean it," she reassured their son. "Go outside and play with your sister. Darling," she chided, "please be careful of what you say. Children often speak out of turn."

Meryt departed for a few moments. She returned with a carafe of wine mixed with honey. Filling a goblet with the beverage, she handed it to her husband. Maya drained it at a gulp.

"It's hell being a treasurer these days," he said, wiping his lips. "Everyone wants Pharaoh's money."

"Did you get back the silver?"

"Some was missing, but we'll make up the deficit. I'm glad Pharaoh takes no interest in the affairs of state now, but I do wish for a return to Thebes."

"That's good news about the silver. At least there are still some honest men left."

"They're all thieves!" said Maya, storming off to the bathroom. "I wish I had known before coming to this accursed place!"

"Why don't you talk to Horemheb?" she called out. "You two could work out an alliance to protect the king. Aten knows he needs it!"

A sullen silence, interspersed with splashing and scrubbing, floated through the walls.

"Good idea," Maya growled from amidst the soapsuds.

***

"Hey, Hump!"

A faint call echoed across the hills. General Horemheb scoured the landscape, until his sharp gaze settled on a rotund shape. He was in the desert rabbit hunting. There was no one with him, except a few companions, which included Ramesses and his son.

"If I'm not mistaken, it's our mutual friend, Maya," Ramesses said.

The brigadier swung his chariot before the onslaught of the profusely sweating official, who was trudging through the dust to their party.

"It's the king's treasurer," Seti chirped from the comfort of his father's knee. Placing plump child's arms on the chariot rail, he gaily waved at the court official whose round face mirrored his own innocence.

"Seti knows how to win important contacts, even at this age," his father said proudly.

Puffing strenuously, Maya reached the group. Rivulets of perspiration coursed down his brow and into his mouth. Seti jumped up and down in the chariot. Unlike most courtiers, Maya acknowledged the child.

"Caught any bandits?" he asked the little boy cheerily, mopping his brow.

"Not yet, but we shall," was the confident reply.

Ramesses tried to control his spirited steeds.

"How can we help you?" he asked.

"I'm not sure," Maya responded, his eyes fixed firmly on Horemheb.

Realising he was an impediment to free conversation, Ramesses wheeled his chariot towards the army barracks nestled in a valley below the cliffs. Giving Horemheb a farewell salute, he galloped downhill, while the childish protests of his son floated across the wind.

"That little chap is always with his father," Maya noted.

"Ram thinks he's learning. Far be it for me to complain."

"Mark my word, he'll be a general before he's sixteen."

"I have no doubt. Do you know he took the reins of his father's horses last week at Thebes in order to show him a speedier method of negotiating Amenhotep's chariot track?"

"Isn't that dangerous?"

"They slammed into the north wall, but with the technique Ram won the memorial race. I don't think anyone had the gall to come within a chariot's length of him!"

Both men guffawed in the blazing afternoon heat.

"Will I see you at the bank tomorrow?" Maya asked after they had both recovered.

"I have to see action first," Horemheb replied gravely.

"Are we at war?"

"It's ... complicated. I would appreciate your discretion in this matter."

"I shall await your return."

The two men chatted easily for some minutes before parting, the courtier to his waiting litter bearers in the cliffs, and Horemheb home to his barracks for a drink with Ramesses and his disappointed son.

***

37.

GENERAL HOREMHEB

Battle lines divided. Skirmishes under the moon. Submerged, in Nile water. Flicking through reeds under the black-and-white night. My blade cuts grass, cuts human. The warm earth fills with water and blood.

***

"We can't pull this off," Horemheb said to his visitor.

Ay chewed his watermelon slice meditatively.

"You're sweating, Horemheb." The older man wiped his fingers with an embroidered napkin.

"A raiding party is one thing, but this is a foreign king's army. We need military tactics."

"Are you in charge of boy scouts, or an army?"

"What I mean –"

The Divine Father cut him short.

"You *are* the army, Horemheb. Strike at dawn and strike hard."

"It's too difficult."

Ay was baffled by the response. It was unlike the general to flinch from action. The wily councillor decided on a different tack.

"My daughter, Mut tells me that you have been visiting her regularly, even though you are a married man. Is that true?" Horemheb turned plum red under his swarthy skin. "I don't think Pharaoh would mind if you resisted Aziru," the older man continued.

"But His Majesty hasn't given me any orders!"

"It's not necessary for you to have Pharaoh's express permission." Ay rose stiffly from the leather army couch. "I must return home."

The sound of crickets grew louder. A gecko trekked its way across a lintel. Flicking out its tongue momentarily, it caught a fly.

Horemheb took a sip of brackish water. Gusts of wind blew around his bare shoulders, but he hardly noticed. Twelve hundred men camped about him in the chilly desert evening.

Despite Pharaoh's apathy towards his enemies, the general, with Ay's permission, was about to repel a group of brigands. He drained the pottery cup, and turned to survey his soldiers. They were arrayed in small groups behind rocks where horses snorted and whinnied. With the waiting he became increasingly irritated. It was not possible to conduct an effective ambush with noise.

Disgusted, he threw away his bowl. A soldier swiftly stooped to retrieve the shards.

"Leave it!" Horemheb ordered, striding away to his tent. It would be dismantled in a few minutes, but for now he chaired a meeting for a small group of officers. "Ramesses, you are to take the left wing." His friend bowed in silent acknowledgment of his orders. "Ata-Hotep the right and Asural ..." He paused. "South."

Later, squadrons took their positions. The moon started to rise. Horemheb eyed the skyline. Sure enough, there was a group of black dots amassing in the distance. Several officers spotted a white haze. It was dust from horses. These wild men rode bareback. A thought occurred to Horemheb as he watched with dispassion, born of experience. The raiders were travelling at such a speed they would never hear Pharaoh's chariots. Neither did they expect opposition.

Horemheb smiled. It would be an easy victory.

***

The last of the sun touched the western hills above the altar of the Aten.

"My God! My God!" Akhenaten wept at the foot of his temple steps.

Although bad news was never appreciated by Pharaoh, Ay felt his sovereign was overdoing it.

"Not all our troops were wiped out," he comforted.

The king turned glazed eyes on his father-in-law, who involuntarily took one step backwards. There was something eerie in those slanted eyes, and the vizier dropped his gaze, hoping his fear would be interpreted as respect.

"I didn't order an attack."

"Many events take place which His Majesty does not directly command," Ay began smoothly, "but are, nevertheless ordered within Pharaoh's scope of duties."

"What's that supposed to mean?" Anger caused the frail figure to focus. "We have fought thousands of battles, and look where it's got us! Gold and stability for whom? For Amon! It's his wretched priests who benefitted. Egypt's throne was nearly conquered by those men before I stepped in." Ay knew better than to dispute with his master, and remained silent. "Order Horemheb to withdraw his soldiers and get back to Thebes."

The courtier's eyes flickered with pleasure, but he opted to feign concern for an old comrade.

"He is a guest of Your Majesty. You wanted him here."

"Not any longer," Akhenaten replied wearily.

Ay bowed and backed away from the temple. Only the Aten had heard them, and the god without a face did not exist, anyway. The Divine Father's footsteps grew lighter with each stride. He now had one less powerful rival removed from Pharaoh's ear.

It had been a good day.

***

Horemheb was dismayed.

"Why did you tell him our troops were destroyed?"

"I couldn't tell him we'd won. Pharaoh sees every military victory as potentially another one for Amon. However, Egypt thanks you."

Ay took the pliable hands of the younger man into his withered palms. He gazed deeply into the general's eyes with what he hoped would be construed as sincerity. So, this was how the game was to be played, Horemheb thought. No matter; while Pharaoh's father-in-law consolidated his power base at Akhet-Aten, he would work from the older base of Thebes.

"So be it," the general mumbled stiffly. "Remember, you are always welcome to visit my humble abode in Thebes."

"I shall," replied the wily courtier, who needed no prompting to spy on a rival.

The general clicked the heels of his boots together, inclined his head to what was surely the most powerful man in Egypt, and left swearing vengeance under his breath.

***

38

Darkness fell across the city as two men wandered from the nobles' quarter to the necropolis. Turning down an artisan's street they passed the sculptor, Tuthmosis' studio. At the end of a lane the shorter man paused for breath. His companion, by contrast was lithe and fit, carrying little excess fat on his frame.

"How much farther?" the dumpy individual gasped, dabbing his brow with an expensive handkerchief.

"About quarter of a mile."

Impatience tinged the man's deep baritone. He was carrying an unlit torch and wanted to be about his business. As darkness reduced the traces of blue in the sky, hundreds of oil lamps lit the men's way. Eventually, they arrived at the end of the settlement and headed into the desert wastes, which were plunged in darkness.

"I think a scorpion bit me, Hump."

"If a scorpion bit you, Maya, you wouldn't be talking."

"Maybe it was a rattlesnake," the courtier puffed. "I'm beginning to wonder if this was a mistake."

"We have to find out where your silver has gone."

They reached the graveyard. Before them stretched the noblemen's tombs, most of them unfilled. General Horemheb trudged confidently towards a large rock sepulchre.

"This is it," he declared. Lighting his firebrand, he walked through the northern entrance. Pushing aside a large boulder without difficulty, he knelt at its opening. "We need to crawl through to the next chamber. Are you up to it?"

Without waiting for an answer, he handed the torch to his companion and wriggled through. He turned, and pushing aside limestone chips, Horemheb widened the entrance through which his friend followed. Taking back his torch, the general raised it high above their heads. The portly official sat down on a piece of rough-hewn rock.

Horemheb found a niche for their light, dusted his palms, and sat next to him.

"It's only a suggestion, but I think Ay's either got his own savings plan, or is buttering up the odd priest." Maya heaved a deep sigh. "I've never seen a tomb like this."

"That's because you've never inspected one, apart from your own." Horemheb wiped the sweat from his eyes.

"As a matter of interest, what's yours like?"

"I'm not telling you. You might pilfer it after I'm gone!"

"You can inspect mine if you like. It's nice," the courtier added simply.

Narrowing his eyes, Horemheb touched a painted surface.

"Bother!"

"Still wet?"

"I've smudged a mural."

"It'll be fixed. The painters will blame it on themselves. Have you found what you were looking for?"

But the general had frozen.

"Be still," he ordered, straining to hear. "Someone's coming in through the workers' entrance."

Hurriedly, the general grasped his torch. Dousing its flames in limestone dust, he hid behind a stone pillar. Quickly, Maya joined him.

In the silence they heard distant voices. As they grew louder, Horemheb began mentally separating them. He detected three men speaking a coarse peasant dialect. Oaths and imprecations peppered their speech.

"Be careful of the paint," one of them snarled. "I worked on that mural today."

"My hand is covered in sticky goo."

"Terrific – fingerprints – just what we need!" one artisan muttered. "Has anyone got a light?"

Clad only in a loincloth, a third party struggled through a rocky tunnel. He carried an oil lamp. Its linen wick wavered slightly in a gust of wind. The man shielded its flame.

"The northern entrance is open," he remarked laconically.

"It's those lax necropolis workers. Stay here."

The second man, who appeared to be bearing a club of some type, headed towards the opening the king's men had recently come through. The sound of a large boulder rolling over it stopped Maya's heart.

Returning, the second intruder said gruffly: "I'm going to sort out my workers tomorrow. They're always leaving their tools about, and the front door open." With one arm he wiped the perspiration pouring off his face. "Can you see the burial chamber?"

"We have the layout of the place, Bak."

"*Bak*?" Horemheb and Maya mouthed silently to one another.

While the men bent over a plan, Horemheb peered from behind the pillar. He made out the dimly lit figures of three individuals dressed in dusty loincloths. Two had shaved heads. One, with curly locks, was bathed in sweat as if from fever. With a sinking heart he detected the traitorous artist. The man, who was one of the king's oldest friends, brandished a club comfortably like any criminal.

Eventually, the small party left, shoving a slab of rock over the entrance.

"So that's how they do it," Maya said admiringly. "Wasn't it odd how one of them had the same name as our old crony?"

"A great coincidence," Horemheb replied grimly.

"I'd have your house of eternity inspected after this."

"Tomorrow we'll catch them. For now, I need to light this torch."

"We don't have any flint, but there's a ray of light coming through the stone block."

"Which means the robbers are still here," Horemheb deduced. "They were carrying an oil lamp."

Maya crawled towards the slab to avoid tripping in the darkness. As he placed his hands on the reassuring firmness of the rock, the light faded.

"I think they're gone," he whispered.

"Give them ten minutes."

"It's cold down here."

"Cheer up, we have something to tell Ay."

"I wouldn't." Maya attempted to push back the slab he had seen used by the tomb robbers for their exit. "Let the thieves plunder the old dog's last resting place. It would serve him right for stealing in his lifetime."

"I do believe you're jealous."

"Since I can't see you, you won't receive the punch on the nose you so richly deserve. By the way, I think you should follow my voice if you want to get out."

Horemheb followed Maya's ample posterior. Bumping into a pillar, the general sat down heavily.

"I can't see you," he whispered aggrievedly.

"You're to the left of me, about fifty yards."

Horemheb inched across the wall until he felt the touch of the treasurer's pudgy fingers.

"Have you got a grip on the rock door?"

By way of reply, Maya pushed the block aside, and moved forward, before falling headfirst down a ledge.

"I suspect we're in the annex," he observed, not moving.

"Better still, we're almost out of this accursed place," replied Horemheb, feeling the rush of desert air as he crawled past his friend. Cautiously descended a few feet to the next level. "Give me your hand and jump."

Maya took the proffered hand.

"Can you see the thieves anywhere?" he asked, dusting himself down after his jump. "My robe is ruined," he added.

"You should have worn a loincloth like our friends," the general retorted, scouting the area for robbers. "Don't talk till we get to the town," he adjured. "These rocks can throw an echo a mile out and we don't know where those men are."

"I know a shortcut to the workers' village."

"You're full of surprises, Maya. I'll inspect that place tomorrow. I intend to catch the tomb robbers. They deserve to have their right hands cut off."

"That's a bit harsh."

"What do you suggest I do with thieves?"

"They haven't stolen anything. The vizier has on many occasions. I spend most of my time cooking the books, while Abner-el commits criminal acts in order to keep the king's treasury intact. I say let natural justice take its course. Ay's corpse will be violated in any case."

"Have you finished?"

"I'll silence myself for your sake."

"We need to get to our hideout before daybreak."

The two made their way over the rocky terrain to the necropolis.

***

MAYA AND HOREMHEB

Hawk like intent.

"I hate him."

Fluting.

"You can't say that."

Maya pours wine with his own hand. Eccentricity loves genius. Horemheb does not notice. He has a good friend, date-beer, and doughy bread which the general does not like, although it goes well with his drink.

***

"Do you have a problem with this, Hump?"

"The meat is stringy, the beer thin on hops and I swear a rat went past as we came in."

"You're a soldier – you should be used to this." Flopping on a hard pallet, Maya tucked his arms behind his head. "At least no one will find us here."

"You're right about that. No one would credit us with surviving a night in this wretched hole!"

290

Downing the last of his beer, Horemheb prepared for bed. Gingerly, he lay on his bunk sideways.

"Mind you don't snore," he warned.

Something scurried in the darkness.

"This is an empty peasant's hut," Maya whispered. "Think about it, Hump, we have the perfect opportunity to obtain an insight into how the other half lives."

"I don't need educating. I live like the other half most of the time."

"How interesting to be in your position, and yet have such a full picture of the human condition!" Regarding the thatched roof above their heads, Maya pointed. "I can see the sky," he announced. Settling into his pillows he continued: "This sort of thing makes me feel like bursting into song."

"Please refrain. The mice are frightened enough as it is."

"I shall commence with a moonlight lay, followed by 'Suggestions of Starlight'."

"Suggestions of what?"

"Starlight. It's a poem I wrote to Armenia from you."

"If the poem's from me I should know about it."

"Precisely." The accountant folded his small hands atop his belly. "I think it will put you both in the mood for conjugal bliss when you share it with her."

"I can't wait," was the sarcastic rejoinder.

But, as the nobleman's lilting tenor swept over their humble room, Horemheb grew pleasantly sleepy. The melody, soft and haunting, complemented the moonbeams shining through the thatch. The general soon forgot about Lord Ay. Instead, he noticed the stars of which his friend had spoken. Everything grew still. Even the mice did not stir.

As the pressures of court life, and army duty melted away, the hardened military man was aware of being in a state he could only recall from his earliest childhood. He was purely in the moment, and it was a pleasant one. Peace knocked on the door of Horemheb's troubled heart, and he slipped into a fitful slumber.

The Divine Father walked briskly down a gaily painted corridor. His ebony staff, inlaid with gold, a gift from Pharaoh, tapped to the rhythm of his impatient footsteps.

"Maya!" The courtier, who was ambling ahead at his own pace, glanced up furtively. "I need to see you," declared Ay, catching up.

"I was on my way to afternoon tea with Prince Smenkhare," Maya said, reluctant to engage himself in any communication with the king's father-in-law.

"My great-nephew can wait."

"I was expected ten minutes ago."

"And *I* have pressing business with you," Ay snapped, in a manner so reminiscent of Queen Tiye, that Maya conceded without another word. Meekly, he followed the vizier into a side chamber, which ran off the corridor. "Now," Ay began, as his shrewd eyes penetrated the room for possible spies, "we both know you are the most powerful noble in the land."

"That honour belongs to Your Lordship," Maya hedged.

"Quit the flattery. Rumour has it that my everlasting place of rest was recently disturbed."

"So I believe, by robbers."

"Rather by certain noblemen of the court, who think I have stashed hidden reserves of Pharaoh's gold underground!"

Maya swallowed.

"I see."

"I am not a thief."

"No."

"The size of my tomb proves how much favour I hold with the king. Why should I want more riches?"

"Why indeed?"

The Divine Father glared at the diminutive accountant, who was infuriating him with his vague responses.

"If I hear of trespassers in my tomb, or on my property, I will seek recourse from our justice system."

"I think that's wise."

"Now, since you are late for a royal audience, you should allow me to accompany you to Smenkhare's apartments. He can hardly complain if I'm the one who kept him waiting."

"The Divine Father is most generous."

On hearing himself formally addressed Ay winced. Maya breathed a sigh of relief. The old crow would never approach him in such a manner again. To do so would risk alienation from an important sector of the court. All that remained was to inform General Horemheb, who would know what defensive action to take.

***

On the roof of a house, in the worker's village of the royal necropolis, Bak showed his accomplice's son how to paint a shabti. The faience figurine, shaped like a mummy, was meant to do the work of its tomb owner.

Royal tombs had thousands of shabtis, some fashioned in precious metals. Only the wealthy could afford to stock multiple figures, which magically turned into servants in the afterlife. Everyone, however, wanted at least a few to help out with work in the next world. The manufacture of such figurines was big business, and it made sense to learn how to make them while still a young artist.

Having recently burgled the tomb of Amenhotep-the-Second in the Valley of the Kings, Bak's band of tomb robbers was back at Akhet-Aten. They were, enjoying a day off in the knowledge that the loot was being dispersed on the black market for a price close to outrageous. Down in the narrow alleyways other artisans exchanged vegetables and ducks from their wage packets in order to balance their respective larders. As the morning wore on, the hubbub grew louder.

Around noon pandemonium struck, as a group of chariots raced down the narrow alleyways. Before the villagers could gather their wits, a posse of armed men forced themselves into the house which Bak was visiting. Rapidly, he farewelled his host's bewildered child, and shinned down the outside wall of the mudbrick house. Turning one way and that, he soon found it useless to flee and was hacked to pieces on the spot.

***

"There was no trial, General," Abner reflected aloud in the empty hall. "We've lost a master craftsman."

Horemheb spoke coldly: "There are plenty of other skilled artists, who are not thieves."

"Your logic finds its mark with me. However," the Chief Minister pressed an index finger to his lips, "the reason for his execution without trial escapes me."

"He was pillaging tombs, or rather planning to do so."

"There is a world of difference between robbery and wishful thinking. Do you have any proof?"

"There is a concealed passageway in Lord Ay's tomb from which robbers might enter after it was sealed."

"And how did you come across this knowledge?"

"I have been inspecting the noblemen's tombs at Akhet-Aten to ensure they have the same security as their counterparts in Saqqara and Thebes." Horemheb turned his military gaze squarely onto Abner. "Including my own."

"And Ay's differs from yours?" A faint quiver played on the minister's lips.

"And yours."

"How so?"

"I cannot reveal that. However, Your Lordship's Saqqara tomb is the safest I've seen."

Abner waved to the scribe sitting at his feet to put down his stylus. The man ceased to record the meeting.

"Your zeal in serving Pharaoh and his people is most commendable." Abner stroked his forehead with thumb and forefinger. Horemheb noticed a batch of new lines criss-crossing the minister's brow. "It's Akhenaten you have to worry about. Bak was one of his oldest friends.

294

For my part, I thank you. That infidel was against our Pharaoh's religious revolution from the start. Even as a child, he did not support His Majesty's theories on God. Now give me twenty-four hours in which to put in a good word to the king. In the meantime, keep a low profile."

***

"I believe you punished our artist, without my permission, General," Akhenaten said gravely.

"I executed him."

Nefertiti, who was seated next to her husband, gasped. Contempt crossed Horemheb's face, but he held back from venting his true emotions. He had long since realised that Akhenaten's informality, and apparent accessibility, were only skin-deep. The king was as autocratic as any of his forebears.

While he droned on, running through a multiplicity of rules like a lawyer, the general stopped listening. He stared ahead at Nefertiti, glassy-eyed, wondering if the love of his life was pregnant with another child. Then thoughts of his own unborn children - those Armenia had miscarried, those very little ones he would have welcomed as his own – filled his mind. Standing there in a mixture of pain, humiliation, and frustration, Horemheb felt the core of his soul harden. In fact, he reflected, he might turn into a limestone cliff, not unlike one of those at the entrance to the Valley of the Kings he had inspected under Queen Tiye's orders.

"I see you are repentant," Akhenaten concluded, noticing the sheer misery on his general's face.

Horemheb wiped away two tears which had run down his cheeks. Meritaten was tugging her father's robe discreetly. Only Nefertiti remained impassive. In a flash, Horemheb's lingering love for the lady turned to hatred. Feeling overwhelmed by the vehemence of his emotion, he prostrated himself in what appeared to be respect for the king.

"Be of good cheer," Akhenaten consoled. "On behalf of lords Ay and Abner, I commend your actions to secure our afterlife." Pharaoh

295

was animated, as if his lecture had strengthened him. "Please grace our table at dinner."

Exchanging glances with the queen, Akhenaten squeezed her hand. Horemheb felt a surge of gratitude towards Meritaten, who had brought the audience to an end.

Outside, he saw Abner, who was waiting for his horses in the shade of a portico.

"How was it?" the Chief Minister asked.

"I have a dinner invitation."

"You did the right thing. Now go back to work, General. The empire needs you."

Abner's gold-plated chariot arrived, followed by the general's red leather car. If Abner retired from court life, Horemheb reflected, as he gathered up his own horses' reins, he could find employment as a counsellor for the wounded in spirit. Noting the minister's team of white stallions heading for the treasury, he sighed. No doubt, he and Maya had to cook the books for another day.

***

PART IV:
The Court of Akhet-Aten

39.

SMENKHARE

Father thinks the world is ruled by a loving creator. I never join him at worship. Only his immediate family do that. We pray later with the harem, although I personally don't participate.

***

"I am not sure how we can overcome this, Maya."

Ay deftly removed two pawns from the *senet* board.

"You'll think of something.'

The latter moved a blue piece towards the end.

"Hoping to finish the race is one thing." Ay neatly knocked down an ivory foot soldier, and shifted it to one side to stand with the rest of his defeated foes. "But how to play the game?" Finished, he sat back and placed his fingers together in a pyramid. "Do you have any ideas?"

"I am completely loyal to Pharaoh," the accountant replied. "And I must ask to be excused. My wife expected me home hours ago. You may come if you wish. We're having duck, and there's a plentiful supply of beer." He beamed. "I brewed it myself."

"Another time, perhaps," Ay demurred. Rising from his chair he bowed courteously to the nobleman, who trotted away into the evening shadows. Resuming his seat, the vizier began toying with a gold *senet* piece. An hour passed. "Fool!" he spat furiously at last.

Angrily regarding the remains of their board game, the king's father-in-law reflected that Maya was so preoccupied with his happy home life, he had scarcely time to be embarrassed about his defeat.

After his rift with Horemheb, the older man assumed it would be an easy matter to worm his way into Maya's confidence. He could not have been more wrong. Having been unable to weave his web of intrigue, Ay was unsure who had lost in his chamber today.

"Excuse me, Uncle, may I join you?"

The Divine Father never bowed to the royal heir. They knew each other too well. Perhaps one day, when the lad became supreme monarch of Asia, their familiarity would change.

"Would you like a game, Smenkhare?"

Gold and ivory pieces were swiftly arranged on the board. Smenkhare looked down his long nose.

"Maybe just one."

"What brings you here?"

"Boredom," the prince replied, taking one of his great-uncle's white pieces. He held it up to the light and brushed it fastidiously. The Divine Father grimaced. No wonder Tutankhaten hated his brother. He beckoned to a servant to bring refreshments. The youth's carefully shaped eyebrows rose a fraction.

"We should have been served wine the moment I entered," he remarked. "You're too soft with the slaves."

Ay concentrated on how to avoid being eaten alive by Smenkhare's board tactics.

"Manners, my boy, are free. Besides, I always get what I want from the kitchen and more."

"You eat like a bird." Smenkhare moved his first piece to the end to side-swipe his opponent's pawn. "Why would you be interested in the kitchen?"

"It's the hub of the house. You would be surprised at the information you can pick up."

"Indeed."

Smenkhare finished the game. He sat back idly, and picked a small pimple at the end of his elbow.

"Stop that!" Ay slapped the boy's hand. The youth snickered. Hugging himself, he grinned, almost flirtatiously. The vizier exhaled in exasperation.

Wine arrived, and was deftly poured by two maidens.

"The service is faster than at Pharaoh's table," Smenkhare commented, ogling the girls. He scooped up a handful of nuts which had been provided.

"For Aten's sakes," Ay exploded "Stop gawking! It's rude. Never be rude." He shelled a nut. "You may not realise, but I have –"

"One of the largest houses in Akhet-Aten – I know."

"Theoretically," Ay assented. "But as generous as Pharaoh is, he didn't put the mortar and bricks together."

"I hope you're not saying what I think you are."

"It's exactly the same principle used for building the pyramids."

"Oh, come on!" Smenkhare laughed loudly. He stopped abruptly, catching the eye of one of the girls.

"I was generous with the workmen. All it took was a bit of extra beer and bread, but I tell you what," Ay leaned towards the prince. "My house is the only one with perfect lines."

"Rubbish!" Smenkhare's arrogant eyes turned very slowly away from the girl to his host. "My father, the king, gave no bonuses. Yet his house lines are precise, and his temples are perfect."

"You are not." Ay waved impatiently at the maids in a gesture of dismissal. Suddenly, he reached out, and slapped Smenkhare soundly on both cheeks. "I'm fed up," he hissed. "You're the heir, yet you don't rise in the morning. You refuse to worship Aten, preferring to chase girls, but you treat each one callously."

"They're servants." The crown prince wiped a tear from one corner of his eye. "That really hurt."

"Now you know how your brother feels."

"What do you mean?"

Ay looked seriously angry.

"The way you bully Tut is nothing short of torture. I wonder what sort of king you're going to be."

Smenkhare rose, nursing his flushed cheek.

"You'll find out soon enough," he snarled.

The Divine Father rearranged the board. He always ensured he lost to the heir.

"I doubt it," was the rejoinder.

As Smenkhare flounced out of the stately home, a strange smile twitched at the corners of Ay's mouth.

***

Maya plumped himself into a cushioned seat by the boat's railing. "I'm not moving."

"We have to get off," Abner pointed out.

"It's horribly hot in the city."

"Why must you insist on behaving like a child?" Horemheb interjected.

The treasurer placed diminutive hands on his stomach.

"I wasn't aware toddlers could come and go as they pleased," he answered insolently.

After seven months he had only recently decided to speak to Horemheb again. Abner rubbed one greying eyebrow.

"This boat is going back to Thebes. You may do as you wish, but I need to disembark."

Waving his ebony cane, he walked in a dignified fashion, down the gangplank. Horemheb regarded his plump friend with annoyance.

"Are you coming?" he asked.

"I think I'll stay here. The stench is less putrid than onshore."

"Play your games, if you wish, but maybe you could spare a thought for how I might have felt, bringing Bak to justice. He was my friend, too."

Briefly, he stepped aside for a white-robed woman who boarding their vessel. Then, the general marched off, accompanied by his retinue, which included Ramesses and the young Seti.

"You're a monster!" Maya yelled, his eyes swimming with tears. "Bak was like a brother to us all, and a better friend than you. Your

301

concept of friendship revolves around political expediency. When are you going to behead me? Next month? Next year? Be assured, Horemheb, you won't take me so readily!"

His high-pitched words floated across the jetty. The general's hands tightened around the hilt of his dagger. Inside, his heart pounded. He wanted to cry out in grief and frustration. Maya was his only true friend. Could the butterball not see that? Did he not realise how many nightmares the general had experienced over the last hundred, mournful days?

Horemheb steeled himself to turn away from his incensed friend, who remained on the boat. He gave orders to his entourage in clear, calm tones. Some picked up their luggage, which was deposited on the jetty by the boat crew. Others found the waiting horses and chariots which were assigned to their party.

"I never picked our treasurer for being prone to tantrums," confided Abner, who had not heard the content of Maya's vituperation. "The porter must have mislaid his luggage in the hold. Look, he's still jumping up and down over there!"

"I don't think it's temperament," Horemheb replied coldly. "And his luggage is in Thebes. Tiye needs our chief treasurer's services for another week to fill out the temple tax returns."

"So why did he come all this way to Akhet-Aten with us? It's a waste of the king's resources."

Horemheb shrugged.

"Our friend enjoys boat rides. Pays for them himself. Queen Tiye gave him some time off, so he's indulging in his favourite pastime."

"Is he coming back again?" Abner asked uneasily. "We require a treasurer in Akhet-Aten. The palace needs to put aside seven years' worth of grain."

"Oh, he's bound to cease chugging up and down the Nile in time for your famine relief programme. By the way, it's a marvellous idea."

The minister ventured a small smile. Unable to think of anything to say, he made his way to the palace at Akhet-Aten.

"Is Maya eccentric, or were you two pulling Abner's leg?" asked Ramesses throwing his cap on the barracks sofa.

Horemheb sipped his wine.

"The palace treasurer is on holiday."

"May I ask why His Lordship refused to get off the boat?"

"Dowager Queen Tiye requires his services. He's balanced the books, and collected temple tax up here. Abner's possessed with a plan to save as much grain as possible in the event of a famine. Maya needs a well-deserved break before he attacks the books at Thebes. They're in a mess since the royal court moved its top personnel here. Besides," the general winked, "his wife's on board."

"Meryt?"

"The veiled woman who boarded as we were alighting with our troops."

"That was discreet!"

"Maya's inordinately fond of his wife. It's something I can't profess to understand. Do you?"

"Yes!" Ramesses' reflex action caused both men to smile.

"I should be conversing with that lady-killer son of yours. I would have received a more unsentimental response from our illustrious soldier, Seti."

"He's *young*, my lord."

"And I'm a battle-hardened veteran. I've blocked love out."

Horemheb drained his glass.

***

Ay's brows were contracted in consternation. He was standing with General Horemheb in the king's audience hall, waiting to make a full report on the affairs at Thebes.

"Where's Maya?" he asked.

"Thebes. Queen Tiye wants him there, although he'll be back for his weekend party."

Ay rubbed his chin. Unwilling to verbalise his spies' contrary information, he hesitated. Abner's stray comment to one of them about Maya's loss of temper with Horemheb must have been no more than an outburst. Clearly, the two old colleagues had settled their grievances.

And now Maya was cruising from one end of the Nile to the other for reasons of his own.

"I must find an accountant," he muttered.

"Abner's good with figures," Horemheb ventured.

Ay curled his lip with ill-concealed contempt.

"I daresay."

***

40.

Tapping his cane on the brick floor of the International Records House, the Divine Father was asking questions.

"What do the letters say?" he asked a scribe.

"Many of the vassals request gold. There's war on, too."

"Between foreigners, or against us?"

"Between our allies. The king of Canaan is a menace."

Ay bit his lip.

"I can't do anything," he said in a strained voice. "His Majesty does not wish to be hard on the king of Canaan. Please just ... file them."

The scribe stacked the letters in their boxes, a defeated expression on his face.

***

Horemheb banged down several bags on Maya's desk.

"What's this?" the accountant asked as a line of foot soldiers traipsed past.

"Silver."

"Is this a bribe, or are you contributing on behalf of Ramesses?"

"Neither. It's loot confiscated from Bak's cellar."

"R-really?" Maya's voice quivered.

"To steal on this scale is a crime, but surely even a dullard like you can understand the implications of Bak taking from his childhood friend, now our king. I hope it disgusts you as much as it does me."

Overcome with an excess of emotion Maya placed his head in his hands and sobbed freely. Dismayed, Horemheb clenched his fists. Everyone was staring at the pair.

"What are you crying about? I've done His Majesty, our *friend*, a great service, and all without his knowledge."

"It wasn't for himself," Maya hiccupped, wiping red eyes on his perfectly pleated robe.

"No, it was for the poor!" Horemheb scoffed.

"It was for the *resistance*."

"If such a movement existed, my intelligence agents would have informed me, and I would have executed him sooner. Dead as a thief, or dead for treason, I would have caught him."

"Abner rounded up the Mazoi Police who arrested the others. They made a sworn statement."

Horemheb was silent. All he had wanted was vindication. Now Maya was informing him that Akhenaten's police were superior to his intelligence agency.

"Do you know anything about this cover-up?" he asked.

"Before you implicate me, don't think I don't know about your dealings with Amon's spawn!"

Horemheb was taken aback.

"I was merely asking."

"If anyone can sympathise with Bak it's the great General Horemheb. You may not realise, but you have shared the same agenda for years. You both wanted the old regime back in power. *'I have done a great favour for King Akhenaten.'* Balderdash! It's through people like you that his dynasty will be destroyed." Maya leaned over the plain wooden table Bak had fashioned for him as a teenager, and which he carried with him everywhere from Thebes to Akhet-Aten. Horemheb's neck was strangely contorted as he bent back under the onslaught. "How dare you condemn a man for acting out what you will do in ten years' time, Hump!"

"I have no idea what you're babbling about."

"You're a liar – a liar, and a plotter against His Majesty!"

"And you're a fat old fraud!"

"Have I interrupted something?"

The false pleasantness could only belong to one person.

"I was just leaving, Lord Ay," Horemheb responded wearily.

"Your tribute gets heavier with each visit," remarked the Divine Father in a pleased tone. "Our Lord Maya is possibly working for his salary for the first time in his life."

"Not that he appreciates it," the general replied bitterly.

"Unlike us, these nobles have soft hands," Ay said.

"Who has soft hands?" a new voice queried.

"Lord Abner!" Maya exclaimed with relief.

"We were discussing old army days," Ay continued sweetly. "You see, unlike many at court, we were trained in a barracks which could only be described as hell on earth."

"I concur," Abner said in an even smoother voice than Ay's. "Amon knows, I could never do it, but then I'm a true aristocrat." Turning from the aged vizier, whose face was the colour of beetroot, he addressed Maya brightly. "Let's count our worthy general's tribute, shall we?"

***

Sitting in silence, Maya and Horemheb watched the evening prayers. King Akhenaten lifted his hands to the setting sun. Nefertiti and several of his daughters followed.

Smenkhare, as usual, was conspicuous by his absence. Tutankhaten was sleeping in the nursery, enjoying the end of his siesta before dinner. While Meritaten and Ankhsenpaaten rattled their sistrums in the last rays of the dying sun, Horemheb watched the queen sadly.

From the corner of his eye Maya caught the line of his friend's gaze. Suddenly, compassion swept over the little courtier. It was a known fact Armenia could not have children, but perhaps things could have been different. Love changed all. Maya felt a guilty pang, remembering his speech at the mortuary temple of Amenhotep-the-Magnificent. He had extolled the virtues of love at the monument of a man both he and the current pharaoh called "Father".

Maya moved his chair closer to Horemheb. The general turned irritably at the sound of the chair scraping against the stony desert floor.

Maya gave a pleasant smile. Horemheb frowned. He returned to watch the lovely queen, but his concentration was broken. The king's arms fell to his sides as he pronounced the last "amen".

Leaving the dais, the royal family joined the congregation. In a few moments everyone was walking, or taking their chariots back to the palace. Maya noticed Horemheb had chosen to walk. Maya too, found sunset the time of day when he liked to venture out into the fresh air and forget his troubles at the office.

Making a bold move the treasurer started to walk alongside his friend. Horemheb did not chide him.

"How is His Majesty these days? Maya enquired.

"Exceptionally gracious. Odd, considering –" He broke off in mid-sentence. Horemheb had wanted to mention Bak. Instead, they continued in silence. Once at the palace, the pair walked aimlessly down the corridors, unsure of what to say. Eventually, Horemheb stopped.

"Where are we going?"

"I've been asking myself that very same question for the last mile." Maya stopped for breath. "I do wish to take this moment of blessed immobility to ask you round for a night of dancing."

"I don't dance."

"Even at parties?"

"I'm too old for parties."

Maya clutched his arm.

"My friend," he said seriously. "Don't let this death affect you."

"I wasn't thinking about that accursed man until you brought it up," the general replied crossly.

"Bak was a common thief. You were harsh, but fair, Hump. Please, however, spare a thought for me. Every time you have someone put to death, you turn to granite for months, and Armenia complains of your frigidity to my wife."

Horemheb looked aghast while his colleague nodded meaningfully.

"If you weren't my long-term comrade, I would rebuke you in a manner becoming a military man," he spluttered.

"I suggest getting drunk and taking up with a dancing girl."

"Have you ever had one?" the general asked, wondering why on earth he was interested.

"I've never experienced any woman except Meryt," his friend confessed. Horemheb's eyebrows shot up.

"Don't you ever crave variety?"

"Before I was married, I was very ... frustrated. Girls are never attracted to the fat ones. They prefer your type."

"True."

Maya rubbed his snub nose.

"I didn't marry Meryt because she was the only person who would accept my marriage proposal, you understand."

Horemheb's lip trembled.

"Of course not."

"She's wonderful in the bedroom," the accountant enthused.

"I don't really want to know, especially if I'm coming to your house on Friday."

"So, you will? Excellent!"

The treasurer beamed with satisfaction.

***

Beer and wine flowed at Maya's party. He had finished his business at Thebes where he had spent much of the time renovating the palace. Taking up quarters in the bedroom he had once shared with the king, he had enjoyed renovating it and sleeping until noon in their old cots.

Reassured that the splendid palace in which he had spent many happy hours as a child, was coming back to life, Maya was now in the best of moods.

Back in Akhet-Aten he put on a lavish repast. Everyone at court, including friends and enemies, was in attendance. Even Ay seemed to be enjoying himself. Without Pharaoh the guests were able to be less self-conscious and indulge in a variety of conversational topics.

During the evening, Lord Ay joined Horemheb and Ramesses. They sat in a group, while dancers performed on the lawn. All wore

their best linen, which became saturated with perfume from the melting wax cones placed atop their wigs. The pleasant fragrance offset the
rank smell of sweat and garlic-laden foods, and gave the appearance of
everyone being fresher than they really were. It was certainly helping
out the teenagers who were groping in the bushes, Ay observed. He was
sharing the third carafe of Mycenaen wine with Horemheb.

"We need a strong army," Ay said.

Horemheb cracked a macadamia. It shattered in pieces, causing the
older man to start.

"The army is ready for anything." He crunched his double-bar-
relled nut, secretly pleased Ay was on edge. "What are you really saying, Your Lordship?"

"Our pharaoh refuses to read his overseas mail."

"Maybe they're our queen's love letters. Heaven knows she has
many admirers from across the world."

Ay shot the general a peculiar look. Horemheb had imbibed more
than usual. Every time it happened, the general's thoughts turned to the
beautiful lady he had once loved, and now hated more than any Hittite.

"There are things going on that need to be addressed."

"Short of killing him, what do you suggest?"

Ay licked his lips. He was as sober as if he was drinking fruit juice.

"Keep things under control. And plan a return to Thebes."

***

It was morning as the soldiers sauntered through the king's gardens, feeling slightly worse for wear.

"Did you hear him?" Ramesses asked, matching Horemheb stride
for stride.

"Hear what?"

"Ay doesn't discount murder! He didn't bat an eyelid at your comment about disposing of Akhenaten."

"Ram, you're a wonderful soldier – the best," his friend said patiently, "but Ay knew I was joking. You don't think *I* was serious, do you?"

"He's dangerous. Can't you see? Even his own grandchildren are afraid of him!"

"That's just the Divine Father. He's been looking sinister for the last quarter of a century."

"You should be careful of him. I would hit home before he does."

Horemheb stopped walking. He looked at his bare feet, a result of doffing his sandals during a wild dance at Maya's. Gazing across the sweeping gardens of Akhet-Aten's palace, a rush of fragmentary thought sluiced through his mind. Several pictures of the Divine Father skimmed through his imagination in quick succession. He saw the man's entire life from his cadet days to those in court. In a few moments, Ay's career flashed past.

Then he remembered Maya. In his mind's eye, Horemheb saw the familiar figure of his friend, bustling about the gardens of the late King Amenhotep's home where he weeded, and even renovated old buildings. In a few seconds, his vision was over. He rubbed his forehead vigorously.

"Ever since we visited that accursed Karnak temple, I've had problems."

"They're *revelations*," Ramesses spelled out in a strong voice. "It's the god speaking to you. What did he say?"

"That you're right." The general looked at his feet. "I forgot my sandals."

"They're by the lotus pond with Maya." Ramesses wagged a finger. "That fat friend of yours has known all along. Why do you think he hardly talks to the Divine Father, and makes time for you?"

"Ay's a bore who talks all the time, while I'm a well-mannered friend, willing to listen."

"Ay's more polite than you on any given day of the week. However, that tub of lard has more brains in his little finger than you and Tiye put together. I suggest you both devise a scheme because Egypt is sinking fast."

"Calm yourself, Ram."

"Formulate a plan. I don't want to be on the same boat as Ay when we all go down. Now, I must retire to the barracks."

Horemheb watched in amazement as the tall soldier, weary from his exertions, limped to the outer gate where his horses awaited.

***

"At last!" Maya exclaimed as the general approached the tree under which he was sitting. "I've been holding these for you. You left them at the party last night in your haste to flee Lord Ay."

He handed Horemheb his gold-embossed sandals. The latter eyed him warily.

"You're sitting in the shade," he commented, looking about. "That's wise."

"It's hot at this time of day."

"You're near water too," Horemheb continued in a suspicious tone.

"Have a swim. It might relax you."

"Why do you think I might need relaxing?"

"Your friend's gestures were very animated."

Horemheb sat down in the emerald grass with a thump.

"I do wish you'd stop spying."

"I'm not, I'm noticing."

"What's the difference?"

"Spying's what our Divine Father does. I'm just a treasurer having a day off from counting the king's gold."

"And I've had just about enough of people babbling about Ay. Why are you all so obsessed with him?"

"Most powerful man in the land. What do you make of an individual who rises from lieutenant to Divine Father?"

"I find it disconcerting."

"I bet you do," his friend agreed with zest. "*You* should be the most powerful man in Egypt." The accountant sprawled in the grass. "That's so much cooler," he mumbled, shutting his eyes.

"*You're* the one with your hands on the purse strings."

"Indeed I am. At your disposal twenty-four hours of the day."

"Are you making me an offer?" the general asked.

"I don't make offers of Pharaoh's money to honest men."

"Do you make them to dishonest men?"

"Never! I would have gone out of business. Actually, His Highness' treasury has made a profit, mainly through your raids."

"My raids? I've never given you a penny!"

"Ramesses has. And thanks to our tomb investigation, the Divine Father dares not steal from Akhenaten." Maya propped himself against a tree trunk. "Wake up, Hump. There's a race on for Egypt's throne and you're out in front."

***

"I can't sleep," the general moaned. Throwing aside his bedsheet, he dangled his legs. Calloused feet touched cold cedar floorboards. Hurriedly he retracted them. *"Maybe I have a fever,"* he thought. "Armenia," he called sleepily, as he made his way through the house. His wife rubbed her eyes.

"Horemheb? What are you doing at my door at this time of night?"

"I can't sleep."

"Well, I've had enough lovemaking for a week," she declared strongly. "Go back to bed and try."

"I didn't come for that." He flopped on the floor rug. "It's the court – it's driving me crazy."

Armenia sat up in her bed.

"What's wrong?" she asked.

"Everyone's conspiring against everyone else."

"That's normal. If you can't handle it, go back to the front."

"It's more serious now," Horemheb said gloomily. "There is something very wrong with Egypt."

"There has been for the last decade."

"Do you think so?" There was a telling silence. "I wish you'd told me," her husband continued tetchily. "Because I received an update this afternoon."

"From whom? Pharaoh?"

313

"Everyone: Ay, Ramesses ... Maya. They say the throne's in trouble."

"And?"

"They think returning to Thebes would be a good idea. It's all very confusing."

"You obviously have a lot on your mind. Why don't you go into the kitchen? I'll make us something to eat."

"We have cooks, Armenia."

His wife twisted her hair into a bun, lit an oil lamp, and put on her soft slippers. Her husband had gifted them to her last winter on his return from battling Hittites.

"This way we can talk undisturbed," she said. Glancing at her husband, she flirtatiously rumpled his thick dark hair. "And who knows what might happen later?"

***

41.

"You're in a good mood this morning," Ay commented.

"Every morning is good." Horemheb rubbed his hands vigorously.

"Especially when you're in shape," Maya quipped.

The general gave a rare guffaw. His bright teeth splashed across a face which bore few lines. The trio waited while hundreds of people took their seats at court. The noise built to a crescendo. When Pharaoh was announced, the audience fell to their faces like sheaves of wheat.

Wearing the double crown of Egypt, Akhenaten appeared taller than his five foot, six inches. As he took his throne, all in attendance rose from their posture of submission. Involuntarily, Horemheb took a sharp intake of breath. For Akhenaten seemed more haggard than usual. Pharaoh's emaciated frame bore a yellowish hue, and in parts where he had lost condition, the flesh sagged.

"Welcome, Horemheb," greeted the king.

Despite his physical condition, Akhenaten's smile was one of such extraordinary beauty and sweetness that the general was momentarily dazed.

"Report time," Maya whispered. "Stop staring. He's been fasting."

Horemheb scowled, and was about to say something, before he found his feet moving of their own volition across the floor.

"Your Majesty: Life! Health! Prosperity!"

Suddenly, the doors flung open. A man in rags hurled himself across the court floor. Two guards instantly crossed their spears, causing him to fly in the opposite direction of Pharaoh, and out the doors.

"I'm from Thebes," he cried, as they attempted to gag him. "Help us, Your Majesty, we're starving!"

"As I was saying," Horemheb continued unruffled. "Your city is as you would wish it. The soldiers are in charge, and the priests continue to be suitably subdued."

"Who is that man?" Akhenaten asked.

"A priest."

"A priest?" The king looked about him, dazed. "Last time I checked, they were fed and clothed." A ripple of nervous laughter ran through the crowd. Pharaoh continued to exhibit genuine bewilderment. "A poet, perhaps," he muttered. "A Greek bard – yes, that must be it. Guards, bring him back!"

"That would not be wise," Horemheb interjected.

"He's an Amonite, Your Majesty." Ay leaped smoothly to the rescue. "He stowed away on the royal ship."

"He doesn't resemble an Amon priest," Akhenaten said. "BRING HIM BACK!" he ordered, suddenly imperious.

Maya noticed the king's eyes had lost their dullness. Instead, they were sparkling as they once did when he was a child in the middle of pulling the wool over some unsuspecting teacher's eyes. In a trice, the king collected himself, and reverted to his fatigued, weakened state. The stranger was ushered in, and forced into a prostration with which he seemed unfamiliar.

"Who are you?" Akhenaten leaned forward, gazing into the man's burning eyes.

"My name is Joseph," he said. "I am a Jew."

"Then it's settled." Akhenaten turned to his court. "He does not serve Amon."

"I sailed up from Thebes on a boat. They are making us work." The court began to jeer. "There are forced labour camps in Your Majesty's birthplace," the man clarified with the desperation of one who has nothing to lose. He swallowed hard, but his spittle had dried up.

"Who's forcing you to work? Are you a criminal?"

"I'm *Hebrew*, Your Majesty."

Abner, standing on Pharaoh's right, flinched.

"Would someone give this man a drink of water?" Akhenaten called stridently. "Are you telling me you are in forced labour because you're Jewish?" The man nodded, grasping a proffered cup, and draining it on the spot. "Why? I made no such edict. Jews are Egyptians."

"Your father ordered it."

A glimmer of fury flickered in the king's eyes.

"This is monstrous," he muttered. "Arathamon, Ipy, get this man to his quarters." The two men rushed forward. "Make sure he's bathed, rested, and given food. I want to see him in the morning – alive," he added harshly. "Thank you, General Horemheb," Akhenaten continued in a lighter tone. "We will sleep better knowing your army has prevailed."

The military man remained as immobile as granite. Ay attempted to make eye contact with him to ensure he removed himself from the king's presence, to no avail. Finally, he coughed and the general, realising he was dismissed, blinked and reluctantly returned to his seat.

"That was close," Maya whispered. "Are you alright?"

Horemheb sat rigidly upright.

"I've been set up."

***

"Pass the salt," Abner said quietly.

His wife shifted a gold saucer across a dainty wooden dining table, inlaid with mother-of-pearl. The two sat in silence on their verandah, overlooking their private garden. The children were in bed, and the sun was setting in a glorious splash of yellow, green, and pink. Abner cut a lime and sprinkled half of it with salt. He sucked it thoughtfully. Eventually, his wife cleared her throat.

"I heard a stowaway Jew from Karnak made an appeal at court."

"Pharaoh is investigating the incident."

Abner's wife sat in silence next to him until the sun had completely set. It was only when the stars spangled the warm night sky, and servants placed shawls around their shoulders, that she began to converse.

"What is happening in the treasury?"

"Ay and Horemheb are accumulating wealth. When Akhenaten dies, they will race for the throne."

"Meryt said the silver and gold from Akhenaten's treasury is being divided equally. The Divine Father is also rumoured to be looking for a skilled accountant."

The hairs on Abner's spine prickled.

"Then we shall have two kings."

With a shaking hand he placed more salt grains on the other half of his lime.

***

Across the courtyard, lengthening black shadows leapt up against cold white walls. A rotund figure tried to blend in unsuccessfully with a tree it was hiding behind.

Towards moonrise, another shadow sauntered from the palace kitchens to the encircling mud-brick fence. Looking from left to right, the figure lifted its long robe, and climbed delicately over the stile at its furthest end. Then, it melted into blackness under a tamarisk bush.

High in the sky, the moon was only a sliver, but the night torches, and whiteness of Akhenaten's palace lit up everything for miles.

"Have you got it?" a low voice questioned of the shadow under the bush.

"All forty pieces, Meryre," a high-pitched whisper replied. "Information, please."

"Lord Ay definitely wants the throne."

"How do you know?"

"He's hired me to spy on Horemheb."

"He isn't king!"

"He could be if Akhenaten was killed. Remember, he controls the army."

"Only Pharaoh oversees the army. He made sure of that when he created his new city."

"Akhenaten is in charge of nothing! The Mazoi police answer to his every whim, it's true, but their loyalty is to Horemheb."

"I'm not talking about the Mazoi. I mean the real armed forces in Thebes."

"Is that what you call it?" was the sneering reply. "Since when did you become Greek?"

318

"Since Tuthmosis-the-Great started opening up the glass trade with our Greek neighbours."

"Greece has always bowed to us, Maya. Why do you think the late King Amenhotep portrayed them as bound captives on his monuments?"

"Akhenaten was taught by Greeks."

"It's true, he changed Egypt's ways. Next thing he'll be taking boys into his harem." The tree's leaves shuddered in the evening wind as this last comment produced a violent spate of invective from the incensed accountant. "Can I have my payment now?" was the weary question, after Maya had run out of words.

"For what? You haven't given me anything!"

"On the contrary, I have bestowed upon you the most important piece of information you'll ever receive."

"That you are the most useless spy I've ever had the stupidity to hire for silver!" Maya made to leave in a huff, but was quickly restrained by a slender hand covered in rings.

"The future is composed of two possibilities, that of Akhenaten's dynasty and the other, without it. Ay has already decided on replacing the king with himself. Your friend, Horemheb is likely to oppose him. You can choose to protect the heirs Smenkhare and Tutankhaten, but you will have to stop following Akhenaten in order to do it."

Maya was so shocked, he stood staring at Meryre for a full minute. The normally smooth-talking individual had the look of an avenging harpy, he thought, his mind spinning back to Heliopolis where he had learned under the redoubtable Orestes, long after Akhenaten was expelled.

"You're out of your mind," was all he could say.

One apologetic hand extended towards him.

"It's for my son's education," Meryre explained.

The chink of silver concluded their meeting.

***

42.

THE ROYAL APARTMENTS

In the dim solitude of his study Akhenaten gave way to hearty laughter. There was no one to hear him as his slim shoulders heaved under a new red linen jacket. No one to know that he had eaten a full meal with wine and dessert.

Not a soul to know his thoughts.

***

In the days that followed, hundreds of skiffs rowed upstream. The inhabitants of Akhet-Aten swelled by fifty thousand. Tents and makeshift shelters were erected hastily in the back lot of every quarter, regardless of location.

Through the upheaval Akhenaten, looking fitter than usual, conducted personal visits to the grateful refugees. His bodyguards became fraught with anxiety over the king's all-too frequent surprise inspections. Laws became consolidated with a surer display of authority. It was as though Pharaoh had found a new confidence in his destiny for the country and its religious path.

"I'm hazy on these details," Ay remarked haughtily.

"It's all there." Maya turned the papyrus towards him and stabbed a column with one short finger. The older man held the document at arm's length. After his fiftieth year, he no longer saw as he once did. "Permit me to read the figures, Your Lordship."

"Then I won't be able to see them."

"Allow me to place the paper under a piece of glass. It magnifies the numbers." The Divine Father grumbled his thanks as the plump official fussed pleasantly over his task. "There, I think you will find that quite satisfactory."

"I was told that we were not to part with any gold," Ay said. "Here we have clear evidence of gold going out and none coming in. Can you explain this?"

Maya controlled his thudding heart.

"It's for the Jews," he said as calmly as possible.

The vizier's eyes narrowed.

"What Jews?"

"The ones coming to the city. Pharaoh wishes to welcome them."

"And no one's been told?"

Maya shrugged.

"I do the accounts."

"So you do," Ay agreed. "So you do."

He fixed the chief treasurer with a disconcertingly frank stare.

***

Throwing up his hands, Ay stormed around his palatial residence, cursing in a fit of pique.

"He drives me crazy!" he shouted, hurling a pottery vase against a mural.

"Darling," Tee finally said, with exaggerated patience, after this had been going on for an hour, "how long are you going to behave like a madman?" She stood in the middle of their living room. Despite her short stature, she made an imposing figure. Ay ground his teeth, and she noticed the insanity in his eyes. "You're drooling like a rabid dog," she remarked. Silently, her husband wiped the froth from his lips with his handkerchief. "When you've composed yourself, dinner awaits. And please don't break any more of our furniture," She left the room. "What are you doing?" she addressed a woman hovering in the corridor.

"Pardon me, ma'am, but I'm supposed to clean that room."

"There's a lion in there," Tee responded with equanimity. "Do it later. If he refuses to vacate the premises, leave it till morning."

The maid thanked her mistress, and scurried past the room. She glimpsed the lean figure of her master standing silently in a corner, banging his head against a wall.

Taking a deep breath, she closed her eyes and ran all the way down the garden lane to her house, where she bolted the door for the night.

***

"I love apples in the spring!"

Enthusiastically, Maya bit into the crisp rind, spattering Horemheb's torso in the process. Sitting in the royal gardens the pair were having a day off from the pressures of court life. The latter grimaced.

"Do you have a towel?"

The courtier obliged by taking part of his linen shift. He began wiping the dark torso.

"My, what well-developed abs you have this summer, Hump!"

"That's what happens when you fight Hittites." Horemheb pushed his friend's dumpy hands away.

"Are we fighting Hittites?" Maya spun the fruit around while he munched. "One never gets the news around here."

"It's not news," Horemheb rejoined sharply. "It's a job. Mine. I protect Egypt's borders."

"Generals give orders without getting their hands dirty at the front."

"I go."

Sighing, Maya tossed his apple core into the bushes.

"Then you're a fool." Dipping his fingers into the wild papyrus pond next to them, Maya dried them on the hem of his garment. "I don't see why an illustrious general need get himself killed when he has others capable of going to the front lines."

"You courtiers wouldn't know anything about the army," Horemheb retorted in a surly fashion, wrenching at a stray grass stalk. He slumped onto his elbows and shaded his eyes.

"I see Nefertiti," Maya commented.

"The Great Wife hasn't come out of the palace for months. Since Akhenaten decided to axe all witchcraft practices, she only attends the minimum of banquets with him for the sake of appearances. I knew she'd tire of his purity," Horemheb added smugly.

"I must have been dreaming," replied the accountant, ignoring his friend's words. "It's Prince Smenkhare. He looks *so* like Nefertiti. I thought she couldn't have sons."

The pair watched a young man moving about the garden with a woman of his age. Surrounded by palace staff, he was concentrating on a group of trees.

"Keen gardener?" Horemheb ventured, craning his head forward.

"He and Meritaten want a set of acacias for their new palace. They're landscaping."

Maya glanced at his friend as if he had seen him for the first time.

"What's he like?" Horemheb asked, sliding forward in the grass on his elbows.

"Abner thinks the prince is arrogant, which is strange. I've never heard the Chief Minister say a bad word about anyone." Maya glanced at Horemheb again as though re-assessing his words. "I personally like him. He loves military pursuits."

"It is rumoured Smenkhare has no love for the Aten."

"It's not a rumour. He never attends worship."

Horemheb gazed sadly at Smenkhare.

"I would give anything to be watching my child picking out trees for his garden. I wouldn't care if he had no faith."

"This doesn't sound like you at all."

"Do you know why I go to the front?"

"I'm sure you're going to tell me." Maya sat close to his friend in the hope of comforting him with his bulk.

"I play a game with myself. It goes like this: You're a mighty warrior. It is good for you not to have progeny because you're combatting Egypt's enemies. It would be an awful thing for a son to lose his father. Or a daughter." Horemheb let the green stem drop into the soft sedge.

"That's why I fight. If I stayed away it would mean I could have a family. There would be no excuse."

Maya placed a sympathetic hand on the general's shoulder.

"Would you like to adopt?"

"Never!" The plump hand dropped from the muscled shoulder. Horemheb shook himself. "But thank you for the thought." He forced a smile.

"Not at all. I have a naughty son to give away!"

"If he's anything like you, he'd be snooping in my barracks and gossiping with the servants."

"Unlike me, he's very athletic."

"Then there's hope."

"You know, there may be a reason why the gods have not given you children," Maya stated, glancing in Smenkhare's direction. "And it might not be a bad thing."

"No?"

"You are much freer to engage in warfare as you pointed out. "And," he screwed up his round face, "there might be something coming up later which you don't understand."

"I can't think what."

"There's always a reason for things. Nothing happens by accident."

"I wish I had your faith, Maya. Then I could sit around all day and twiddle my thumbs."

"Hump," his friend continued, ignoring the hurtful comment, "try for babies, but don't eat yourself up over it. Life's for living."

"That's all very well for you to say. You have a family. I don't even have parents."

Horemheb choked back his tears.

"Dear me!" Maya rubbed his back vigorously. "Roll on Friday's party! Look," he said in a flash of inspiration. "Pharaoh has everything, but he's cut himself off from the world to read religious texts and fast. It would be a joke if it wasn't so sad."

"You can't say he's heirless. And he still has Nefertiti."

Horemheb looked up at the royal group, which had moved to another part of the garden. Smenkhare, who appeared to be giving orders, paused briefly to regard the pair at the papyrus pool.

"Who are they, Meritaten?" he asked.

"I can't see, darling, but they're definitely from the palace."

"I think it's a man and woman, but I don't recognise them."

"They're probably in love, like us."

She kissed Smenkhare's cheek. They chatted for the remainder of the morning, taking care not to disturb one of the garden's couples.

***

PART V:
Let My People Go

<h1 style="text-align:center">43.</h1>

Lamps flickered across the darkened lawns of the king's palace. Hundreds of yellow, red, and blue flowers towered in bunches on square trestles which groaned with wine and food.

Lotus scent wafted across the hedgerows and parks. It was the king's birthday, and he had called for the festivities to begin after dark.

No one saw either Akhenaten or Nefertiti after the banquet. It freed the visitors to be informal, which had been the king's intention. Besides, the royal couple had retired early with what was rumoured to be a huge amphora of dry white.

"The problem, Seti," the Divine Father confided, "is that Jews are a nuisance on several counts. Unlike the Hyksos, who adopted our traditions, these people worship an entirely different god from us."

"Worse than my Seth?" the boy laughed, alluding to his family god, which was often associated with evil and chaos.

"Much worse," Ay replied. "They have *one* god to the exclusion of others."

"Like our king." The boy thought for a moment. "Some say Aten is their god with a different name."

"Nonsense," was the firm rebuttal. "Furthermore, if Jews multiply, they will be most prolific in *your* lifetime."

The pair continued to discuss matters of race and religion as the evening unfolded.

Incense was brought out to repel mosquitoes. Crowds gathered in the forecourts, and spilled into the gardens where a cool breeze blew in from the Nile.

"Who is that charming man?" a girl enquired behind Maya's left ear.

The official swallowed a meat patty.

"Where?" he asked, looking about him. A delicate arm gestured discreetly in Ay's direction. The accountant could scarcely conceal his shock. "That's Ay." He gulped and surveyed the girl. "He's *married*."

"He would be."

The young lady returned to conversing with her mother, who sat on her right.

"You have the appearance of someone who has stubbed his toe," Horemheb noted, joining the treasurer.

"I never cease to be amazed by women." Maya cast an eye over his shoulder to ensure the Divine Father's admirer was real. "Only just now an attractive member of the fair sex showed an interest in our king's father-in-law."

"He's powerful. Women like that."

"She had no idea of who he was."

"That's simply frightening."

"By the way, are you fully reconciled with our king's policy on the Jews?"

"If he wants to care for his subjects, it's none of my concern."

"It should be," Maya rejoined. "I also hear you take care of Karnak when I'm not renovating Malkata Palace."

"You have much free time."

Sipping a glass of red wine, the general surreptitiously studied the Divine Father.

"What I'd kill to know," said Maya, "is why these Hebrews were conscripted for hard labour. We never built on the scale of the late Amenhotep. In fact, his son was at pains to give everyone tiny blocks instead of great gobs of sandstone to work with. I can't recall Akhenaten's father giving an order to oppress Jews, either."

"But they are probably leftover conscripts from Amenhotep's time. They must have been forgotten in the fuss of the revolution." The general turned away. "Have you seen Ramesses?"

Maya sighed.

"No. And I've been sitting all alone as usual, since our dazzlingly attractive mutual friend chose to hog the general's son, instead of me."

Paying no heed to his friend's feelings, Horemheb excused himself in favour of Ay's table. The Divine Father and Seti made room in the cramped confines of the main garden bower, which Akhenaten, as usual, had filled to capacity.

"You're wearing a new robe," Ay noted. "It suits you."

"I'm not used to these things." Horemheb wrestled with a piece of fabric which had become caught under a chair. "What are we discussing?"

"Jews," Seti responded brightly.

"We've been combing through a vast array of topics," the king's father-in-law interjected smoothly, turning his stool away from Seti to face Horemheb. "You look well after your trip to Thebes. I hear it's quite habitable now."

The two men continued to chat. Seti grew quiet. Bashfully, he finally excused himself.

"Come over here," Maya offered the downcast boy as he walked by. "No one wants to talk to me either. I'm just not that interesting."

"But you must be! All the country's wealth comes to you. Do you really stack thousands of gold-dust bags on your shelves as Father says?"

"Quite often," Maya beamed.

"I've never even seen a gold ingot."

"Are you doing anything on Saturday?"

"Nothing," replied the youth, his eyes gleaming with anticipation.

"Visit my house. You can meet my wife, Meryt, and our children. We could dine after inspecting the bank." He craned his head closer to the eager lad. "I might let you handle some of the bullion."

"It sounds wonderful!"

A delicate finger tapped Maya's shoulder.

"Who is your friend?"

"I must ask for your name, Miss."

"Tuya. My father is on the dais conversing with His Majesty."

"This is Seti, Ramesses' son. His father is a great friend of General Horemheb." Maya turned to face the girl. "Weren't you admiring Ay half an hour ago?"

"This is my first time at the court of Akhet-Aten. I grew up with Queen Tiye's children. Naturally, I'm curious about the character of everyone I see."

"In that case you should realise that Ay is a very rude old man, who throws items of furniture about when things aren't going his way, while young Seti here is an eligible bachelor. I gather you're available?" he addressed the boy.

"I'm single, if that's what you mean," Seti said, blushing.

"Come and sit with him, Tuya," the accountant said in a matter-of-fact tone. "And let me talk to your mother."

***

Horemheb drew his brows together and pursed his lips as he studied the map which outlined his strategy. He had recently equipped a large army to protect Egypt's Delta ports, and wanted Ramesses' presence in the area.

"Which battalion you are leading, Ramesses?"

"I have no idea. The king made me Captain of Every Circuit of the Aten. It puts me in a difficult position. I'm not physically able to be in the Delta and Akhet-Aten at the same time. You might also recall you expressed a desire for my company in Thebes."

Horemheb tugged his ear.

"You'll have to juggle your commitments like the rest of us."

"I was wondering if it would be proper for Seti to take my place in the Delta."

"An excellent plan."

"His Majesty also requested new patrols at Akhet-Aten."

"We have the Mazoi. Let them take care of the city."

"I could join you in Thebes in a fortnight's time."

"I'm campaigning against Hittites next week."

"I need at least four days for Pharaoh's work."

"What is so pressing about a border patrol? This is a city of peace. You could delegate the job to one of your juniors."

"There are several hundred Jews arriving from the Delta and a thousand from Thebes. His Majesty expects me to place them."

"Do what Pharaoh demands," was the curt reply.

Dreamily, the king trailed his fingertips in the clear water. Boating on the Nile was the only way to escape the heat.

"The air is fresh," remarked Nefertiti, who was thinking about the state of the Two Lands. "I hoped to discuss foreign policy with you."

Akhenaten retrieved his hand from the water and wiped it on his pleated robe.

"My position is as it has always been – to let Egypt look after herself."

"A difficult task when she insists on our leadership."

"We became indebted to Amon due to our colonial yearnings."

As if noticing it for the first time, the king picked up the tassel of his robe and twirled it aimlessly. Its silver sheen caught a rainbow of colours which delighted his wandering mind.

"Some of our vassals demand gold, which all Egyptian kings give."

"I refuse to discuss it."

Sprawling on his back, Akhenaten closed his eyes. Recently, Nefertiti noticed the aging process had speeded up in her husband.

Her throat constricted. She glanced enviously upstream at the peasant women slapping clothes against large rocks.

Their voices floated across the wind while they gossiped and laughed.

A crocodile slacked its jaws, and slid rapidly down the opposite bank.

The royal boatmen turned the skiff shoreward where waiting attendants were ready to assist the ailing king to his litter.

Rubbing his eyes, the Divine Father focused on his wife.

"I have nothing but contempt for that man."

"I know you don't like Pharaoh, but just *try*," Tee pleaded.

"He drives me insane."

"You're the one behaving like a madman," she retorted.

"What do you mean?"

"At court you're the model of calmness, while at home you break the furniture. Our children will be scarred for life, not to mention the household staff. Only last week one of them abdicated in favour of Maya's rooftop. He's still embarrassed to face me at the palace!"

"Who cares about the staff? They're *servants*, Tee."

"I do," she responded firmly. "I want our home to be a happy, carefree environment, so that our children can grow up to be decent citizens."

"There is no happiness in life. You've been brainwashed by Akhenaten. As for our staff, let them run off to Maya. Everyone knows he wastes his money on extra rations for the likes of them."

"This is my house," Tee stated. "I demand that it be free of strife, and women."

Puzzlement crossed the courtier's brow.

"I don't entertain women."

"All I know is that there are four exceptionally beautiful girls in this house, and I have no idea how they came to be here!"

"They all look the same to me," Ay replied tetchily. "I wouldn't know one staff member from the next. Wait!" He lifted his hand as if struck by a revelation. "Isn't young Seti staying in our spare living quarters?"

"He moved in a fortnight ago."

"That lad is a notorious womaniser. He should have been born Pharaoh."

"What a thing to say! He's just a child."

"He's *fifteen*, Tee. Every girl from here to Karnak is attracted to those good looks of his."

"I'd actually forgotten about the lad," his wife confessed. "He's so quiet, and no bother at all."

"He likes privacy for his escapades. I'll talk to him tonight and flush out those hussies, whoever they are." Ay rose from his chair. "I'll also have a word with Abner. We have barbarians on our doorstep, and Akhenaten couldn't care less. I do believe he thinks he's Jewish these days."

"We're all Egyptian."

Ay waved his hand as if brushing away a pesky fly.

"It's beyond me. I apologise for bringing my problems into our home. There will be no more tantrums."

Without further ado, Ay grasped his ebony cane and walked with determination down the rambling pathway to the palace.

***

44.

Stroking Bessie's velvety ridges made her purr in alternating high-pitched bleeps, giving Akhenaten immense pleasure. She was a *plesiosaur maximus* he reflected; a happy dinosaur, who was soon to make him a grandfather. Her purple-and-orange boyfriend, Skate, was snoozing among the lilies. After an exhausting three-week courtship, the mother would shortly be delivered of twins.

Walter sauntered into the bower of bliss.

"Do these creatures lay eggs, or give birth?" the king asked.

"Not sure," replied Walter, stepping gingerly to one side. "They *do* have twins." On hearing another human voice, Bessie pricked up her small, well-formed ears and, squeaking with joy, slithered across the grass to plant a wet kiss on the archaeologist's cheek. "Ugh," he grunted, falling backwards under the seaweed breath.

"Come on, girl, behave," the king admonished, patting her wide tail, but the giant sea-slug was clapping her new friend between wide flippers. "She wants to play," he explained.

"I'm not a ball," Walter gasped. "Get her off, before she kills me!"

"You can't die in this realm," reassured Akhenaten, pulling his guest to his feet with surprising strength.

"You're already dead, but I don't think the rule applies to me."

"Bessie has lots of human friends, including my great-grandchildren. Nobody's ever expired from being embraced by a whale."

"She's not a whale, she's a ruddy eight-hundred tonne dinosaur with sharp teeth and bad breath!"

Just then a large clap to the side of his head felled Walter. Thinking she had found a playmate, the huge dinosaur was pushing him across the patio with her nose. Before he had time to feel pain, protest, or fight back, Walter had disappeared into the pharaoh's pool with a splash. Surprisingly, he did not go under, but floated, while the *plesiosaur* sat on the ground beside him and clapped her flippers.

334

"Go inside!" Akhenaten commanded. Bessie scuttled away, head down and with her tail dragging behind her. "Sorry about that. She's attracted to the sound of male voices." The king scooped Walter out of the water with a large pole, and the firm grip of his sinewy dark hands, tanned by years of sun worship – or so Walter thought. "I don't worship the sun," Akhenaten corrected softly.

Smiling agreeably, he led his soaked and dripping guest indoors. To Walter the house seemed bigger than last time. At the end of an enormous living room sat Bessie under a chandelier, clearly in a huff.

"Don't worry, she won't bother us," Akhenaten soothed cheerfully, pointing to towels shelved neatly in a cabinet.

"Why doesn't that blessed monster sit outside with her boyfriend?" asked the disgruntled scientist, disrobing without a thought.

"Oh, I like having her around. Bessie's a pet, you know."

Gratefully, Walter accepted the large whiskey sloshed into a tumbler by the over-generous monarch.

"So, did you prove I was Moses?" Pharaoh asked casually.

"No."

It was as if Walter had broken wind. Silence ensued, punctuated by the dinosaur's reproachful glances at her master.

"Ah well ..." Akhenaten glanced at a painting he had just completed. As usual it was ugly, expressionistic, and very, very good. "Lunch?"

***

"My heart's burning."

Clutching his chest, Akhenaten fell to his knees. His daughters screamed.

"Fetch a doctor!" Tee called, while her son-in-law's skeletal fingers groped for a hold on the nearest armchair.

Meritaten was the first to collect herself.

"Quick, run!" she ordered an attendant. Setepenre began to wail. "Go to the playroom," her elder sister ordered. "NOW!"

The child shook her head. Frustrated, Meritaten summoned two of the other little girls. Forcing them to link hands, she sent them down the hall. Meanwhile, the nurse held her king in an awkward embrace. Unable to lift the dead weight of his body, she remained with Akhenaten on the cold floor. He sat, propped awkwardly against a mixture of a whitewashed wall, and ebony furniture.

"I can't breathe," he complained.

Tee unclasped his heavy collarette. As she did so a clatter of gold and semi-precious jewels fell onto the tiles. She hardly noticed the odd glint in one bright eye.

Scuffling in the corridor brought a motley of guards, priests, and several doctors. At the door, a man was propelled forward by a sentry, intent on having Pharaoh cured as quickly as possible.

"His breathing is shallow, Doctor Yuti," Tee explained, attempting to disengage herself from the dazed monarch. Crouching next to Akhenaten the healer looked gravely into the opaque eyes. He checked for a pulse and deduced that it was irregular. "Is he dying?"

"Only a mild heart attack," the doctor pronounced. "We need to make him comfortable here for a while." The guards clanked their arms menacingly, as if ready to guard the royal patient with their lives. "Fetch me a cushion," he ordered. "The one the princesses have in their room would be ideal."

Immediately, Meritaten, who was hovering in the doorway, disappeared on her errand. Running into the nursery, she grasped the thick, overstuffed purple pillow. Beloved by the children, her father had commissioned several portraits of them playing atop its bulk. Now, the doctors eased it under the frail, supine body of her father.

"He hasn't been poisoned," Yuti intoned blandly to the guards, who were gripped by panic over their jobs. "It's his heart."

"How do you know?" Smenkhare's abrupt voice heralded the regent's entry. Standing solemnly above his father, tears welled in his eyes. "Is he alive?"

"His Majesty is breathing. You may hold his hand if you like."

Gently, several attendants placed a compress on the monarch's forehead. Akhenaten groaned slightly. His breathing was stertorous.

Dutifully Smenkhare intertwined his fingers with those of his father, only to find them caught in a vice-like grip by the ailing king. Briefly, he cried out. The grip relented, but only slightly.

Shaken, the co-regent sat cross-legged next to the barely conscious figure. Meritaten joined him.

"How long does he have to stay like this?" the prince asked.

"Until evening, or when his heart returns to normal."

Swiftly, Yuti took the regent's hand and placed it on Akhenaten's neck.

"Feel that?" he asked. The boy nodded dumbly. "That's your father's heart. Sense the difference in rhythm to yours?" Again, a nod. "We must wait."

Smenkhare sat by his father. Accepting a cup of wine brought by a solicitous attendant the youth took a grateful sip.

"How long?" he asked.

"You don't have to stay with him," Yuti said, "but Pharaoh is still conscious. He feels your presence."

As if in agreement, Akhenaten grunted.

"Of course," Smenkhare acquiesced. Pulling Meritaten beside him, he drew her hand close to the thin neck of her father. "It's his pulse." She drew it away rapidly.

"I know," she replied, unwilling to touch the ashen figure.

Several doctors began grinding herbs, while a nurse massaged the stone-cold feet. Slowly, Pharaoh's tortured expression relaxed, and colour returned to his cheeks. He slept.

***

Tee placed a strand of hair over one ear. Her face's pallor matched the recently decorated living room decor.

"I'm vexed."

"Sit down," her husband pointed to a divan. "You need rest." His wife obeyed, stretching across the couch. Ay fetched a pillow and tucked it behind her grey head.

"It took a full ten minutes for palace security to arrive with help. His Majesty could have died."

"There's nothing you could have done." Beckoning to a servant, Ay silently mimed an order for sustenance. "We will double the guard. Why were you alone with him? There should always be nurses and doctors around my son-in-law."

"You know what Pharaoh is like. He came into the children's nursery unannounced, to play with Baby Tut."

"Ah, yes – how is the little fellow?"

"Full of beans, but he fell sound asleep at midday. I put him down. Then we walked into a new room His Majesty is currently decorating for the children. That's when it happened."

As her body tensed, the Divine Father leaned forward.

"You helped as much as you could."

He stretched out a hand to stroke his wife's shoulder.

"There's no need for that," she said. "I'm fine."

"You need to rest. The palace children are being taken care of."

"I don't need to sleep. I'm as strong as an ox."

"You're as white as a sheet." Ay's voice sounded like a caress.

"You do fuss," his wife replied faintly. "A nap wouldn't do any harm I suppose."

***

NEFERTITI

Death comes quickly on the Nile.

My husband was buried in his tomb. Clasping my beloved on his bier in a final embrace, before they took him away to the embalmer's, I shed copious tears. His body looked so small in comparison with my everyday memory of him. Akhenaten was full of vitality – always breathing visions, worshipping, never sitting still, until recently when illness arrested his body and memory.

I don't have sons and I'm afraid. The harem supports Smenkhare. No relative of Kia will rule while I'm alive. I know their plan – a return to Thebes. Do you know, not once in twenty years, have I seen that young man at worship?

***

45.

AKHENATEN

There is another story. That I simply fled, Jews in tow.

***

Rising from his couch, Akhenaten rubbed his eyes. Lord Abner stepped forward.

"Are you ready?"

"I can't find my staff, Abbie."

"It's outside in your chariot. Please hurry, I can't keep Horemheb away from here much longer."

Lifting himself off the hard mattress, the king stumbled to his feet.

"How long have I been out?"

"A day." Abner placed a dark blue cloak around him. "The potion was strong. You missed your own funeral."

"Ha!" Akhenaten slipped on his shoes and tottered outside. Hundreds of people stood clumped under the palace eaves. Their breath collected in steam above their coats. Catching sight of their leader, a low cheer issued from the crowd. "Did you get the money, Abbie?"

"As you know, we've been pilfering your coffers for some time," Abner chuckled. "You should be able to walk out with half of Egypt's wealth, thanks to your father-in-law. We had to keep Maya out of the loop, on account of his friendship with General Horemheb."

"Give my best to the Divine Father." Akhenaten took his position at the head of the gathering. "Make sure he protects Nefertiti and the children when I'm gone." Lifting slender arms against the night sky, Akhenaten fractured the new moon's thin rays of white. "My people," he addressed the horde in a clear voice, "let us go."

***

EPILOGUE:
The Conversation

Puffing under the weight of his papyrus scrolls, Amenhotep Junior trudged up the dusty hillock to the well. Sweat poured down his brow and into his eyes. Squinting in the blazing sunlight, he noticed a figure looming up ahead.

A lone stranger was sitting on the circular mudbrick wall by the waterhole. The boy's heart skipped a beat, and his load seemed to lighten.

"Do you mind getting me a drink?" asked the prince, dumping his books by his feet.

"If only you knew of whom you were asking –"

"I just want a cup of water. I've been lectured to all afternoon by wise men, who are stupid because they think they know everything."

The man sighed. A drinking cup, attached to a rope, was sitting next to him. He picked it up and dropped it into the depths of the well. After a few moments, he reeled up the cup, now filled with cool water. Amenhotep drank thirstily, slopping the liquid over his dusty muslin vest.

"I know what you mean," the stranger said. "I used to discuss religion with the priests."

"The priests?" Amenhotep Junior took off his wig. He perched his plump bottom on the circular wall next to the man. "Are you an acolyte?"

"No, I'm a king."

The boy wrinkled his nose.

"Of Mitanni?"

"No."

"Syria?"

"No."

"Kush?"

"No."

A terrified glint appeared in the boy's eye.

"Of Hatti?" he squeaked.

"No."

The stranger smiled mysteriously and for some reason the child did not press further. They sat in silence for a few minutes, listening to the faraway cries of men, and the occasional braying of a donkey.

"Are you hungry?" Amenhotep suddenly asked.

Without waiting for a reply, he pulled up his satchel from where it lay at his feet, and started rummaging through its contents. Triumphantly, he pulled out two pieces of flat bread. Taking one for himself, he offered the other to the stranger.

"Ah, yes." The man politely accepted the snack from the little boy. "You know, this doesn't satisfy."

"I'm sorry," the prince said with his mouth full. "I forgot you were a grownup." He tore his pancake in half, and pushed the larger piece towards the man. "Help yourself."

"Thank you," replied the stranger somewhat amused, "but that wasn't what I meant. After a while you'll get hungry again, won't you?"

"I guess."

"But what if you could have bread that satisfied so that you wouldn't have to eat again?"

"I don't know." Amenhotep looked greedily at his new friend's uneaten victuals. "I rather like eating," he remarked.

"Go ahead," the man encouraged. "I'm not hungry." The prince wolfed down the loaves. "The bread I'm talking about is the bread of life, and the water I offer –"

"Could I have another drink, please?" asked the child, wiping his mouth, and holding out the empty cup. Again, it plunged into the well's dark depths before returning to the thirsty prince's hands. "I just had a thought," Amenhotep said. "If you're a king and I'm just a prince, why are you serving me?"

"Because the greater always serves the lesser."

The cup halted halfway to the boy's lips.

"That's the most preposterous thing I have ever heard!"

"Aah!" said the man in a pleased fashion. "That's a big word for such a small child."

"I'm a poet."

"I thought you were a prince."

"I am that, too."

"You are right in saying that you are both a prince and a poet. One day you will be a king and write a great poem in praise of my father."

"You know what?" said Amenhotep. "You remind me of me."

"Oh, and why is that?"

"Neither of us makes any sense!"

The little child grinned up at the man, displaying a set of perfectly straight, white teeth. It seemed that the man's body gleamed in response as they sat together and talked amiably in the stillness of the Nile afternoon.

***

Appendix 1:
AKHENATEN'S 'HYMN TO THE ATEN'
(Tomb of Ay)

I

You rise glorious at the heaven's edge, O living Aten!
You in whom all life began.
When you shine from the eastern horizon
You fill every land with your beauty
You are lovely, great and glittering.
You go high above the lands you have made,
Embracing them with your rays,
Holding them fast for your loving son.
Though you are far away, your rays are on the Earth;
Though you fill men's eyes, your footprints are unseen.

II

When you sink beyond the western boundary of the heavens
The Earth is darkened as though by death;
Then men sleep in their bedchambers,
Their heads wrapped up, unable to see one another;
Their treasures are stolen from beneath their heads
And they know it not.
Every lion comes out of its lair,
All serpents emerge and sting.
Darkness is supreme and the Earth silent;
Their maker rests within his horizon.

III

The Earth brightens with your rising.
With the shining of your disc by day.
Before your rays the darkness is put to flight.
The people of the Two Lands celebrate the day,
You rouse them and raise them to their feet.
They wash their limbs, they dress themselves,
They lift up their arms in praise of your appearing,
Then throughout all the land they begin their work.

IV

Cattle browse peacefully,
Trees and plants are verdant;
Birds fly up from their nests
And lift up their wings in your praise.
All animals frisk upon their feet.
All winged things fly and alight once more –
They come to life with your rising.

V

Boats sail upstream and downstream.
At your coming every highway is opened.
Before your face fish leap up from the river.
Your rays reach the Green Ocean.
You it is who place the male seed in woman.
You who create the semen in man;
You quicken the son in his mother's belly,
Soothing him so that he shall not cry.

Even in the womb you are his nurse.
You give breath to all your creation,
Opening the mouth of the newborn,
And giving him nourishment.

VI

When the chick chirps within the shell
You give him breath that he may live.
You bring his body to readiness
So that he may break from the egg.
And when he is hatched he runs on his two feet,
Announcing his creation.

VII

How manifold are your works!
They are mysterious in men's sights.
O sole, incomparable god, all-powerful,
You created the Earth in solitude
As your heart desired.
Men you created, and cattle great and small,
Whatever is on Earth,
All that tread the ground on foot.
All that wing the lofty air.
You created the strange countries, Khor and Kush,
As well as the land of Egypt.
You set every man in his right place
With his food and his possessions
And his days that are numbered.
Men speak in many tongues,
In body and complexion they are various,
For you have distinguished between people and people.

VIII

In the Netherworld you make the Nile-flood,
Leading it out at your pleasure to bring life for the Egyptians.
Though Lord of them all, Lord of their lands,
You grow weary for them, shine for them,
The sun, disc by day, great in your majesty,
To far lands also you have brought life,
Setting them a Nile-flood in the heavens
That falls like the waves of the sea,
Watering the fields where they dwell.
How excellent are your purposes, O Lord of Eternity!
You have set a Nile in the sky for the strangers,
For the cattle of every country that go on their feet,
But for Egypt the Nile wells from the Netherworld.
Your rays nourish fields and garden.
It is for you that they live.

IX

You make the seasons for the sake of your creation,
The winter to cool them, the summer that they
May taste your heat.
You have made far skies so that you may shine in them.
Your disc in its solitude looks on all that you have made,
Appearing in its glory and gleaming both near and far.
Out of your singleness you shape a million forms –
Towns and villages, fields, roads and the river.
All eyes behold you, bright disc of the day.

X

There is none other that knows you, save Akhenaten,
Your son.

You have given him insight into your purposes;
He understands your power.
All creatures of the world are in your hand,
Just as you have made them.
With your rising they live;
With your setting they die.
You yourself are the span of life.
Men live through you,
Their eyes filled with beauty till the hour of your setting,
All labour is set aside when you sink in the west.

XI

You established the world for your son,
He who was born of your body,
King of Upper Egypt and Lower Egypt,
Living in Truth, Lord of the Two Lands,
Neferkheprure, Wanre,
The Son of Ra,
Living in Truth, Lord of Diadems,
Akhenaten, great in his length of days,
And for the King's Great Wife,
She whom he loves,
For the Lady of the Two Lands, Nefernefruaten-Nefertiti,
May she live and flower for ever and ever.

***

Appendix II:
PSALM 104 (Attributed to Moses, King James Bible)

1 Bless the Lord, O my soul. O Lord my God, thou art very great; thou art clothed with honour and majesty.

2 Who coverest thyself with light as with a garment: who stretchest out the heavens like a curtain:

3 Who layeth the beams of his chambers in the waters: who maketh the clouds his chariot: who walketh upon the wings of the wind:

4 Who maketh his angels spirits; his ministers a flaming fire:

5 Who laid the foundations of the earth, that it should not be removed for ever.

6 Thou coveredst it with the deep as with a garment: the waters stood above the mountains.

7 At thy rebuke they fled; at the voice of thy thunder they hasted away.

8 They go up by the mountains; they go down by the valleys unto the place which thou hast founded for them.

9 Thou hast set a bound that they may not pass over; that they turn not again to cover the earth.

10 He sendeth the springs into the valleys, which run among the hills.

11 They give drink to every beast of the field: the wild asses quench their thirst.

12 By them shall the fowls of heaven have their habitation, which sing among the branches.

13 He watereth the hills from his chambers: the earth is satisfied with the fruit of thy works.

14 He causeth the grass to grow for the cattle, and herb for the service of man: that he may bring forth food out of the earth;

15 And wine that maketh glad the heart of man, and oil to make his face to shine, and bread which strengtheneth man's heart.

16 The trees of the Lord are full of sap; the cedars of Lebanon, which he hath planted;

17 Where the birds make their nests: as for the stork, the fir trees are her house.

18 The high hills are a refuge for the wild goats; and the rocks for the bunnies.

19 He appointed the moon for seasons: the sun knoweth his going down.

20 Thou makest darkness, and it is night: wherein all the beasts of the forest do creep forth.

21 The young lions roar after their prey, and seek their meat from God.

22 The sun ariseth, they gather themselves together, and lay them down in their dens.

23 Man goeth forth unto his work and to his labour until the evening.

24 O Lord, how manifold are thy works! In wisdom hast thou made them all: the earth is full of thy riches.

25 So is this great and wide sea, wherein are things creeping innumerable, both small and great beasts.

26 There go ships: there is that leviathan, whom thou hast made to play therein.

27 These wait all upon thee; that thou mayest give them their meat in due season.

28 That thou givest them they gather: thou openest thine hand, they are filled with good.

29 Thou hidest thy face, they are troubled thou takest away their breath, they die, and return to their dust.

30 Thou sendest forth thy spirit, they are created: and thou renewest the face of the earth.

31 The glory of the Lord shall endure forever: the Lord shall rejoice in his works.

32 He looketh on the earth, and it trembleth: he toucheth the hills, and they smoke.

33 I will sing to the Lord as long as I live: I will sing praise to my God while I have my being.

34 My meditation of him shall be sweet: I will be glad in the Lord.

35 Let the sinners be consumed out of the earth, and let the wicked be no more. Bless thou the Lord, O my soul. Praise ye the Lord.

***

Biography

Sharon Janet Hague is a lawyer and writer with an interest in ancient Egypt. Holding a master's degree in Egyptology from the University of Manchester, she pens articles for various publications, including Nile Magazine.

For more on the author you may visit her website at: https://sharonjanethague.com.

In order to assist other readers, please consider leaving a review.